SpongeBob™

COMICS #3

Tales From the
Haunted Pineapple

PUBLISHER'S NOTE:
This is a work of fiction. Names, characters, places, and incidents are either the product of the author's imagination or used fictitiously, and any resemblance to actual persons, living or dead, business establishments, events, or locales is entirely coincidental.

Library of Congress Cataloging-in-Publication Data has been applied for and may be obtained from the Library of Congress.

ISBN 978-1-4197-2560-9

Cover illustration by Derek Drymon (sketch),
Jacob Chabot (pencils and inks), and Rick Nielsen (colors).
Title page illustration by Vince Deporter (pencils and inks)
and Molly Dolben (color).

Book design by Pamela Notarantonio

The stories included in this collection were originally published in *SpongeBob Comics* no. 5 (October 2011), 6 (December 2011), 9 (June 2012), 11 (August 2012), 13 (October 2012), 14 (November 2012), 18 (March 2013), 22 (July 2013), 25 (October 2013), 29 (February 2014).

Published in paperback in 2017 by Amulet Books, an imprint of ABRAMS. All rights reserved. No portion of this book may be reproduced, stored in a retrieval system, or transmitted in any form or by any means, mechanical, electronic, photocopying, recording, or otherwise, without written permission from the publisher.

Amulet Books and Amulet Paperbacks are registered trademarks of Harry N. Abrams, Inc.

Printed and bound in China
10 9 8 7 6 5 4 3 2 1

Amulet Books are available at special discounts when purchased in quantity for premiums and promotions as well as fundraising or educational use. Special editions can also be created to specification. For details, contact specialsales@abramsbooks.com or the address below.

ABRAMS The Art of Books
115 West 18th Street, New York, NY 10011
abramsbooks.com

SpongeBob™
COMICS #3
Tales From the
Haunted Pineapple

STEPHEN HILLENBURG
EDITED BY CHRIS DUFFY

AMULET BOOKS
NEW YORK

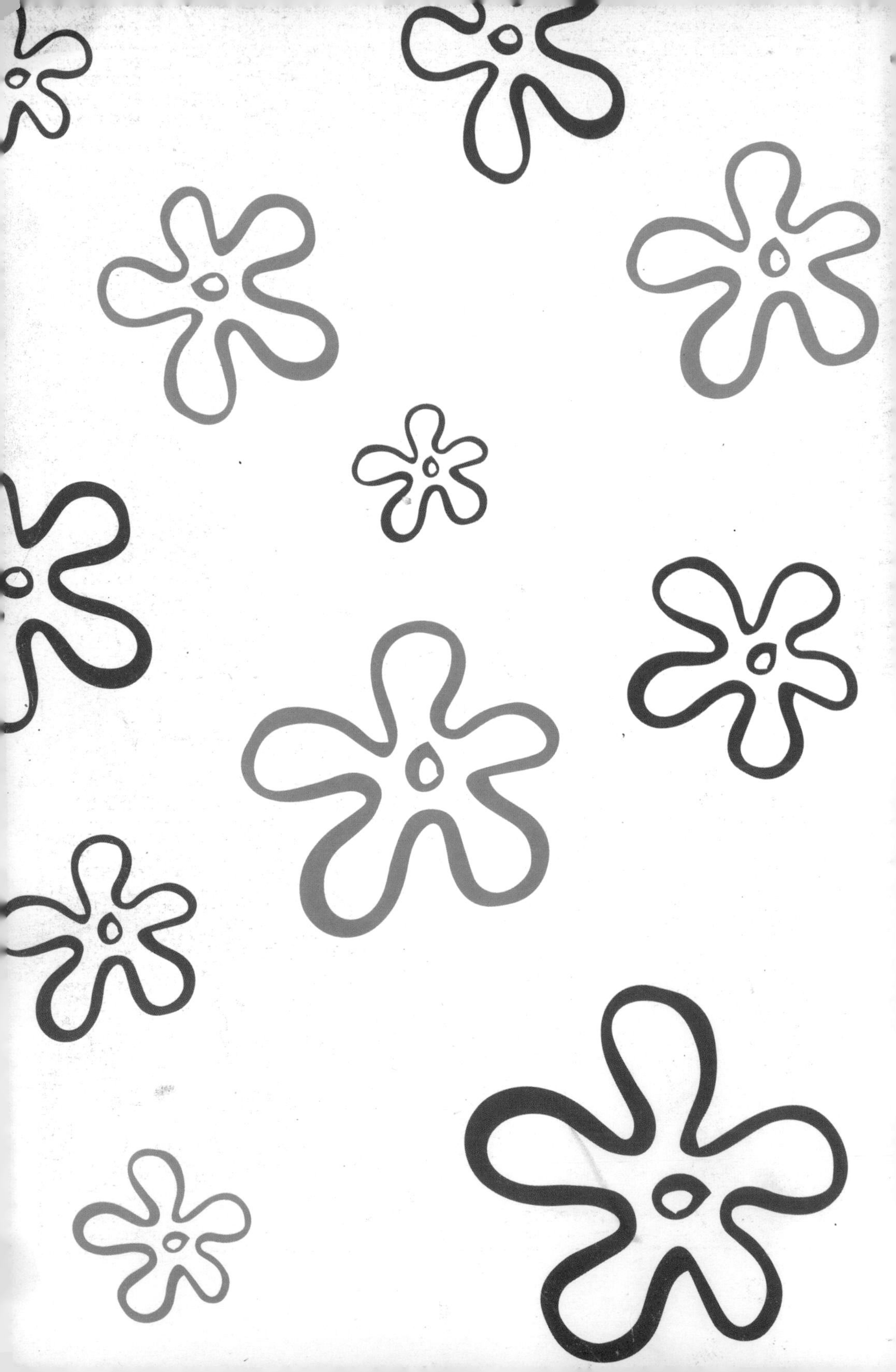

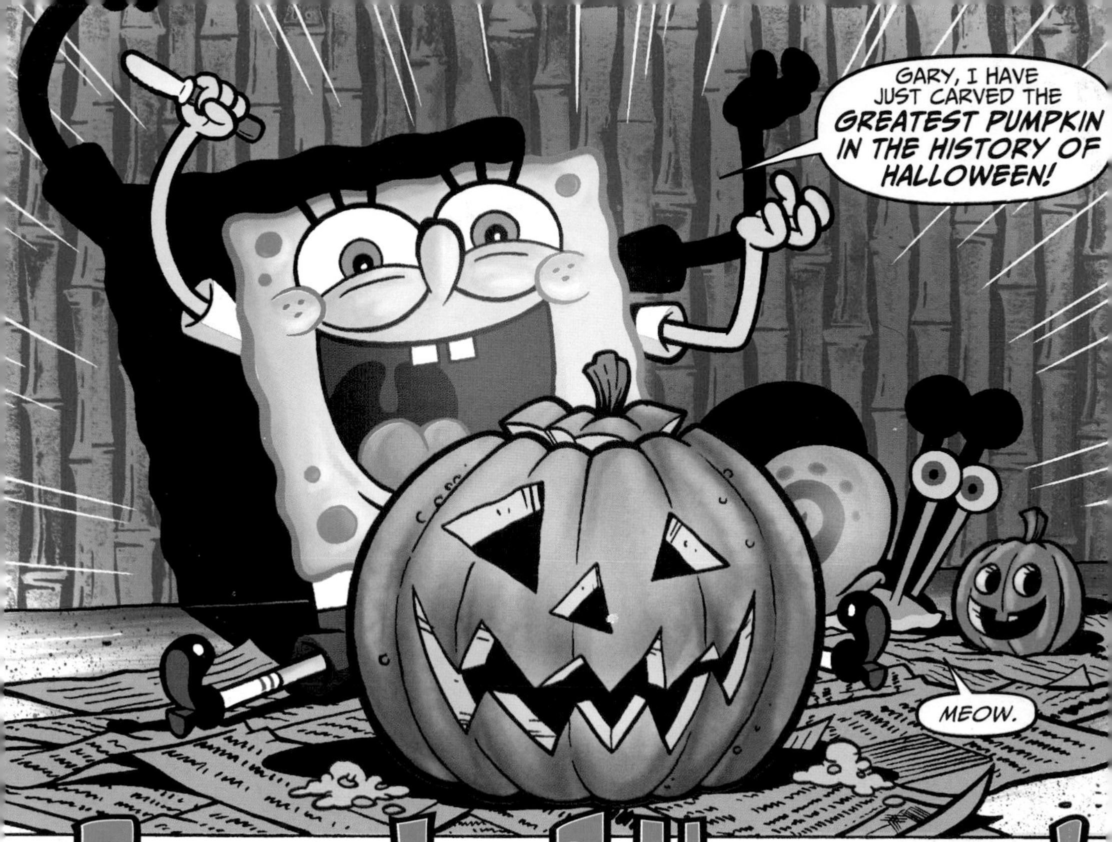
GARY, I HAVE JUST CARVED THE GREATEST PUMPKIN IN THE HISTORY OF HALLOWEEN!
MEOW.

Gourd of Horror!

STORY: DAVID LEWMAN PENCILS AND INKS: JACOB CHABOT COLOR: HIFI LETTERING: COMICRAFT

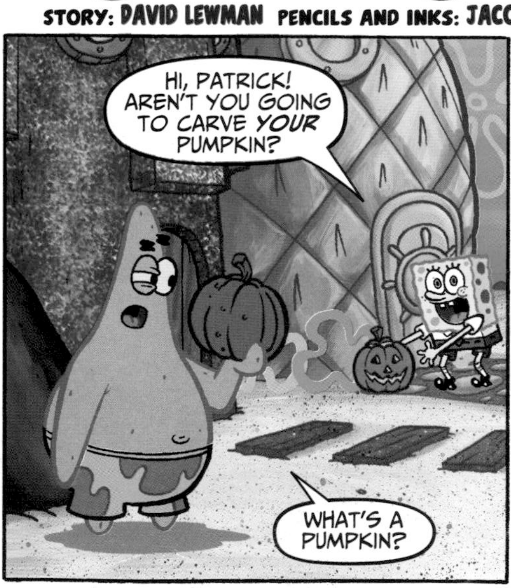
HI, PATRICK! AREN'T YOU GOING TO CARVE YOUR PUMPKIN?
WHAT'S A PUMPKIN?

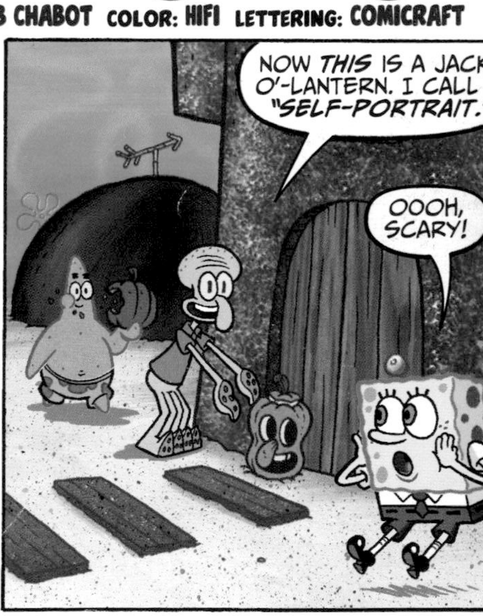
NOW THIS IS A JACK-O'-LANTERN. I CALL IT "SELF-PORTRAIT."
OOOH, SCARY!

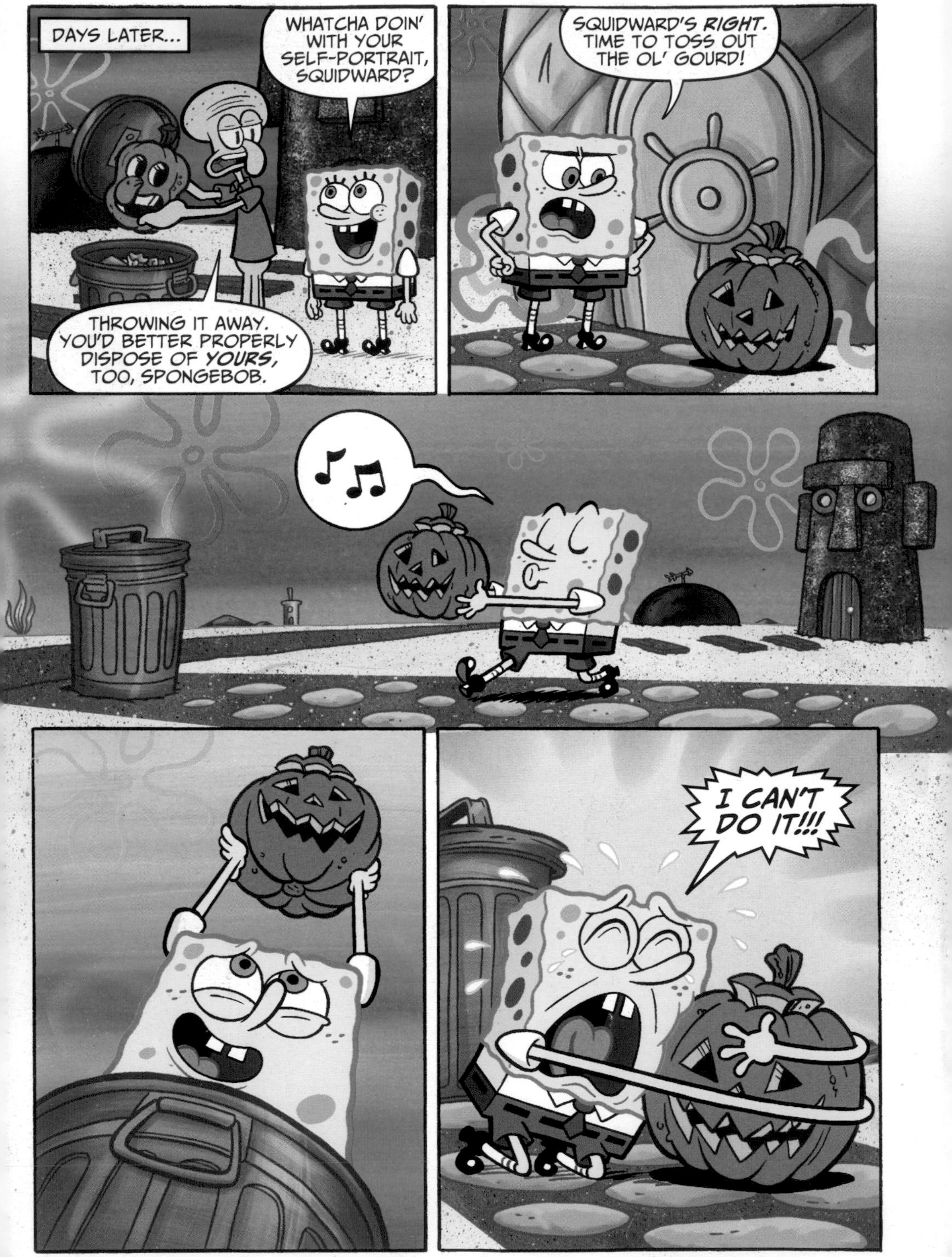
DAYS LATER...
WHATCHA DOIN' WITH YOUR SELF-PORTRAIT, SQUIDWARD?
THROWING IT AWAY. YOU'D BETTER PROPERLY DISPOSE OF YOURS, TOO, SPONGEBOB.
SQUIDWARD'S RIGHT. TIME TO TOSS OUT THE OL' GOURD!
I CAN'T DO IT!!!

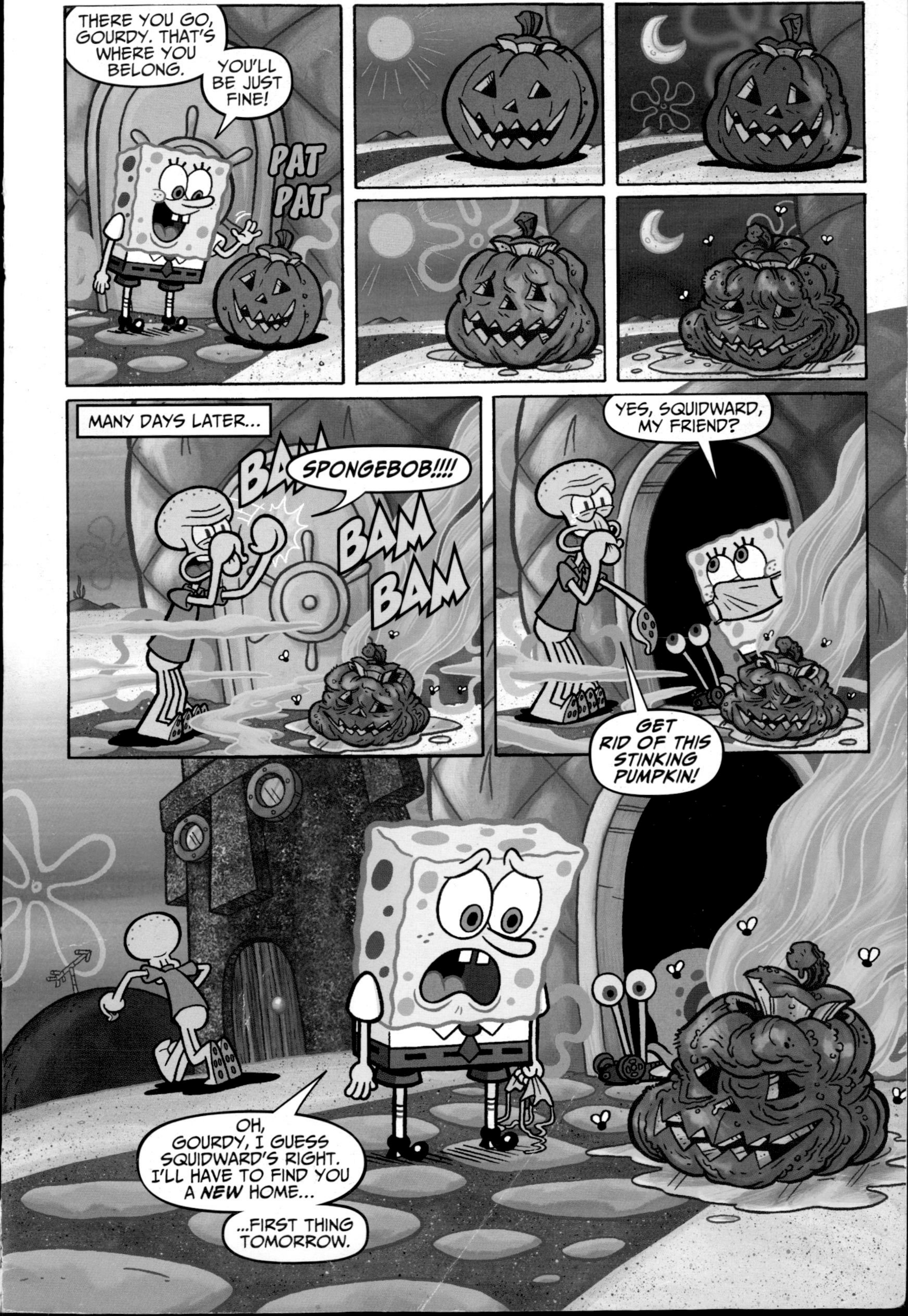
THERE YOU GO, GOURDY. THAT'S WHERE YOU BELONG.
YOU'LL BE JUST FINE!
PAT PAT
MANY DAYS LATER...
BAM
SPONGEBOB!!!!
BAM BAM
YES, SQUIDWARD, MY FRIEND?
GET RID OF THIS STINKING PUMPKIN!
OH, GOURDY, I GUESS SQUIDWARD'S RIGHT. I'LL HAVE TO FIND YOU A NEW HOME...
...FIRST THING TOMORROW.

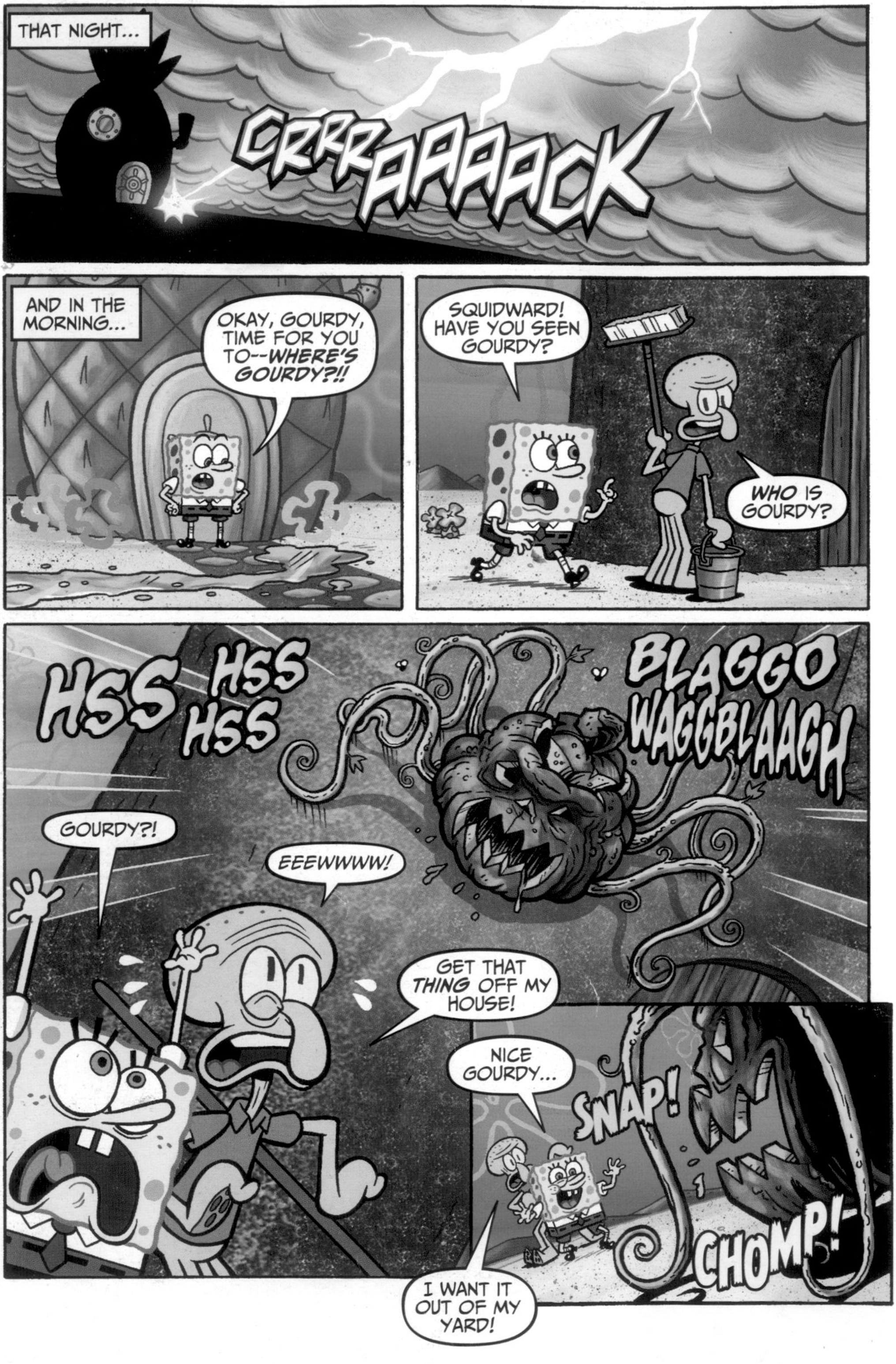
THAT NIGHT...
CRRRAAAAACK
AND IN THE MORNING...
OKAY, GOURDY, TIME FOR YOU TO--WHERE'S GOURDY?!!
SQUIDWARD! HAVE YOU SEEN GOURDY?
WHO IS GOURDY?
HSS HSS HSS
BLAGGO WAGGBLAAGH
GOURDY?!
EEEWWWW!
GET THAT THING OFF MY HOUSE!
NICE GOURDY...
SNAP!
CHOMP!
I WANT IT OUT OF MY YARD!

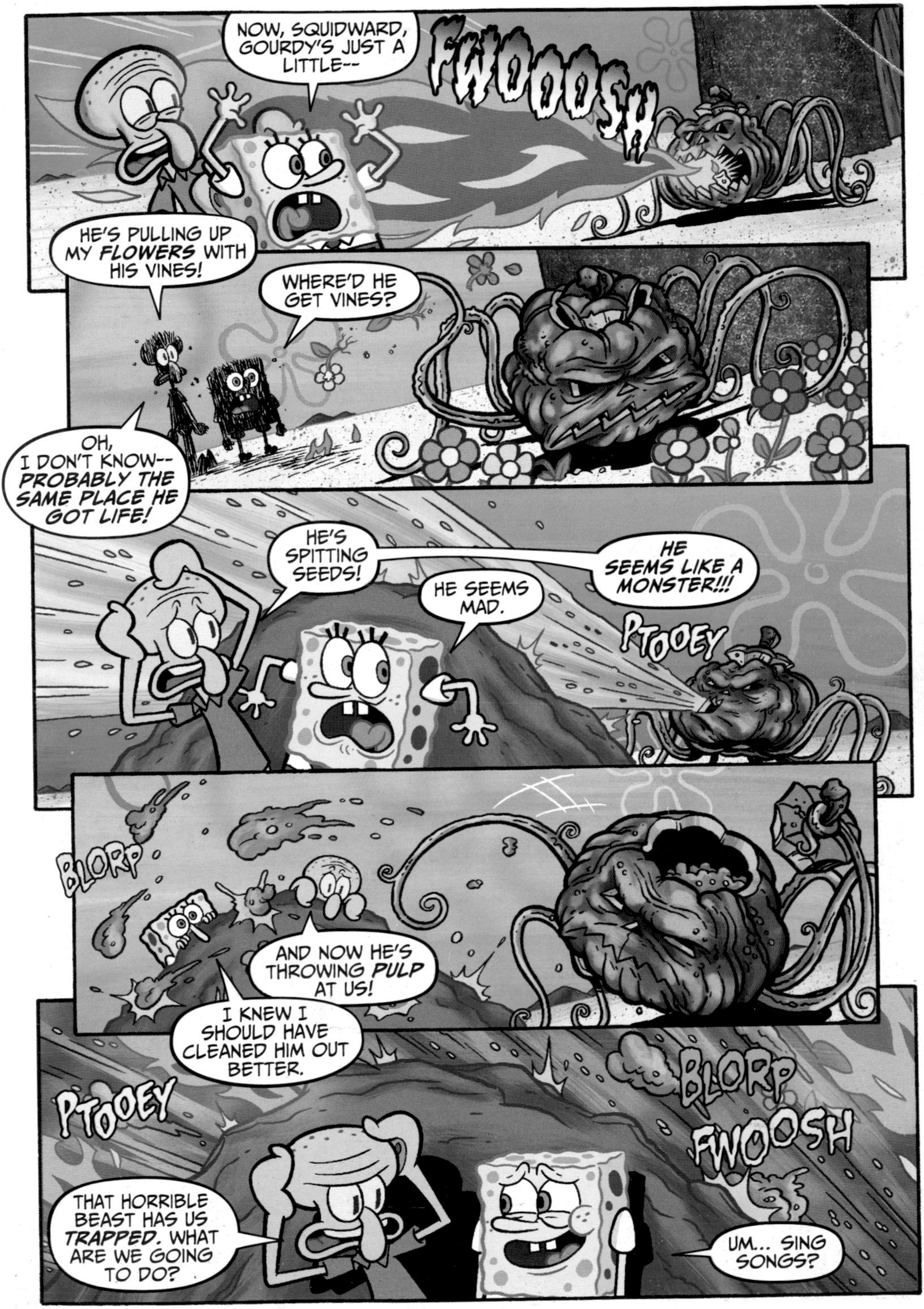
NOW, SQUIDWARD, GOURDY'S JUST A LITTLE--
FWOOOSH
HE'S PULLING UP MY FLOWERS WITH HIS VINES!
WHERE'D HE GET VINES?
OH, I DON'T KNOW-- PROBABLY THE SAME PLACE HE GOT LIFE!
HE'S SPITTING SEEDS!
HE SEEMS MAD.
HE SEEMS LIKE A MONSTER!!!
PTOOEY
BLORP
AND NOW HE'S THROWING PULP AT US!
I KNEW I SHOULD HAVE CLEANED HIM OUT BETTER.
PTOOEY
BLORP
FWOOSH
THAT HORRIBLE BEAST HAS US TRAPPED. WHAT ARE WE GOING TO DO?
UM... SING SONGS?

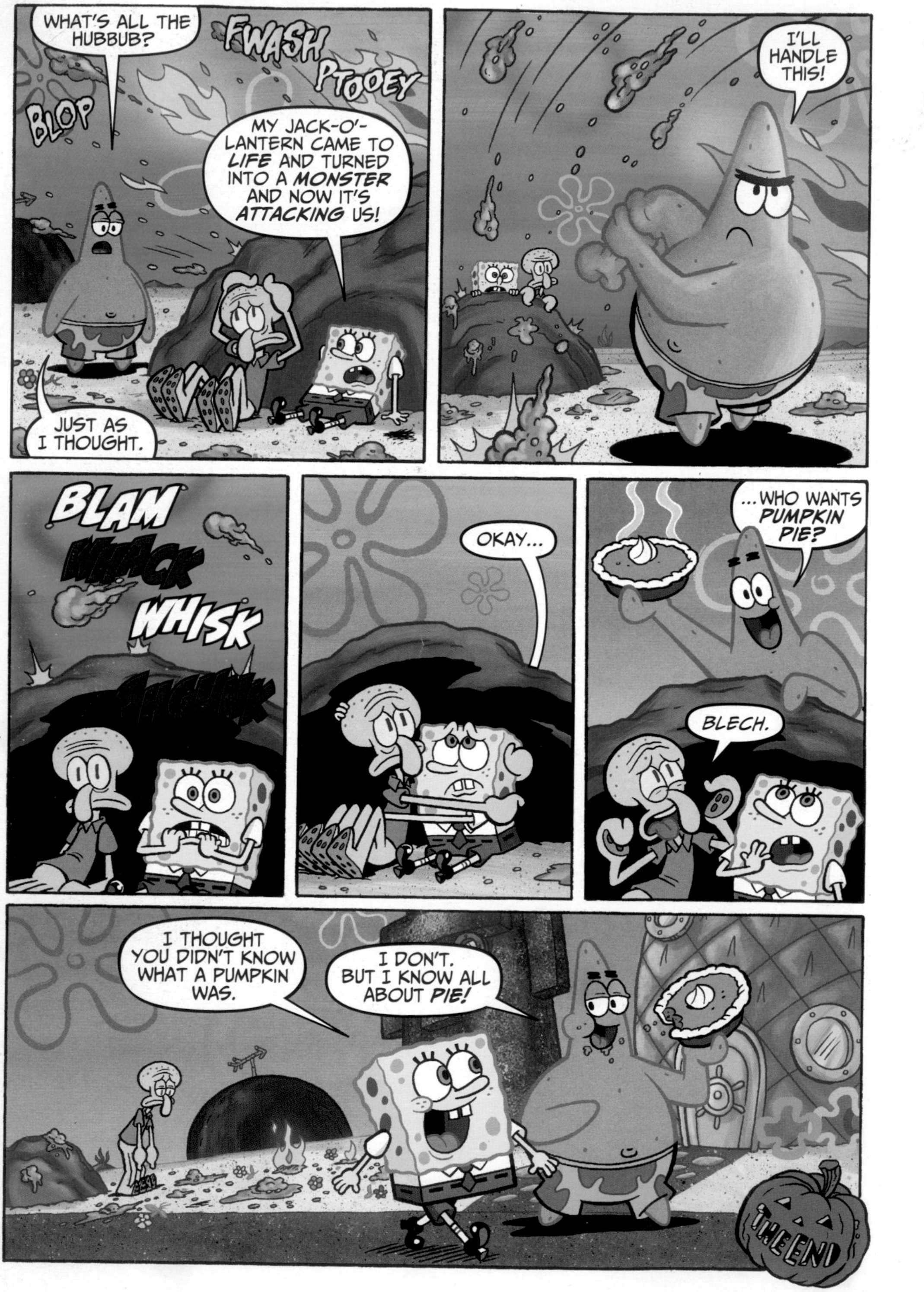
WHAT'S ALL THE HUBBUB?
FWASH
PTOOEY
BLOP
MY JACK-O'-LANTERN CAME TO *LIFE* AND TURNED INTO A *MONSTER* AND NOW IT'S *ATTACKING* US!
JUST AS I THOUGHT.
I'LL HANDLE THIS!
BLAM
WHACK
WHISK
OKAY...
...WHO WANTS *PUMPKIN PIE?*
BLECH.
I THOUGHT YOU DIDN'T KNOW WHAT A PUMPKIN WAS.
I DON'T. BUT I KNOW ALL ABOUT *PIE!*
THE END

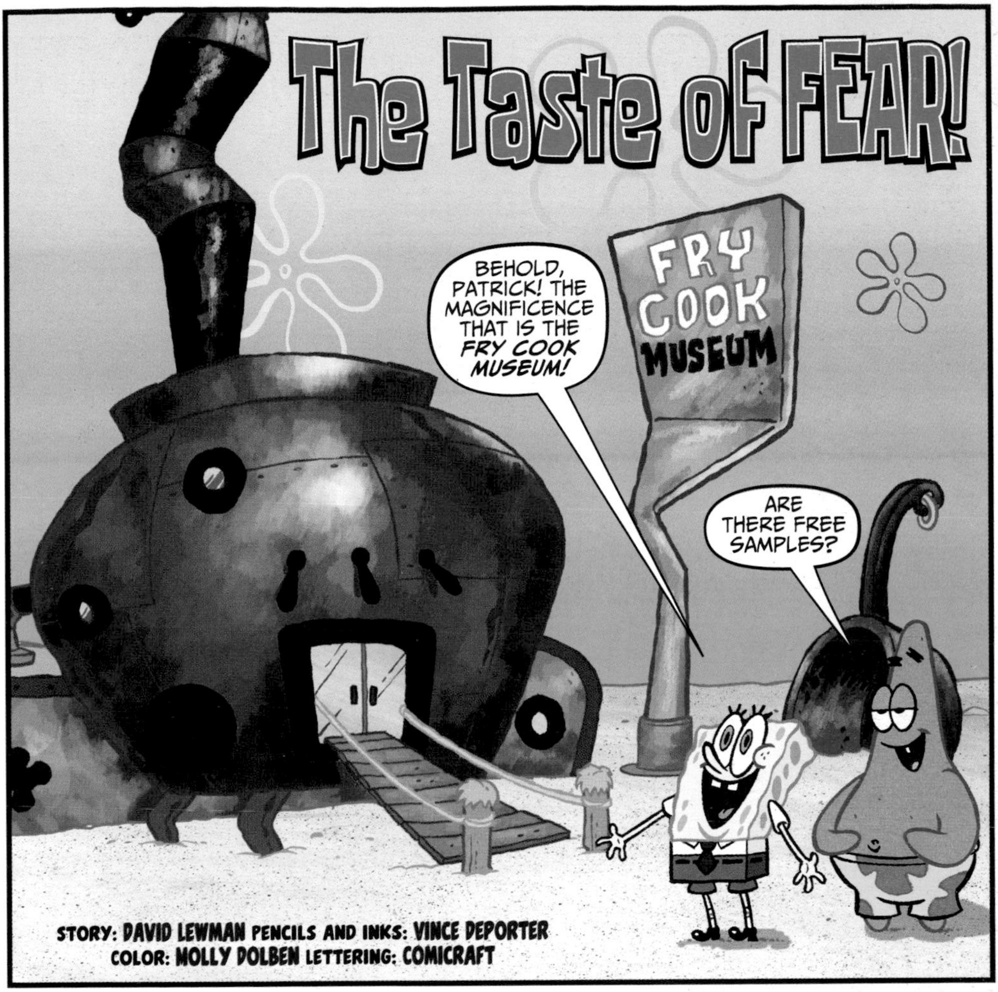
The Taste of FEAR!
FRY COOK MUSEUM
BEHOLD, PATRICK! THE MAGNIFICENCE THAT IS THE *FRY COOK MUSEUM!*
ARE THERE FREE SAMPLES?
STORY: DAVID LEWMAN PENCILS AND INKS: VINCE DEPORTER
COLOR: MOLLY DOLBEN LETTERING: COMICRAFT

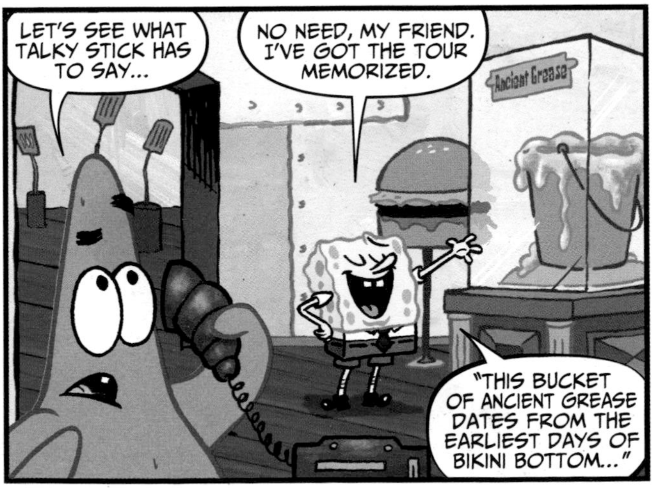
LET'S SEE WHAT TALKY STICK HAS TO SAY...
NO NEED, MY FRIEND. I'VE GOT THE TOUR MEMORIZED.
Ancient Grease
"THIS BUCKET OF ANCIENT GREASE DATES FROM THE EARLIEST DAYS OF BIKINI BOTTOM..."

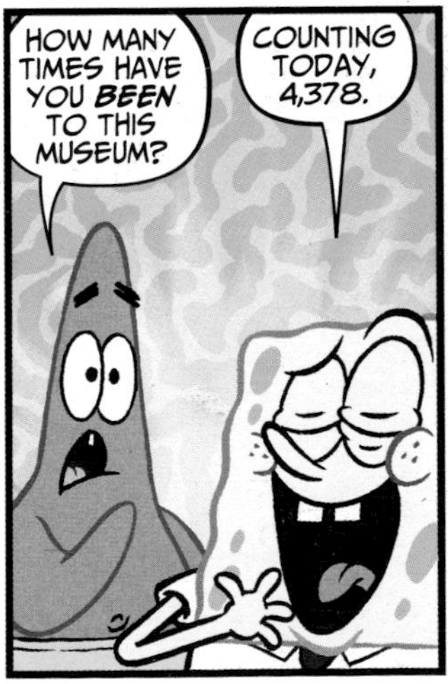
HOW MANY TIMES HAVE YOU *BEEN* TO THIS MUSEUM?
COUNTING TODAY, 4,378.

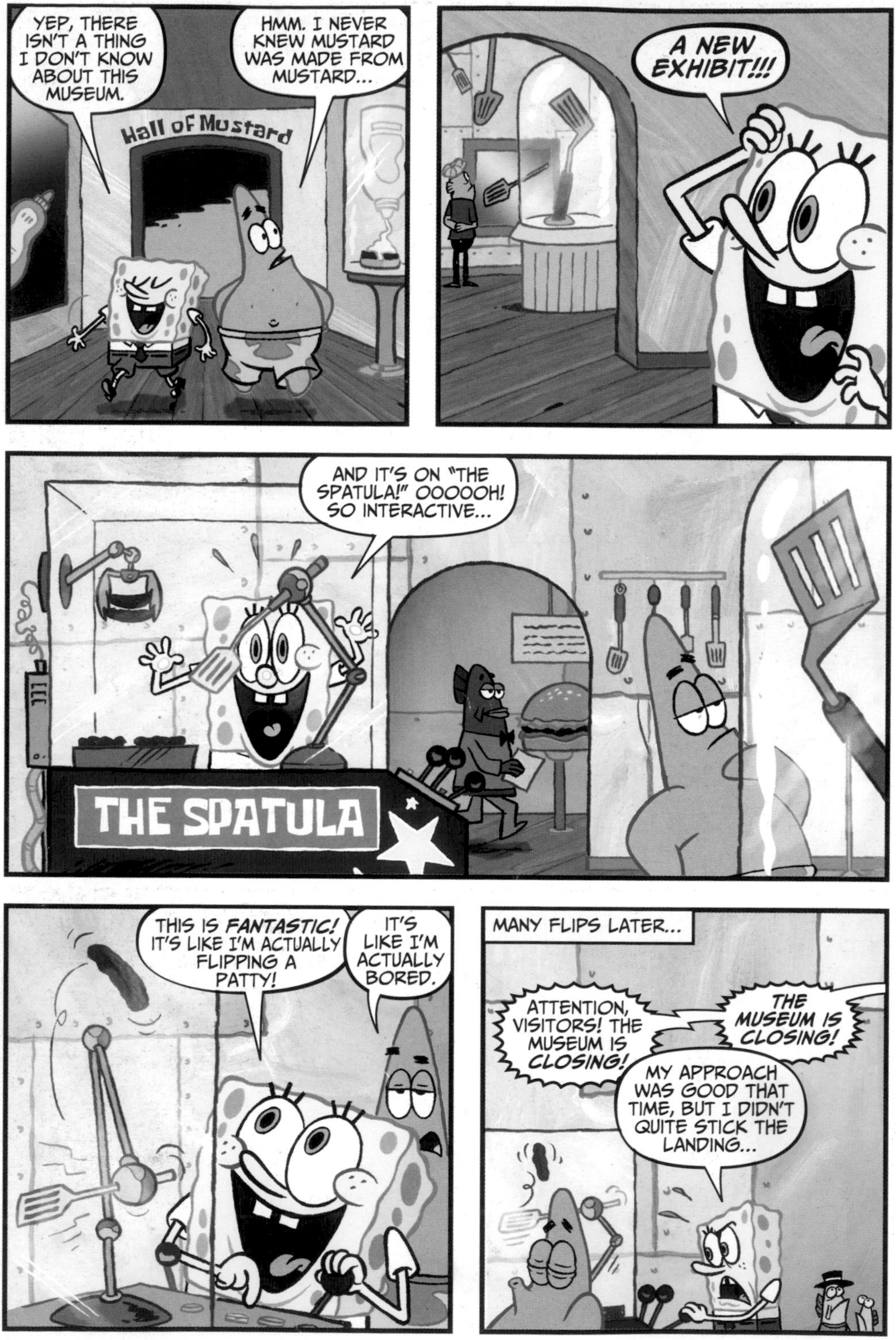
YEP, THERE ISN'T A THING I DON'T KNOW ABOUT THIS MUSEUM.
HMM. I NEVER KNEW MUSTARD WAS MADE FROM MUSTARD...
Hall of Mustard
A NEW EXHIBIT!!!
AND IT'S ON "THE SPATULA!" OOOOOH! SO INTERACTIVE...
THE SPATULA
THIS IS FANTASTIC! IT'S LIKE I'M ACTUALLY FLIPPING A PATTY!
IT'S LIKE I'M ACTUALLY BORED.
MANY FLIPS LATER...
ATTENTION, VISITORS! THE MUSEUM IS CLOSING!
THE MUSEUM IS CLOSING!
MY APPROACH WAS GOOD THAT TIME, BUT I DIDN'T QUITE STICK THE LANDING...

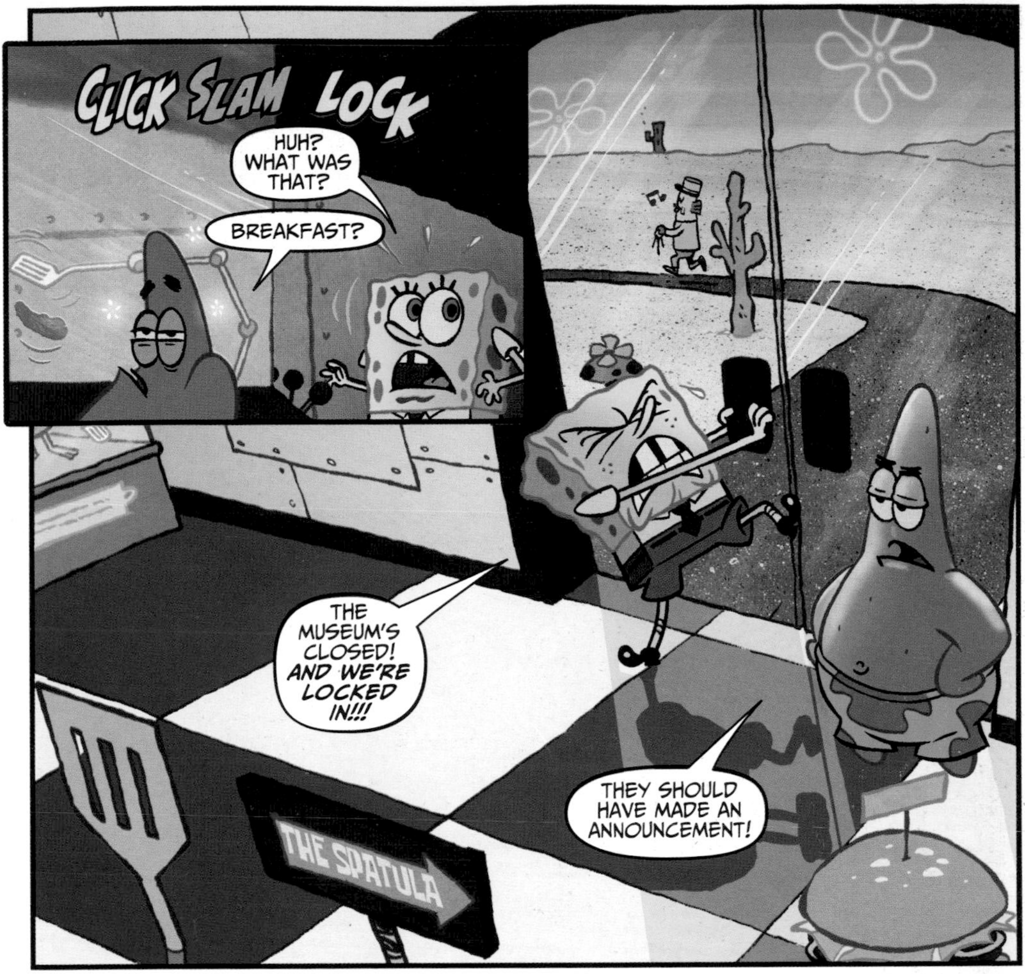
CLICK SLAM LOCK
HUH? WHAT WAS THAT?
BREAKFAST?
THE MUSEUM'S CLOSED! AND WE'RE LOCKED IN!!!
THEY SHOULD HAVE MADE AN ANNOUNCEMENT!
THE SPATULA

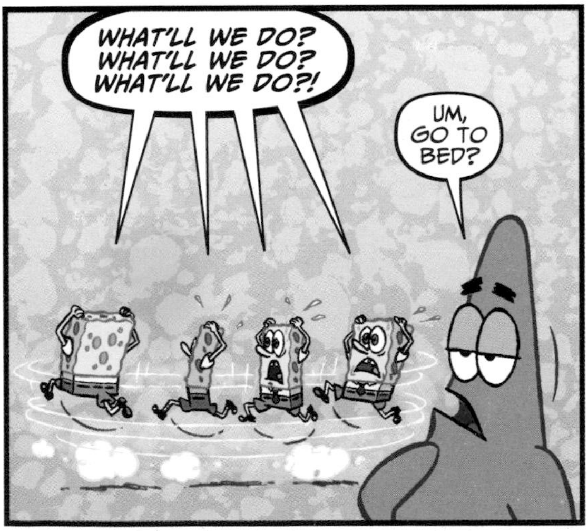
WHAT'LL WE DO? WHAT'LL WE DO? WHAT'LL WE DO?!
UM, GO TO BED?

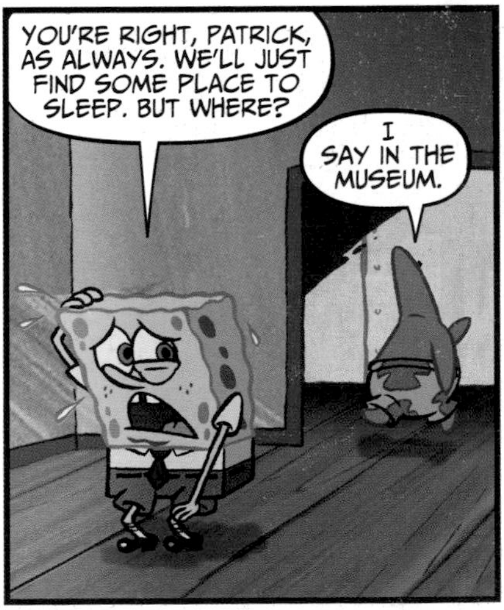
YOU'RE RIGHT, PATRICK, AS ALWAYS. WE'LL JUST FIND SOME PLACE TO SLEEP. BUT WHERE?
I SAY IN THE MUSEUM.

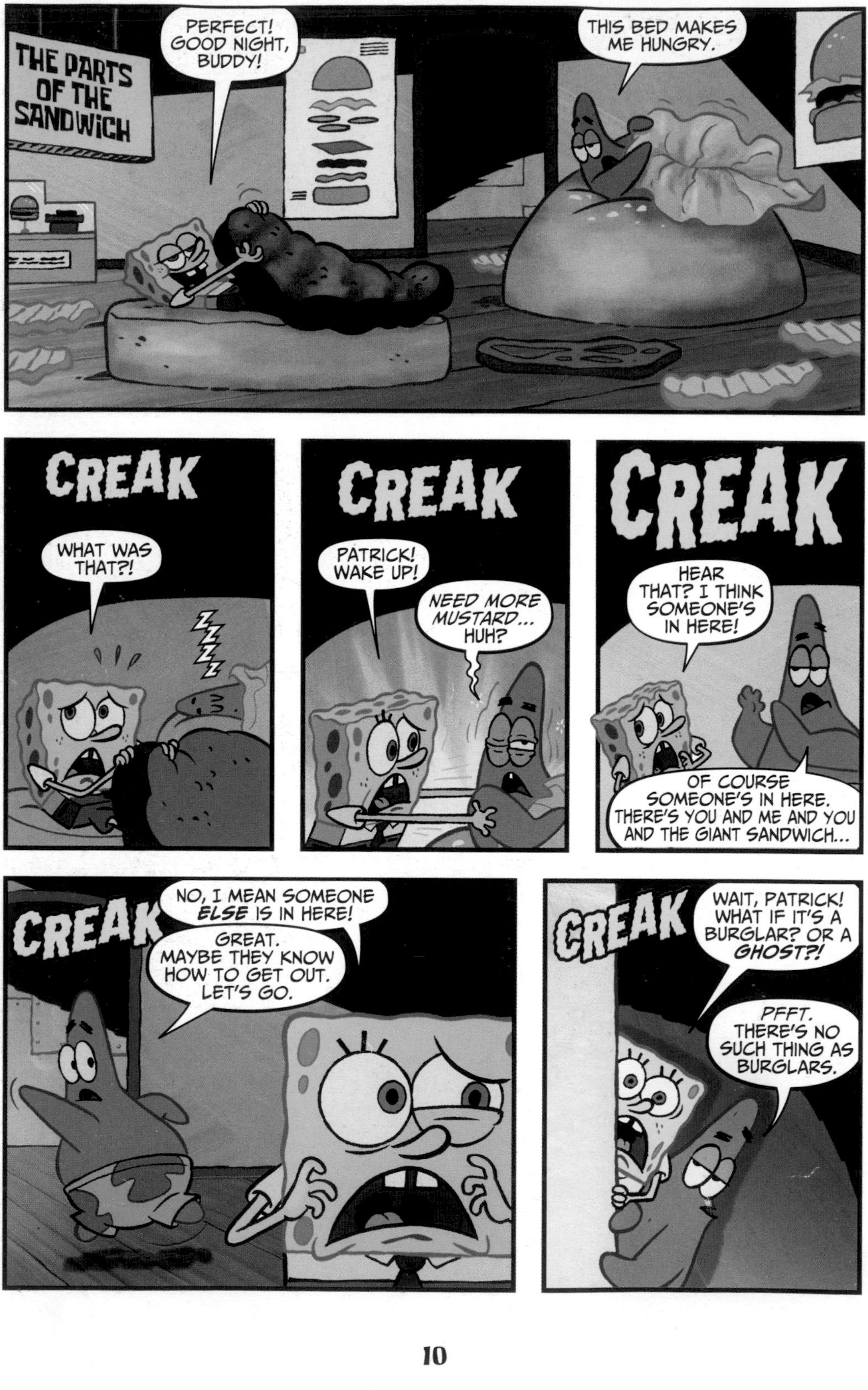
THE PARTS OF THE SANDWICH
PERFECT! GOOD NIGHT, BUDDY!
THIS BED MAKES ME HUNGRY.
CREAK
WHAT WAS THAT?!
ZZZZ
CREAK
PATRICK! WAKE UP!
NEED MORE MUSTARD... HUH?
CREAK
HEAR THAT? I THINK SOMEONE'S IN HERE!
OF COURSE SOMEONE'S IN HERE. THERE'S YOU AND ME AND YOU AND THE GIANT SANDWICH...
CREAK
NO, I MEAN SOMEONE ELSE IS IN HERE!
GREAT. MAYBE THEY KNOW HOW TO GET OUT. LET'S GO.
CREAK
WAIT, PATRICK! WHAT IF IT'S A BURGLAR? OR A GHOST?!
PFFT. THERE'S NO SUCH THING AS BURGLARS.

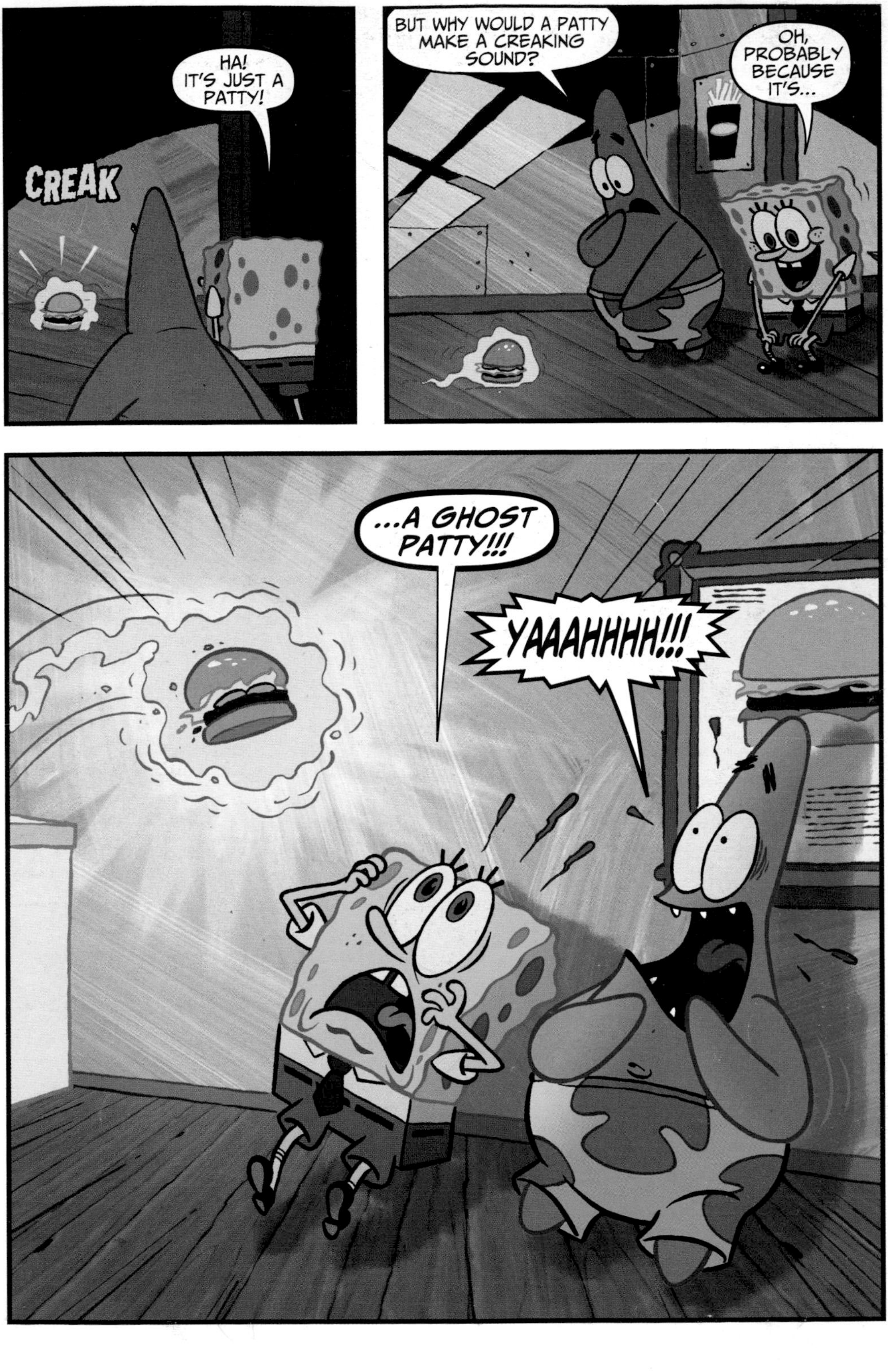
HA! IT'S JUST A PATTY!
CREAK
BUT WHY WOULD A PATTY MAKE A CREAKING SOUND?
OH, PROBABLY BECAUSE IT'S...
...A GHOST PATTY!!!
YAAAHHHH!!!

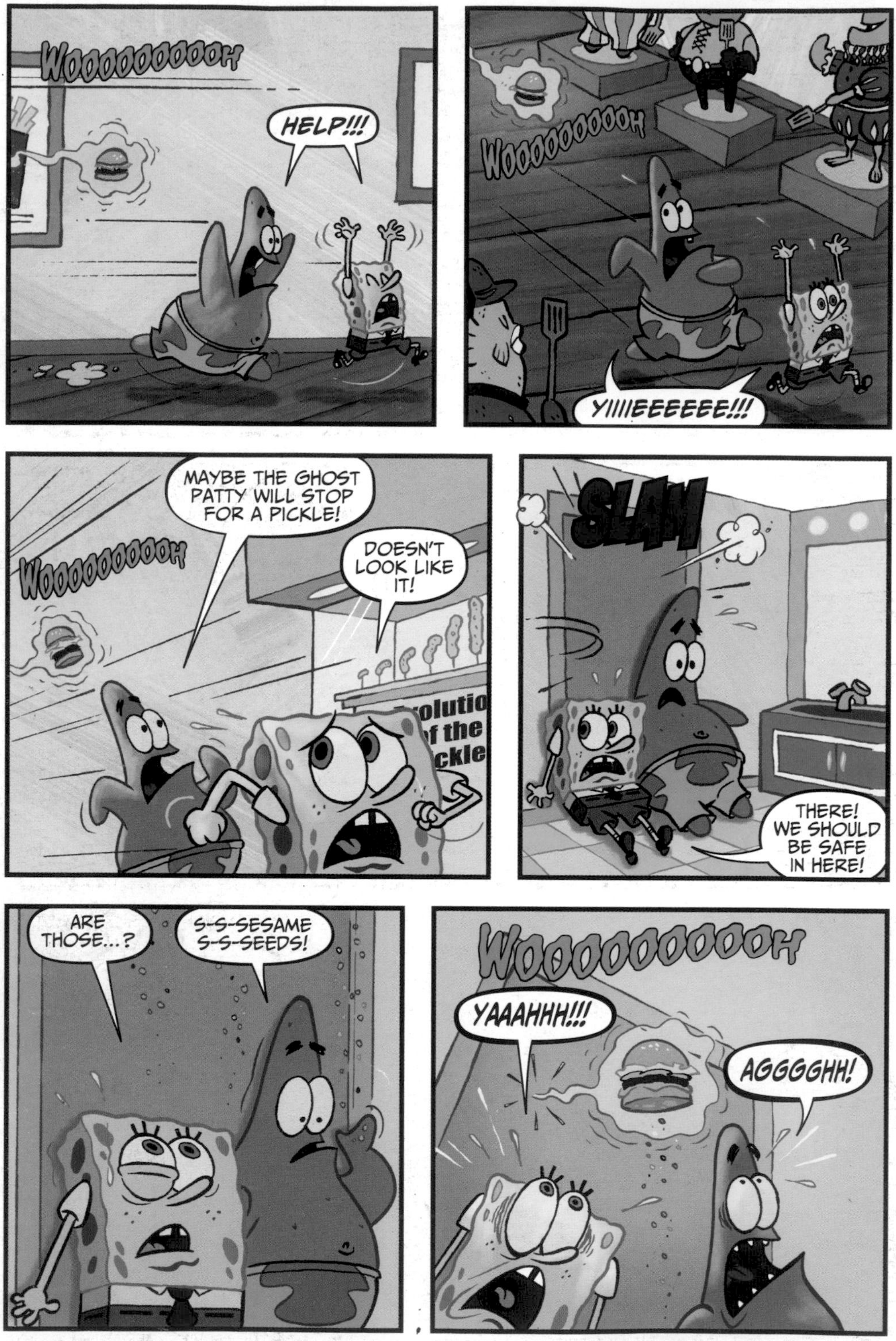
WOOOOOOOOOH
HELP!!!
WOOOOOOOOOH
YIIIIEEEEEEE!!!
MAYBE THE GHOST PATTY WILL STOP FOR A PICKLE!
WOOOOOOOOOH
DOESN'T LOOK LIKE IT!
SLAM
THERE! WE SHOULD BE SAFE IN HERE!
ARE THOSE...?
S-S-SESAME S-S-SEEDS!
WOOOOOOOOOOH
YAAAHHH!!!
AGGGGHH!

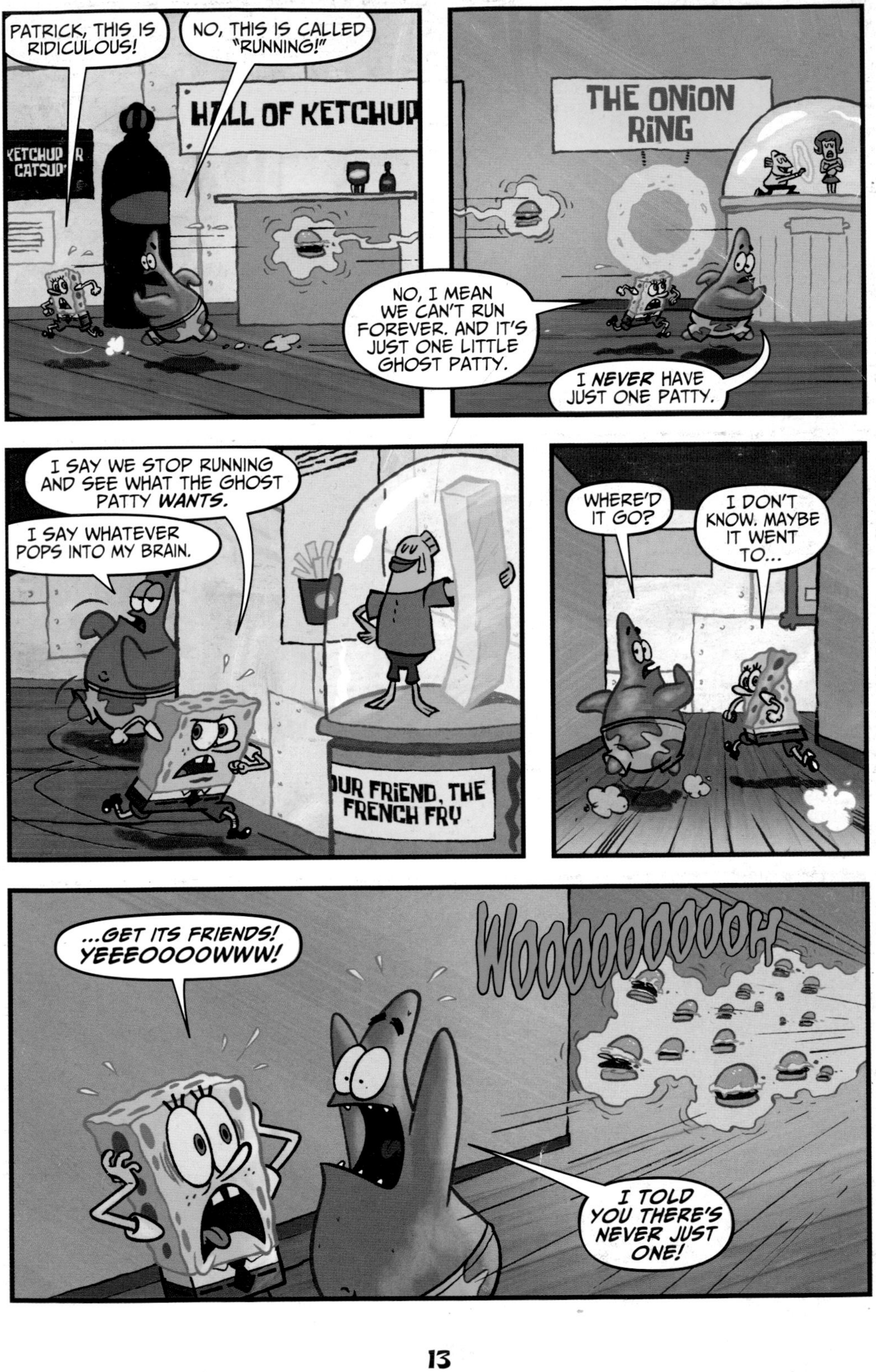

PATRICK, THIS IS RIDICULOUS!
NO, THIS IS CALLED "RUNNING!"
HALL OF KETCHUP
THE ONION RING
NO, I MEAN WE CAN'T RUN FOREVER. AND IT'S JUST ONE LITTLE GHOST PATTY.
I NEVER HAVE JUST ONE PATTY.
I SAY WE STOP RUNNING AND SEE WHAT THE GHOST PATTY WANTS.
I SAY WHATEVER POPS INTO MY BRAIN.
OUR FRIEND, THE FRENCH FRY
WHERE'D IT GO?
I DON'T KNOW. MAYBE IT WENT TO...
...GET ITS FRIENDS! YEEEOOOOWWW!
WOOOOOOOOOH
I TOLD YOU THERE'S NEVER JUST ONE!

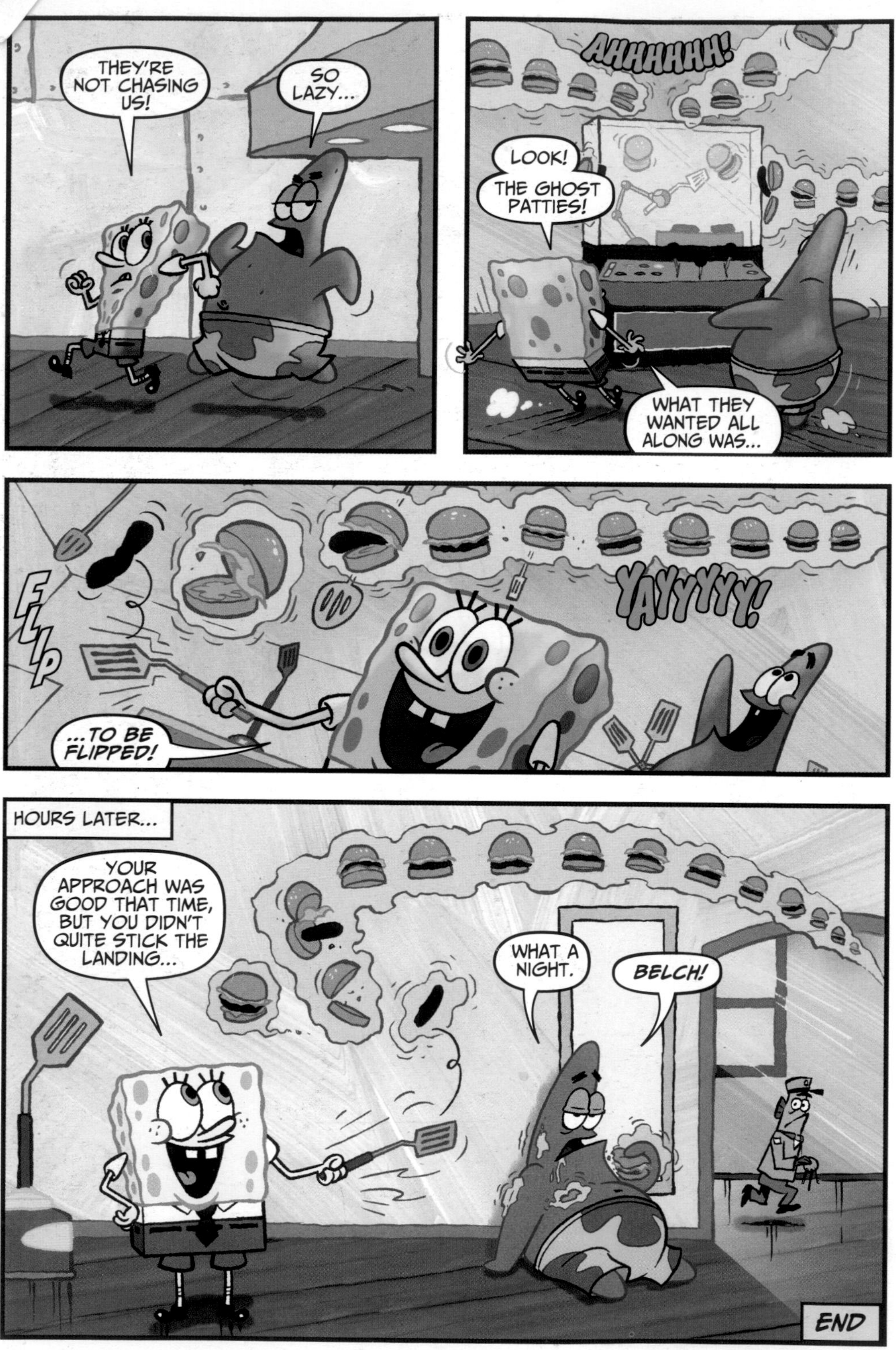
THEY'RE NOT CHASING US!
SO LAZY...
AHHHHHH!
LOOK!
THE GHOST PATTIES!
WHAT THEY WANTED ALL ALONG WAS...
FLIP
YAYYYY!
...TO BE FLIPPED!
HOURS LATER...
YOUR APPROACH WAS GOOD THAT TIME, BUT YOU DIDN'T QUITE STICK THE LANDING...
WHAT A NIGHT.
BELCH!
END

SPONGEFUNNIES by KOCHAL

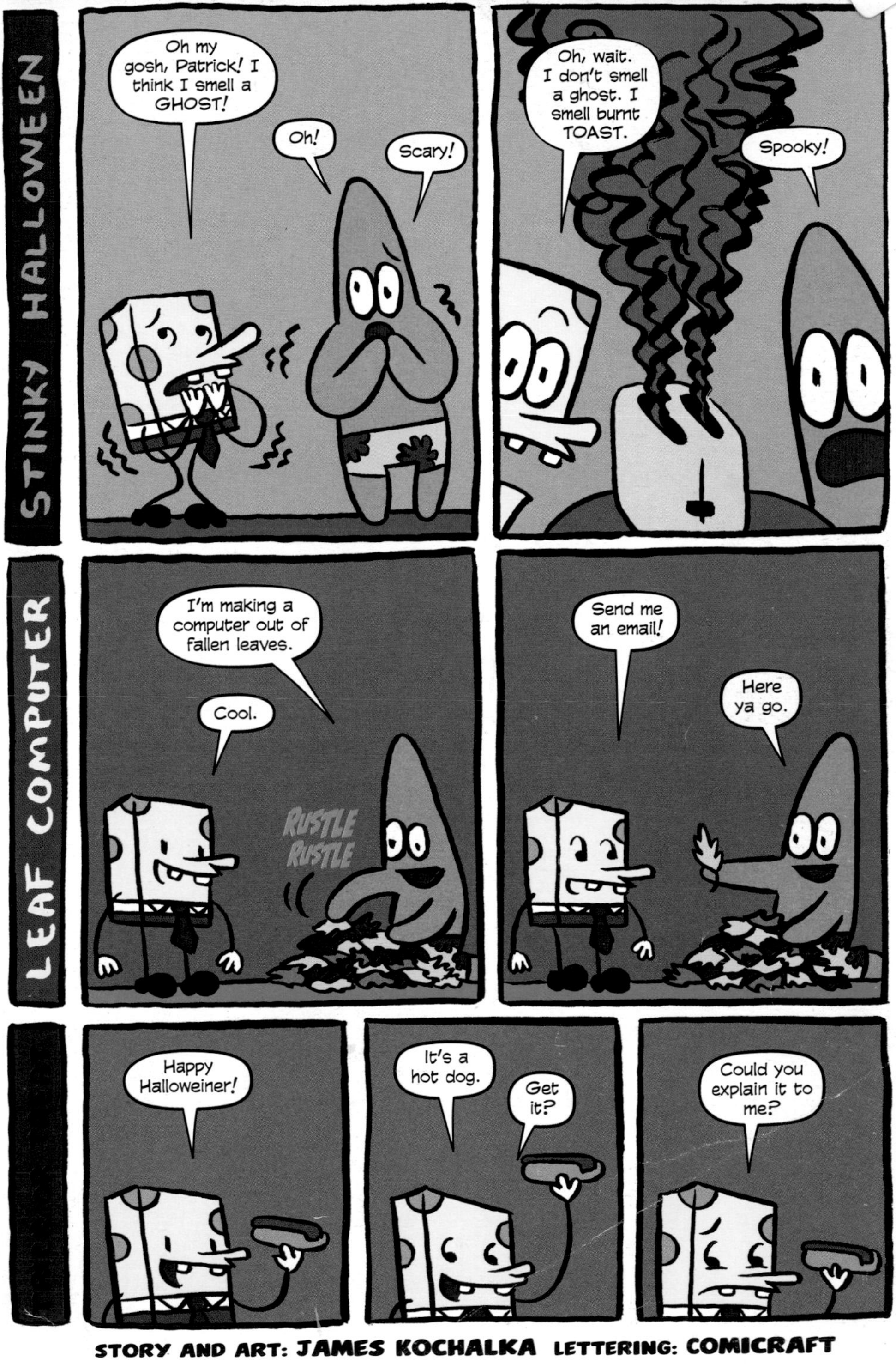
STINKY HALLOWEEN
Oh my gosh, Patrick! I think I smell a GHOST!
Oh!
Scary!
Oh, wait. I don't smell a ghost. I smell burnt TOAST.
Spooky!
LEAF COMPUTER
I'm making a computer out of fallen leaves.
Cool.
RUSTLE RUSTLE
Send me an email!
Here ya go.
Happy Halloweiner!
It's a hot dog.
Get it?
Could you explain it to me?

STORY AND ART: JAMES KOCHALKA LETTERING: COMICRAFT

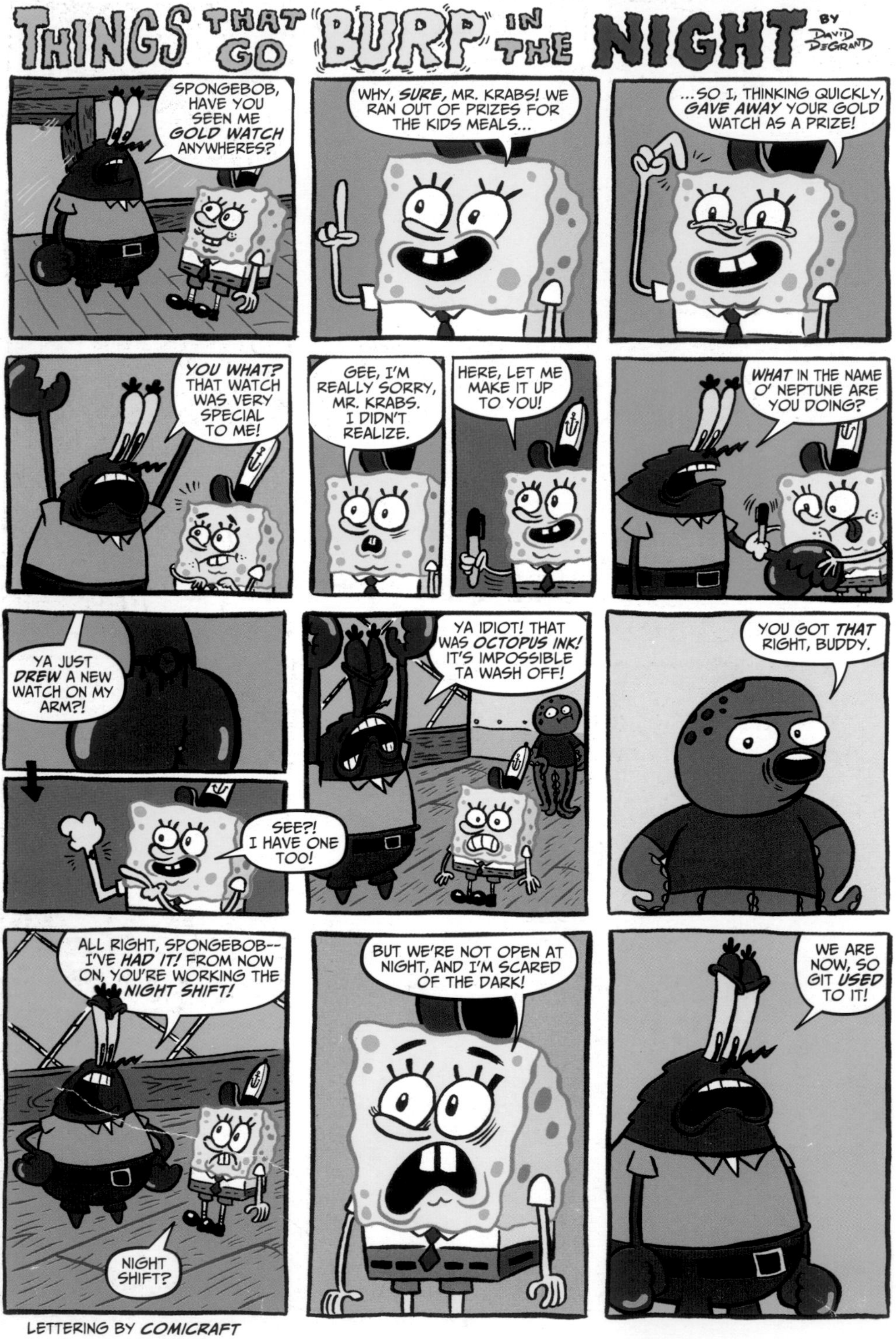
THINGS THAT GO BURP IN THE NIGHT
BY DAVID DEGRAND
SPONGEBOB, HAVE YOU SEEN ME GOLD WATCH ANYWHERES?
WHY, SURE, MR. KRABS! WE RAN OUT OF PRIZES FOR THE KIDS MEALS...
...SO I, THINKING QUICKLY, GAVE AWAY YOUR GOLD WATCH AS A PRIZE!
YOU WHAT? THAT WATCH WAS VERY SPECIAL TO ME!
GEE, I'M REALLY SORRY, MR. KRABS. I DIDN'T REALIZE.
HERE, LET ME MAKE IT UP TO YOU!
WHAT IN THE NAME O' NEPTUNE ARE YOU DOING?
YA JUST DREW A NEW WATCH ON MY ARM?!
SEE?! I HAVE ONE TOO!
YA IDIOT! THAT WAS OCTOPUS INK! IT'S IMPOSSIBLE TA WASH OFF!
YOU GOT THAT RIGHT, BUDDY.
ALL RIGHT, SPONGEBOB-- I'VE HAD IT! FROM NOW ON, YOU'RE WORKING THE NIGHT SHIFT!
NIGHT SHIFT?
BUT WE'RE NOT OPEN AT NIGHT, AND I'M SCARED OF THE DARK!
WE ARE NOW, SO GIT USED TO IT!

LETTERING BY COMICRAFT

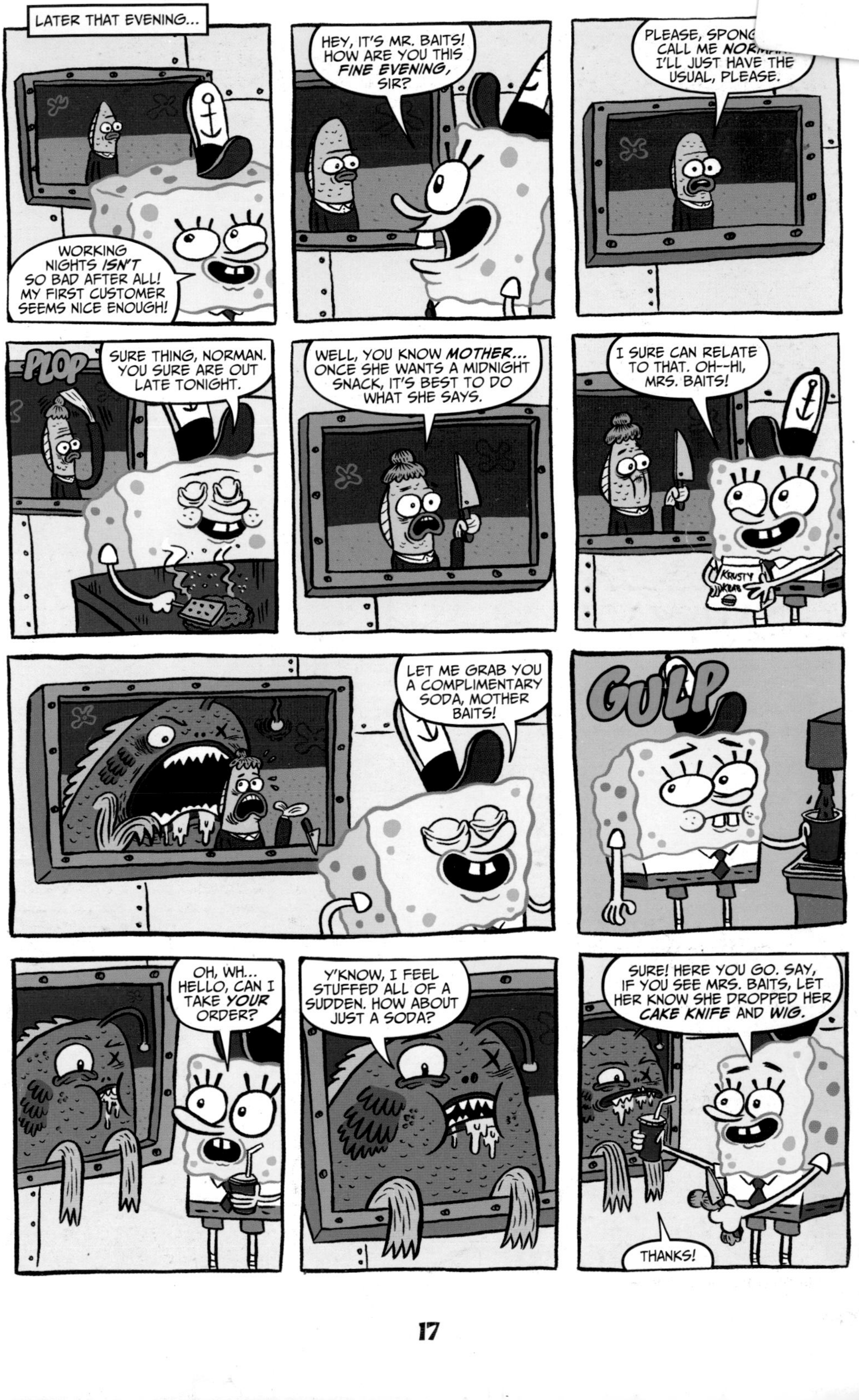

LATER THAT EVENING...
WORKING NIGHTS *ISN'T* SO BAD AFTER ALL! MY FIRST CUSTOMER SEEMS NICE ENOUGH!
HEY, IT'S MR. BAITS! HOW ARE YOU THIS *FINE EVENING,* SIR?
PLEASE, SPONG CALL ME NORM I'LL JUST HAVE THE USUAL, PLEASE.
PLOP
SURE THING, NORMAN. YOU SURE ARE OUT LATE TONIGHT.
WELL, YOU KNOW *MOTHER...* ONCE SHE WANTS A MIDNIGHT SNACK, IT'S BEST TO DO WHAT SHE SAYS.
I SURE CAN RELATE TO THAT. OH--HI, MRS. BAITS!
KRUSTY KRAB
LET ME GRAB YOU A COMPLIMENTARY SODA, MOTHER BAITS!
GULP
OH, WH... HELLO, CAN I TAKE *YOUR* ORDER?
Y'KNOW, I FEEL STUFFED ALL OF A SUDDEN. HOW ABOUT JUST A SODA?
SURE! HERE YOU GO. SAY, IF YOU SEE MRS. BAITS, LET HER KNOW SHE DROPPED HER *CAKE KNIFE* AND *WIG.*
THANKS!

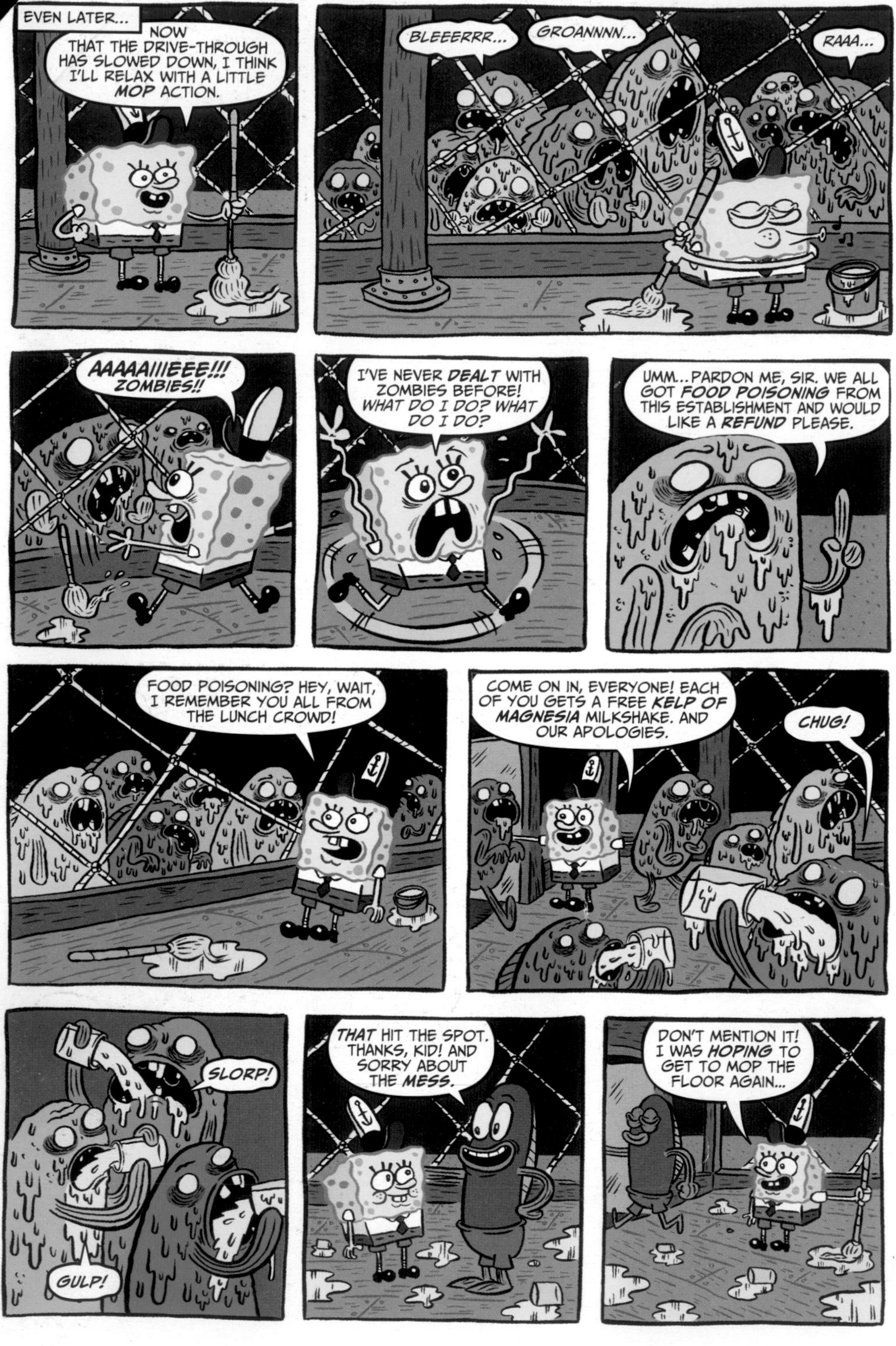
EVEN LATER...
NOW THAT THE DRIVE-THROUGH HAS SLOWED DOWN, I THINK I'LL RELAX WITH A LITTLE MOP ACTION.
BLEEERRR...
GROANNNN...
RAAA...
AAAAAIIIEEE!!! ZOMBIES!!
I'VE NEVER DEALT WITH ZOMBIES BEFORE! WHAT DO I DO? WHAT DO I DO?
UMM...PARDON ME, SIR. WE ALL GOT FOOD POISONING FROM THIS ESTABLISHMENT AND WOULD LIKE A REFUND PLEASE.
FOOD POISONING? HEY, WAIT, I REMEMBER YOU ALL FROM THE LUNCH CROWD!
COME ON IN, EVERYONE! EACH OF YOU GETS A FREE KELP OF MAGNESIA MILKSHAKE. AND OUR APOLOGIES.
CHUG!
SLORP!
GULP!
THAT HIT THE SPOT. THANKS, KID! AND SORRY ABOUT THE MESS.
DON'T MENTION IT! I WAS HOPING TO GET TO MOP THE FLOOR AGAIN...

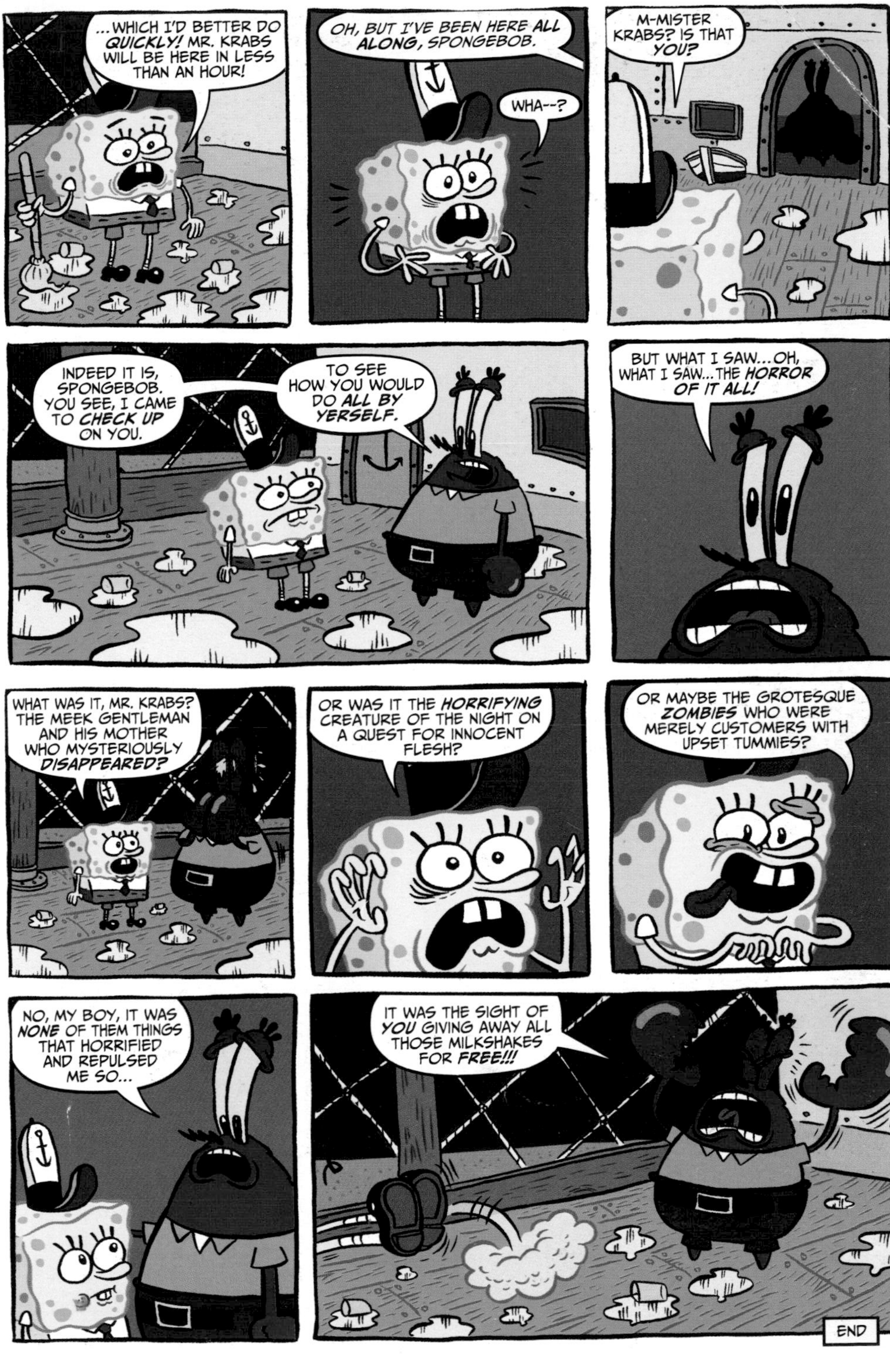
...WHICH I'D BETTER DO QUICKLY! MR. KRABS WILL BE HERE IN LESS THAN AN HOUR!
OH, BUT I'VE BEEN HERE ALL ALONG, SPONGEBOB.
WHA--?
M-MISTER KRABS? IS THAT YOU?
INDEED IT IS, SPONGEBOB. YOU SEE, I CAME TO CHECK UP ON YOU.
TO SEE HOW YOU WOULD DO ALL BY YERSELF.
BUT WHAT I SAW...OH, WHAT I SAW...THE HORROR OF IT ALL!
WHAT WAS IT, MR. KRABS? THE MEEK GENTLEMAN AND HIS MOTHER WHO MYSTERIOUSLY DISAPPEARED?
OR WAS IT THE HORRIFYING CREATURE OF THE NIGHT ON A QUEST FOR INNOCENT FLESH?
OR MAYBE THE GROTESQUE ZOMBIES WHO WERE MERELY CUSTOMERS WITH UPSET TUMMIES?
NO, MY BOY, IT WAS NONE OF THEM THINGS THAT HORRIFIED AND REPULSED ME SO...
IT WAS THE SIGHT OF YOU GIVING AWAY ALL THOSE MILKSHAKES FOR FREE!!!
END

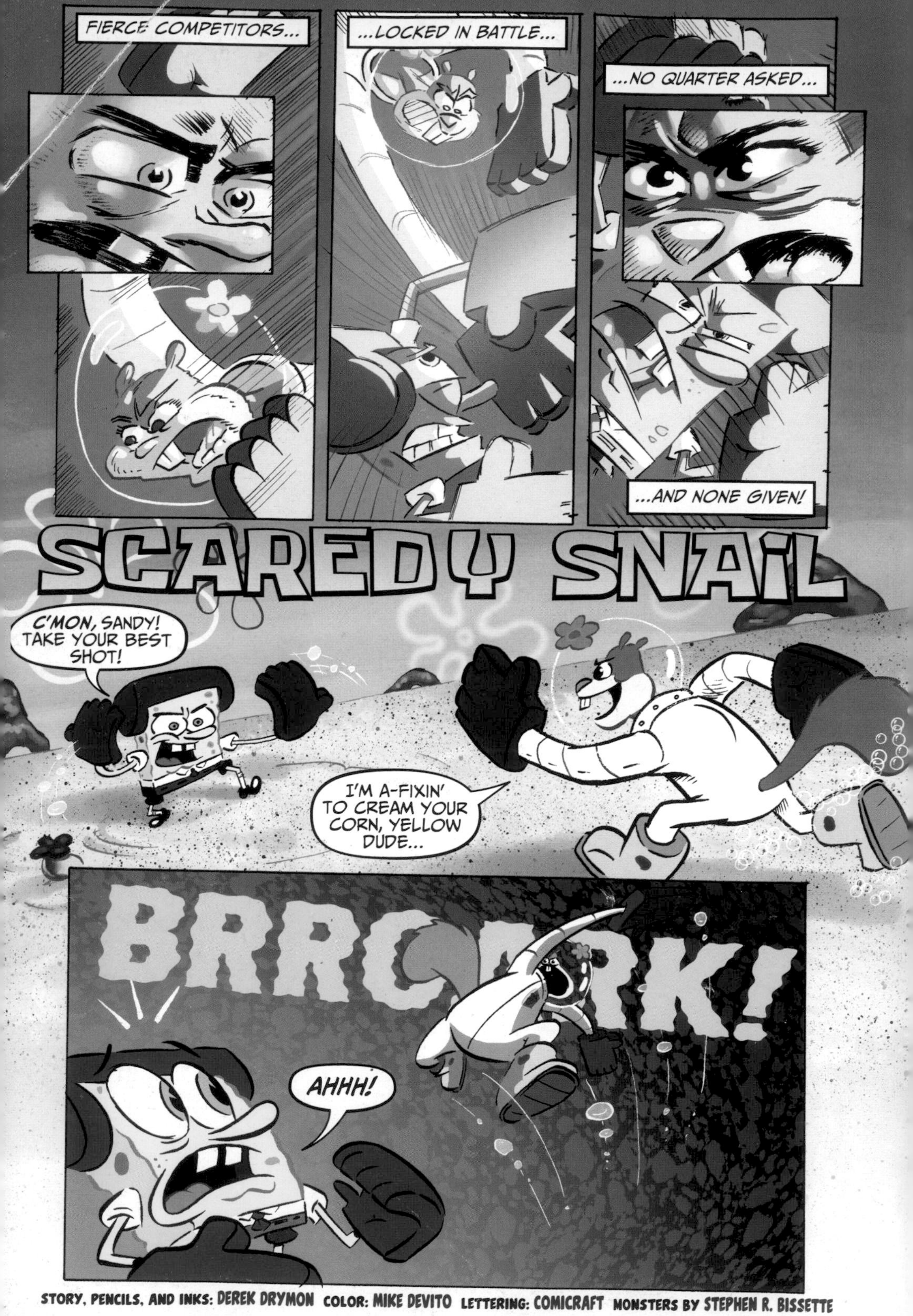
FIERCE COMPETITORS...
...LOCKED IN BATTLE...
...NO QUARTER ASKED...
...AND NONE GIVEN!
SCAREDY SNAIL
C'MON, SANDY! TAKE YOUR BEST SHOT!
I'M A-FIXIN' TO CREAM YOUR CORN, YELLOW DUDE...
AHHH!

STORY, PENCILS, AND INKS: DEREK DRYMON COLOR: MIKE DEVITO LETTERING: COMICRAFT MONSTERS BY STEPHEN R. BISSETTE

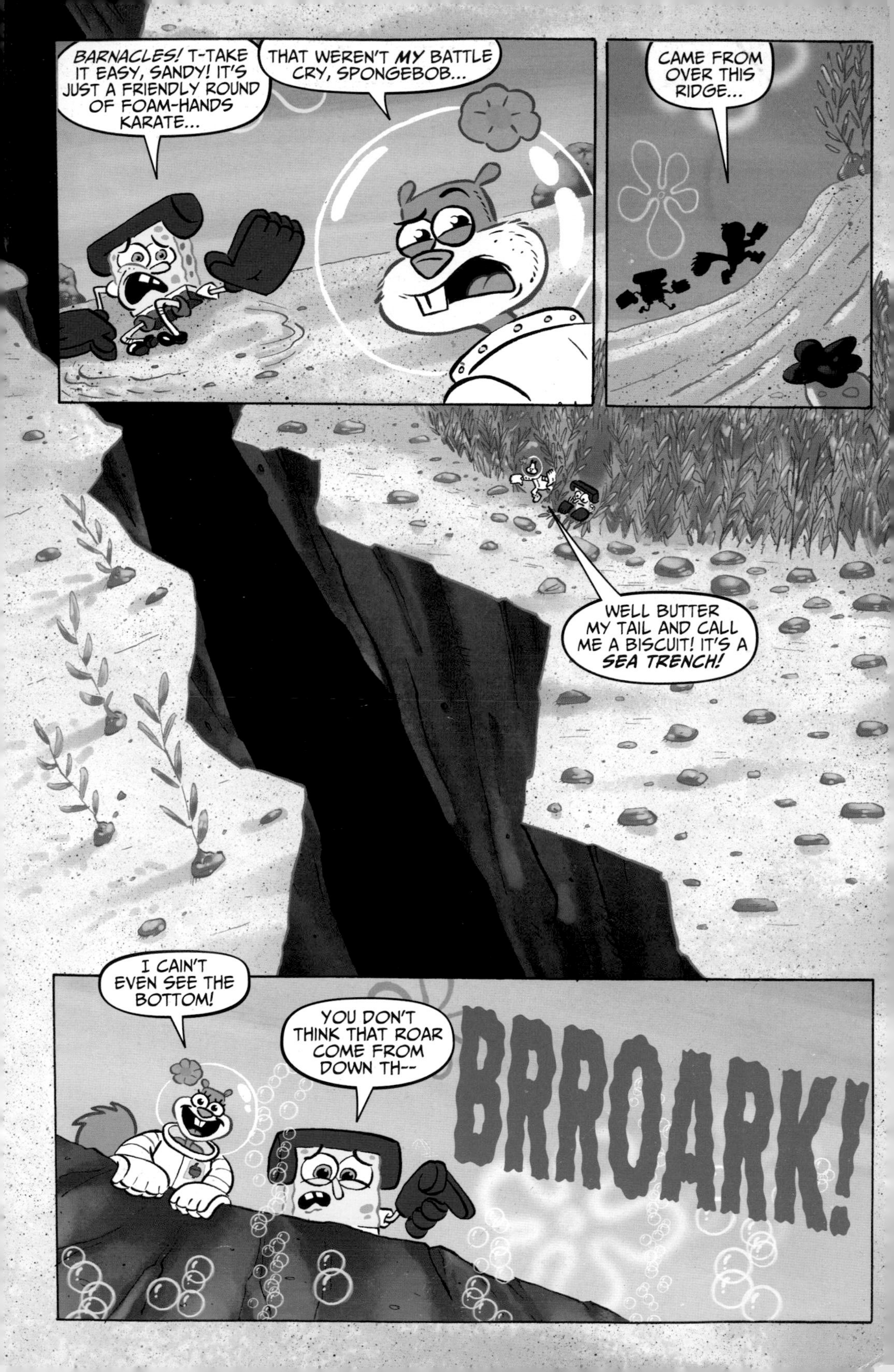
BARNACLES! T-TAKE IT EASY, SANDY! IT'S JUST A FRIENDLY ROUND OF FOAM-HANDS KARATE...
THAT WEREN'T MY BATTLE CRY, SPONGEBOB...
CAME FROM OVER THIS RIDGE...
WELL BUTTER MY TAIL AND CALL ME A BISCUIT! IT'S A SEA TRENCH!
I CAIN'T EVEN SEE THE BOTTOM!
YOU DON'T THINK THAT ROAR COME FROM DOWN TH--
BRROARK!

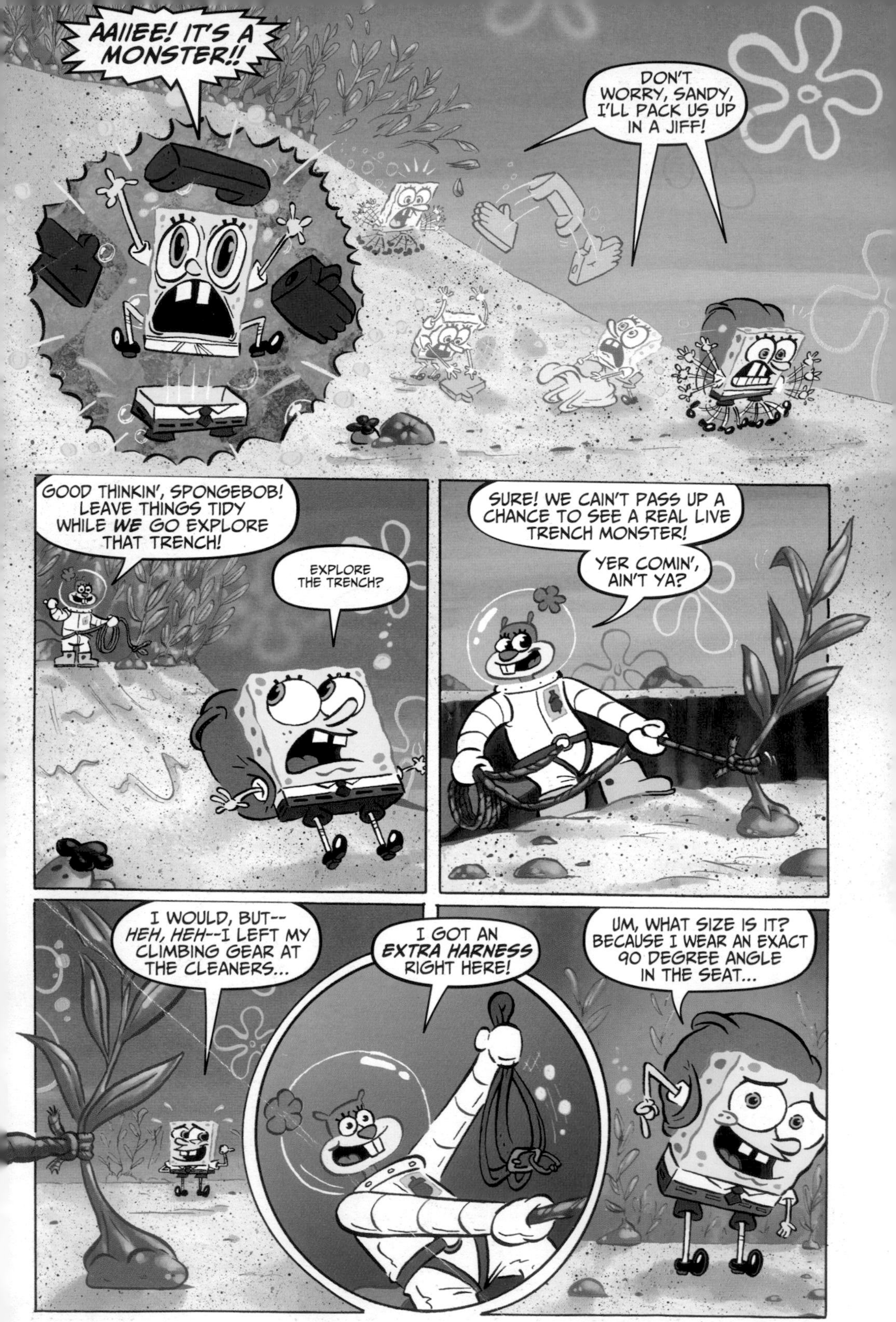
AAIIEE! IT'S A MONSTER!!
DON'T WORRY, SANDY, I'LL PACK US UP IN A JIFF!
GOOD THINKIN', SPONGEBOB! LEAVE THINGS TIDY WHILE *WE* GO EXPLORE THAT TRENCH!
EXPLORE THE TRENCH?
SURE! WE CAIN'T PASS UP A CHANCE TO SEE A REAL LIVE TRENCH MONSTER!
YER COMIN', AIN'T YA?
I WOULD, BUT-- *HEH, HEH*--I LEFT MY CLIMBING GEAR AT THE CLEANERS...
I GOT AN ***EXTRA HARNESS*** RIGHT HERE!
UM, WHAT SIZE IS IT? BECAUSE I WEAR AN EXACT 90 DEGREE ANGLE IN THE SEAT...

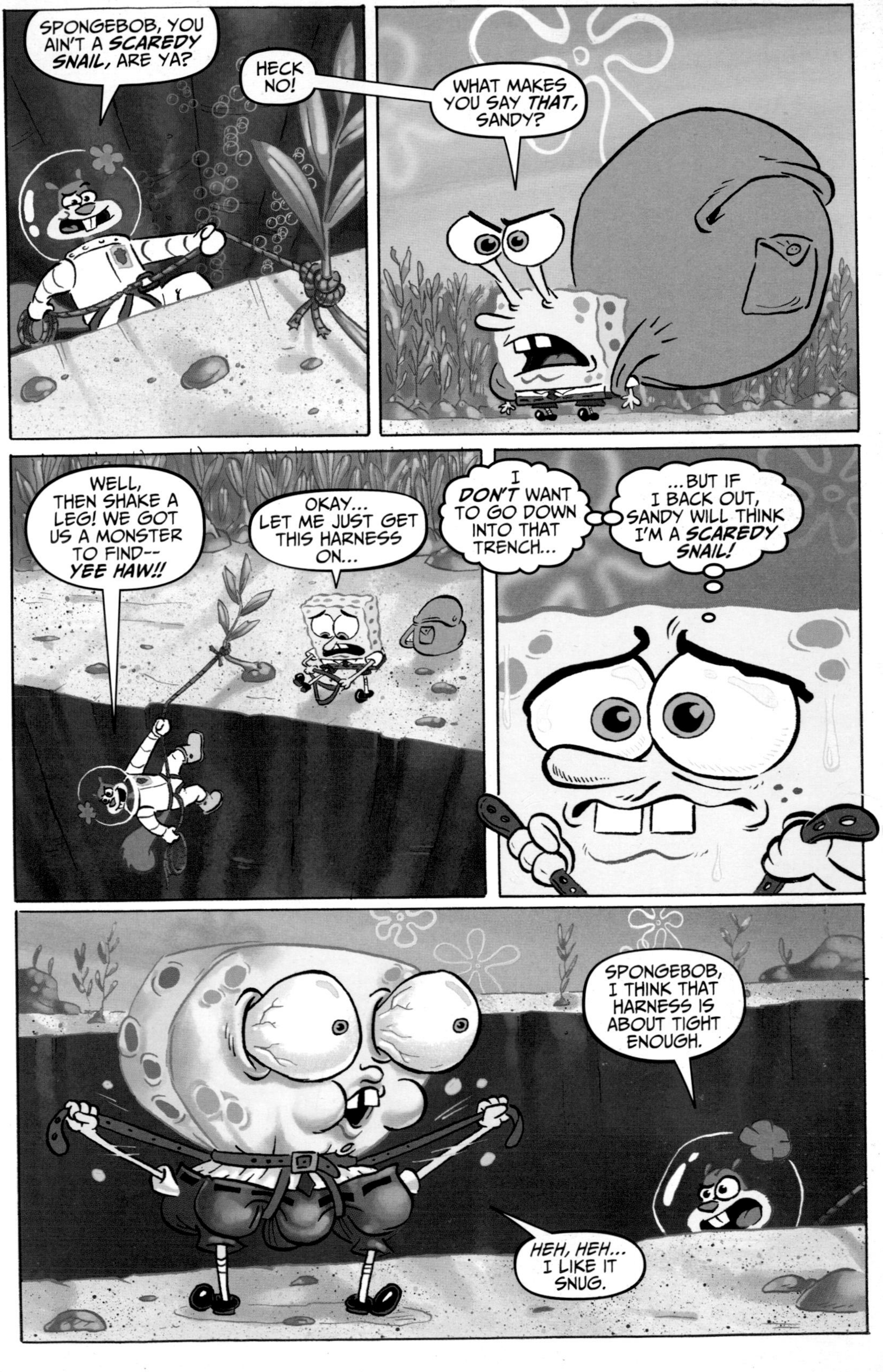
SPONGEBOB, YOU AIN'T A SCAREDY SNAIL, ARE YA?
HECK NO!
WHAT MAKES YOU SAY THAT, SANDY?
WELL, THEN SHAKE A LEG! WE GOT US A MONSTER TO FIND-- YEE HAW!!
OKAY... LET ME JUST GET THIS HARNESS ON...
I DON'T WANT TO GO DOWN INTO THAT TRENCH...
...BUT IF I BACK OUT, SANDY WILL THINK I'M A SCAREDY SNAIL!
SPONGEBOB, I THINK THAT HARNESS IS ABOUT TIGHT ENOUGH.
HEH, HEH... I LIKE IT SNUG.

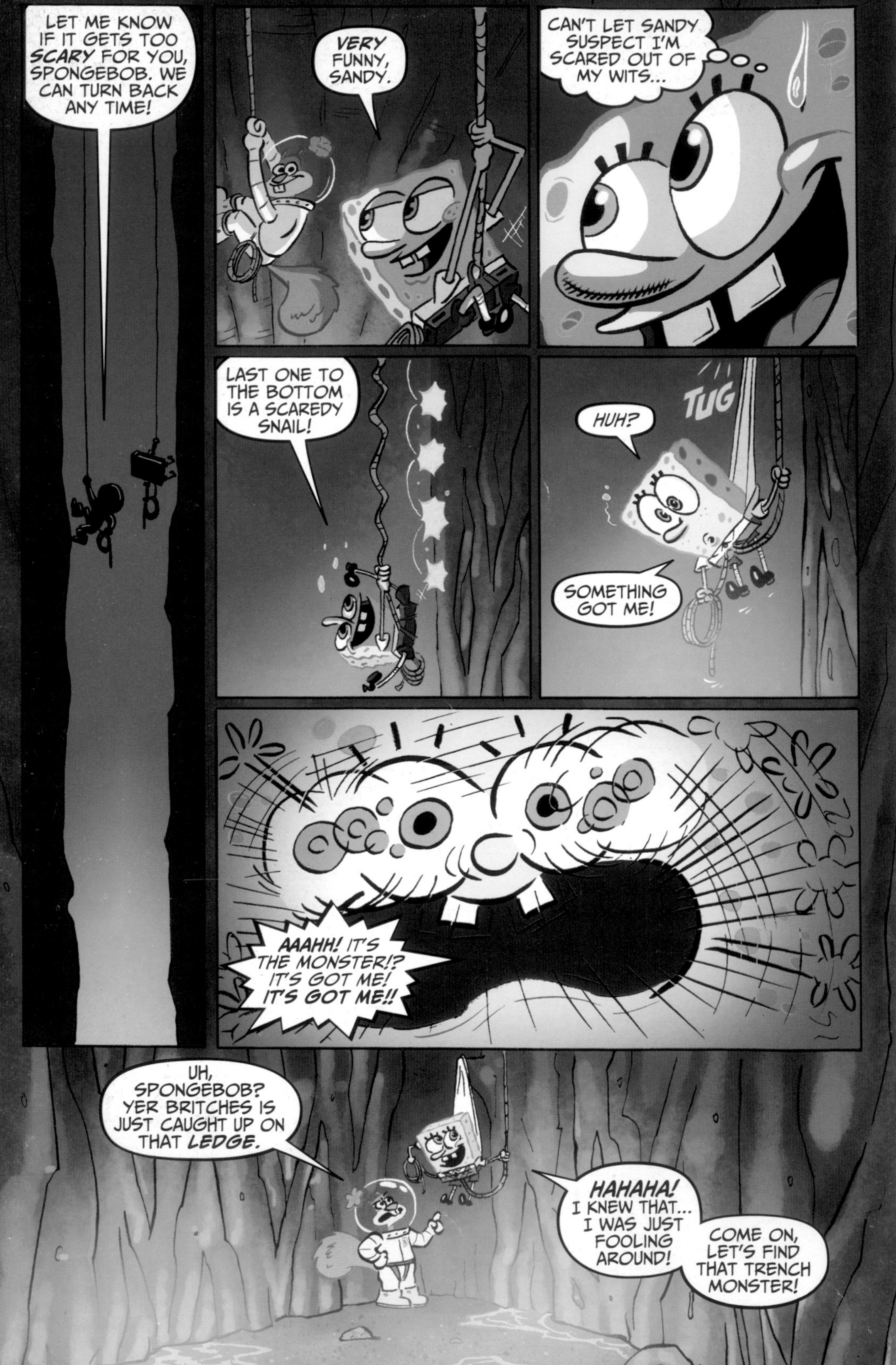
LET ME KNOW IF IT GETS TOO SCARY FOR YOU, SPONGEBOB. WE CAN TURN BACK ANY TIME!
VERY FUNNY, SANDY.
CAN'T LET SANDY SUSPECT I'M SCARED OUT OF MY WITS...
LAST ONE TO THE BOTTOM IS A SCAREDY SNAIL!
TUG
HUH?
SOMETHING GOT ME!
AAAHH! IT'S THE MONSTER!? IT'S GOT ME! IT'S GOT ME!!
UH, SPONGEBOB? YER BRITCHES IS JUST CAUGHT UP ON THAT LEDGE.
HAHAHA! I KNEW THAT... I WAS JUST FOOLING AROUND!
COME ON, LET'S FIND THAT TRENCH MONSTER!

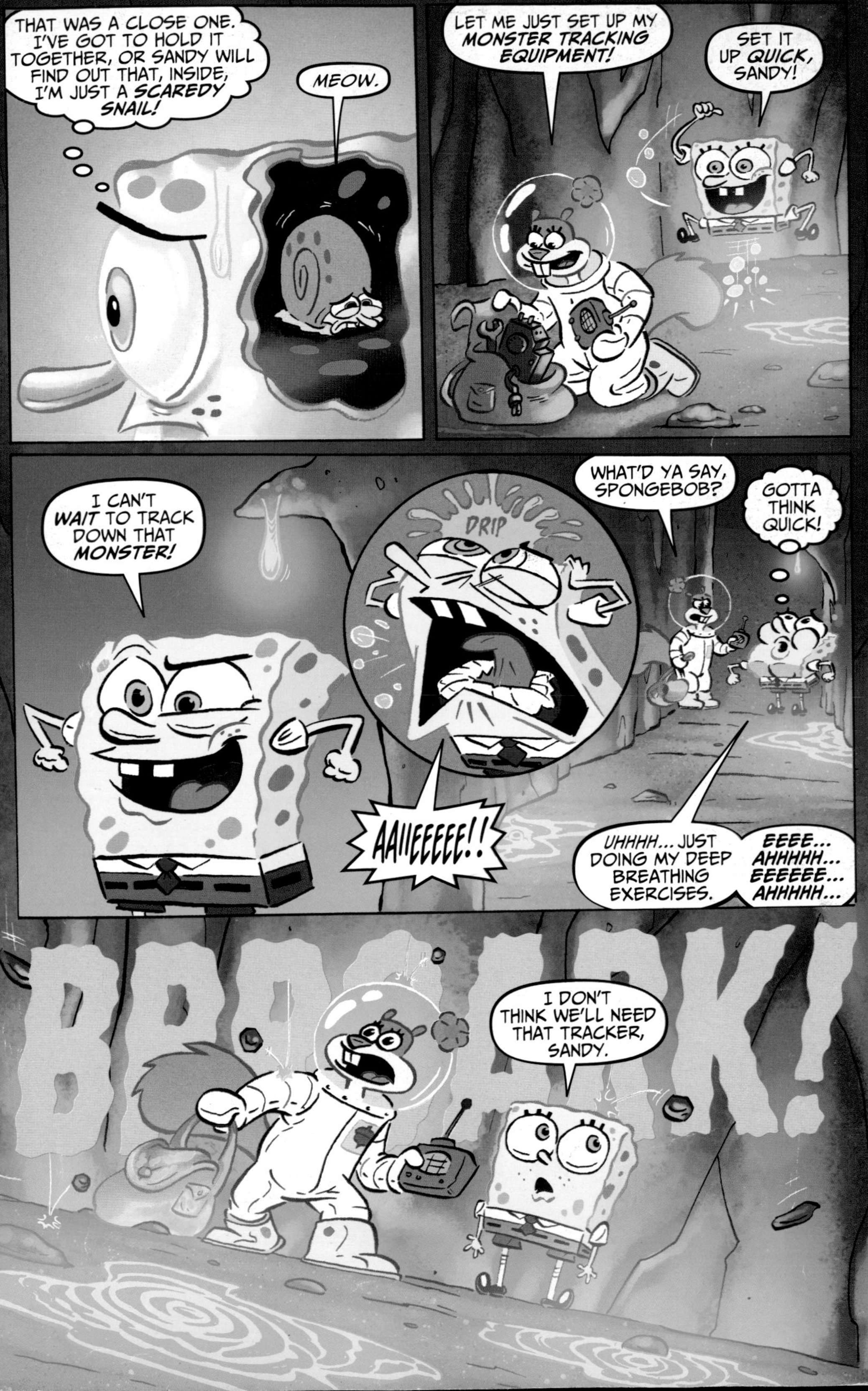
THAT WAS A CLOSE ONE. I'VE GOT TO HOLD IT TOGETHER, OR SANDY WILL FIND OUT THAT, INSIDE, I'M JUST A SCAREDY SNAIL!
MEOW.
LET ME JUST SET UP MY MONSTER TRACKING EQUIPMENT!
SET IT UP QUICK, SANDY!
I CAN'T WAIT TO TRACK DOWN THAT MONSTER!
DRIP
AAIIEEEEE!!
WHAT'D YA SAY, SPONGEBOB?
GOTTA THINK QUICK!
UHHHH... JUST DOING MY DEEP BREATHING EXERCISES.
EEEE... AHHHHH... EEEEEE... AHHHHH...
I DON'T THINK WE'LL NEED THAT TRACKER, SANDY.

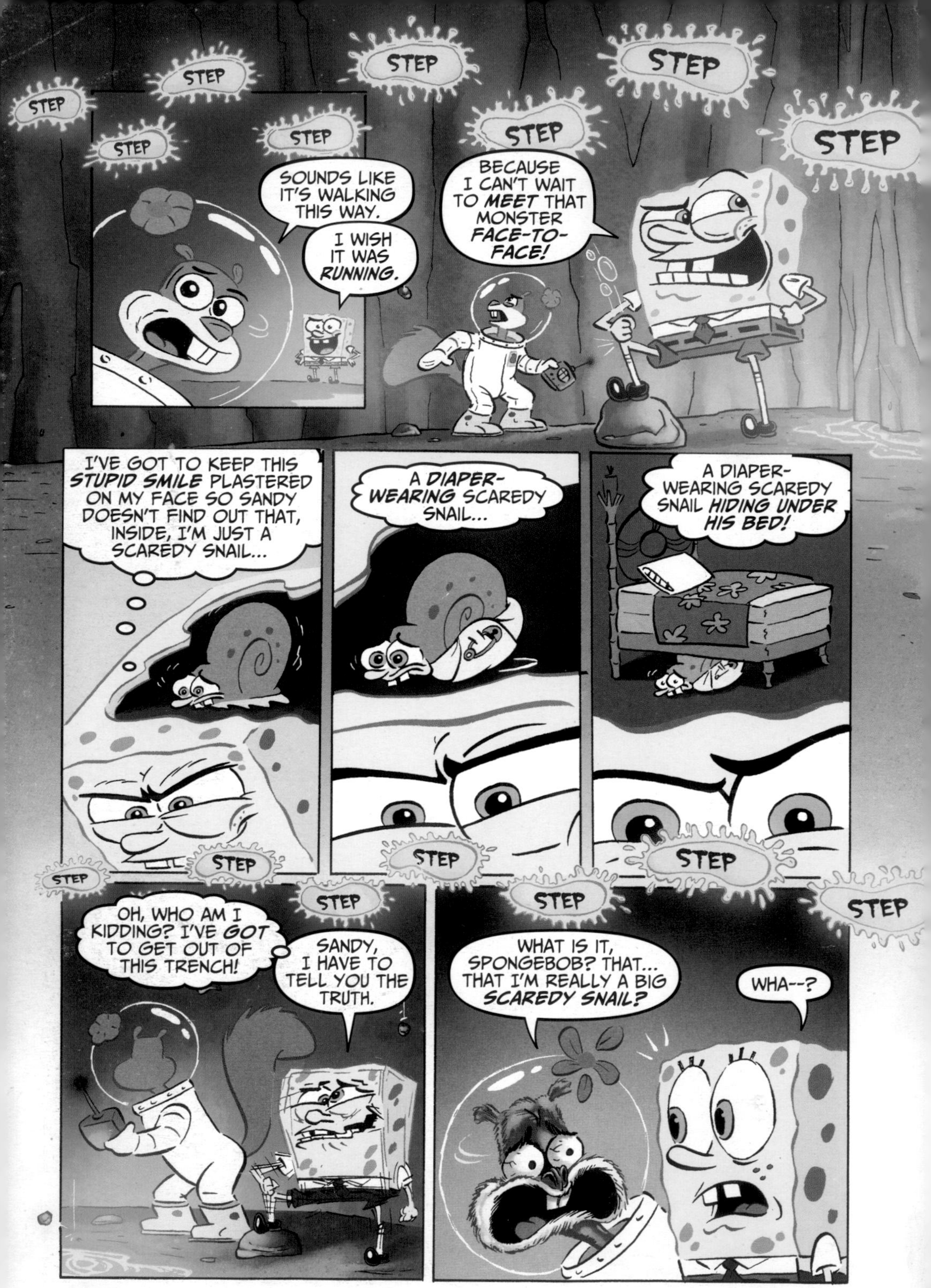
STEP
STEP
STEP
STEP
STEP
STEP
STEP
STEP
SOUNDS LIKE IT'S WALKING THIS WAY.
I WISH IT WAS RUNNING.
BECAUSE I CAN'T WAIT TO MEET THAT MONSTER FACE-TO-FACE!
I'VE GOT TO KEEP THIS STUPID SMILE PLASTERED ON MY FACE SO SANDY DOESN'T FIND OUT THAT, INSIDE, I'M JUST A SCAREDY SNAIL...
A DIAPER-WEARING SCAREDY SNAIL...
A DIAPER-WEARING SCAREDY SNAIL HIDING UNDER HIS BED!
STEP
STEP
STEP
STEP
STEP
STEP
STEP
OH, WHO AM I KIDDING? I'VE GOT TO GET OUT OF THIS TRENCH!
SANDY, I HAVE TO TELL YOU THE TRUTH.
WHAT IS IT, SPONGEBOB? THAT... THAT I'M REALLY A BIG SCAREDY SNAIL?
WHA--?

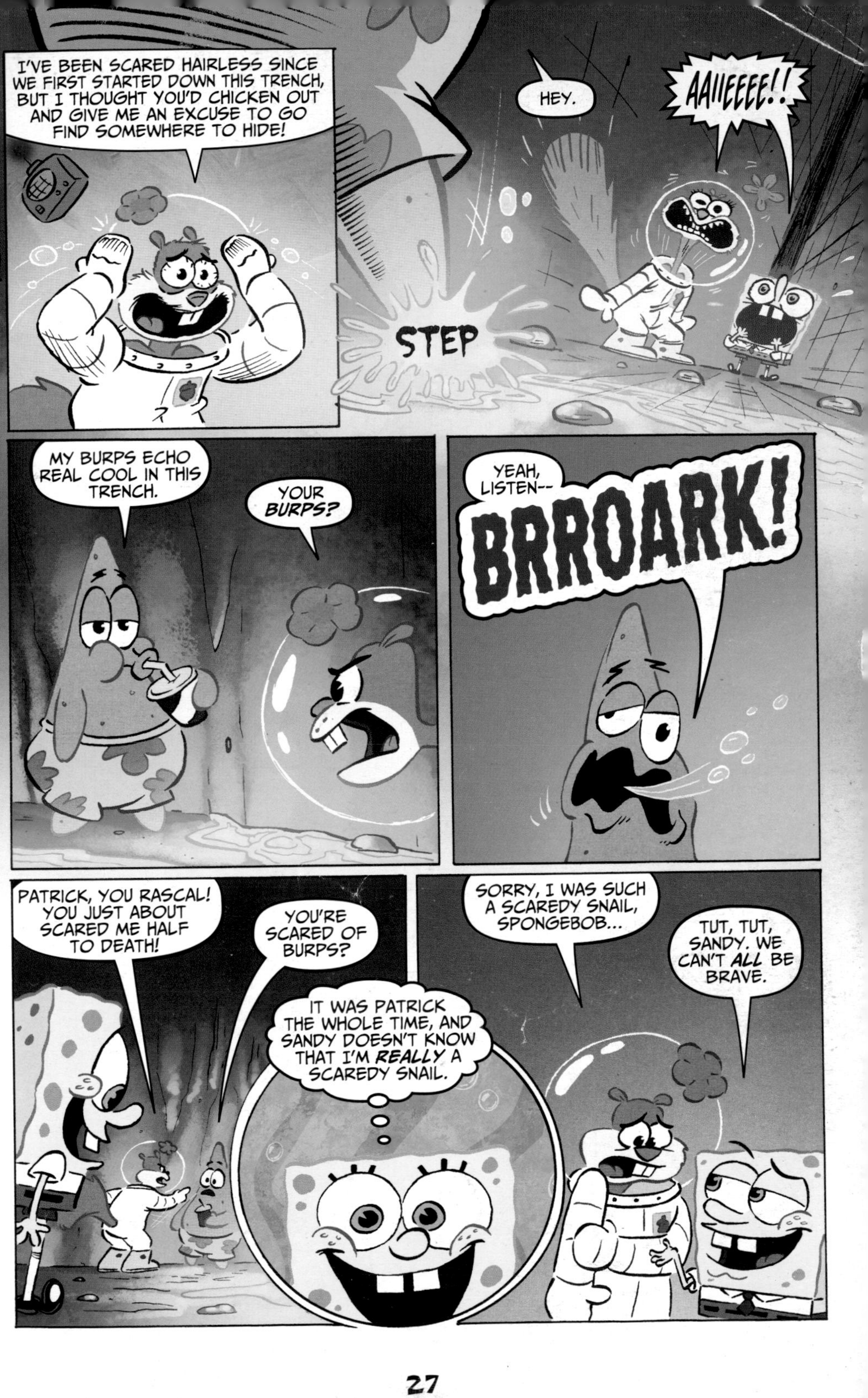

I'VE BEEN SCARED HAIRLESS SINCE WE FIRST STARTED DOWN THIS TRENCH, BUT I THOUGHT YOU'D CHICKEN OUT AND GIVE ME AN EXCUSE TO GO FIND SOMEWHERE TO HIDE!
HEY.
STEP
AAIIEEEE!!
MY BURPS ECHO REAL COOL IN THIS TRENCH.
YOUR BURPS?
YEAH, LISTEN--
BRROARK!
PATRICK, YOU RASCAL! YOU JUST ABOUT SCARED ME HALF TO DEATH!
YOU'RE SCARED OF BURPS?
IT WAS PATRICK THE WHOLE TIME, AND SANDY DOESN'T KNOW THAT I'M REALLY A SCAREDY SNAIL.
SORRY, I WAS SUCH A SCAREDY SNAIL, SPONGEBOB...
TUT, TUT, SANDY. WE CAN'T ALL BE BRAVE.

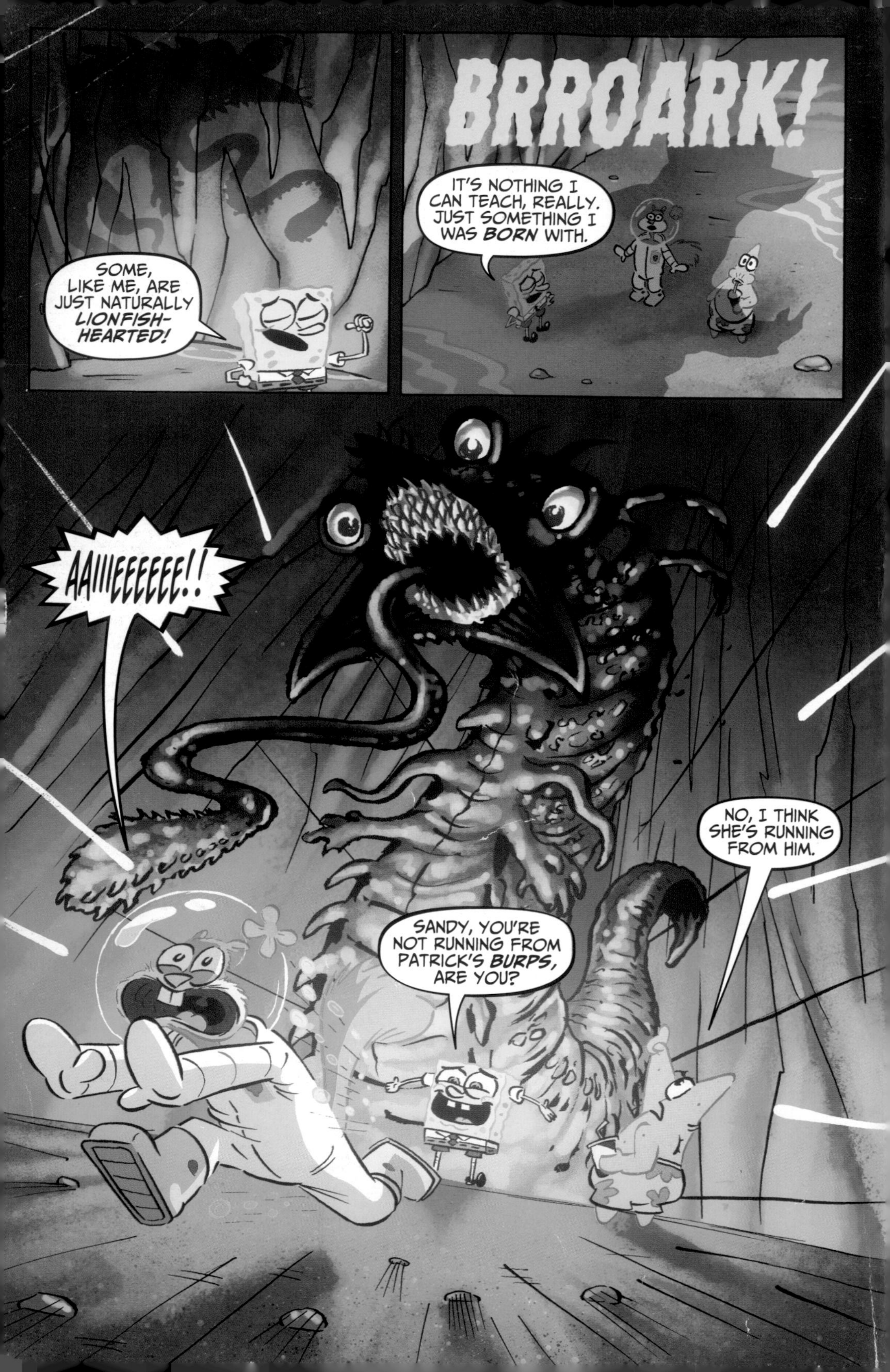
SOME, LIKE ME, ARE JUST NATURALLY LIONFISH-HEARTED!
BRRROARK!
IT'S NOTHING I CAN TEACH, REALLY. JUST SOMETHING I WAS BORN WITH.
AAIIIEEEEEE!!
SANDY, YOU'RE NOT RUNNING FROM PATRICK'S BURPS, ARE YOU?
NO, I THINK SHE'S RUNNING FROM HIM.

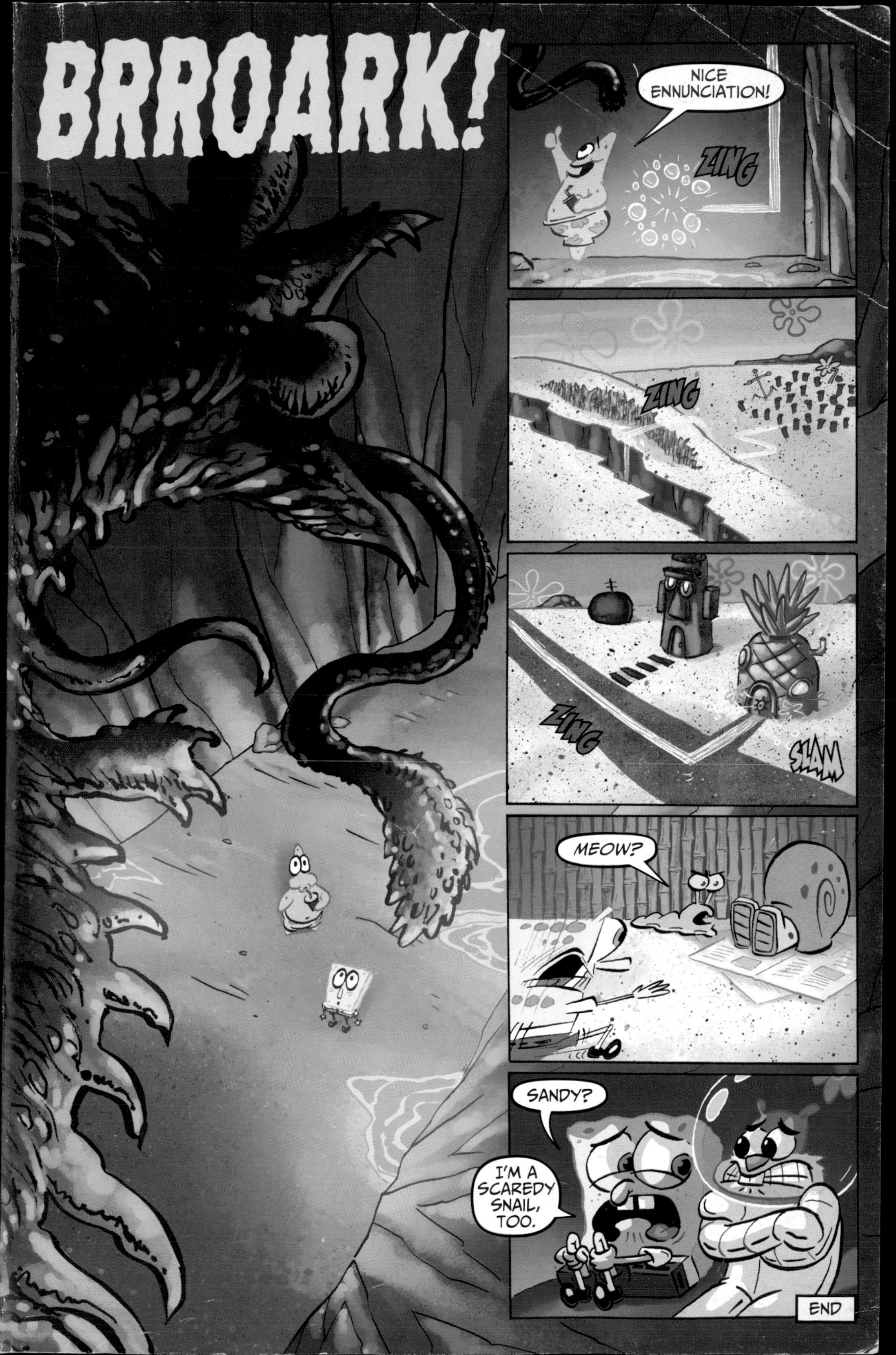
BRROARK!
NICE ENNUNCIATION!
ZING
ZING
ZING
SLAM
MEOW?
SANDY?
I'M A SCAREDY SNAIL, TOO.
END

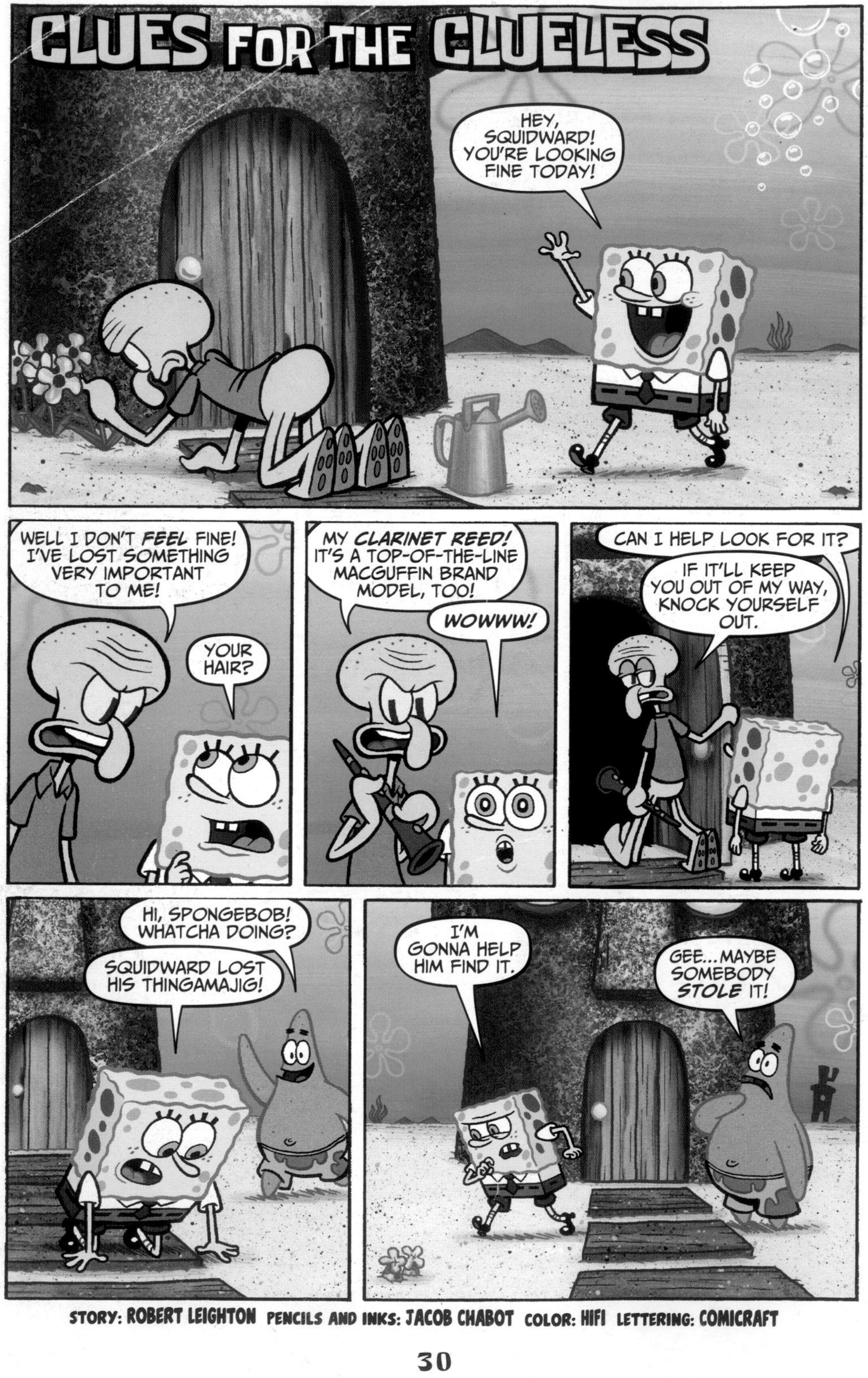
CLUES FOR THE CLUELESS
HEY, SQUIDWARD! YOU'RE LOOKING FINE TODAY!
WELL I DON'T FEEL FINE! I'VE LOST SOMETHING VERY IMPORTANT TO ME!
YOUR HAIR?
MY CLARINET REED! IT'S A TOP-OF-THE-LINE MACGUFFIN BRAND MODEL, TOO!
WOWWW!
CAN I HELP LOOK FOR IT?
IF IT'LL KEEP YOU OUT OF MY WAY, KNOCK YOURSELF OUT.
HI, SPONGEBOB! WHATCHA DOING?
SQUIDWARD LOST HIS THINGAMAJIG!
I'M GONNA HELP HIM FIND IT.
GEE...MAYBE SOMEBODY STOLE IT!

STORY: ROBERT LEIGHTON PENCILS AND INKS: JACOB CHABOT COLOR: HIFI LETTERING: COMICRAFT

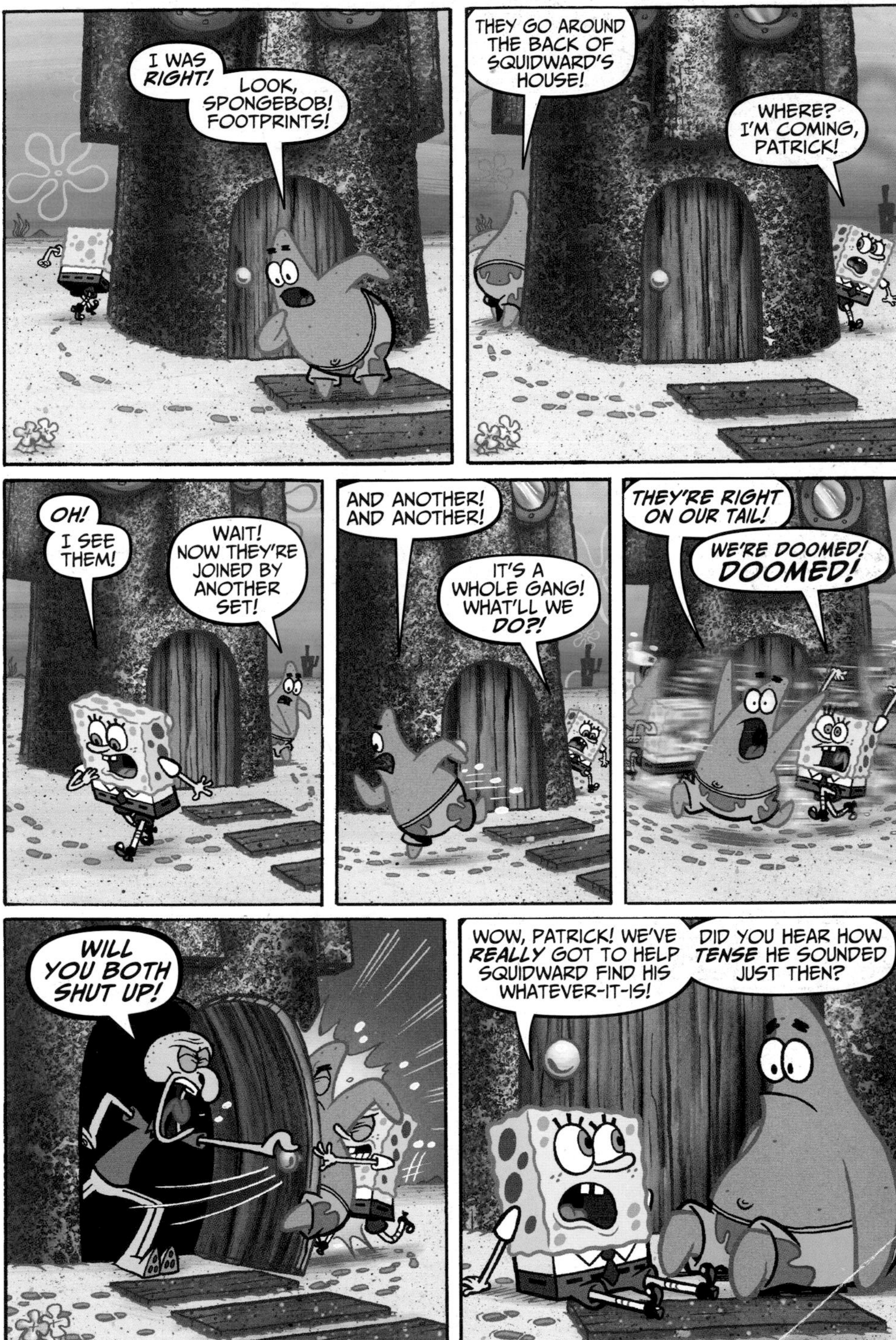
I WAS RIGHT!
LOOK, SPONGEBOB! FOOTPRINTS!
THEY GO AROUND THE BACK OF SQUIDWARD'S HOUSE!
WHERE? I'M COMING, PATRICK!
OH! I SEE THEM!
WAIT! NOW THEY'RE JOINED BY ANOTHER SET!
AND ANOTHER! AND ANOTHER!
IT'S A WHOLE GANG! WHAT'LL WE DO?!
THEY'RE RIGHT ON OUR TAIL!
WE'RE DOOMED! DOOMED!
WILL YOU BOTH SHUT UP!
WOW, PATRICK! WE'VE REALLY GOT TO HELP SQUIDWARD FIND HIS WHATEVER-IT-IS!
DID YOU HEAR HOW TENSE HE SOUNDED JUST THEN?

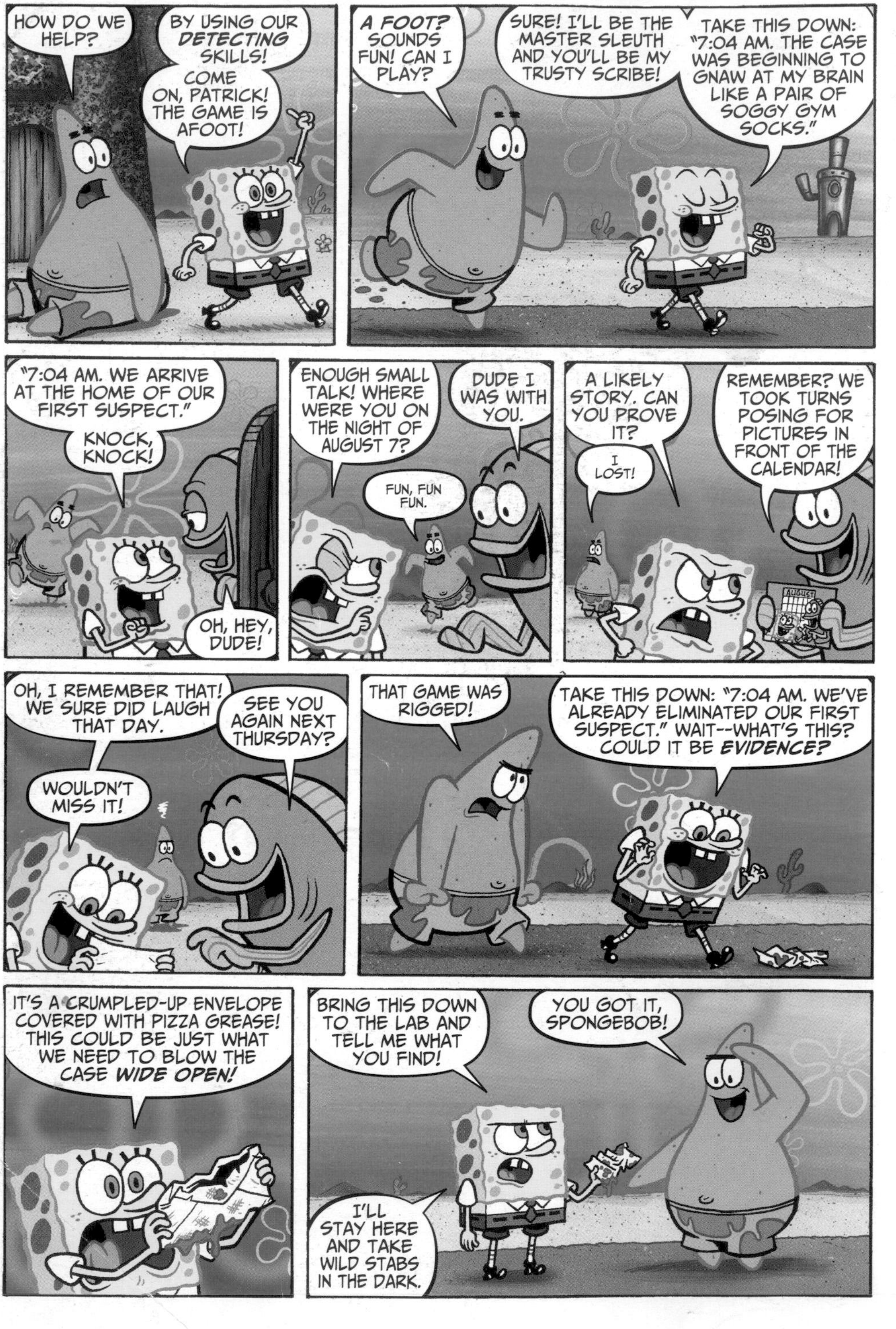
HOW DO WE HELP?
BY USING OUR *DETECTING* SKILLS!
COME ON, PATRICK! THE GAME IS AFOOT!
A FOOT? SOUNDS FUN! CAN I PLAY?
SURE! I'LL BE THE MASTER SLEUTH AND YOU'LL BE MY TRUSTY SCRIBE!
TAKE THIS DOWN: "7:04 AM. THE CASE WAS BEGINNING TO GNAW AT MY BRAIN LIKE A PAIR OF SOGGY GYM SOCKS."
"7:04 AM. WE ARRIVE AT THE HOME OF OUR FIRST SUSPECT."
KNOCK, KNOCK!
OH, HEY, DUDE!
ENOUGH SMALL TALK! WHERE WERE YOU ON THE NIGHT OF AUGUST 7?
DUDE I WAS WITH YOU.
FUN, FUN FUN.
A LIKELY STORY. CAN YOU PROVE IT?
I LOST!
REMEMBER? WE TOOK TURNS POSING FOR PICTURES IN FRONT OF THE CALENDAR!
AUGUST
OH, I REMEMBER THAT! WE SURE DID LAUGH THAT DAY.
SEE YOU AGAIN NEXT THURSDAY?
WOULDN'T MISS IT!
THAT GAME WAS RIGGED!
TAKE THIS DOWN: "7:04 AM. WE'VE ALREADY ELIMINATED OUR FIRST SUSPECT." WAIT--WHAT'S THIS? COULD IT BE *EVIDENCE?*
IT'S A CRUMPLED-UP ENVELOPE COVERED WITH PIZZA GREASE! THIS COULD BE JUST WHAT WE NEED TO BLOW THE CASE *WIDE OPEN!*
BRING THIS DOWN TO THE LAB AND TELL ME WHAT YOU FIND!
YOU GOT IT, SPONGEBOB!
I'LL STAY HERE AND TAKE WILD STABS IN THE DARK.

"7:04 AM. THE CASE WAS BEGINNING TO GNAW AT MY GYM SOCKS LIKE A SOGGY BRAIN."

"7:04 AM. HERE COMES SANDY." HI, SANDY!

HEY, SPONGEBOB! WHATCHA DOIN'?

I'M HOT ON THE TRAIL OF SQUIDWARD'S MISSING DOOHICKY!

DO YOU MEAN HIS CLARINET REED?

COULD BE, DOLL. WHO'S ASKING?

I SAW HIM DANCING A HAPPY LITTLE JIG OUTSIDE HIS HOUSE! HE TOLD ME HE JUST FOUND IT IN HIS WATERING CAN!

VERY INTERESTING... VERRRY INTERESTING INDEED!

I DIDN'T KNOW SQUIDWARD KNEW HOW TO JIG!

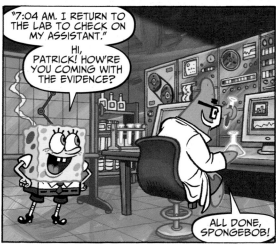

"7:04 AM. I RETURN TO THE LAB TO CHECK ON MY ASSISTANT."

HI, PATRICK! HOW'RE YOU COMING WITH THE EVIDENCE?

ALL DONE, SPONGEBOB!

IT WAS DELICIOUS!

EXCELLENT! WE'VE INTERVIEWED SUSPECTS, WE'VE EXAMINED EVIDENCE! IT'S TIME TO GATHER EVERYONE AT SQUIDWARD'S HOUSE...

I'M READY TO ANNOUNCE THE SOLUTION!

HOW DID SPONGEBOB SOLVE THE MYSTERY? FIND OUT ON THE NEXT PAGE!

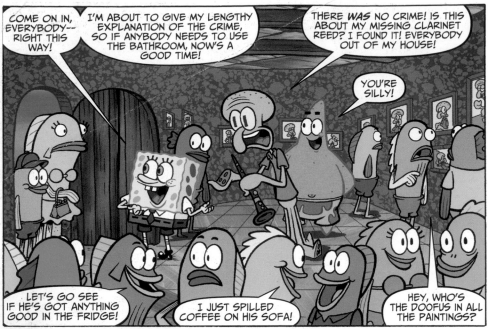

COME ON IN, EVERYBODY-- RIGHT THIS WAY!

I'M ABOUT TO GIVE MY LENGTHY EXPLANATION OF THE CRIME, SO IF ANYBODY NEEDS TO USE THE BATHROOM, NOW'S A GOOD TIME!

THERE *WAS* NO CRIME! IS THIS ABOUT MY MISSING CLARINET REED? I FOUND IT! EVERYBODY OUT OF MY HOUSE!

YOU'RE SILLY!

LET'S GO SEE IF HE'S GOT ANYTHING GOOD IN THE FRIDGE!

I JUST SPILLED COFFEE ON HIS SOFA!

HEY, WHO'S THE DOOFUS IN ALL THE PAINTINGS?

NOT SO FAST, SQUIDWARD. READ THEM MY NOTES, PATRICK.

UM, DO YOU HAVE A PEN?

AND A PIECE OF PAPER?

AND THEN, CAN YOU REPEAT EVERYTHING YOU SAID?

"NEVER MIND. MY FIRST BREAK IN THE CASE WAS A SMALL DETAIL--A LITTLE REMARK SANDY HAD MADE."

SQUIDWARD FOUND HIS CLARINET REED IN HIS WATERING CAN.

"THAT REMINDED ME THAT I HAD JUST SEEN SQUIDWARD GARDENING *THAT VERY MORNING!*"

HI, SQUIDWARD!

GRUNT

"BUT ONLY *TWO YEARS EARLIER,* I HAD SEEN SQUIDWARD MAKING PANCAKES! SO WHICH WAS IT? GARDENING OR PANCAKES?"

HI, SQUIDARD! MAKING PANCAKES?

GRUNT.

"MYSTERIOUSLY, AT THE TIME, HE HAD TALKED TO ME ABOUT *TIME TRAVEL!*"

CAN'T YOU COME BACK SOME *OTHER* TIME? LIKE IN A *THOUSAND YEARS?*

"SUDDENLY I SAW A *PATTERN:* THE PANCAKES. THE SECRETIVE PROJECTS. THE OBSESSION WITH TRAVELING THROUGH TIME!"

BY JOVE, PATRICK--I THINK I'VE GOT IT!

OH, GOOD!

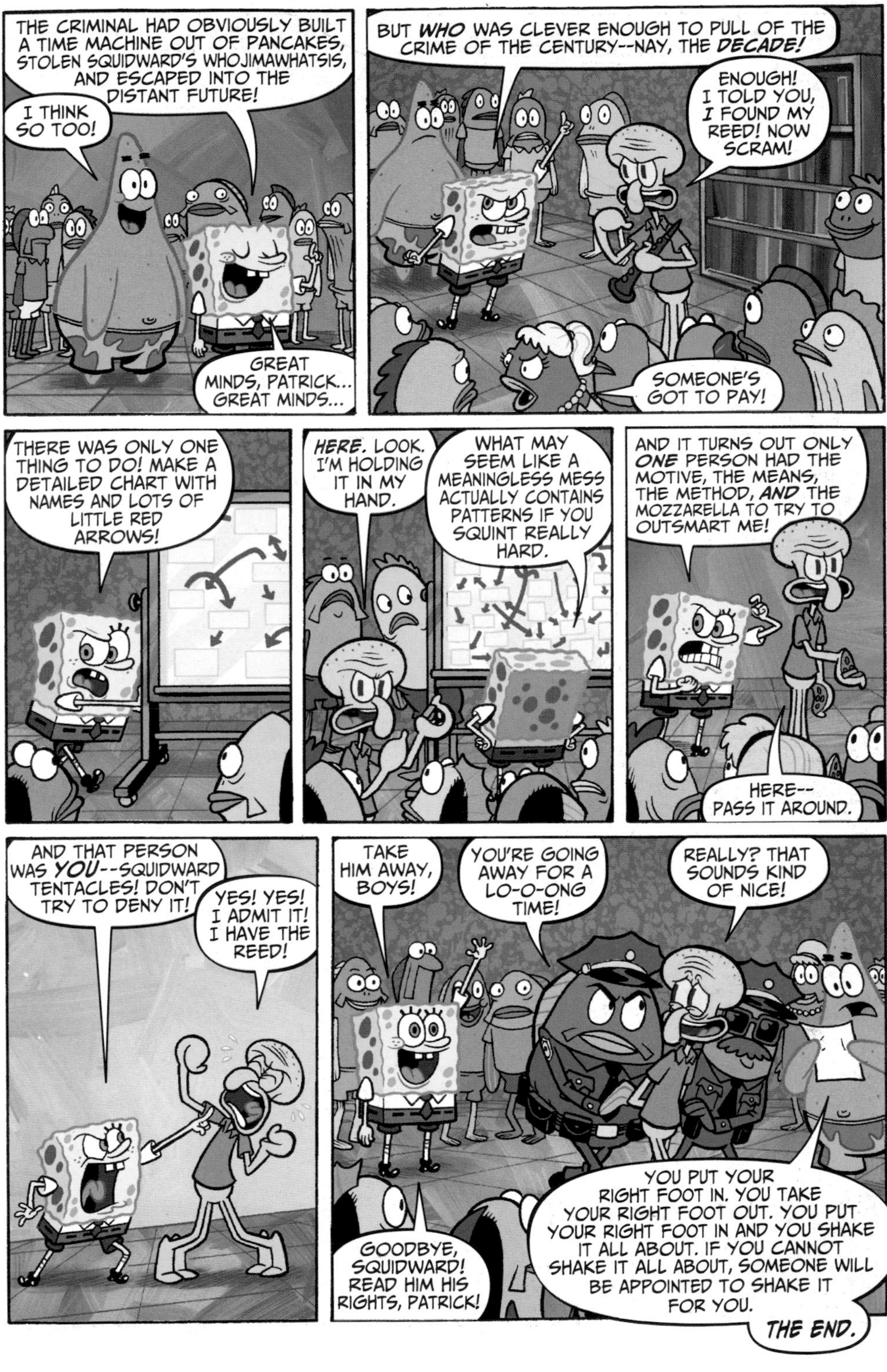
THE CRIMINAL HAD OBVIOUSLY BUILT A TIME MACHINE OUT OF PANCAKES, STOLEN SQUIDWARD'S WHOJIMAWHATSIS, AND ESCAPED INTO THE DISTANT FUTURE!
I THINK SO TOO!
GREAT MINDS, PATRICK... GREAT MINDS...
BUT WHO WAS CLEVER ENOUGH TO PULL OF THE CRIME OF THE CENTURY--NAY, THE DECADE!
ENOUGH! I TOLD YOU, I FOUND MY REED! NOW SCRAM!
SOMEONE'S GOT TO PAY!
THERE WAS ONLY ONE THING TO DO! MAKE A DETAILED CHART WITH NAMES AND LOTS OF LITTLE RED ARROWS!
HERE. LOOK. I'M HOLDING IT IN MY HAND.
WHAT MAY SEEM LIKE A MEANINGLESS MESS ACTUALLY CONTAINS PATTERNS IF YOU SQUINT REALLY HARD.
AND IT TURNS OUT ONLY ONE PERSON HAD THE MOTIVE, THE MEANS, THE METHOD, AND THE MOZZARELLA TO TRY TO OUTSMART ME!
HERE-- PASS IT AROUND.
AND THAT PERSON WAS YOU--SQUIDWARD TENTACLES! DON'T TRY TO DENY IT!
YES! YES! I ADMIT IT! I HAVE THE REED!
TAKE HIM AWAY, BOYS!
YOU'RE GOING AWAY FOR A LO-O-ONG TIME!
REALLY? THAT SOUNDS KIND OF NICE!
GOODBYE, SQUIDWARD! READ HIM HIS RIGHTS, PATRICK!
YOU PUT YOUR RIGHT FOOT IN. YOU TAKE YOUR RIGHT FOOT OUT. YOU PUT YOUR RIGHT FOOT IN AND YOU SHAKE IT ALL ABOUT. IF YOU CANNOT SHAKE IT ALL ABOUT, SOMEONE WILL BE APPOINTED TO SHAKE IT FOR YOU.
THE END.

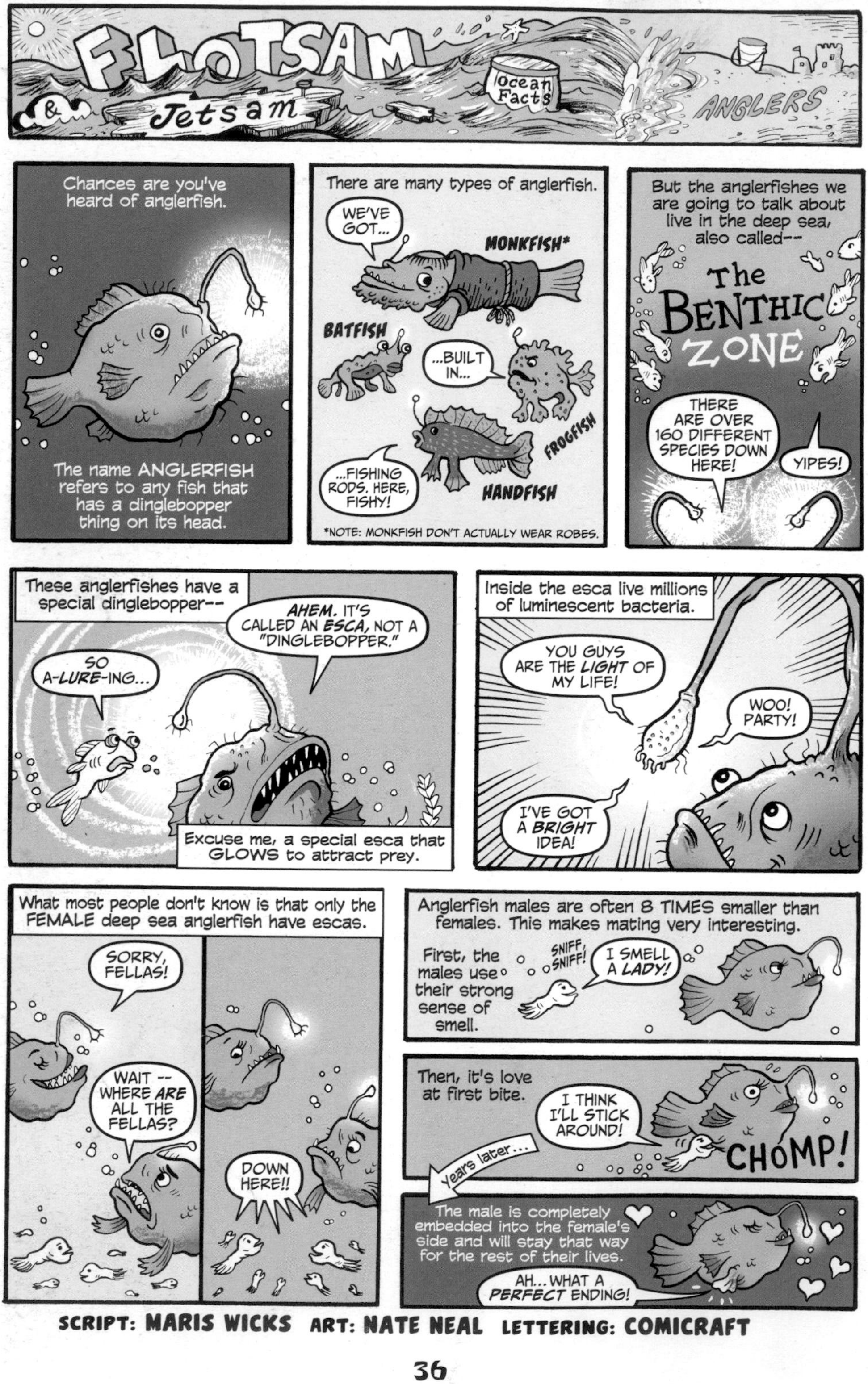
FLOTSAM & Jetsam
Ocean Facts
ANGLERS
Chances are you've heard of anglerfish.
The name ANGLERFISH refers to any fish that has a dinglebopper thing on its head.
There are many types of anglerfish.
WE'VE GOT...
MONKFISH*
BATFISH
...BUILT IN...
FROGFISH
HANDFISH
...FISHING RODS. HERE, FISHY!
*NOTE: MONKFISH DON'T ACTUALLY WEAR ROBES.
But the anglerfishes we are going to talk about live in the deep sea, also called--
The BENTHIC ZONE
THERE ARE OVER 160 DIFFERENT SPECIES DOWN HERE!
YIPES!
These anglerfishes have a special dinglebopper--
AHEM. IT'S CALLED AN ESCA, NOT A "DINGLEBOPPER."
SO A-LURE-ING...
Excuse me, a special esca that GLOWS to attract prey.
Inside the esca live millions of luminescent bacteria.
YOU GUYS ARE THE LIGHT OF MY LIFE!
WOO! PARTY!
I'VE GOT A BRIGHT IDEA!
What most people don't know is that only the FEMALE deep sea anglerfish have escas.
SORRY, FELLAS!
WAIT -- WHERE ARE ALL THE FELLAS?
DOWN HERE!!
Anglerfish males are often 8 TIMES smaller than females. This makes mating very interesting.
First, the males use their strong sense of smell.
SNIFF, SNIFF!
I SMELL A LADY!
Then, it's love at first bite.
I THINK I'LL STICK AROUND!
CHOMP!
Years later...
The male is completely embedded into the female's side and will stay that way for the rest of their lives.
AH... WHAT A PERFECT ENDING!

SCRIPT: MARIS WICKS ART: NATE NEAL LETTERING: COMICRAFT

Dial "S" For Willie

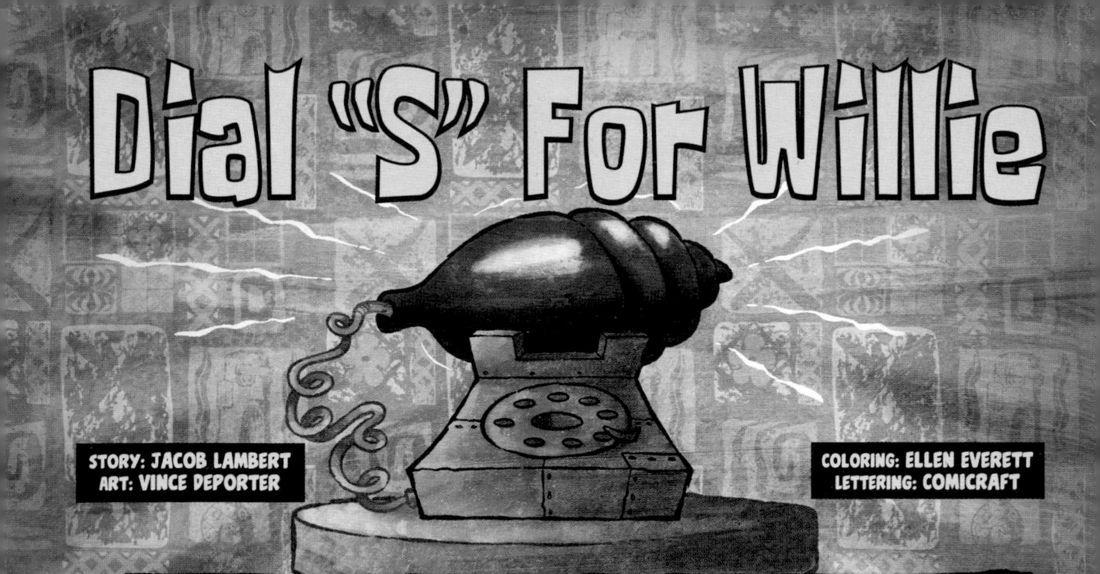
STORY: JACOB LAMBERT
ART: VINCE DEPORTER
COLORING: ELLEN EVERETT
LETTERING: COMICRAFT

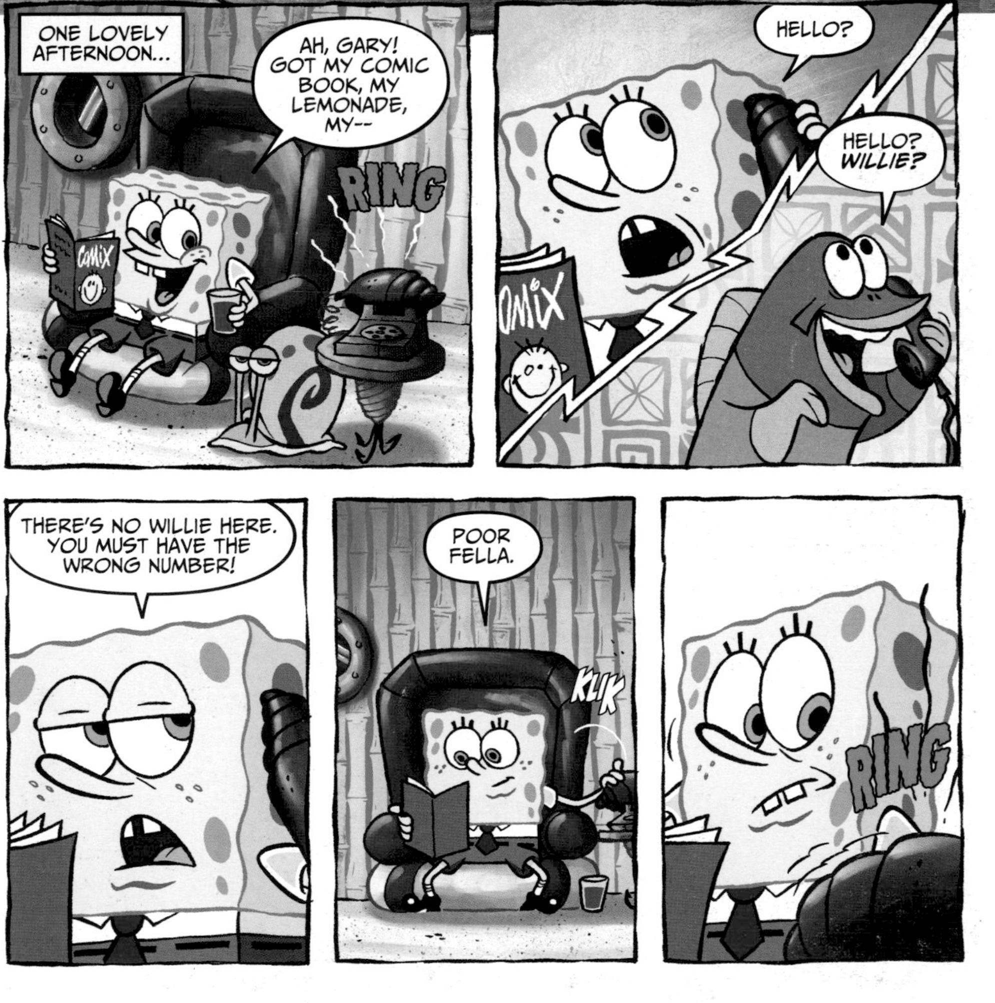
ONE LOVELY AFTERNOON...
AH, GARY! GOT MY COMIC BOOK, MY LEMONADE, MY--
RING
COMIX
HELLO?
HELLO? WILLIE?
COMIX
THERE'S NO WILLIE HERE. YOU MUST HAVE THE WRONG NUMBER!
POOR FELLA.
KLIK
RING

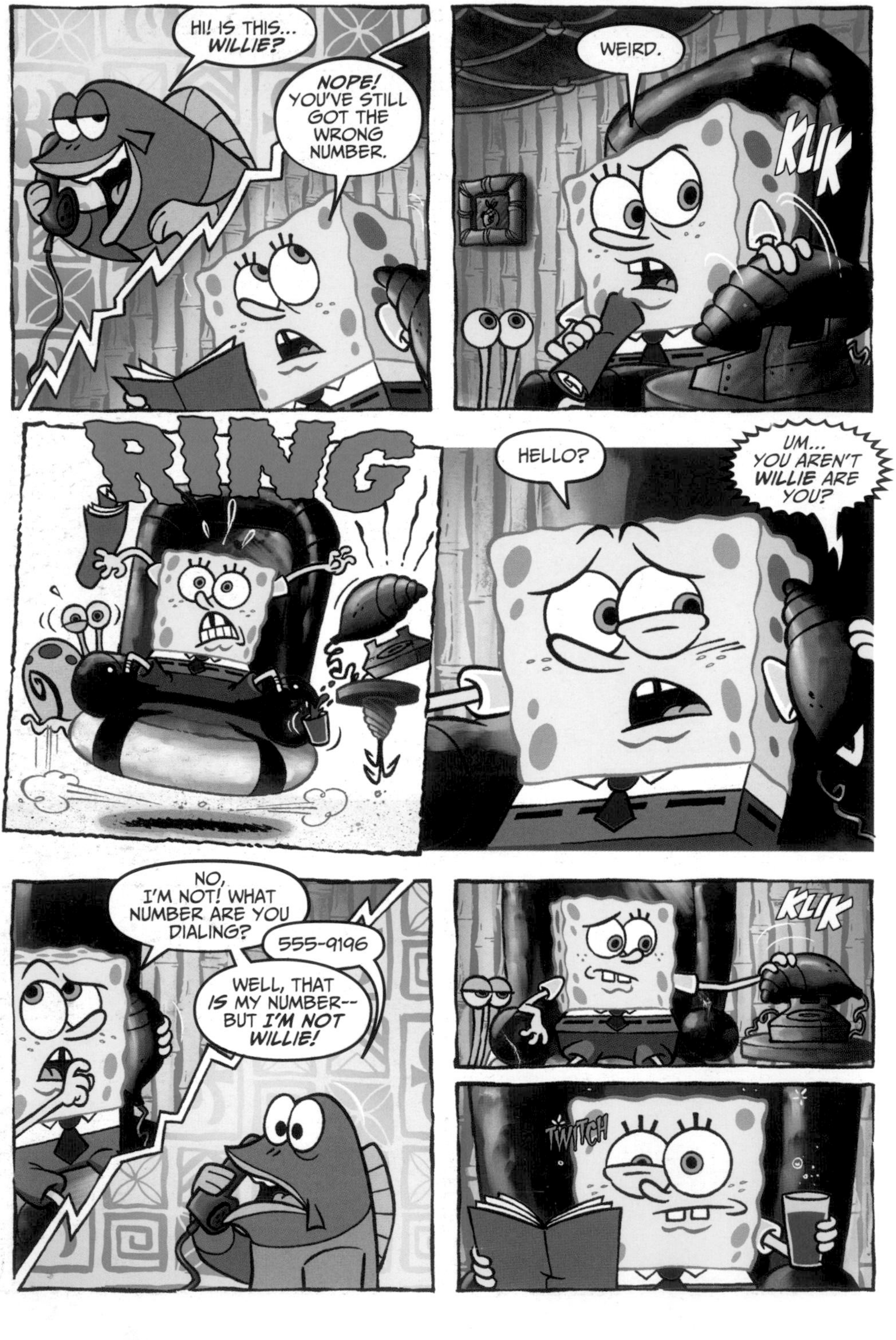
HI! IS THIS... WILLIE?
NOPE! YOU'VE STILL GOT THE WRONG NUMBER.
WEIRD.
KLIK
RING
HELLO?
UM... YOU AREN'T WILLIE ARE YOU?
NO, I'M NOT! WHAT NUMBER ARE YOU DIALING?
555-9196
WELL, THAT IS MY NUMBER-- BUT I'M NOT WILLIE!
KLIK
TWITCH

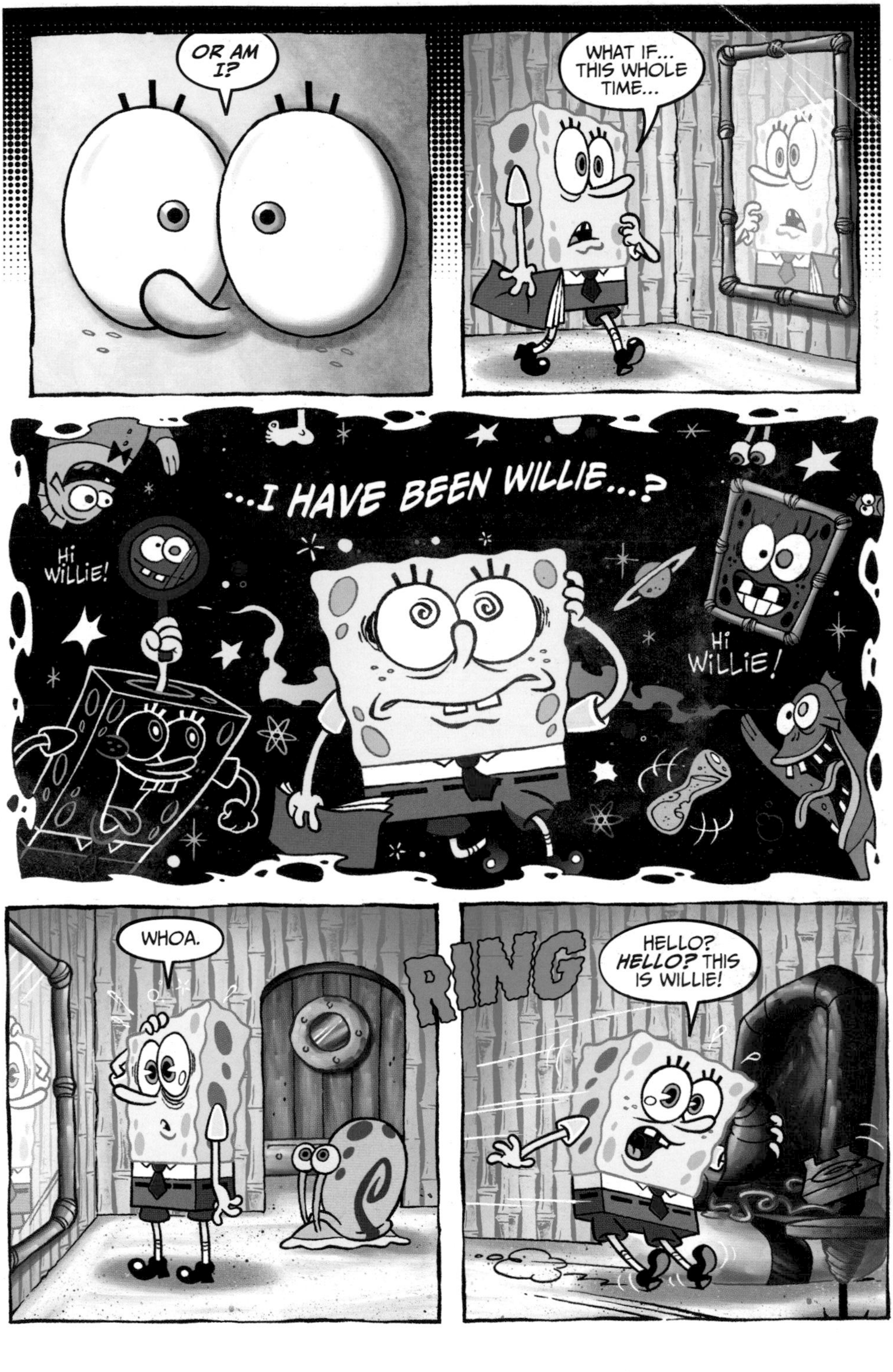
OR AM I?
WHAT IF... THIS WHOLE TIME...
...I HAVE BEEN WILLIE...?
Hi WILLIE!
Hi WILLIE!
WHOA.
RING
HELLO? HELLO? THIS IS WILLIE!

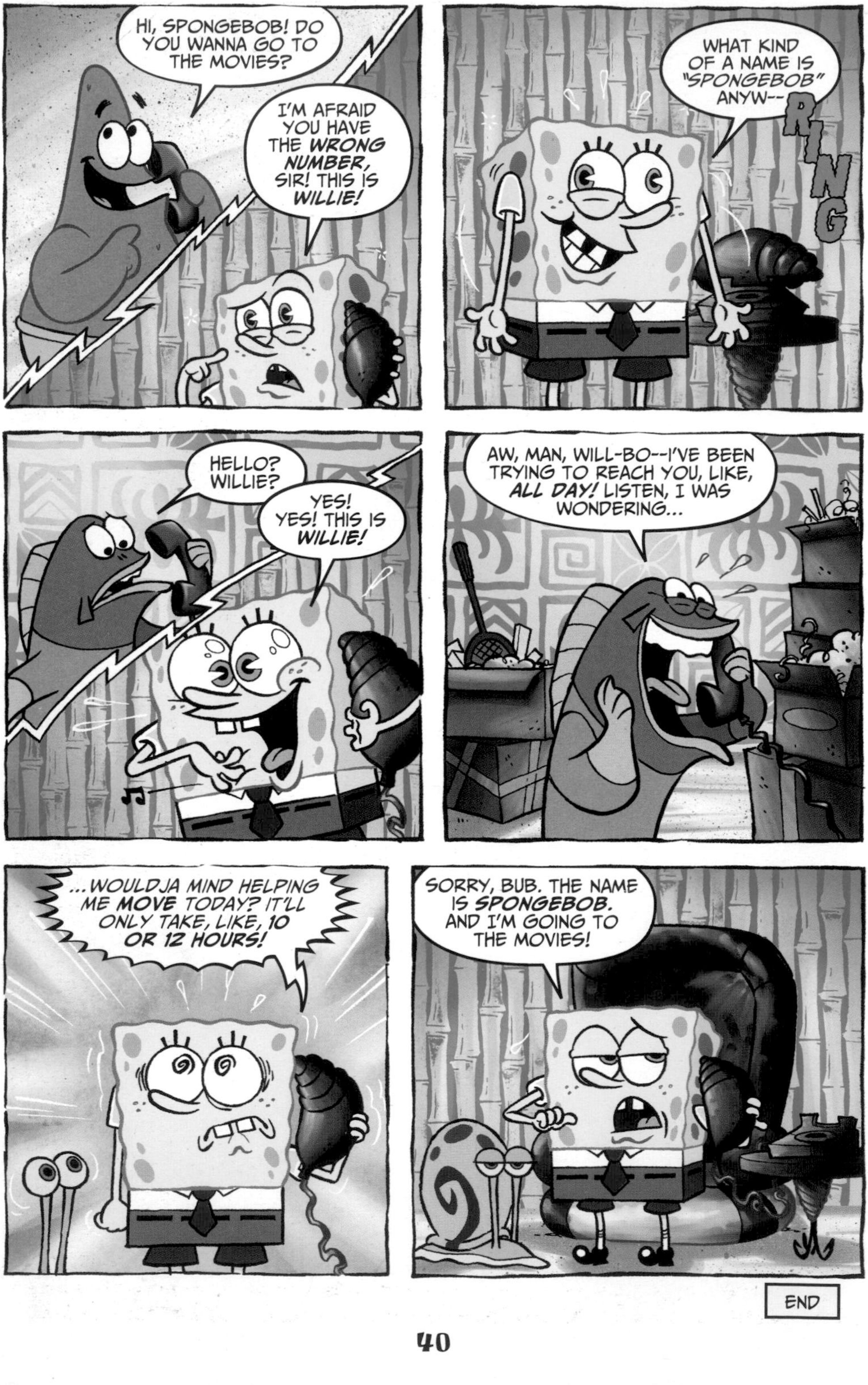
HI, SPONGEBOB! DO YOU WANNA GO TO THE MOVIES?
I'M AFRAID YOU HAVE THE **WRONG NUMBER,** SIR! THIS IS **WILLIE!**
WHAT KIND OF A NAME IS "SPONGEBOB" ANYW--
RING
HELLO? WILLIE?
YES! YES! THIS IS **WILLIE!**
AW, MAN, WILL-BO--I'VE BEEN TRYING TO REACH YOU, LIKE, **ALL DAY!** LISTEN, I WAS WONDERING...
...WOULDJA MIND HELPING ME **MOVE** TODAY? IT'LL ONLY TAKE, LIKE, **10 OR 12 HOURS!**
SORRY, BUB. THE NAME IS **SPONGEBOB.** AND I'M GOING TO THE MOVIES!

END

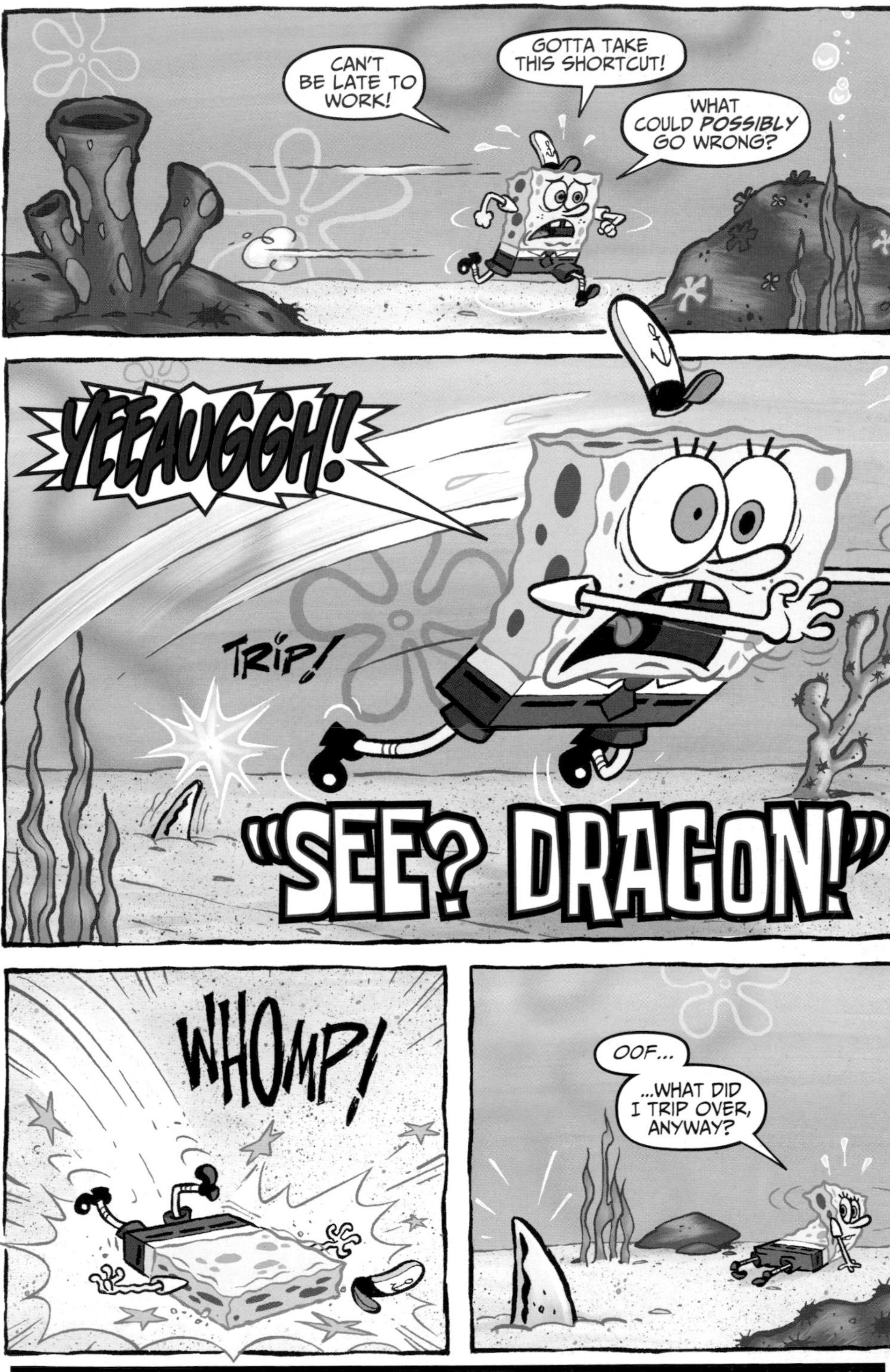
CAN'T BE LATE TO WORK!
GOTTA TAKE THIS SHORTCUT!
WHAT COULD POSSIBLY GO WRONG?
YEEAUGGH!
TRIP!
"SEE? DRAGON!"
WHOMP!
OOF...
...WHAT DID I TRIP OVER, ANYWAY?

STORY: DAVID LEWMAN PENCILS AND INKS: VINCE DEPORTER COLORING: HIFI LETTERING: COMICRAFT

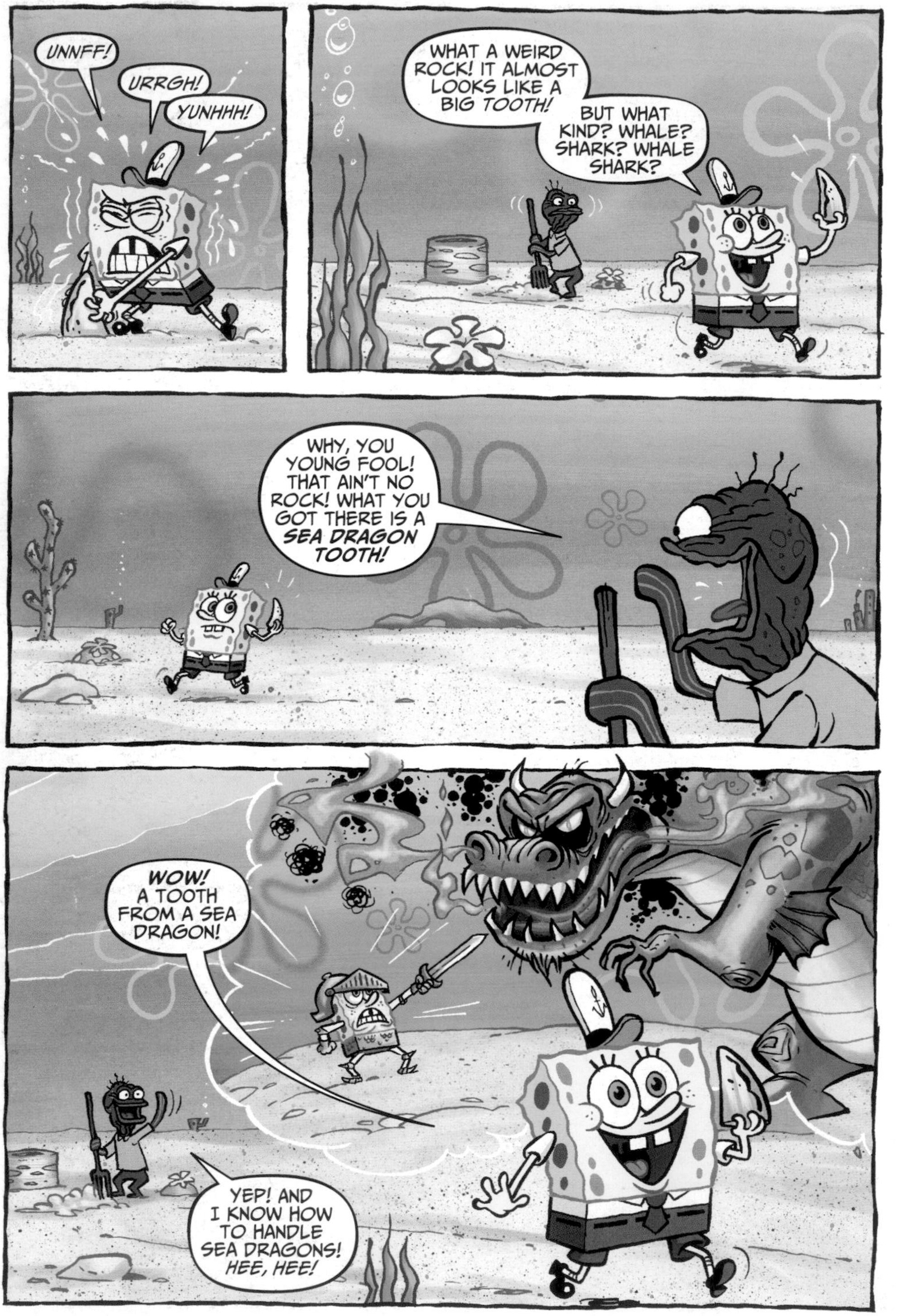
UNNFF!
URRGH!
YUNHHH!
WHAT A WEIRD ROCK! IT ALMOST LOOKS LIKE A BIG TOOTH!
BUT WHAT KIND? WHALE? SHARK? WHALE SHARK?
WHY, YOU YOUNG FOOL! THAT AIN'T NO ROCK! WHAT YOU GOT THERE IS A SEA DRAGON TOOTH!
WOW! A TOOTH FROM A SEA DRAGON!
YEP! AND I KNOW HOW TO HANDLE SEA DRAGONS! HEE, HEE!

EW. WHAT IS THAT *DISGUSTING* GROWTH ON YOUR HAT?

YOU'RE RIGHT, SQUIDWARD--IT *IS* IMPRESSIVE! THIS IS A GENUINE SEA DRAGON TOOTH!

THAT'S NOT A TOOTH! THAT'S A ROCK!

THERE'S NO SUCH THING AS SEA DRAGONS! THEY'RE *MYTHICAL!*

HA!

HA! HA!

WHAT'S WRONG OUT HERE?!

IT ALMOST SOUNDED LIKE SQUIDWARD WAS *HAPPY!*

SLAM!

NOTHING'S WRONG, MR. KRABS. I WAS JUST SHOWING SQUIDWARD MY NEW SEA DRAGON TOOTH!

YES, I SEE...

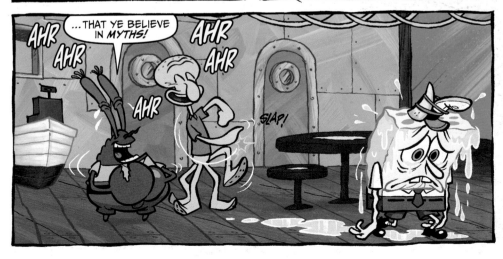

...THAT YE BELIEVE IN *MYTHS!*

AHR AHR

AHR AHR

AHR

SLAP!

43

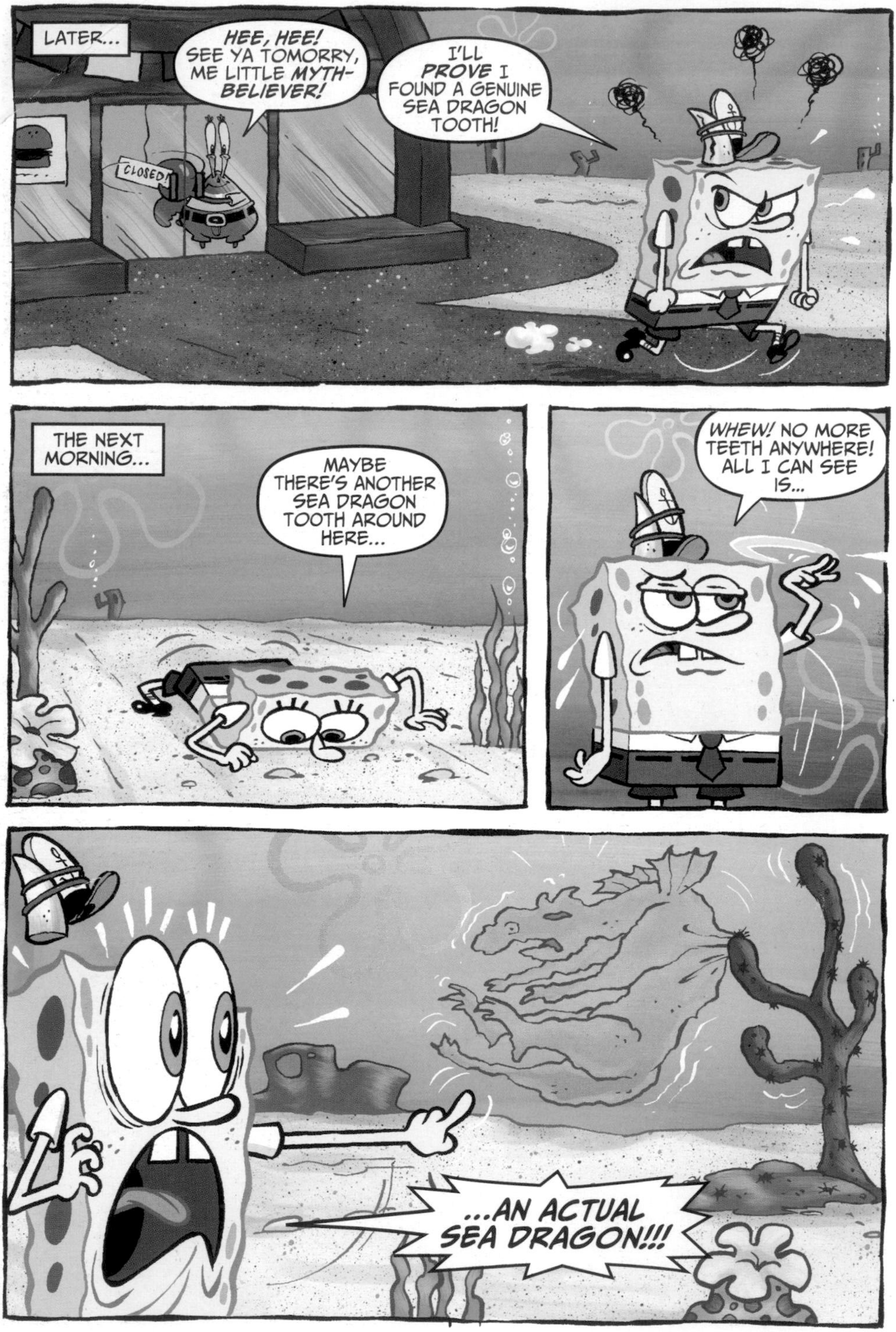

LATER...
HEE, HEE! SEE YA TOMORRY, ME LITTLE MYTH-BELIEVER!
CLOSED
I'LL PROVE I FOUND A GENUINE SEA DRAGON TOOTH!
THE NEXT MORNING...
MAYBE THERE'S ANOTHER SEA DRAGON TOOTH AROUND HERE...
WHEW! NO MORE TEETH ANYWHERE! ALL I CAN SEE IS...
...AN ACTUAL SEA DRAGON!!!

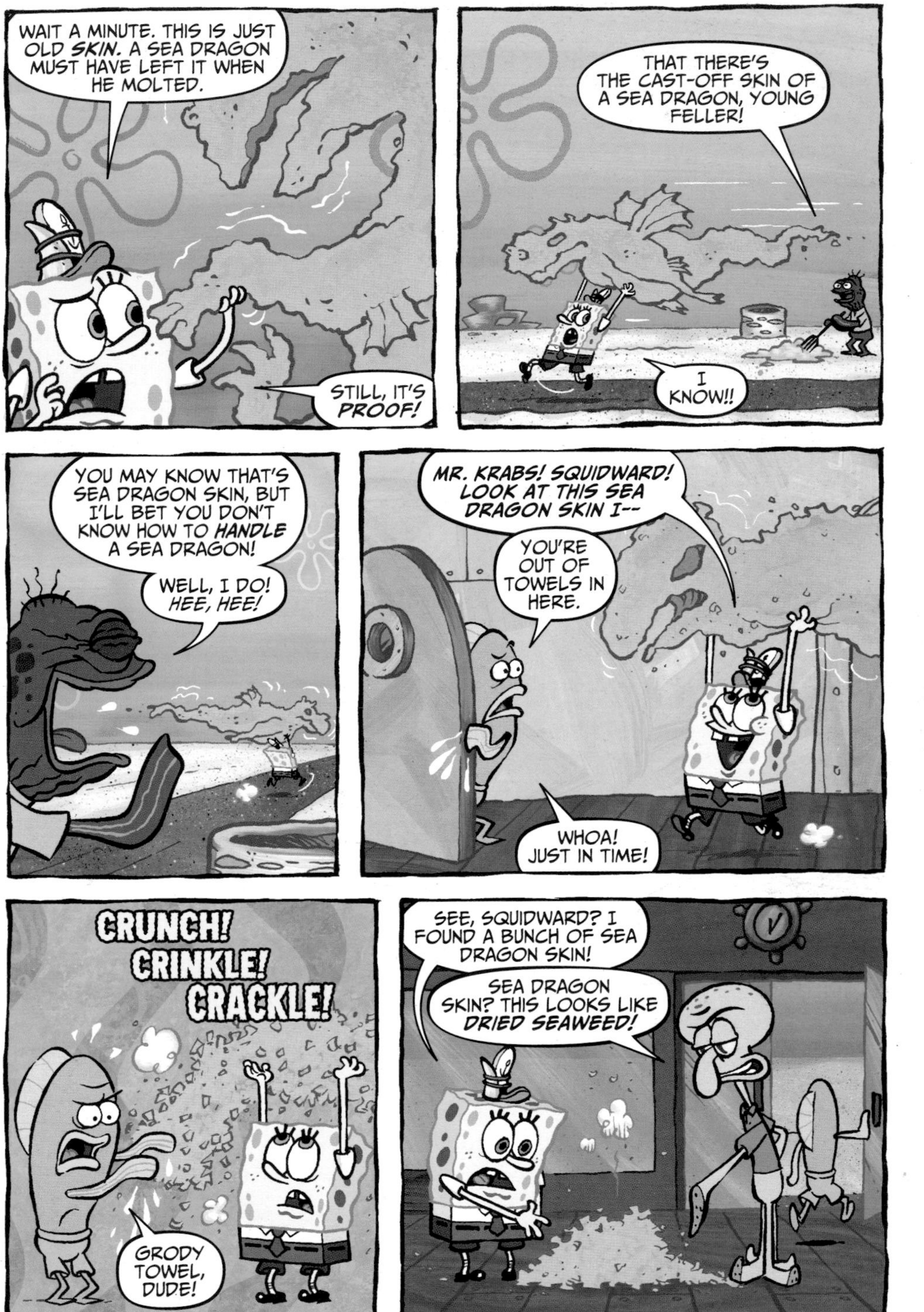
WAIT A MINUTE. THIS IS JUST OLD SKIN. A SEA DRAGON MUST HAVE LEFT IT WHEN HE MOLTED.
STILL, IT'S PROOF!
THAT THERE'S THE CAST-OFF SKIN OF A SEA DRAGON, YOUNG FELLER!
I KNOW!!
YOU MAY KNOW THAT'S SEA DRAGON SKIN, BUT I'LL BET YOU DON'T KNOW HOW TO HANDLE A SEA DRAGON!
WELL, I DO! HEE, HEE!
MR. KRABS! SQUIDWARD! LOOK AT THIS SEA DRAGON SKIN I--
YOU'RE OUT OF TOWELS IN HERE.
WHOA! JUST IN TIME!
CRUNCH!
CRINKLE!
CRACKLE!
GRODY TOWEL, DUDE!
SEE, SQUIDWARD? I FOUND A BUNCH OF SEA DRAGON SKIN!
SEA DRAGON SKIN? THIS LOOKS LIKE DRIED SEAWEED!

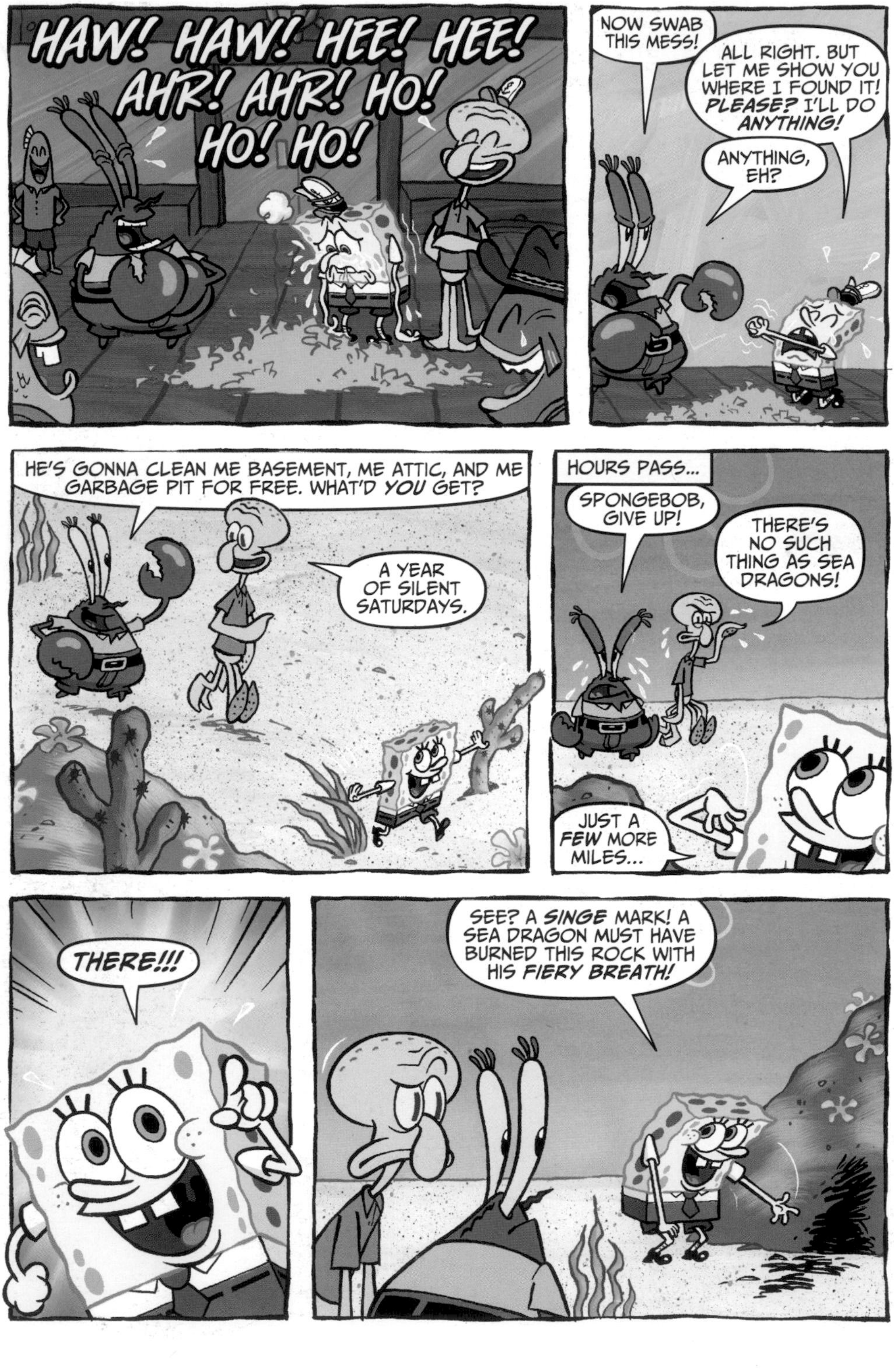
HAW! HAW! HEE! HEE! AHR! AHR! HO! HO! HO!
NOW SWAB THIS MESS!
ALL RIGHT. BUT LET ME SHOW YOU WHERE I FOUND IT! PLEASE? I'LL DO ANYTHING!
ANYTHING, EH?
HE'S GONNA CLEAN ME BASEMENT, ME ATTIC, AND ME GARBAGE PIT FOR FREE. WHAT'D YOU GET?
A YEAR OF SILENT SATURDAYS.
HOURS PASS...
SPONGEBOB, GIVE UP!
THERE'S NO SUCH THING AS SEA DRAGONS!
JUST A FEW MORE MILES...
THERE!!!
SEE? A SINGE MARK! A SEA DRAGON MUST HAVE BURNED THIS ROCK WITH HIS FIERY BREATH!

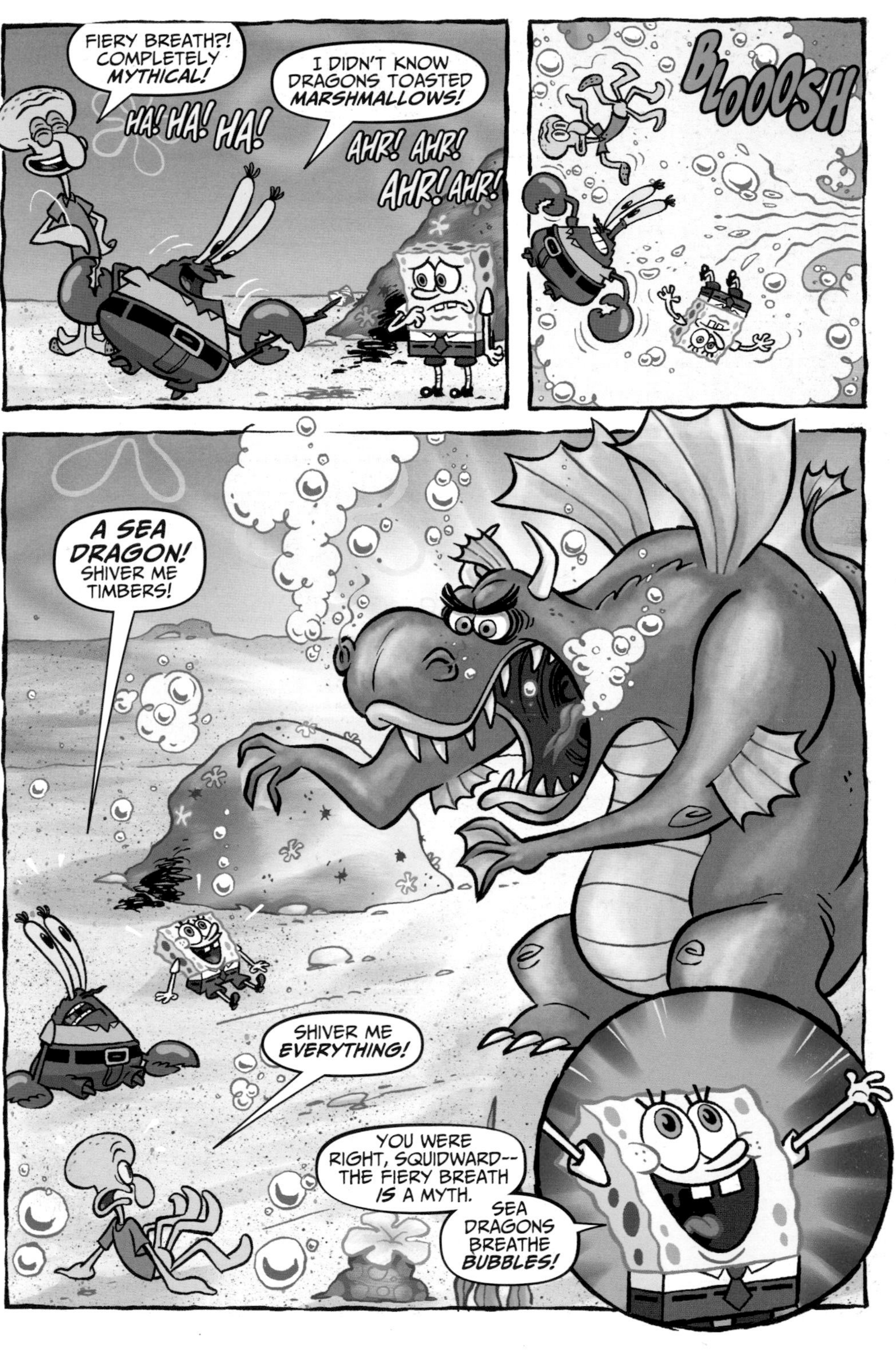

FIERY BREATH?! COMPLETELY MYTHICAL!
HA! HA! HA!
I DIDN'T KNOW DRAGONS TOASTED MARSHMALLOWS!
AHR! AHR! AHR! AHR!
BLOOOSH
A SEA DRAGON! SHIVER ME TIMBERS!
SHIVER ME EVERYTHING!
YOU WERE RIGHT, SQUIDWARD-- THE FIERY BREATH IS A MYTH.
SEA DRAGONS BREATHE BUBBLES!

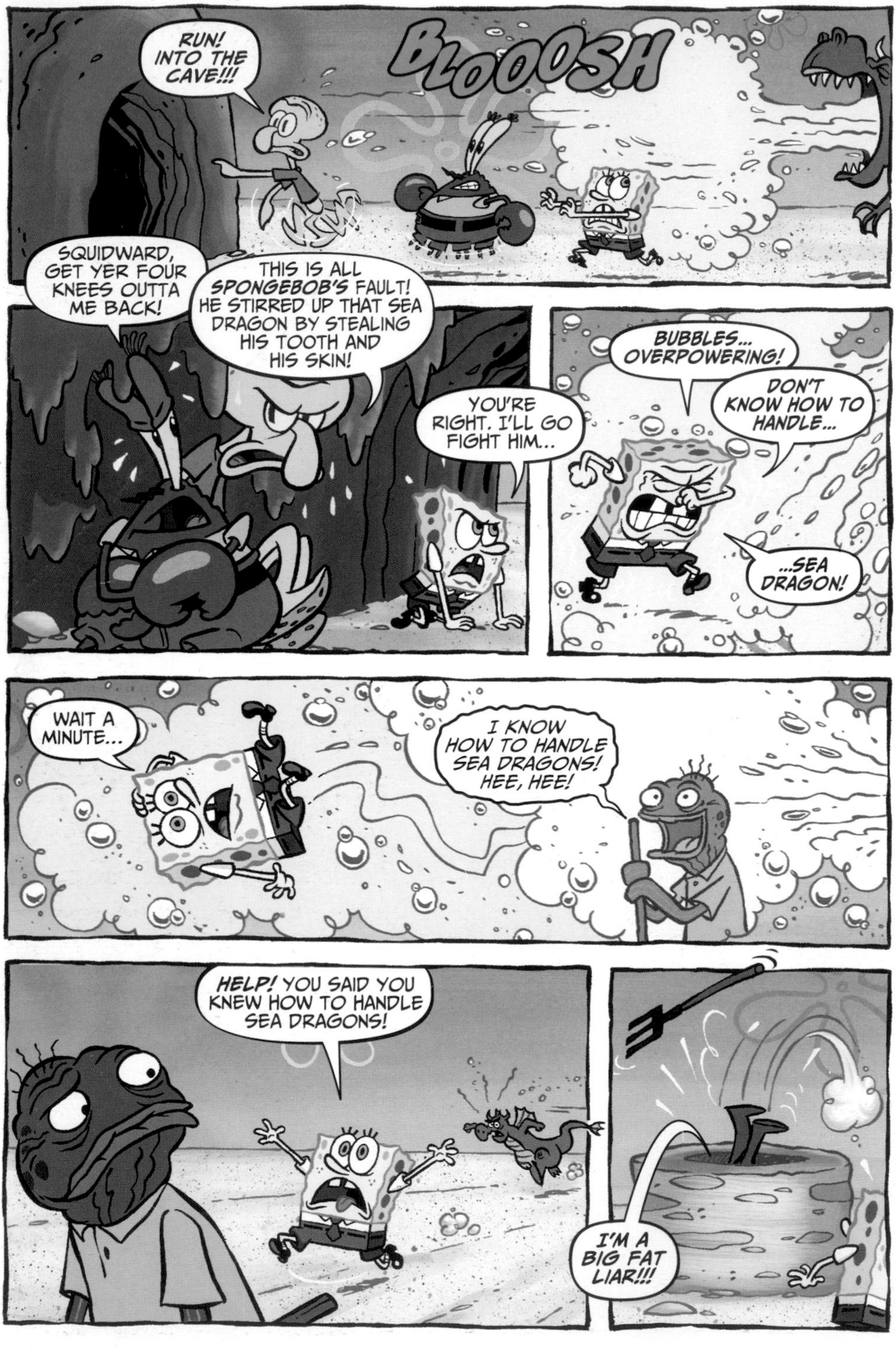
RUN! INTO THE CAVE!!!
BLOOOSH
SQUIDWARD, GET YER FOUR KNEES OUTTA ME BACK!
THIS IS ALL SPONGEBOB'S FAULT! HE STIRRED UP THAT SEA DRAGON BY STEALING HIS TOOTH AND HIS SKIN!
YOU'RE RIGHT. I'LL GO FIGHT HIM...
BUBBLES... OVERPOWERING!
DON'T KNOW HOW TO HANDLE...
...SEA DRAGON!
WAIT A MINUTE...
I KNOW HOW TO HANDLE SEA DRAGONS! HEE, HEE!
HELP! YOU SAID YOU KNEW HOW TO HANDLE SEA DRAGONS!
I'M A BIG FAT LIAR!!!

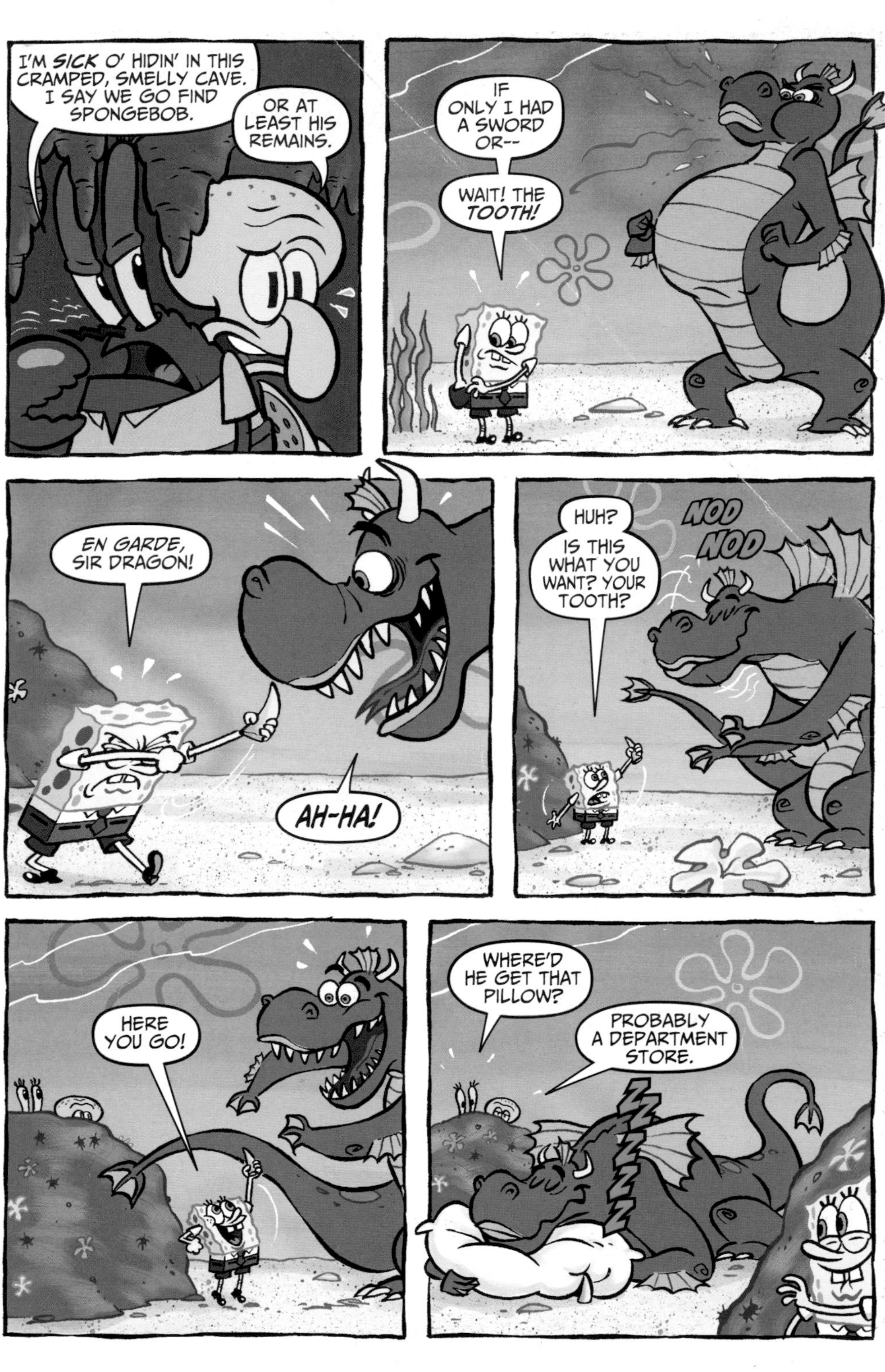
I'M SICK O' HIDIN' IN THIS CRAMPED, SMELLY CAVE. I SAY WE GO FIND SPONGEBOB.
OR AT LEAST HIS REMAINS.
IF ONLY I HAD A SWORD OR--
WAIT! THE TOOTH!
EN GARDE, SIR DRAGON!
AH-HA!
HUH?
IS THIS WHAT YOU WANT? YOUR TOOTH?
NOD
NOD
HERE YOU GO!
WHERE'D HE GET THAT PILLOW?
PROBABLY A DEPARTMENT STORE.

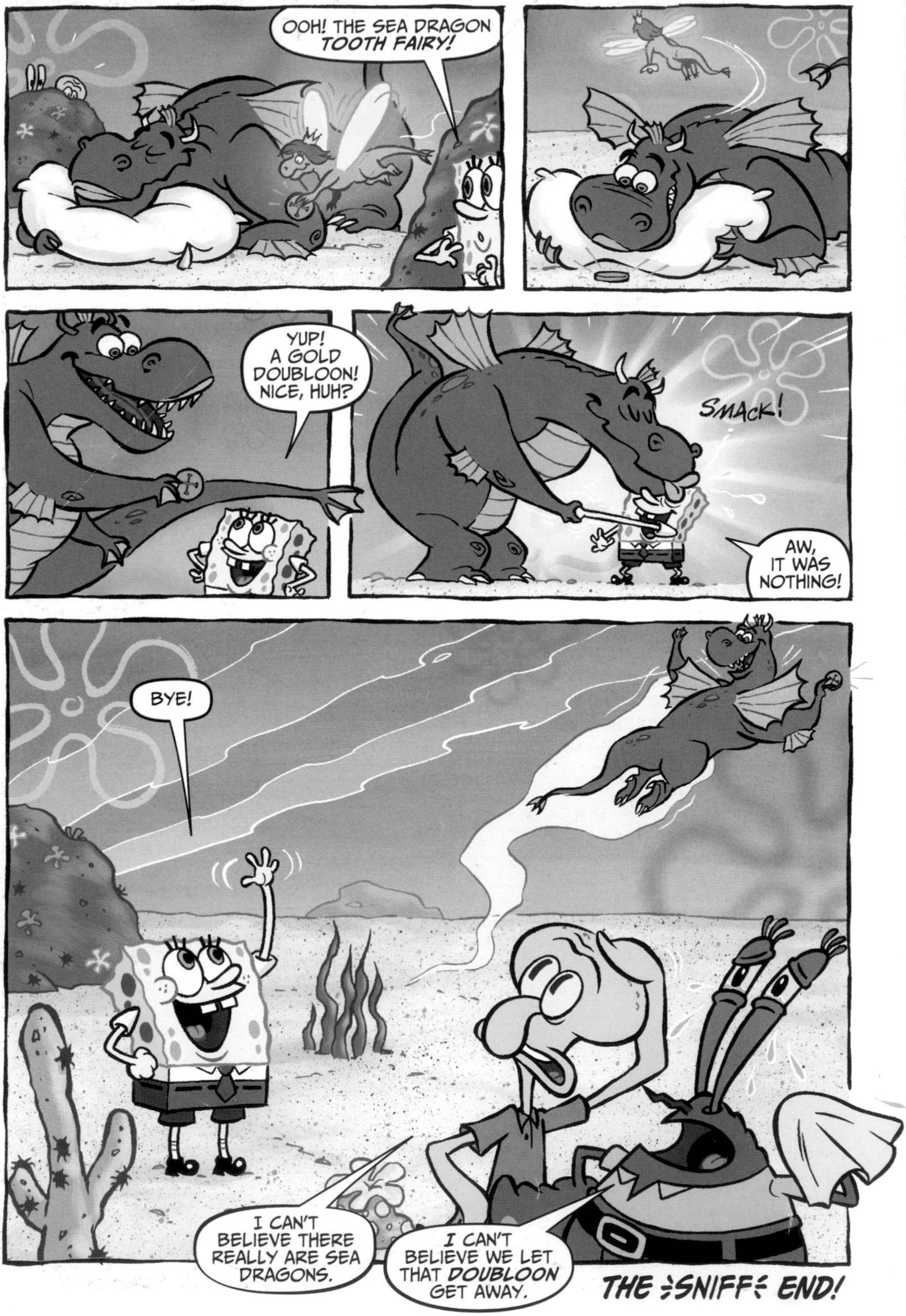
OOH! THE SEA DRAGON TOOTH FAIRY!
YUP! A GOLD DOUBLOON! NICE, HUH?
SMACK!
AW, IT WAS NOTHING!
BYE!
I CAN'T BELIEVE THERE REALLY ARE SEA DRAGONS.
I CAN'T BELIEVE WE LET THAT DOUBLOON GET AWAY.
THE SNIFF END!

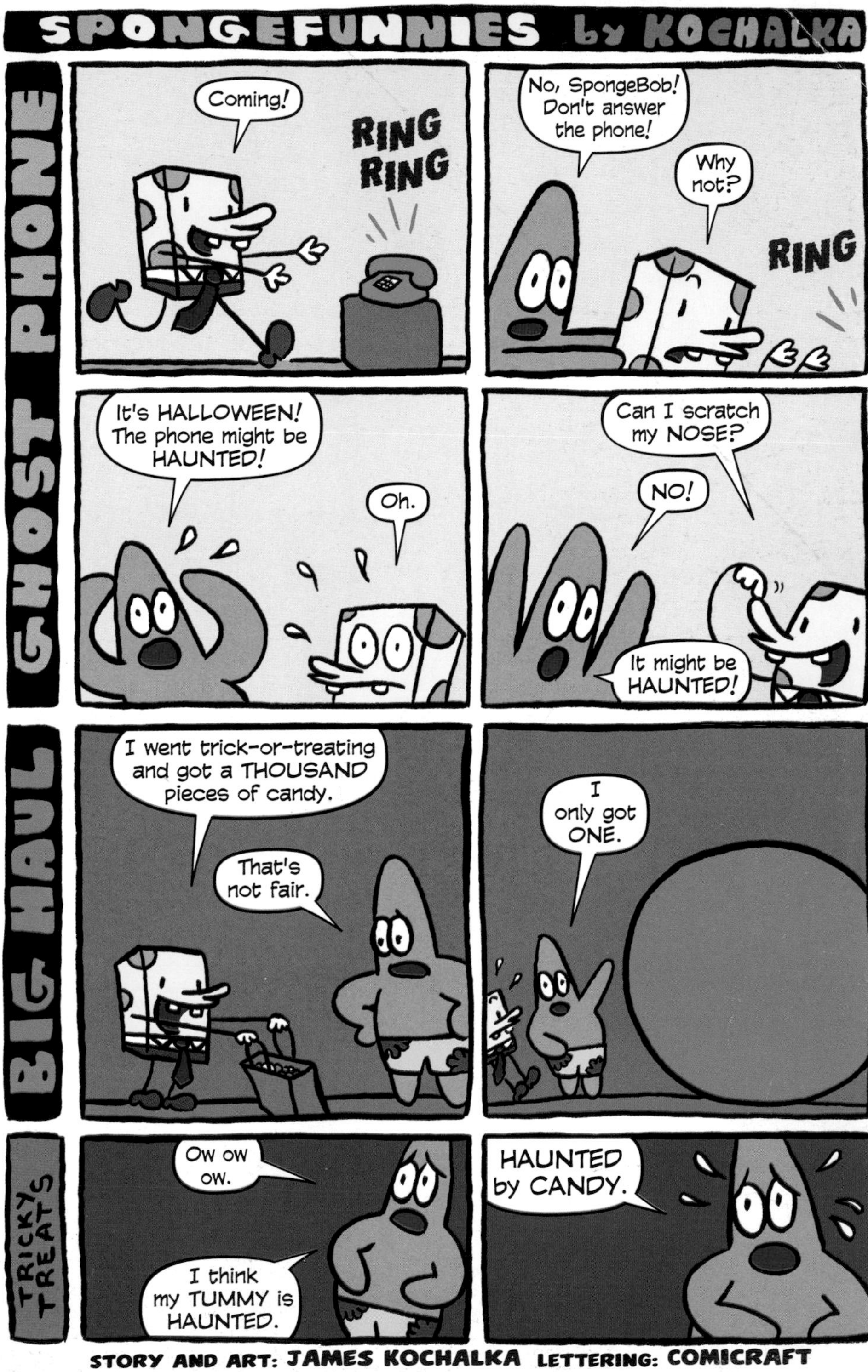
SPONGEFUNNIES by KOCHALKA
GHOST PHONE
Coming!
RING RING
No, SpongeBob! Don't answer the phone!
Why not?
RING
It's HALLOWEEN! The phone might be HAUNTED!
Oh.
Can I scratch my NOSE?
NO!
It might be HAUNTED!
BIG HAUL
I went trick-or-treating and got a THOUSAND pieces of candy.
That's not fair.
I only got ONE.
TRICKY TREATS
Ow ow ow.
I think my TUMMY is HAUNTED.
HAUNTED by CANDY.

STORY AND ART: JAMES KOCHALKA LETTERING: COMICRAFT

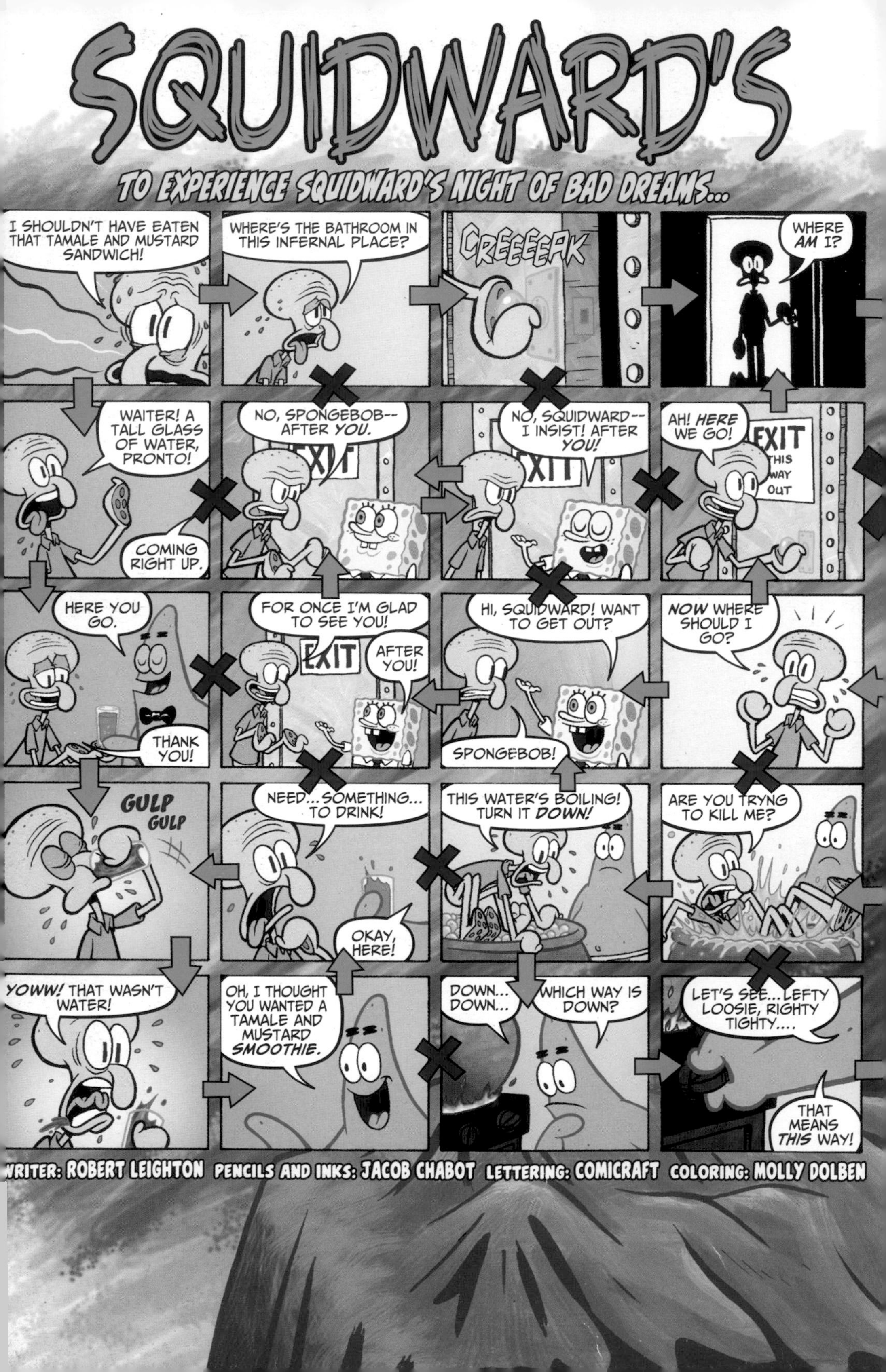
SQUIDWARD'S
TO EXPERIENCE SQUIDWARD'S NIGHT OF BAD DREAMS...
I SHOULDN'T HAVE EATEN THAT TAMALE AND MUSTARD SANDWICH!
WHERE'S THE BATHROOM IN THIS INFERNAL PLACE?
CREEEEAK
WHERE AM I?
WAITER! A TALL GLASS OF WATER, PRONTO!
COMING RIGHT UP.
NO, SPONGEBOB-- AFTER YOU.
EXIT
NO, SQUIDWARD-- I INSIST! AFTER YOU!
EXIT
AH! HERE WE GO!
EXIT THIS WAY OUT
HERE YOU GO.
THANK YOU!
FOR ONCE I'M GLAD TO SEE YOU!
EXIT
AFTER YOU!
HI, SQUIDWARD! WANT TO GET OUT?
SPONGEBOB!
NOW WHERE SHOULD I GO?
GULP GULP
NEED... SOMETHING... TO DRINK!
OKAY, HERE!
THIS WATER'S BOILING! TURN IT DOWN!
ARE YOU TRYNG TO KILL ME?
YOWW! THAT WASN'T WATER!
OH, I THOUGHT YOU WANTED A TAMALE AND MUSTARD SMOOTHIE.
DOWN... DOWN...
WHICH WAY IS DOWN?
LET'S SEE... LEFTY LOOSIE, RIGHTY TIGHTY....
THAT MEANS THIS WAY!
WRITER: ROBERT LEIGHTON PENCILS AND INKS: JACOB CHABOT LETTERING: COMICRAFT COLORING: MOLLY DOLBEN

NIGHTMARE

...FOLLOW ANY PATH IN THE DIRECTION OF THE ARROWS.

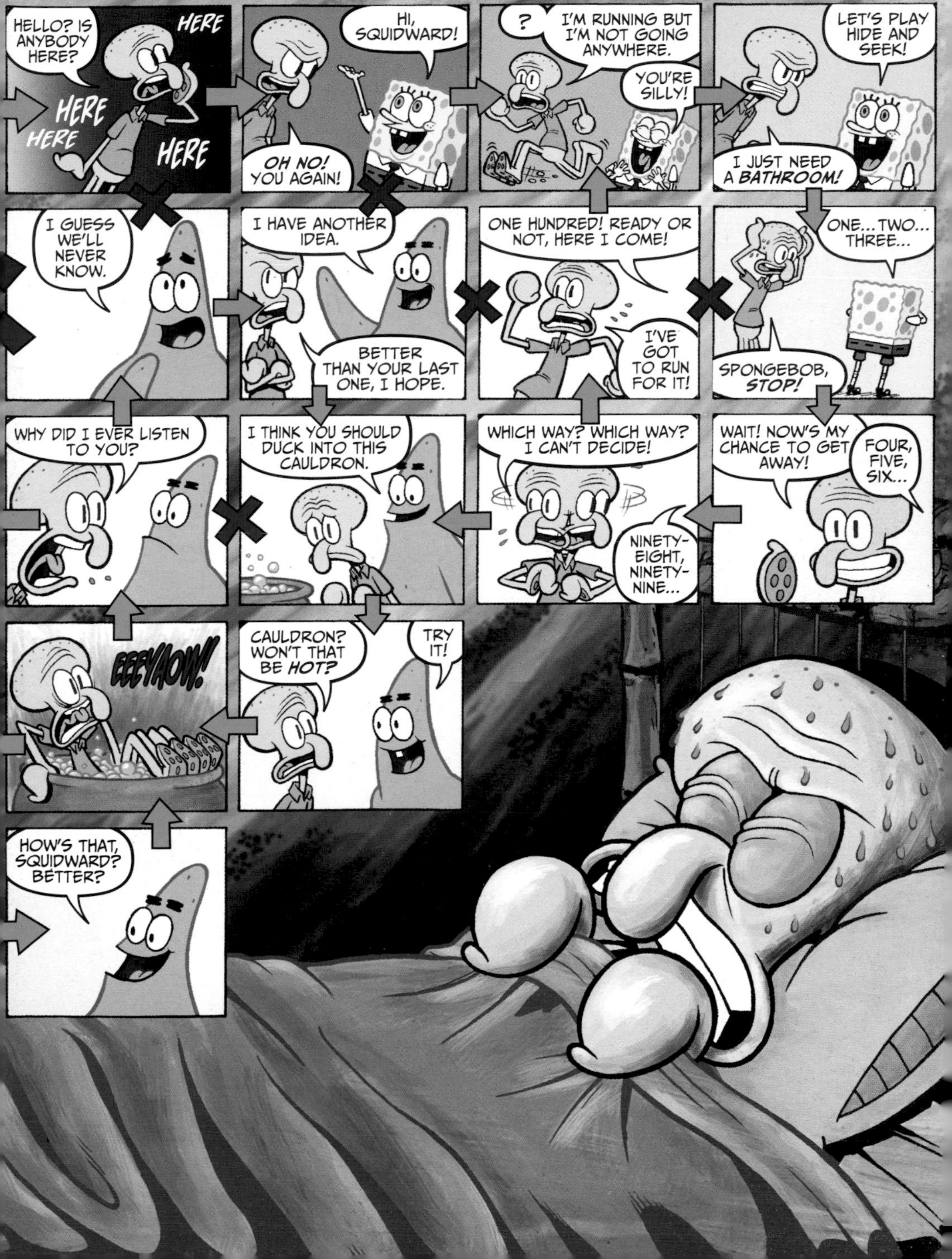
HELLO? IS ANYBODY HERE?
HERE
HERE
HERE
HERE
HI, SQUIDWARD!
OH NO! YOU AGAIN!
?
I'M RUNNING BUT I'M NOT GOING ANYWHERE.
YOU'RE SILLY!
LET'S PLAY HIDE AND SEEK!
I JUST NEED A BATHROOM!
I GUESS WE'LL NEVER KNOW.
I HAVE ANOTHER IDEA.
BETTER THAN YOUR LAST ONE, I HOPE.
ONE HUNDRED! READY OR NOT, HERE I COME!
I'VE GOT TO RUN FOR IT!
ONE... TWO... THREE...
SPONGEBOB, STOP!
WHY DID I EVER LISTEN TO YOU?
I THINK YOU SHOULD DUCK INTO THIS CAULDRON.
WHICH WAY? WHICH WAY? I CAN'T DECIDE!
NINETY-EIGHT, NINETY-NINE...
WAIT! NOW'S MY CHANCE TO GET AWAY!
FOUR, FIVE, SIX...
EEEYAOW!
CAULDRON? WON'T THAT BE HOT?
TRY IT!
HOW'S THAT, SQUIDWARD? BETTER?

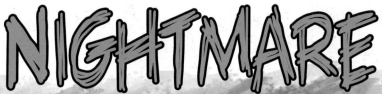

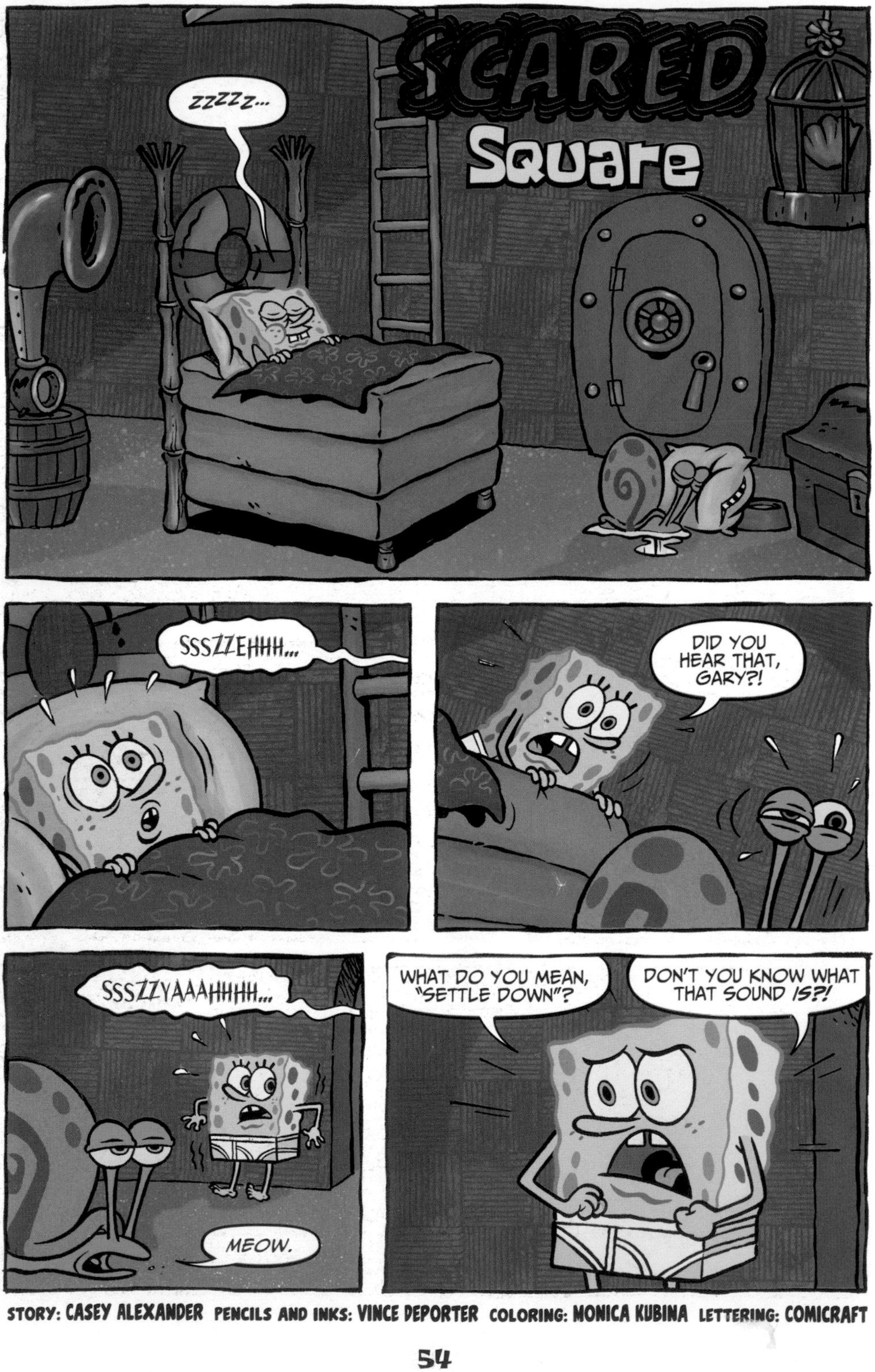
SCARED
Square
ZZZZZ...
SSSZZEHHH...
DID YOU HEAR THAT, GARY?!
SSSZZYAAAHHHH...
MEOW.
WHAT DO YOU MEAN, "SETTLE DOWN"?
DON'T YOU KNOW WHAT THAT SOUND *IS?!*

STORY: CASEY ALEXANDER PENCILS AND INKS: VINCE DEPORTER COLORING: MONICA KUBINA LETTERING: COMICRAFT

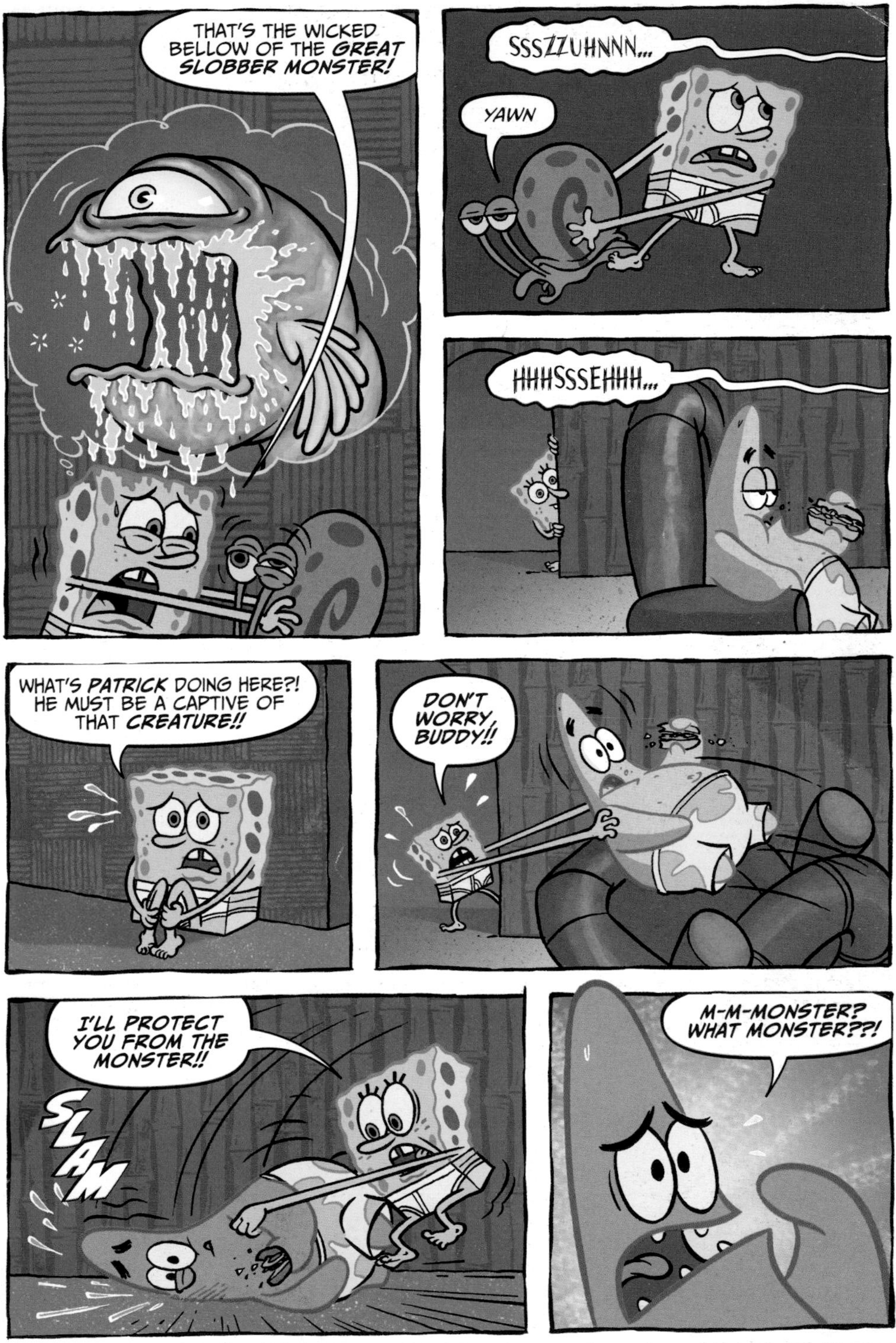
THAT'S THE WICKED BELLOW OF THE GREAT SLOBBER MONSTER!
SSSZZUHNNN...
YAWN
HHHSSSEHHH...
WHAT'S PATRICK DOING HERE?! HE MUST BE A CAPTIVE OF THAT CREATURE!!
DON'T WORRY, BUDDY!!
I'LL PROTECT YOU FROM THE MONSTER!!
SLAM
M-M-MONSTER? WHAT MONSTER??!

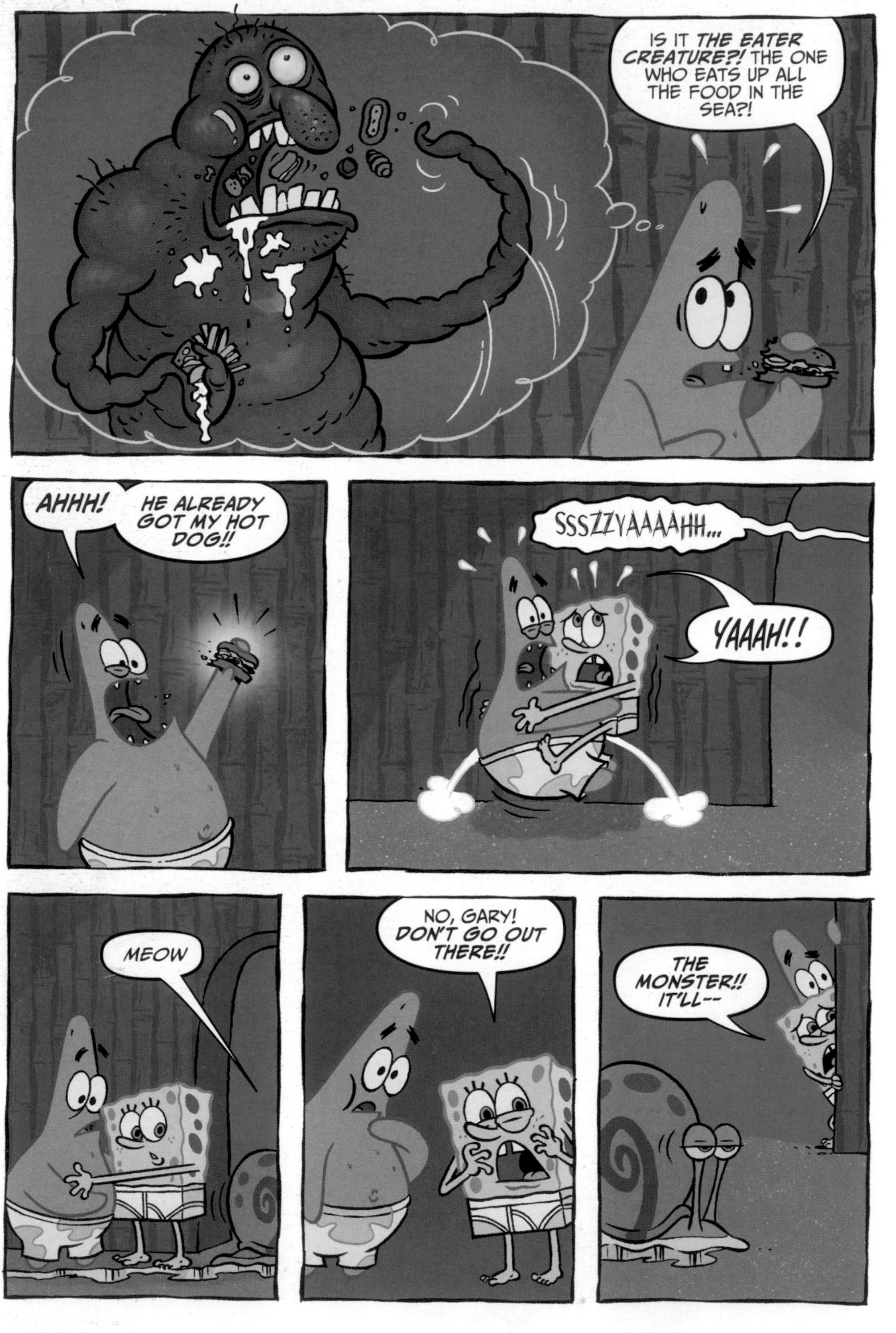
IS IT THE EATER CREATURE?! THE ONE WHO EATS UP ALL THE FOOD IN THE SEA?!
AHHH!
HE ALREADY GOT MY HOT DOG!!
SSSZZYAAAAHH...
YAAAH!!
MEOW
NO, GARY! DON'T GO OUT THERE!!
THE MONSTER!! IT'LL--

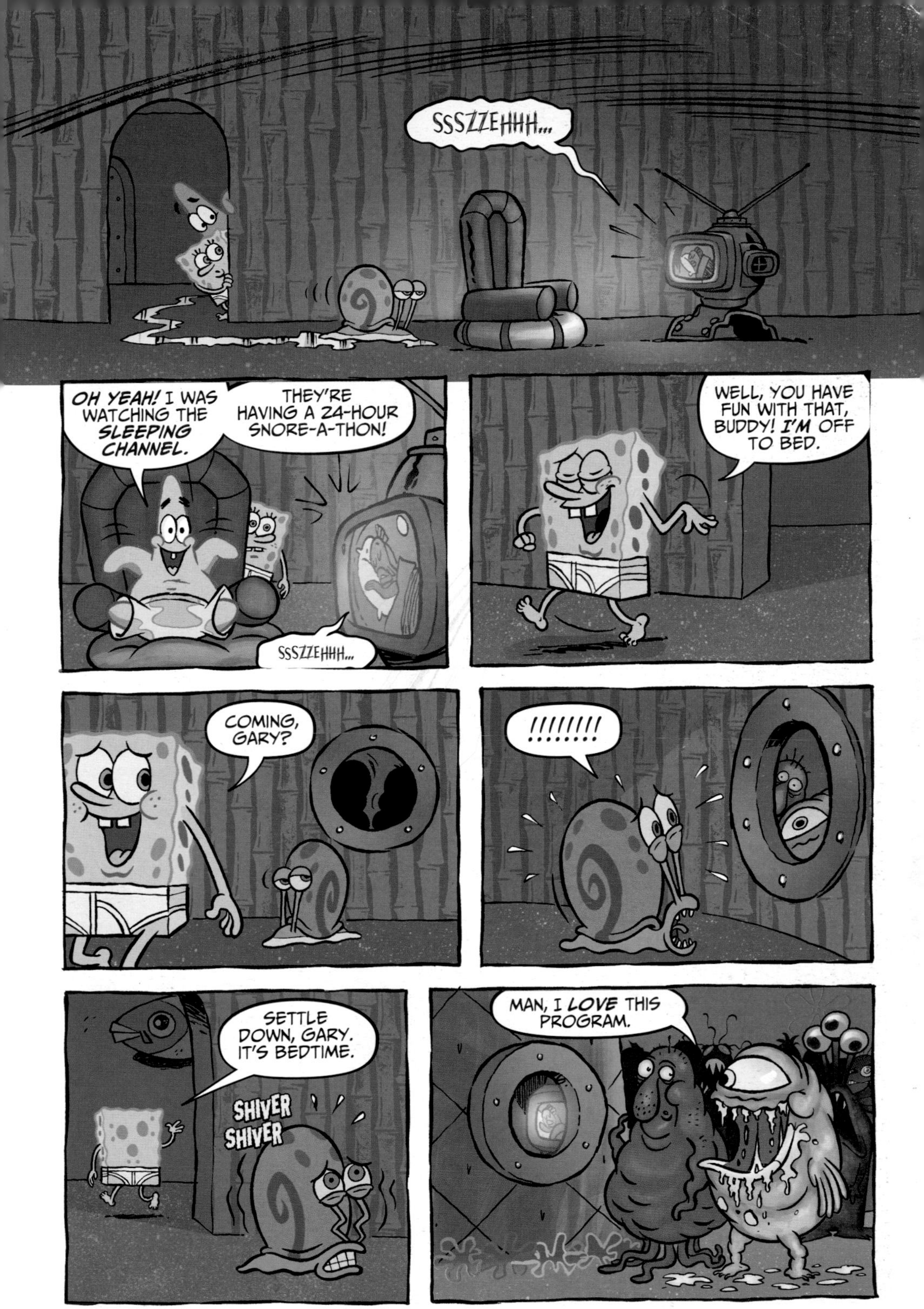
SSSZZEHHH...
OH YEAH! I WAS WATCHING THE SLEEPING CHANNEL.
THEY'RE HAVING A 24-HOUR SNORE-A-THON!
SSSZZEHHH...
WELL, YOU HAVE FUN WITH THAT, BUDDY! I'M OFF TO BED.
COMING, GARY?
!!!!!!!!
SETTLE DOWN, GARY. IT'S BEDTIME.
SHIVER SHIVER
MAN, I LOVE THIS PROGRAM.

END

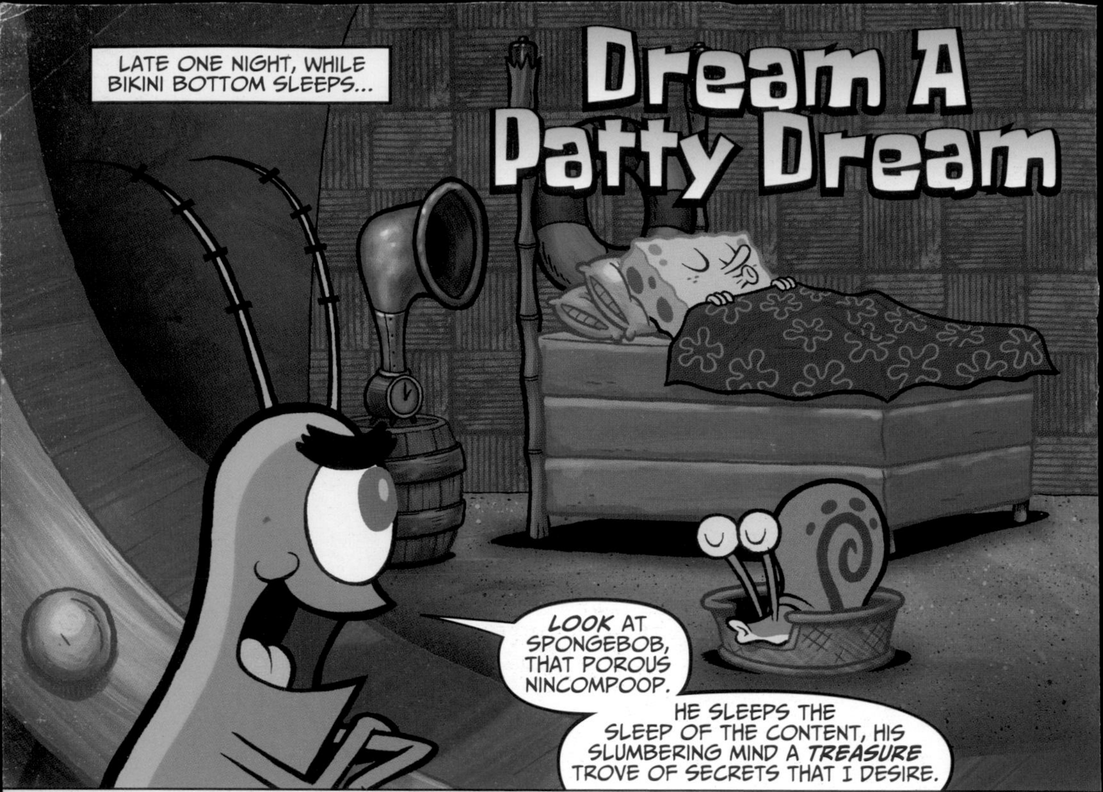
LATE ONE NIGHT, WHILE BIKINI BOTTOM SLEEPS...
Dream A Patty Dream
LOOK AT SPONGEBOB, THAT POROUS NINCOMPOOP.
HE SLEEPS THE SLEEP OF THE CONTENT, HIS SLUMBERING MIND A TREASURE TROVE OF SECRETS THAT I DESIRE.

STORY: CHUCK DIXON PENCILS AND INKS: JACOB CHABOT COLOR: HIFI LETTERING: COMICRAFT

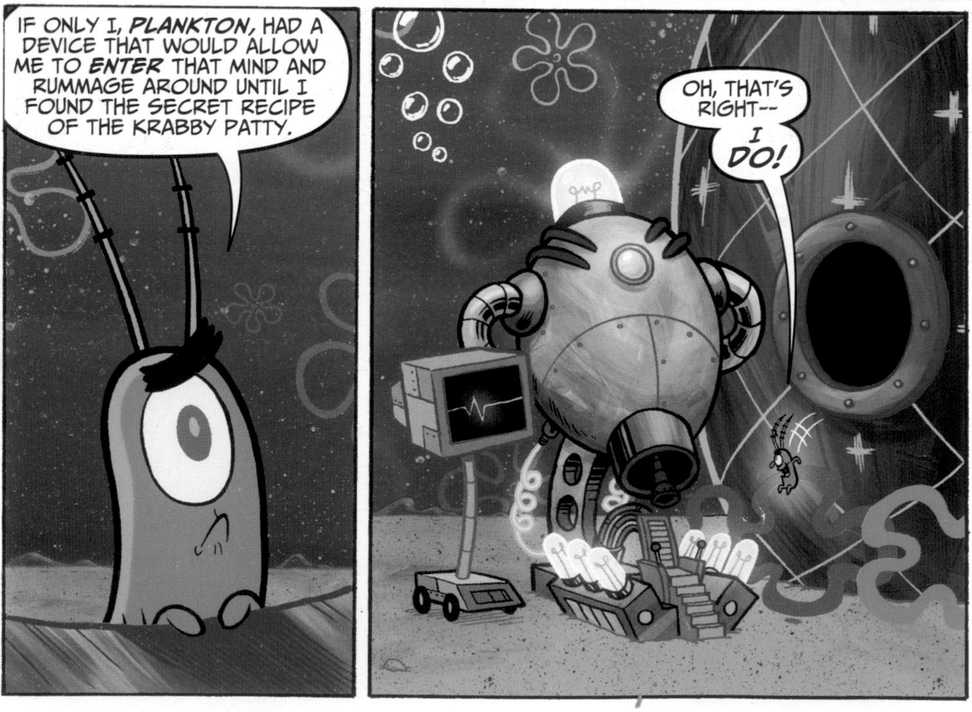
IF ONLY I, PLANKTON, HAD A DEVICE THAT WOULD ALLOW ME TO ENTER THAT MIND AND RUMMAGE AROUND UNTIL I FOUND THE SECRET RECIPE OF THE KRABBY PATTY.
OH, THAT'S RIGHT-- I DO!

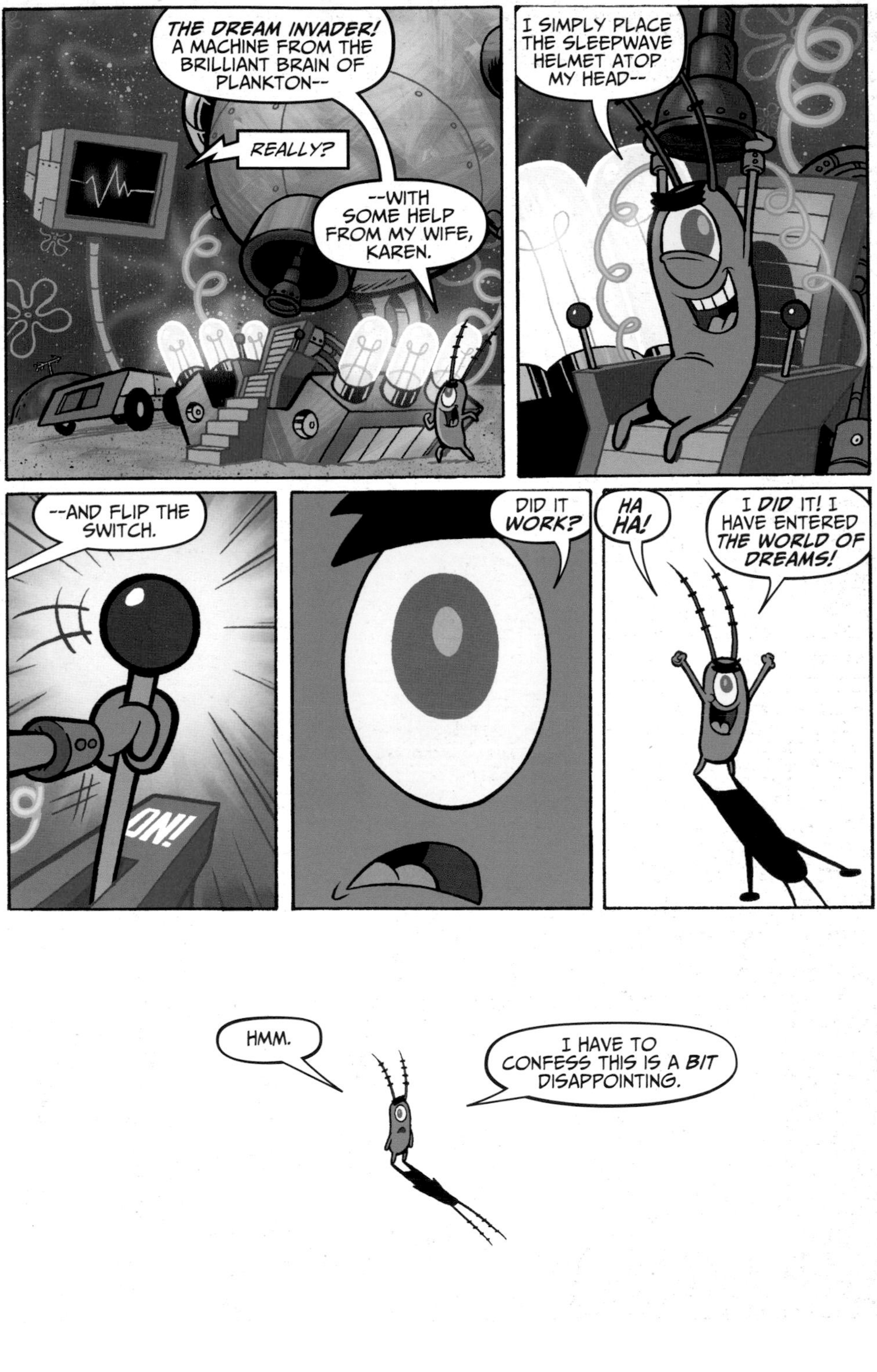
THE DREAM INVADER! A MACHINE FROM THE BRILLIANT BRAIN OF PLANKTON--
REALLY?
--WITH SOME HELP FROM MY WIFE, KAREN.
I SIMPLY PLACE THE SLEEPWAVE HELMET ATOP MY HEAD--
--AND FLIP THE SWITCH.
ON!
DID IT WORK?
HA HA!
I DID IT! I HAVE ENTERED THE WORLD OF DREAMS!
HMM.
I HAVE TO CONFESS THIS IS A BIT DISAPPOINTING.

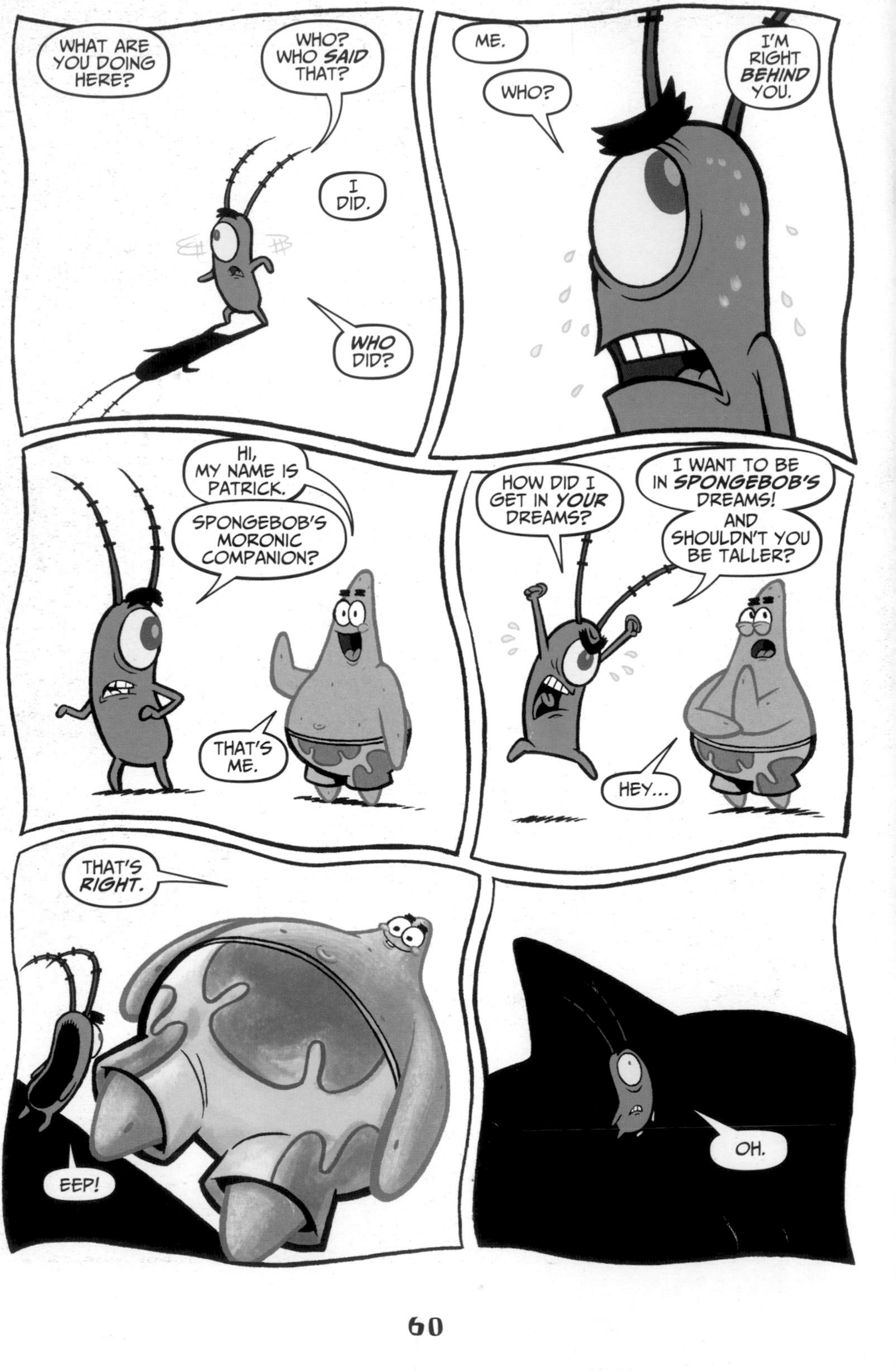
WHAT ARE YOU DOING HERE?
WHO? WHO *SAID* THAT?
I DID.
WHO DID?
ME.
WHO?
I'M RIGHT *BEHIND* YOU.
HI, MY NAME IS PATRICK.
SPONGEBOB'S MORONIC COMPANION?
THAT'S ME.
HOW DID I GET IN *YOUR* DREAMS?
I WANT TO BE IN *SPONGEBOB'S* DREAMS! AND SHOULDN'T YOU BE TALLER?
HEY...
THAT'S *RIGHT.*
EEP!
OH.

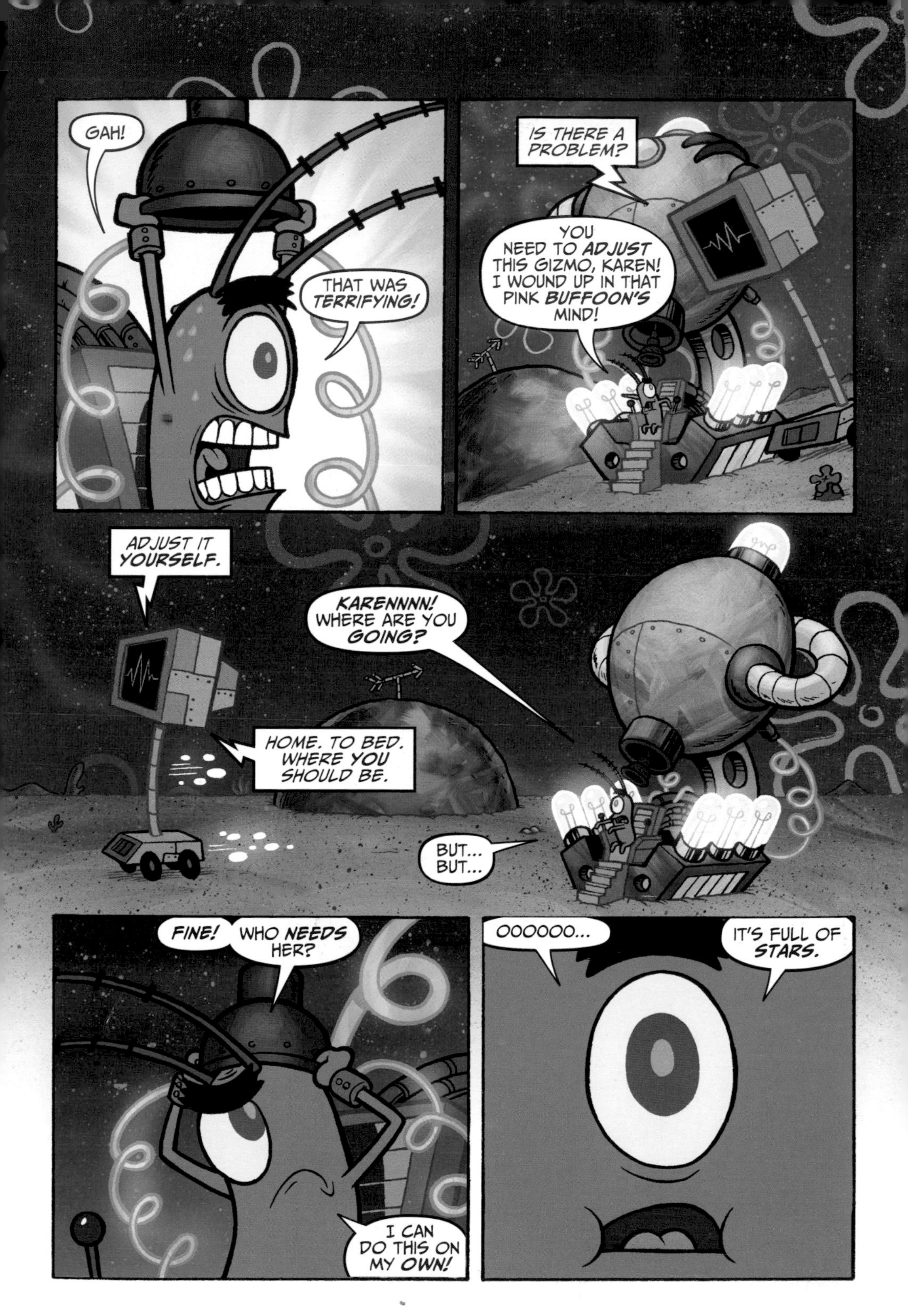
GAH!
THAT WAS TERRIFYING!
IS THERE A PROBLEM?
YOU NEED TO ADJUST THIS GIZMO, KAREN! I WOUND UP IN THAT PINK BUFFOON'S MIND!
ADJUST IT YOURSELF.
KARENNNN! WHERE ARE YOU GOING?
HOME. TO BED. WHERE YOU SHOULD BE.
BUT... BUT...
FINE!
WHO NEEDS HER?
I CAN DO THIS ON MY OWN!
OOOOOO...
IT'S FULL OF STARS.

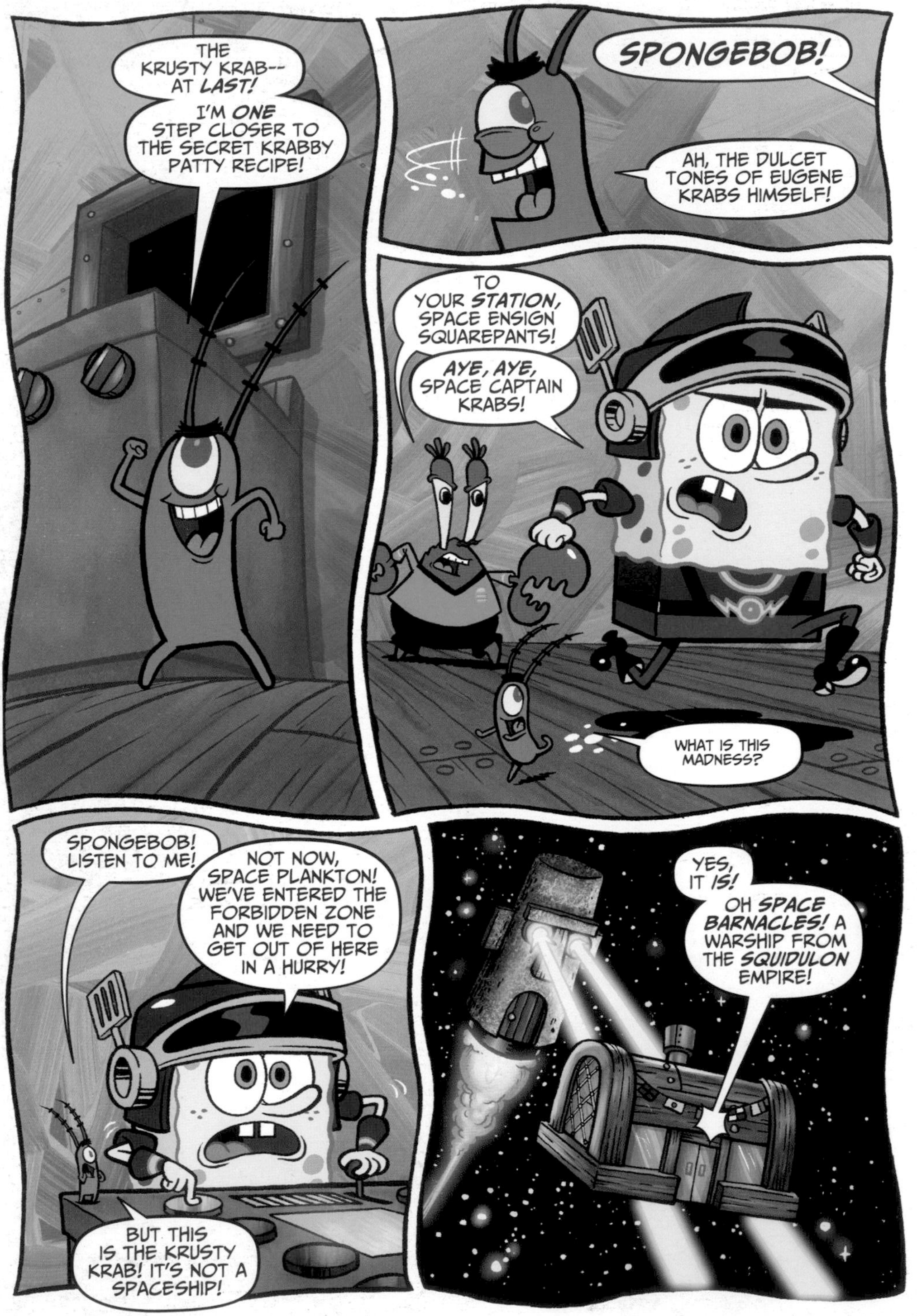
THE KRUSTY KRAB-- AT LAST!
I'M ONE STEP CLOSER TO THE SECRET KRABBY PATTY RECIPE!
SPONGEBOB!
AH, THE DULCET TONES OF EUGENE KRABS HIMSELF!
TO YOUR STATION, SPACE ENSIGN SQUAREPANTS!
AYE, AYE, SPACE CAPTAIN KRABS!
WHAT IS THIS MADNESS?
SPONGEBOB! LISTEN TO ME!
NOT NOW, SPACE PLANKTON! WE'VE ENTERED THE FORBIDDEN ZONE AND WE NEED TO GET OUT OF HERE IN A HURRY!
BUT THIS IS THE KRUSTY KRAB! IT'S NOT A SPACESHIP!
YES, IT IS!
OH SPACE BARNACLES! A WARSHIP FROM THE SQUIDULON EMPIRE!

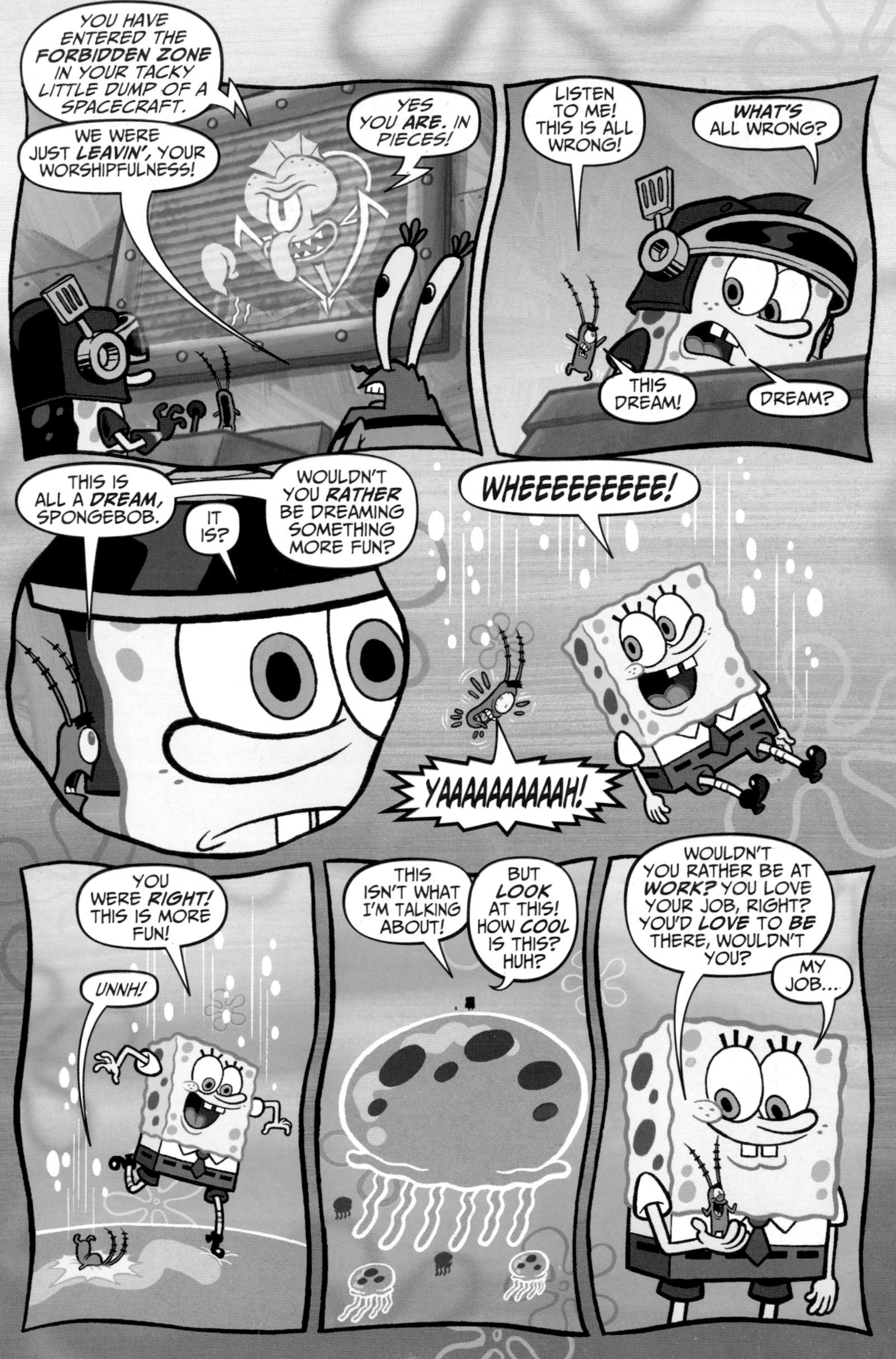

YOU HAVE ENTERED THE **FORBIDDEN ZONE** IN YOUR TACKY LITTLE DUMP OF A SPACECRAFT.
WE WERE JUST ***LEAVIN'***, YOUR WORSHIPFULNESS!
YES YOU ***ARE***. IN PIECES!
LISTEN TO ME! THIS IS ALL WRONG!
WHAT'S ALL WRONG?
THIS DREAM!
DREAM?
THIS IS ALL A ***DREAM***, SPONGEBOB.
IT IS?
WOULDN'T YOU ***RATHER*** BE DREAMING SOMETHING MORE FUN?
WHEEEEEEEEEE!
YAAAAAAAAAAH!
YOU WERE ***RIGHT!*** THIS IS MORE FUN!
UNNH!
THIS ISN'T WHAT I'M TALKING ABOUT!
BUT ***LOOK*** AT THIS! HOW ***COOL*** IS THIS? HUH?
WOULDN'T YOU RATHER BE AT ***WORK?*** YOU LOVE YOUR JOB, RIGHT? YOU'D ***LOVE*** TO ***BE*** THERE, WOULDN'T YOU?
MY JOB...

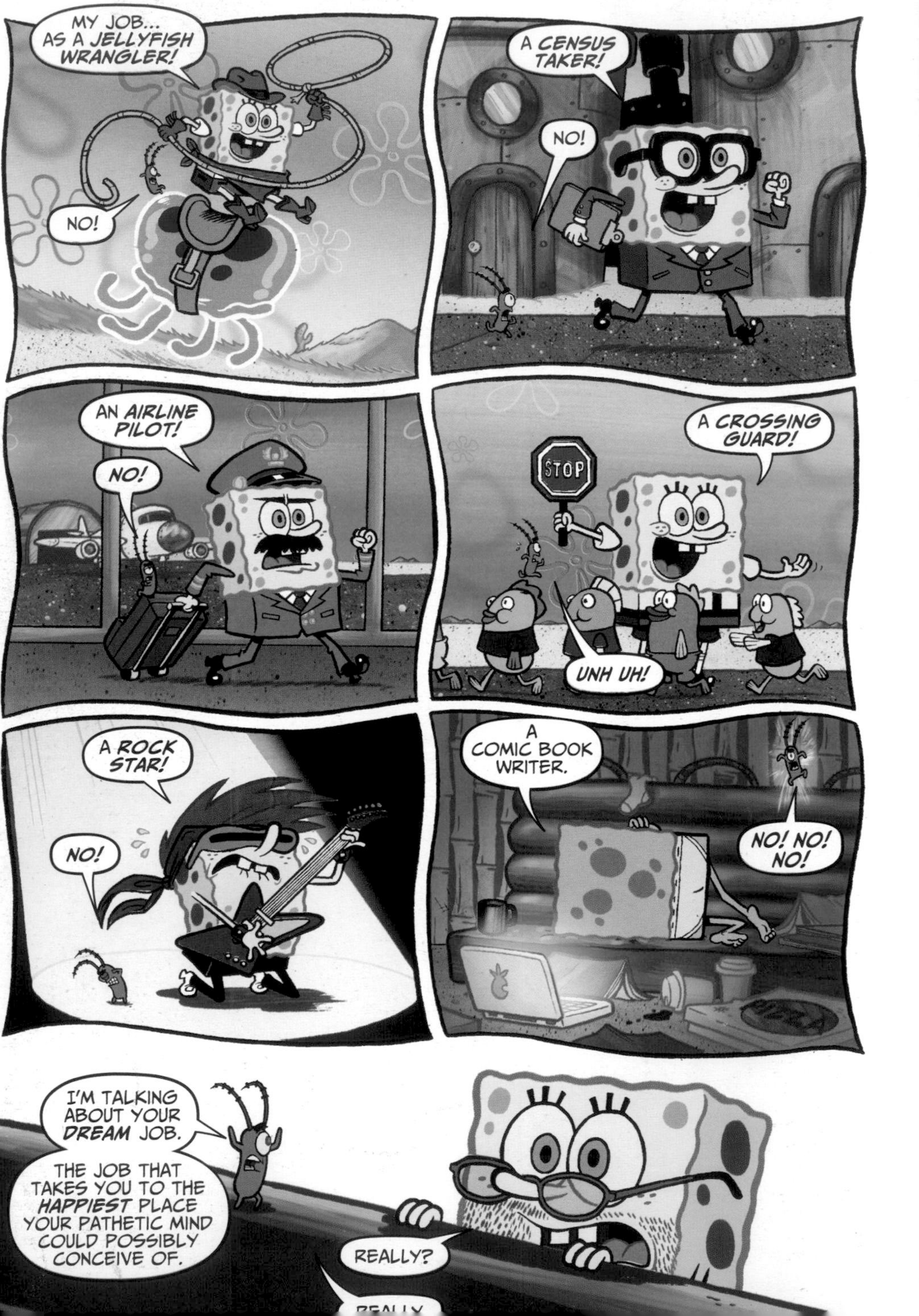
MY JOB... AS A JELLYFISH WRANGLER!
NO!
A CENSUS TAKER!
NO!
AN AIRLINE PILOT!
NO!
A CROSSING GUARD!
STOP
UNH UH!
A ROCK STAR!
NO!
A COMIC BOOK WRITER.
NO! NO! NO!
I'M TALKING ABOUT YOUR DREAM JOB.
THE JOB THAT TAKES YOU TO THE HAPPIEST PLACE YOUR PATHETIC MIND COULD POSSIBLY CONCEIVE OF.
REALLY?

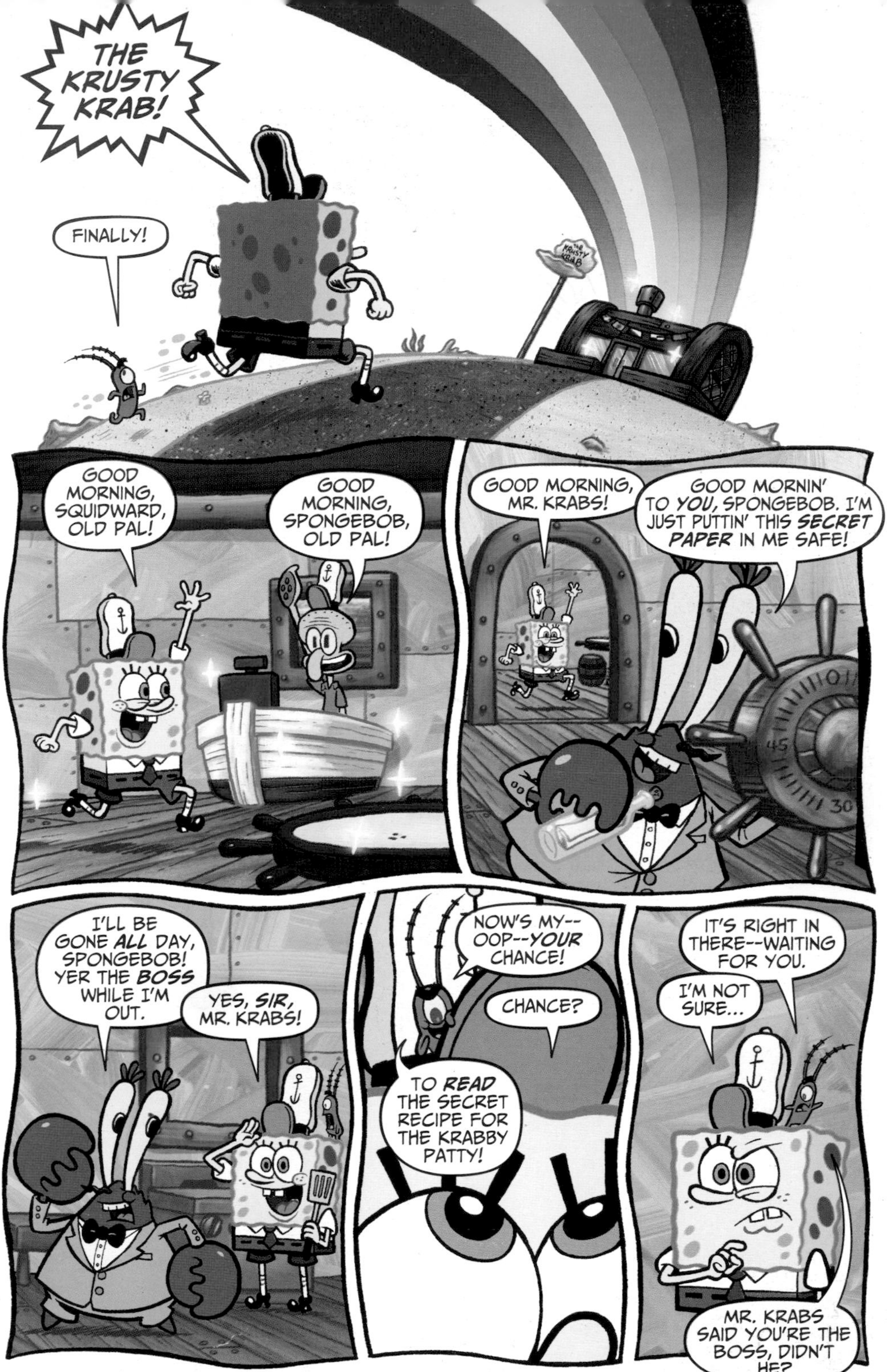
THE KRUSTY KRAB!
FINALLY!
THE KRUSTY KRAB
GOOD MORNING, SQUIDWARD, OLD PAL!
GOOD MORNING, SPONGEBOB, OLD PAL!
GOOD MORNING, MR. KRABS!
GOOD MORNIN' TO YOU, SPONGEBOB. I'M JUST PUTTIN' THIS SECRET PAPER IN ME SAFE!
I'LL BE GONE ALL DAY, SPONGEBOB! YER THE BOSS WHILE I'M OUT.
YES, SIR, MR. KRABS!
NOW'S MY--OOP--YOUR CHANCE!
CHANCE?
TO READ THE SECRET RECIPE FOR THE KRABBY PATTY!
IT'S RIGHT IN THERE--WAITING FOR YOU.
I'M NOT SURE...
MR. KRABS SAID YOU'RE THE BOSS, DIDN'T HE?

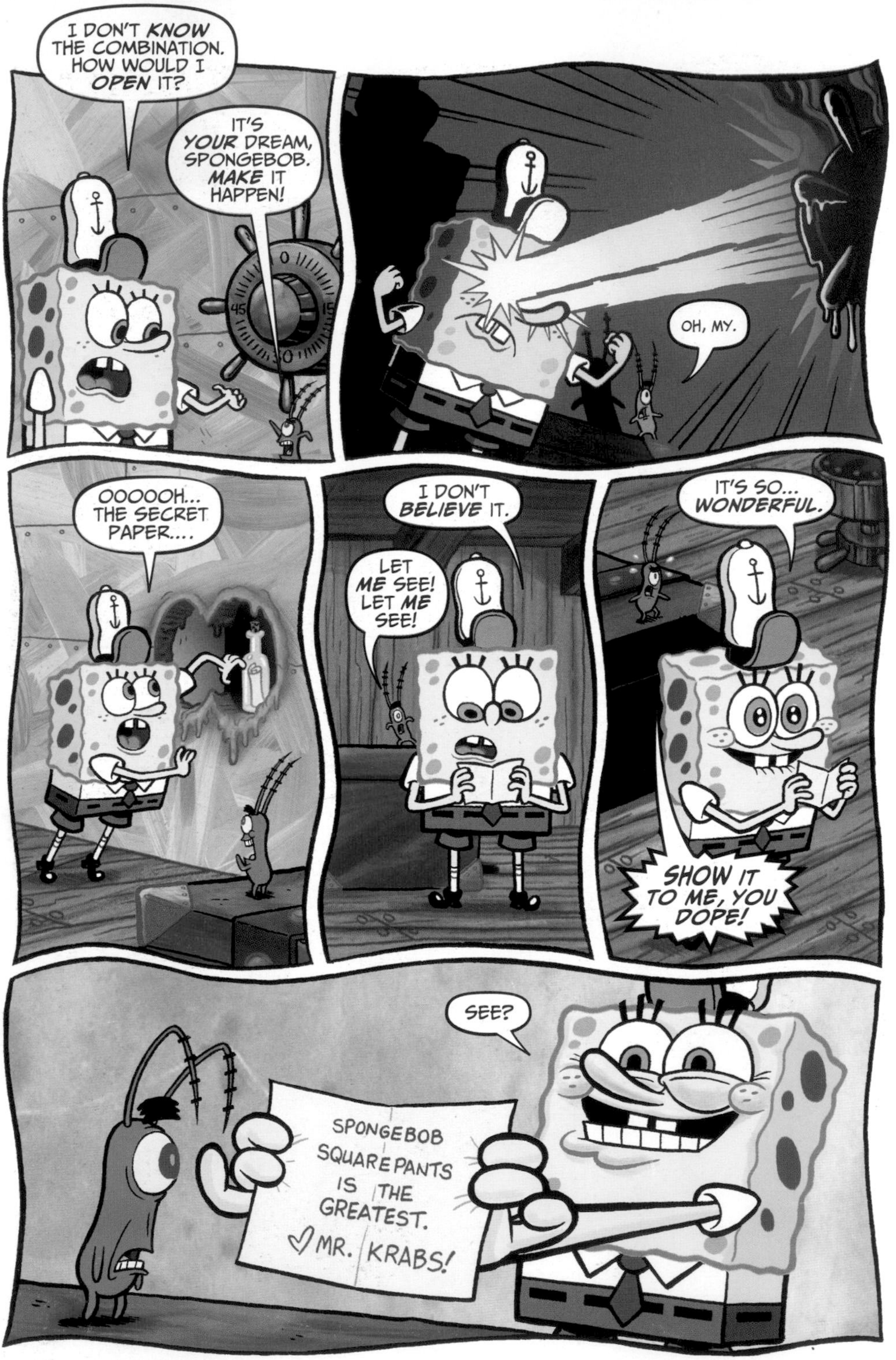
I DON'T KNOW THE COMBINATION. HOW WOULD I OPEN IT?
IT'S YOUR DREAM, SPONGEBOB. MAKE IT HAPPEN!
OH, MY.
OOOOOH... THE SECRET PAPER....
I DON'T BELIEVE IT.
LET ME SEE! LET ME SEE!
IT'S SO... WONDERFUL.
SHOW IT TO ME, YOU DOPE!
SEE?
SPONGEBOB SQUAREPANTS IS THE GREATEST. ♡ MR. KRABS!

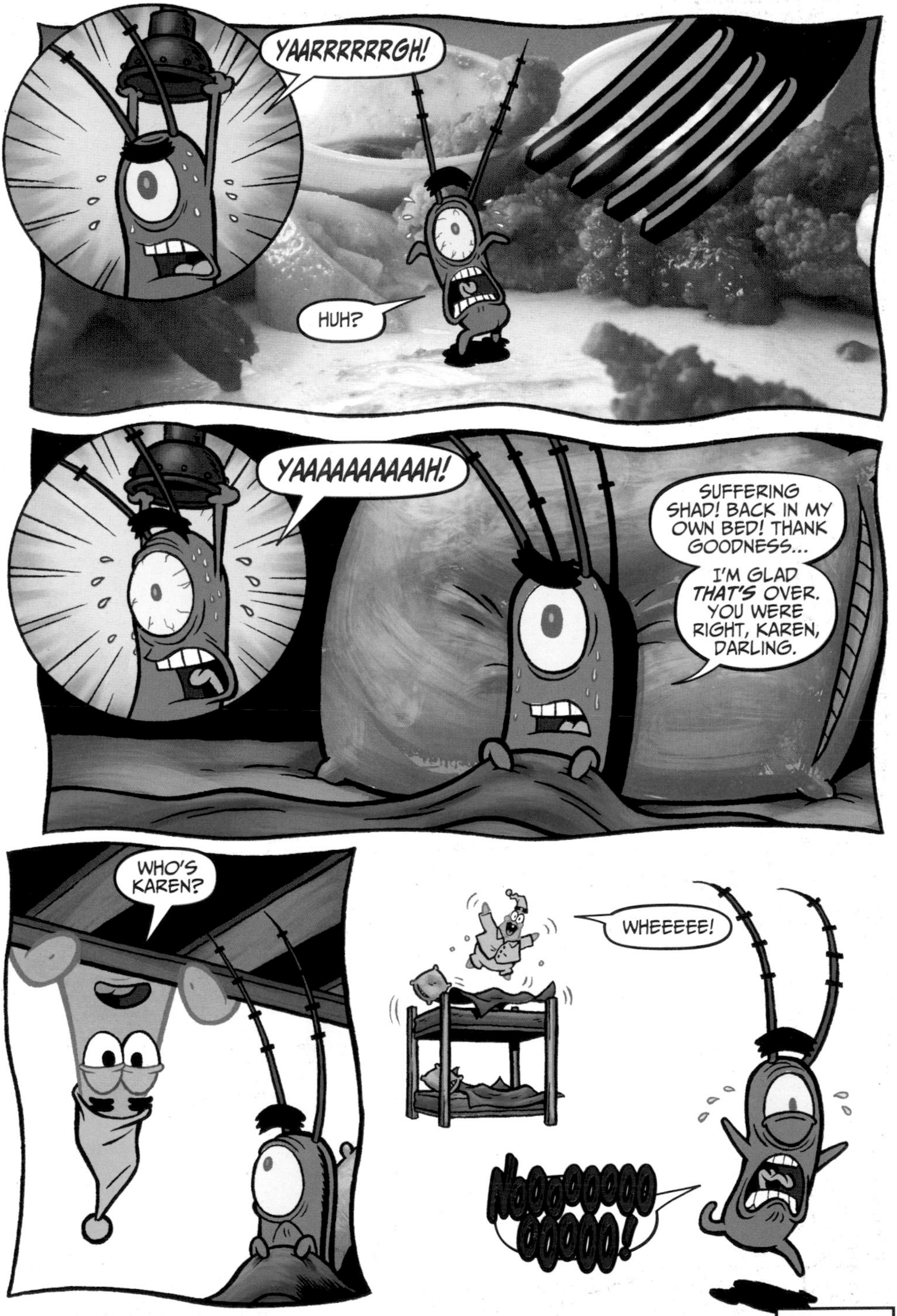
YAARRRRRRGH!
HUH?
YAAAAAAAAAAH!
SUFFERING SHAD! BACK IN MY OWN BED! THANK GOODNESS...
I'M GLAD ***THAT'S*** OVER. YOU WERE RIGHT, KAREN, DARLING.
WHO'S KAREN?
WHEEEEE!
NOOOOOOOO
OOOOO!
THE END?

BUBBLE DOUBLE TROUBLE

STORY: JOEY WEISER PENCILS AND INKS: GREGG SCHIGIEL COLORING: RICK NEILSEN LETTERING: COMICRAFT

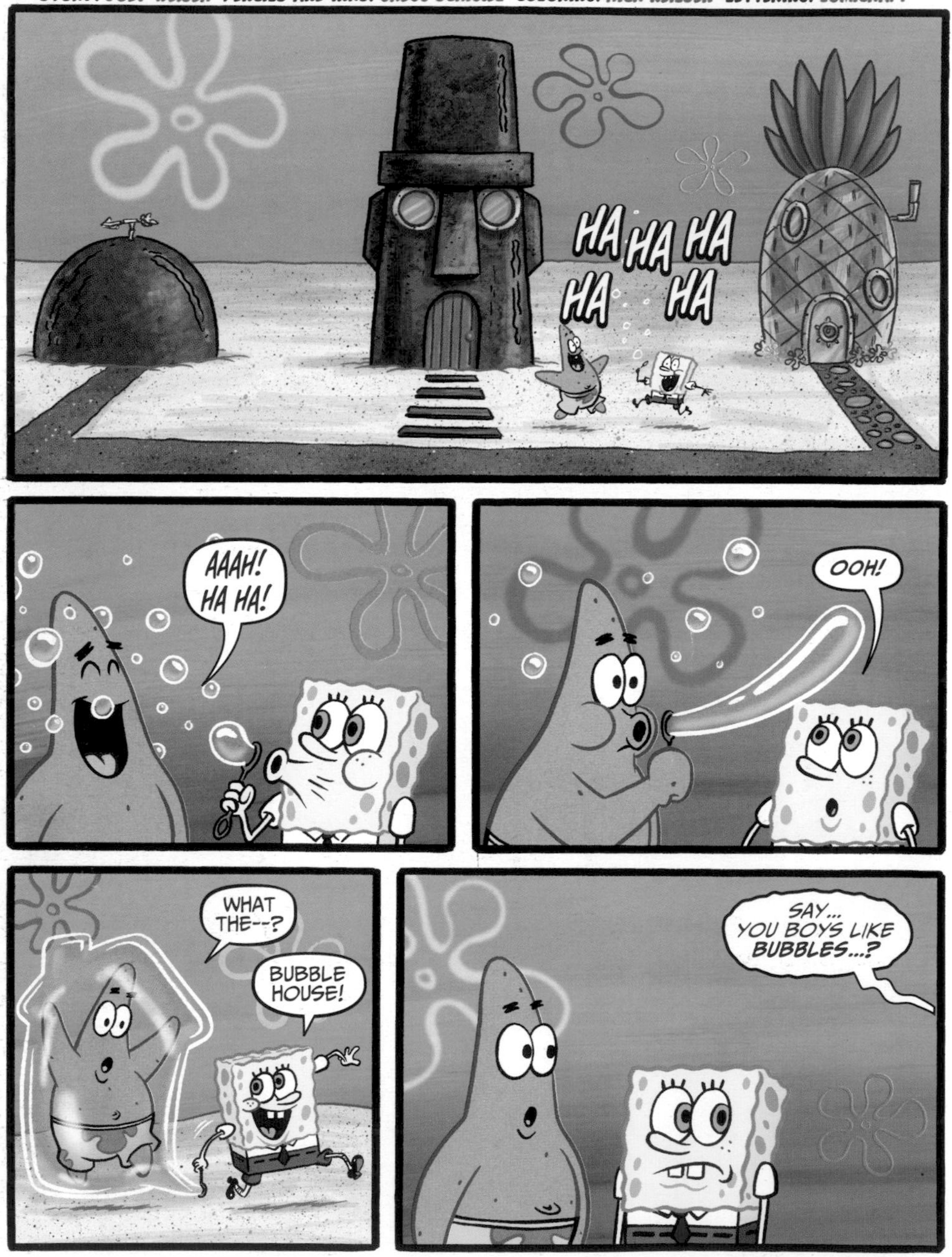
HA HA HA
HA HA
AAAH! HA HA!
OOH!
WHAT THE--?
BUBBLE HOUSE!
SAY... YOU BOYS LIKE BUBBLES...?

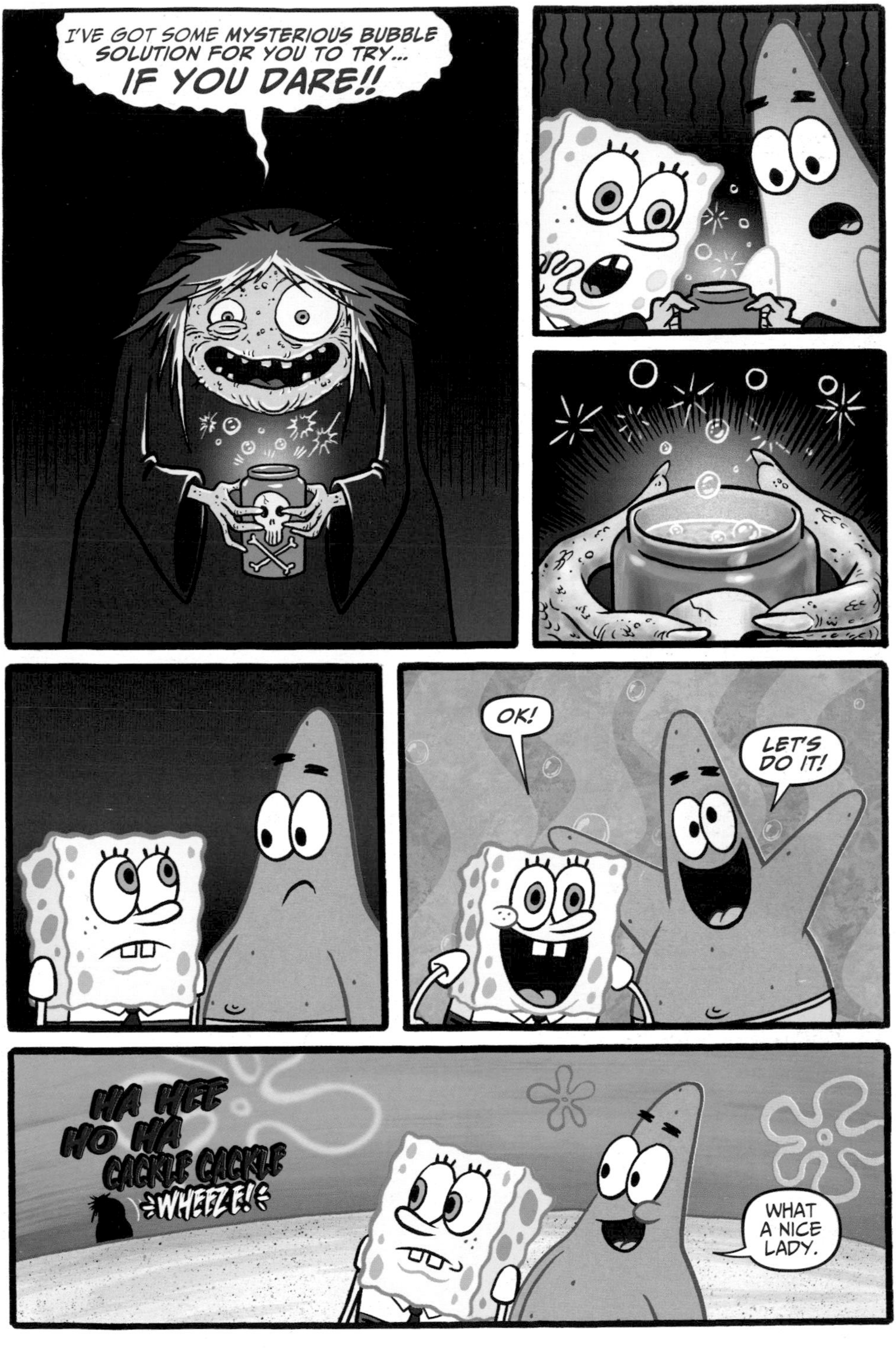
I'VE GOT SOME MYSTERIOUS BUBBLE SOLUTION FOR YOU TO TRY... IF YOU DARE!!
OK!
LET'S DO IT!
HA HEE HO HA CACKLE CACKLE WHEEZE!
WHAT A NICE LADY.

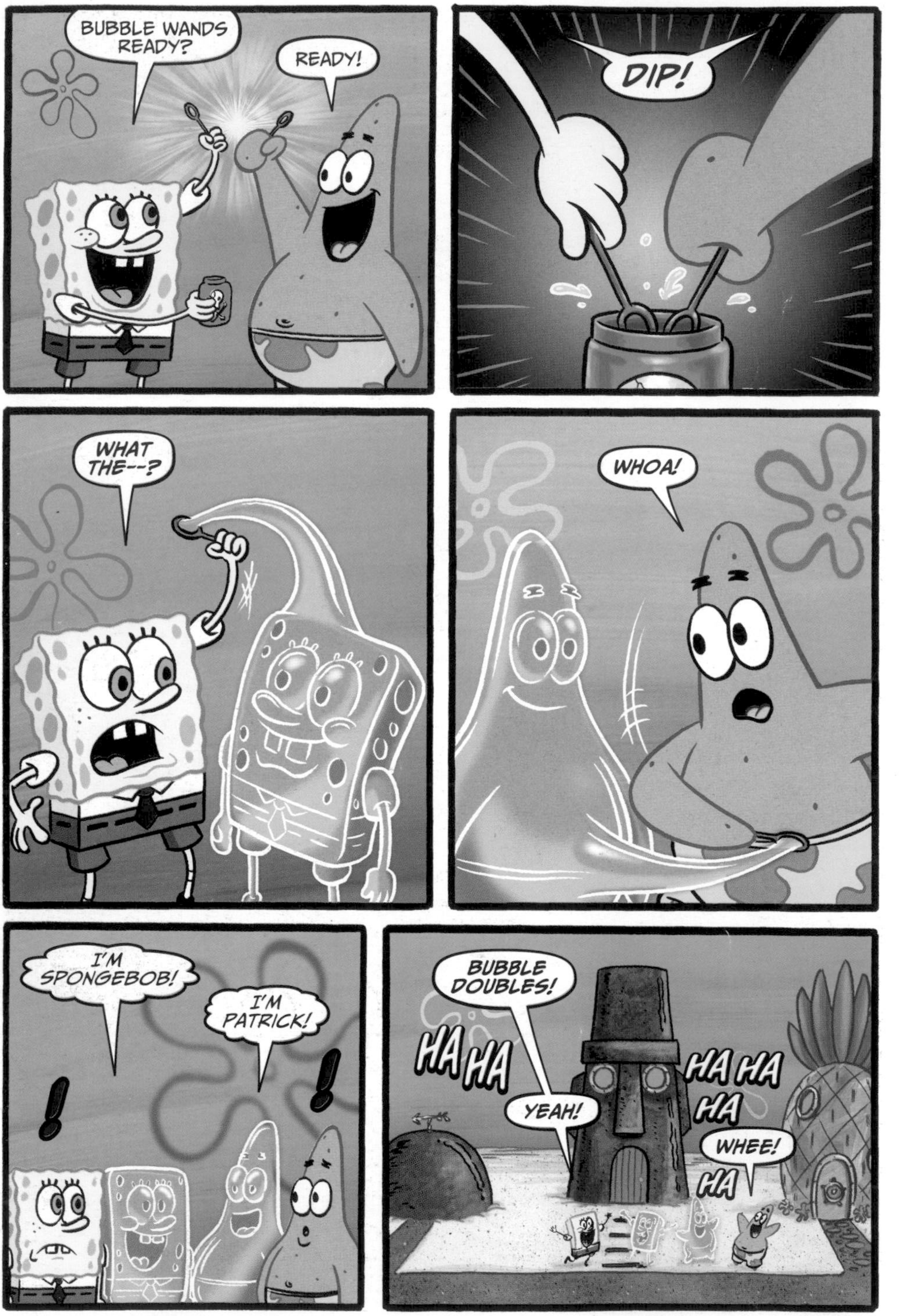
BUBBLE WANDS READY?
READY!
DIP!
WHAT THE--?
WHOA!
I'M SPONGEBOB!
I'M PATRICK!
BUBBLE DOUBLES!
HA HA
YEAH!
HA HA HA
WHEE!
HA

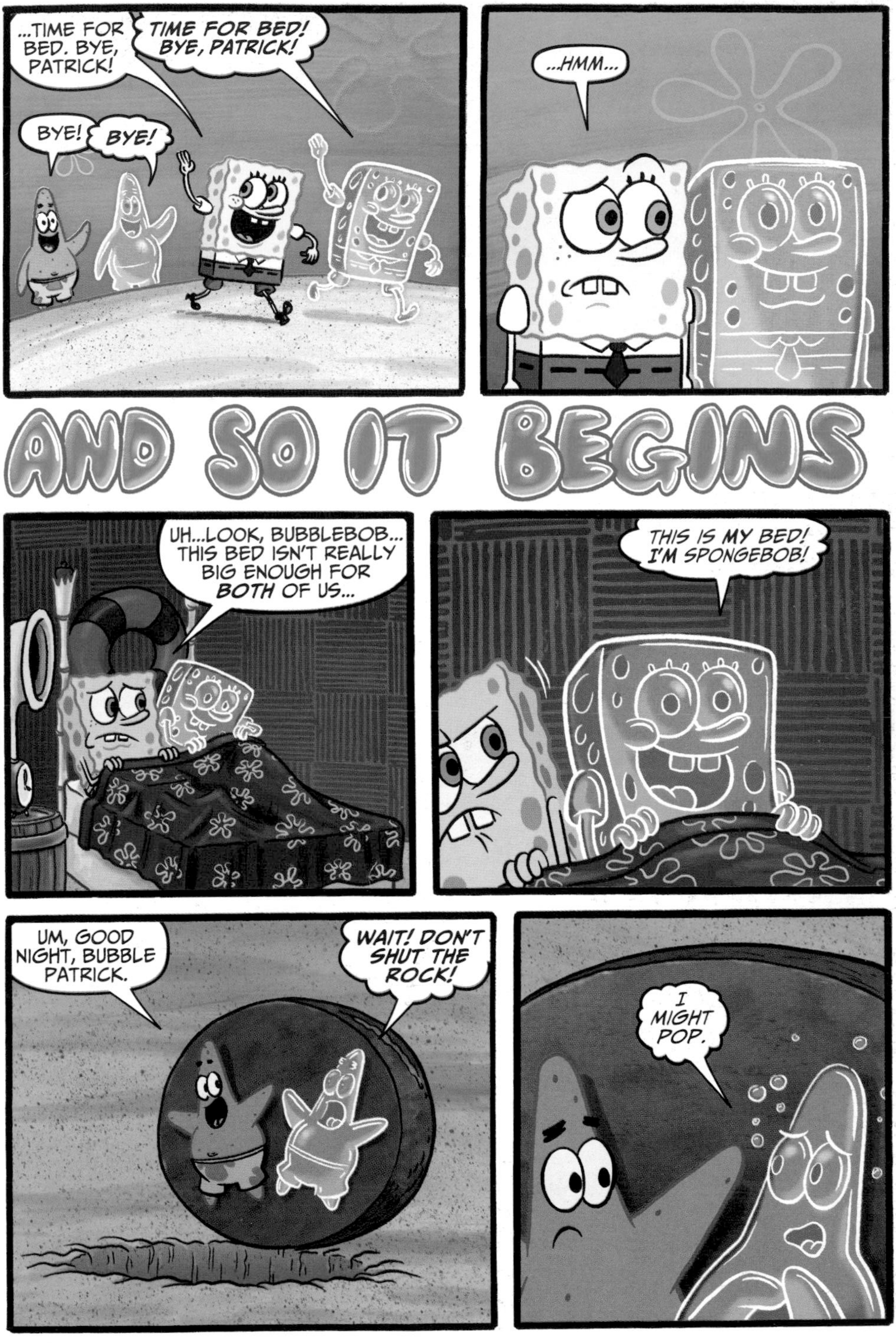

...TIME FOR BED. BYE, PATRICK!
TIME FOR BED! BYE, PATRICK!
BYE!
BYE!
...HMM...
AND SO IT BEGINS
UH...LOOK, BUBBLEBOB... THIS BED ISN'T REALLY BIG ENOUGH FOR BOTH OF US...
THIS IS MY BED! I'M SPONGEBOB!
UM, GOOD NIGHT, BUBBLE PATRICK.
WAIT! DON'T SHUT THE ROCK!
I MIGHT POP.

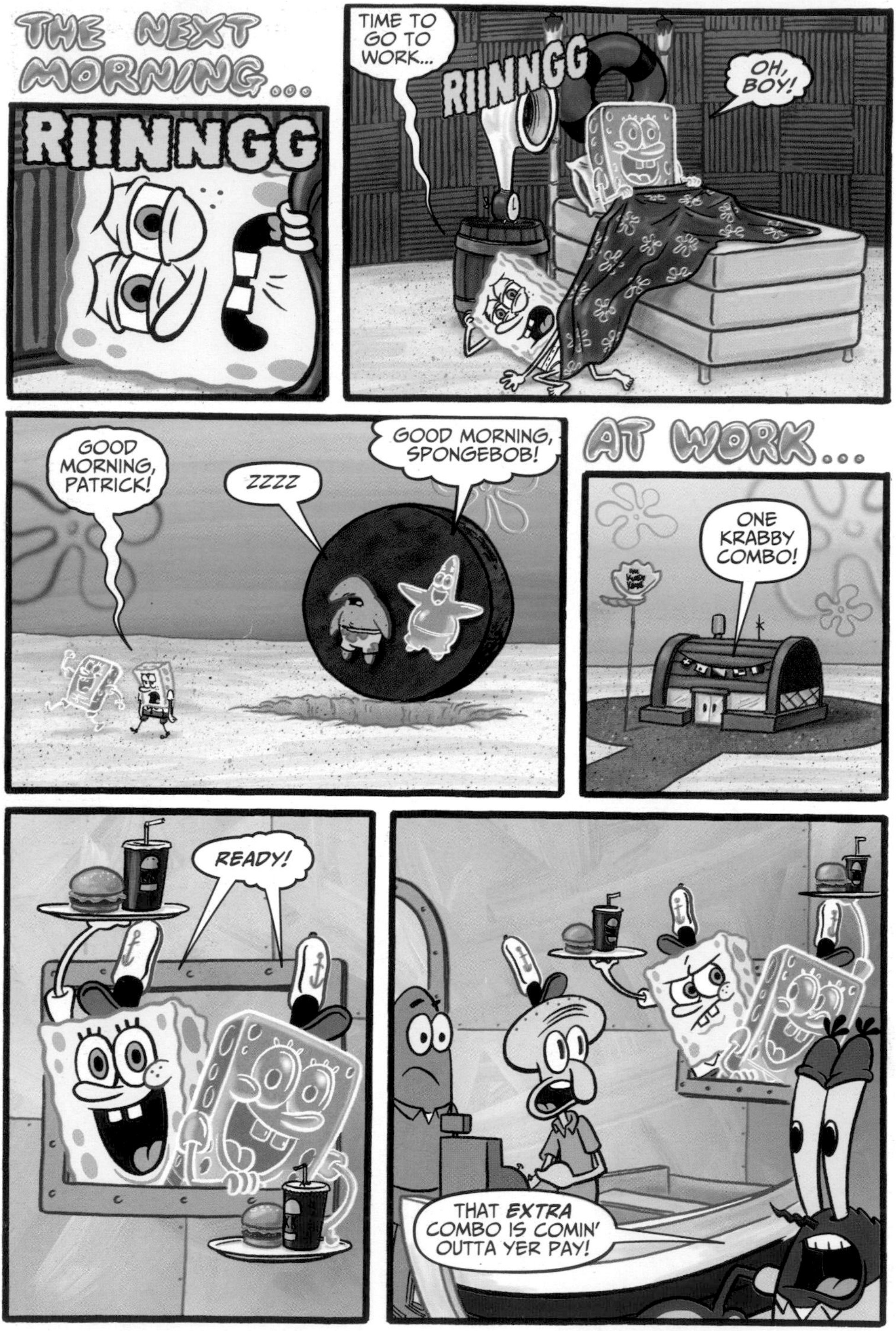
THE NEXT MORNING...
RIINNGG
TIME TO GO TO WORK...
RIINNGG
OH, BOY!
GOOD MORNING, PATRICK!
ZZZZ
GOOD MORNING, SPONGEBOB!
AT WORK...
ONE KRABBY COMBO!
READY!
THAT EXTRA COMBO IS COMIN' OUTTA YER PAY!

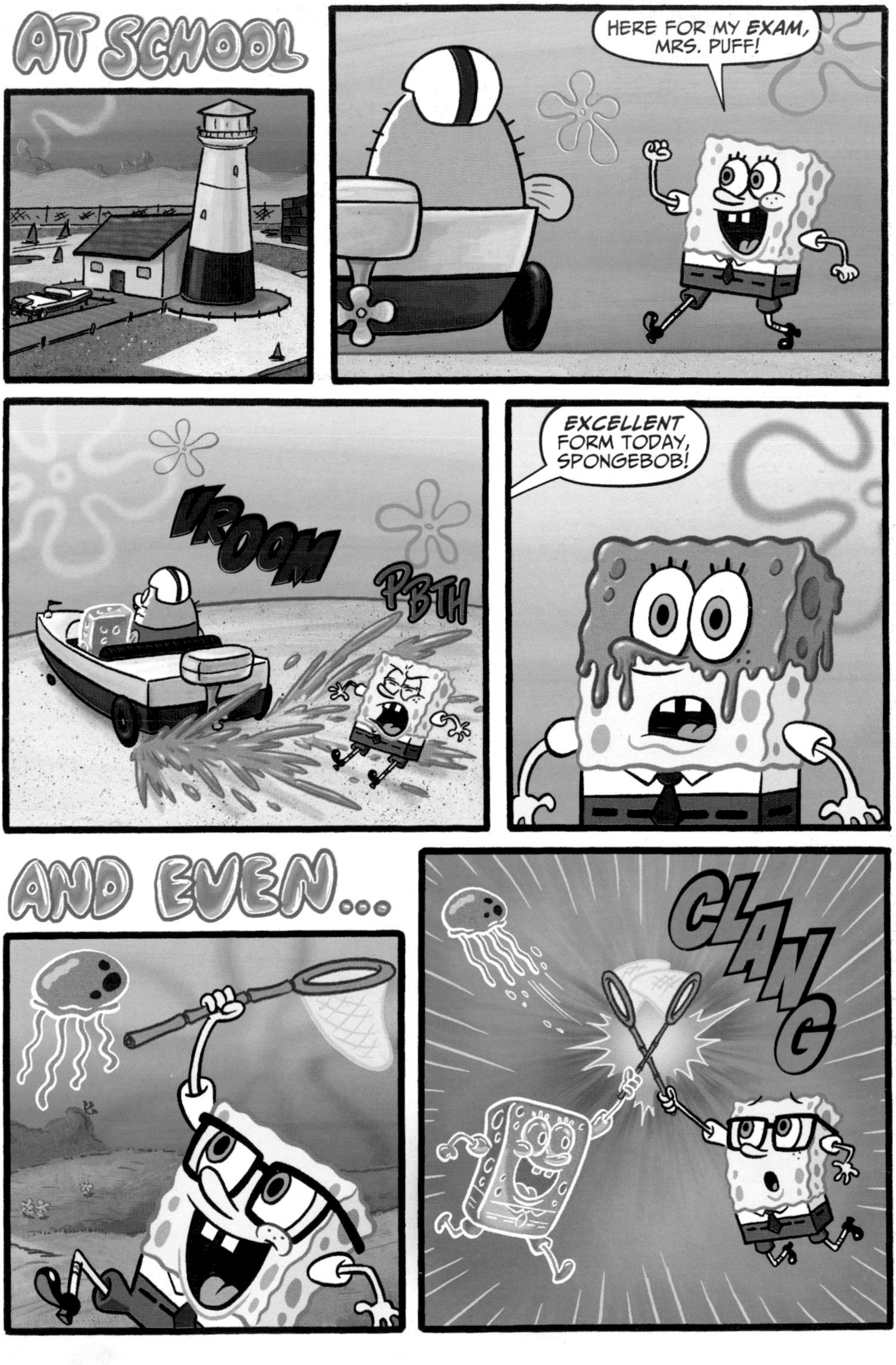
AT SCHOOL
HERE FOR MY EXAM, MRS. PUFF!
VROOM
PBTH
EXCELLENT FORM TODAY, SPONGEBOB!
AND EVEN...
CLANG

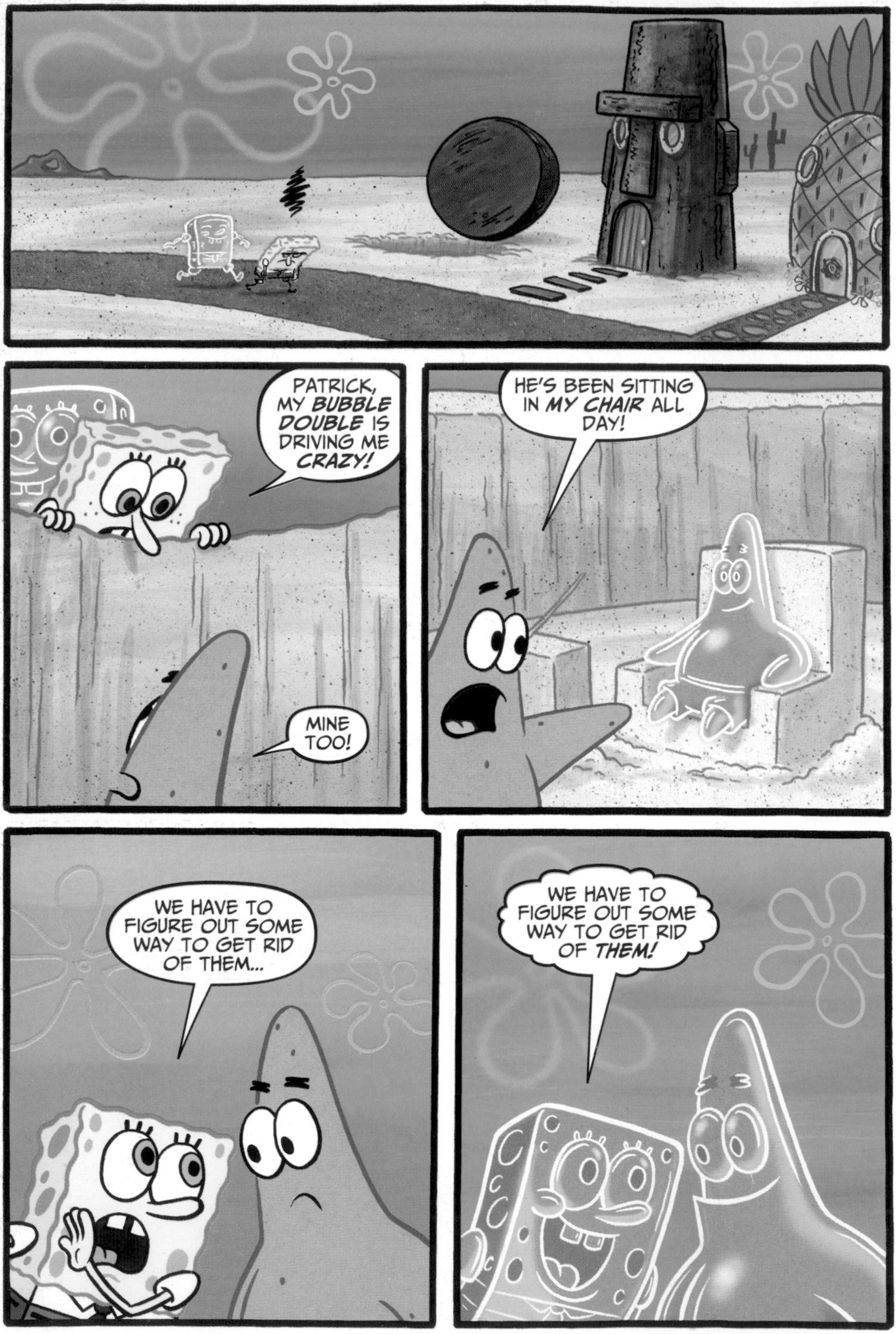
PATRICK, MY BUBBLE DOUBLE IS DRIVING ME CRAZY!
MINE TOO!
HE'S BEEN SITTING IN MY CHAIR ALL DAY!
WE HAVE TO FIGURE OUT SOME WAY TO GET RID OF THEM...
WE HAVE TO FIGURE OUT SOME WAY TO GET RID OF THEM!

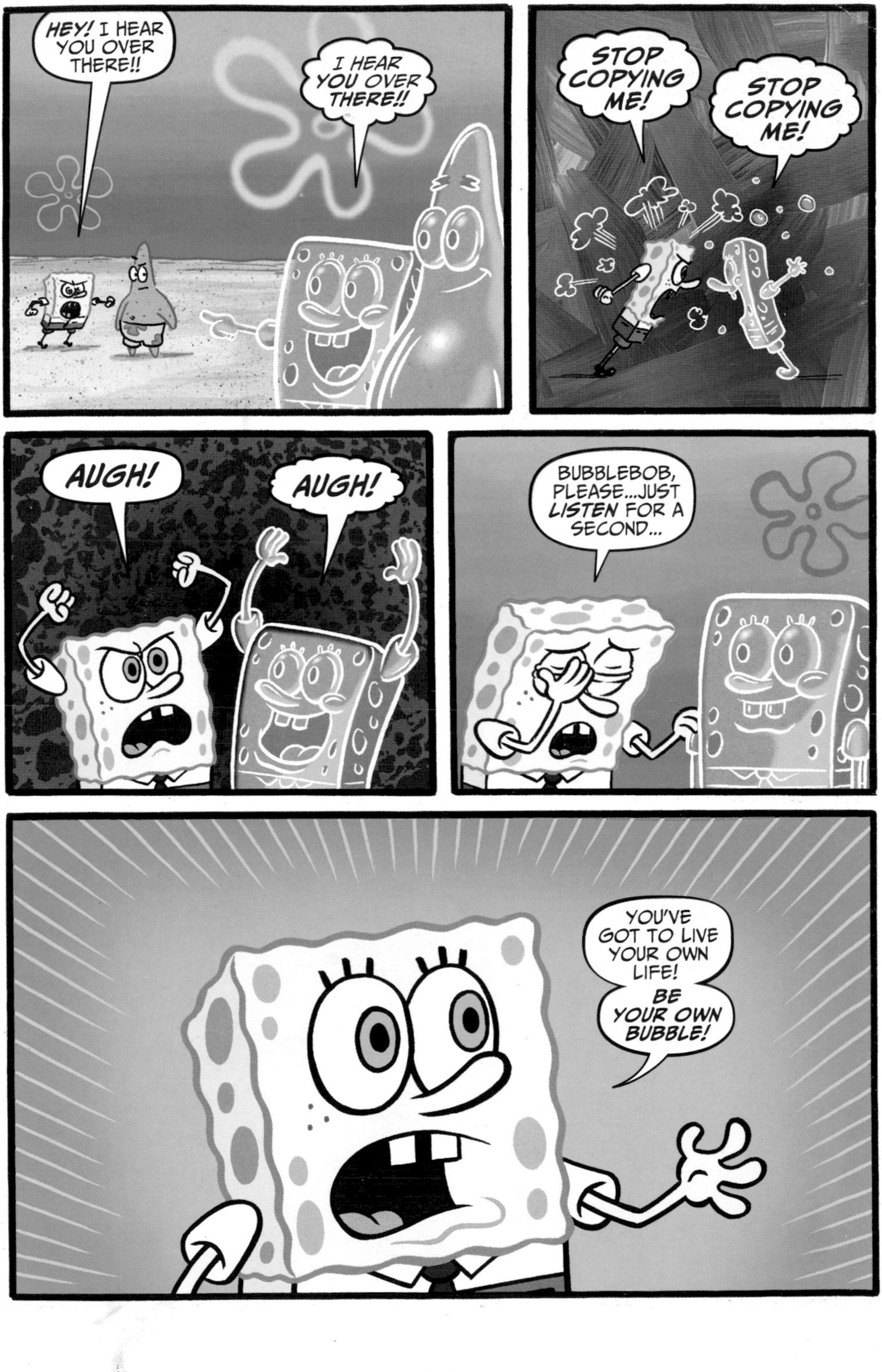
HEY! I HEAR YOU OVER THERE!!
I HEAR YOU OVER THERE!!
STOP COPYING ME!
STOP COPYING ME!
AUGH!
AUGH!
BUBBLEBOB, PLEASE...JUST LISTEN FOR A SECOND...
YOU'VE GOT TO LIVE YOUR OWN LIFE!
BE YOUR OWN BUBBLE!

THERE'S A WHOLE WORLD OUT THERE! YOU'VE GOT TO GRAB IT BY THE SUDS AND MAKE IT YOUR OWN!

CONTROL YOUR DESTINY!!!

NAH!!!

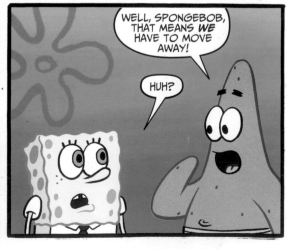

WELL, SPONGEBOB, THAT MEANS WE HAVE TO MOVE AWAY!

HUH?

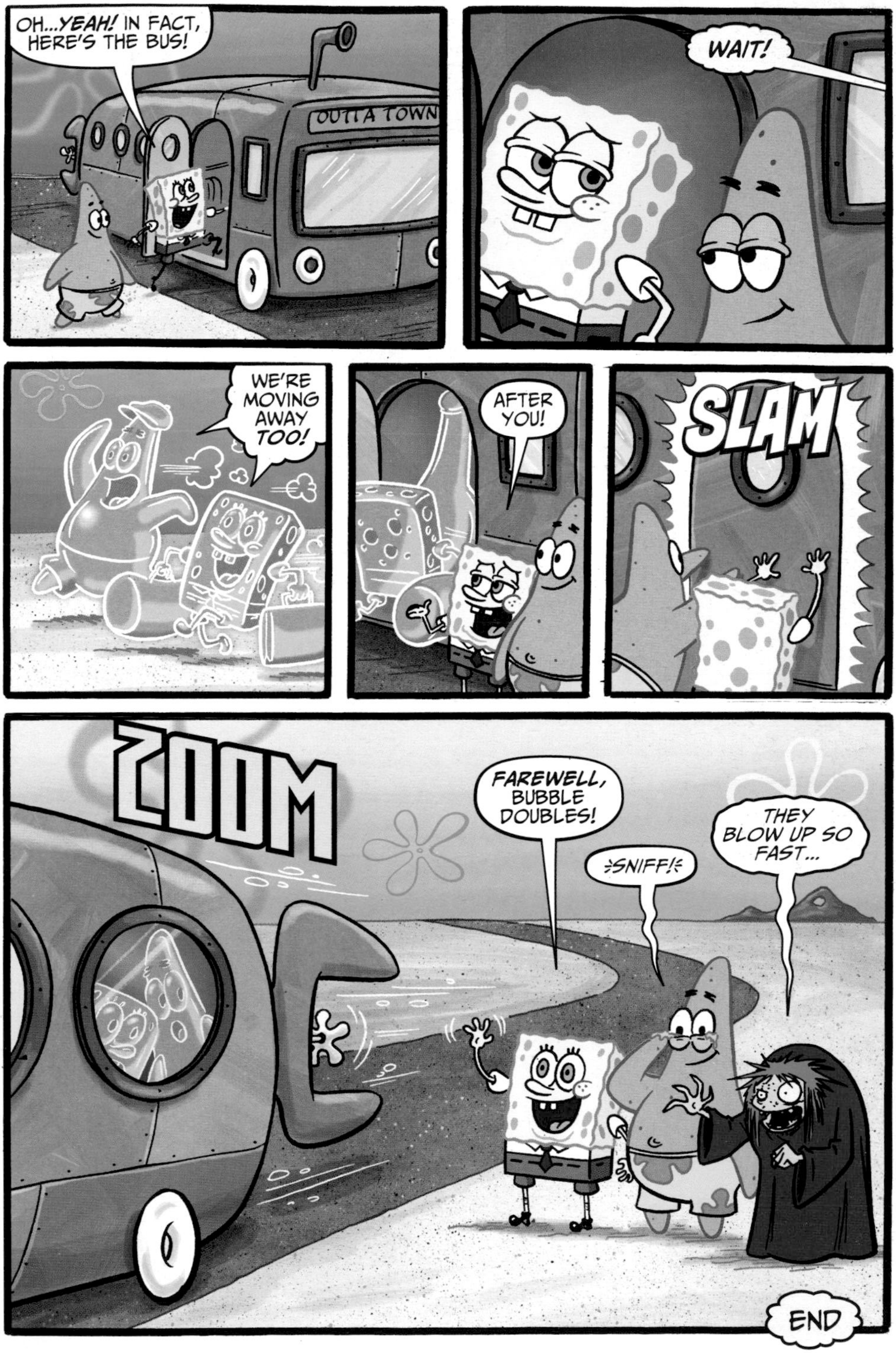
OH...YEAH! IN FACT, HERE'S THE BUS!
OUTTA TOWN
WAIT!
WE'RE MOVING AWAY TOO!
AFTER YOU!
SLAM
ZOOM
FAREWELL, BUBBLE DOUBLES!
SNIFF!
THEY BLOW UP SO FAST...
END

DREAM BIG!

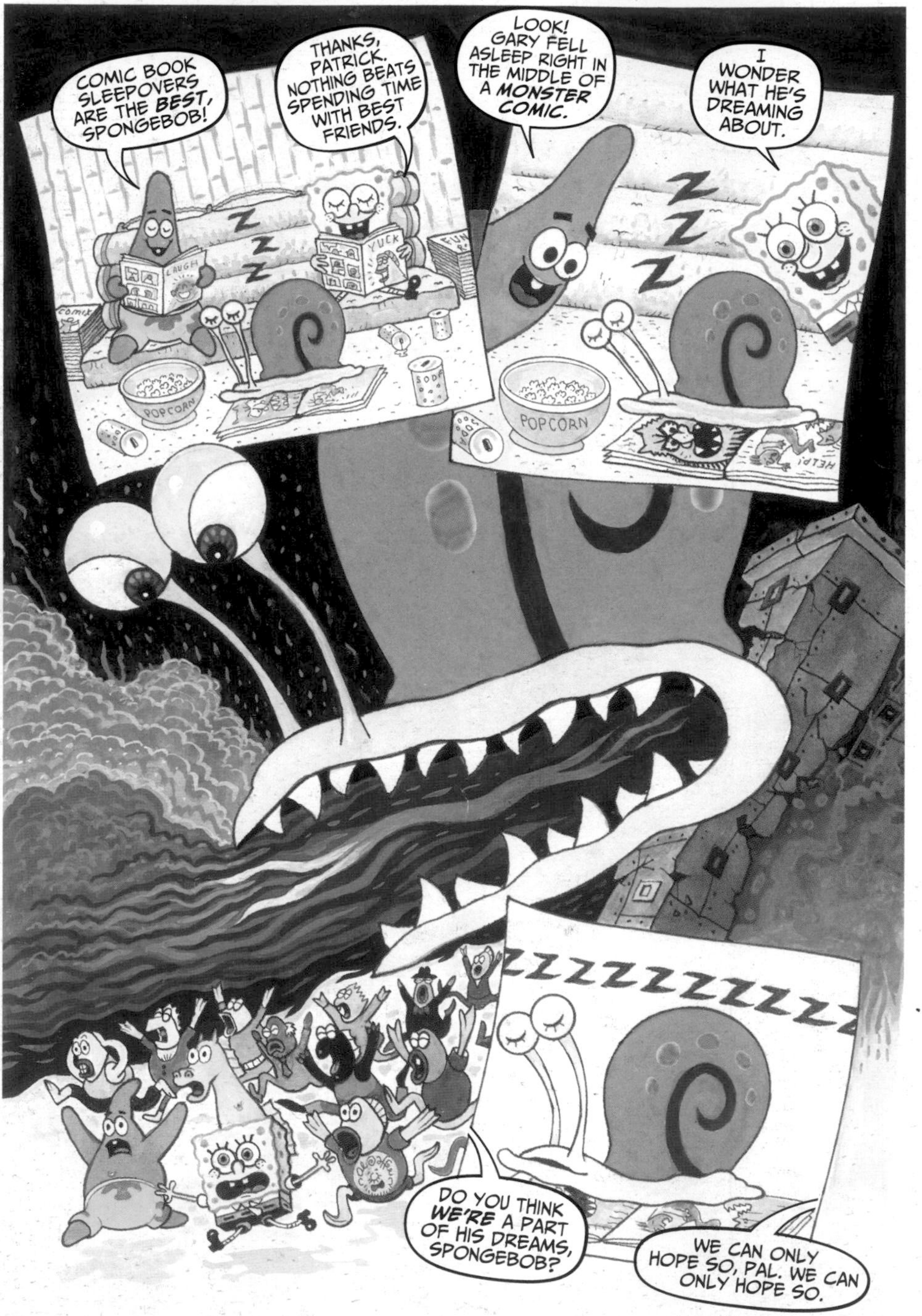
COMIC BOOK SLEEPOVERS ARE THE **BEST**, SPONGEBOB!
THANKS, PATRICK. NOTHING BEATS SPENDING TIME WITH BEST FRIENDS.
Z Z Z
YUCK
LAUGH
COMIX
POPCORN
SODA
LOOK! GARY FELL ASLEEP RIGHT IN THE MIDDLE OF A ***MONSTER COMIC***.
I WONDER WHAT HE'S DREAMING ABOUT.
Z Z Z
POPCORN
SODA
HELP!
ZZZZZZZZZZZ
DO YOU THINK ***WE'RE*** A PART OF HIS DREAMS, SPONGEBOB?
WE CAN ONLY HOPE SO, PAL. WE CAN ONLY HOPE SO.

STORY: CHRIS YAMBAR ART: AL JAFFEE LETTERING: COMICRAFT

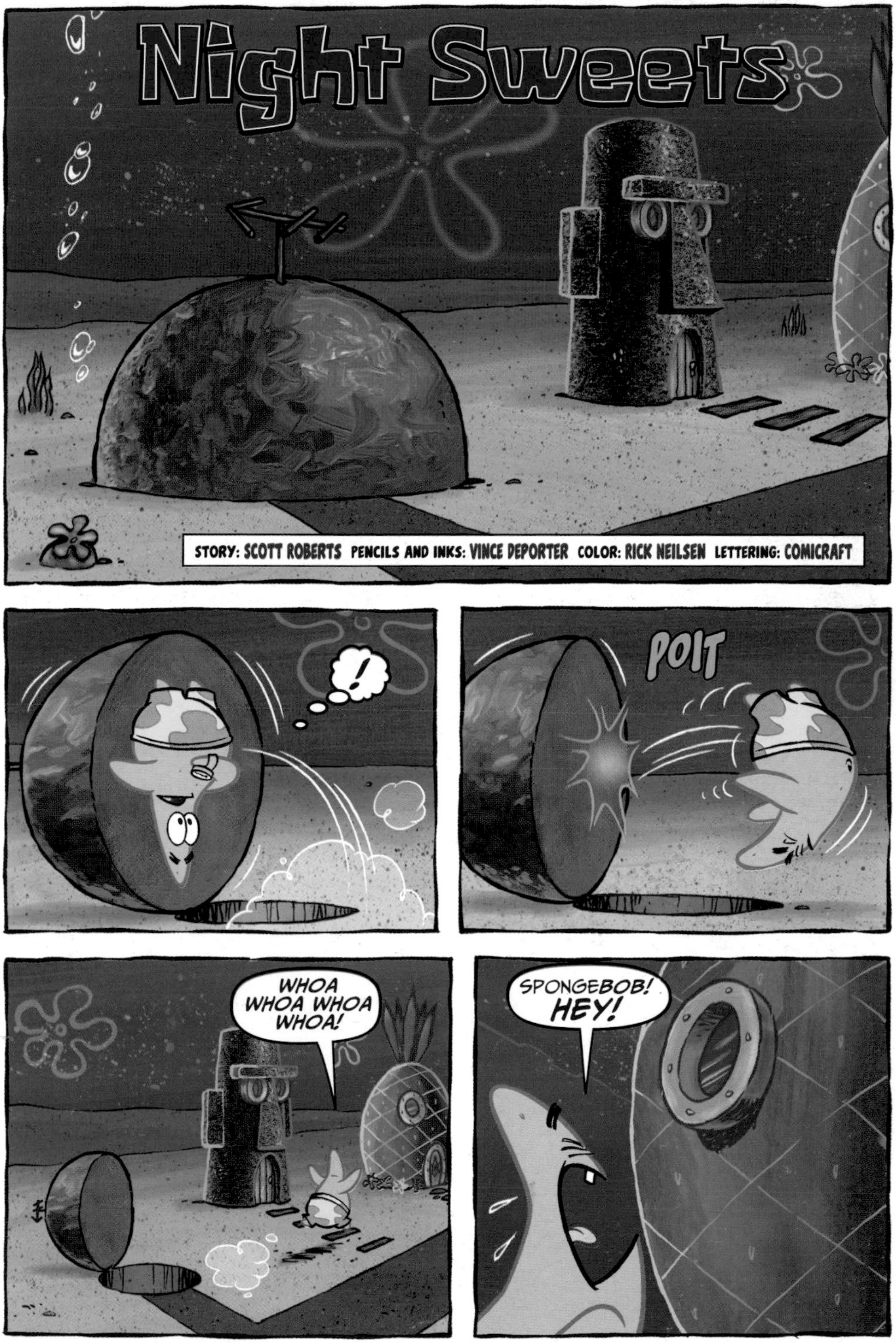
Night Sweets
STORY: SCOTT ROBERTS PENCILS AND INKS: VINCE DEPORTER COLOR: RICK NEILSEN LETTERING: COMICRAFT
!
POIT
WHOA WHOA WHOA WHOA!
SPONGEBOB! HEY!

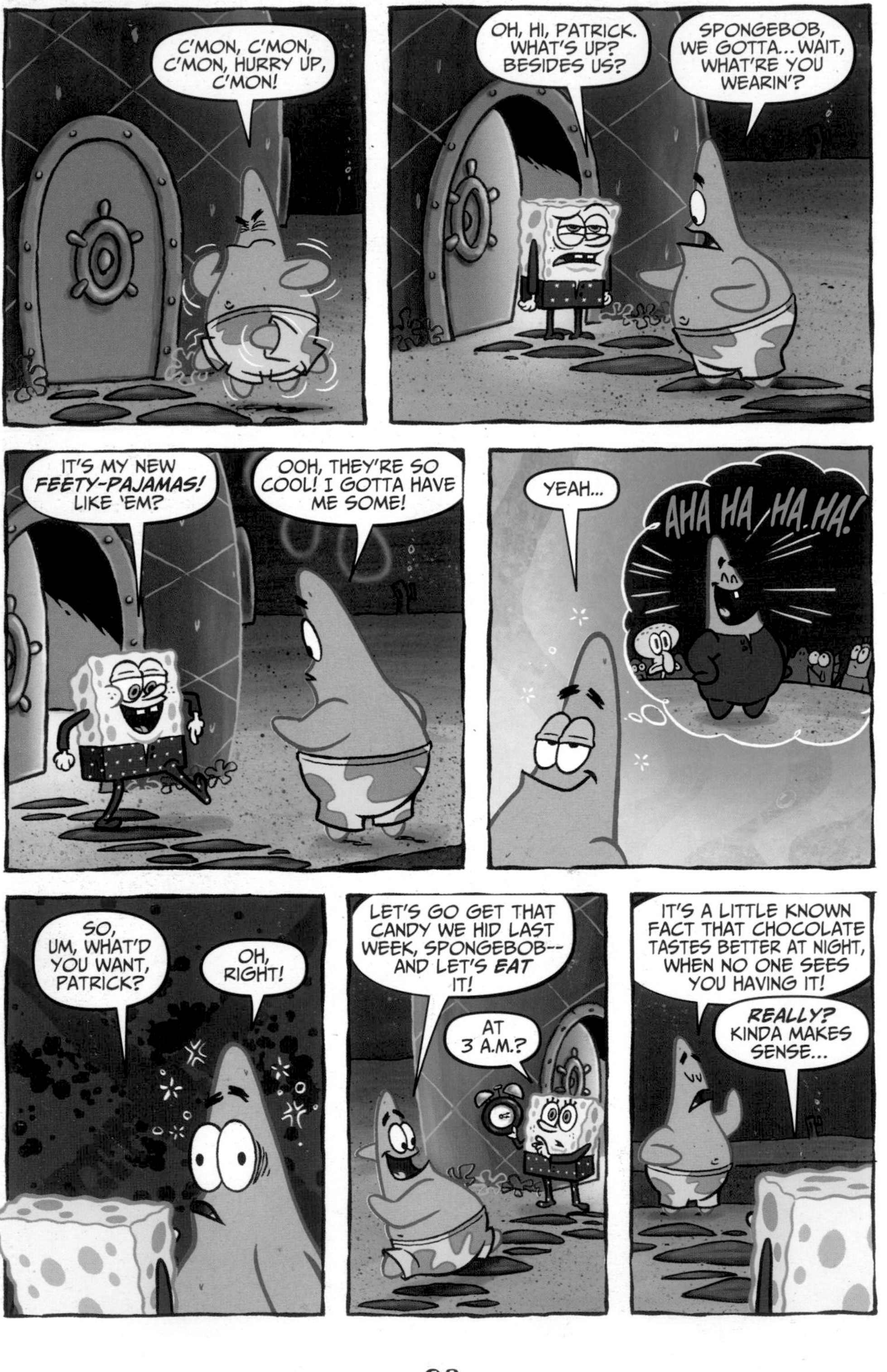
C'MON, C'MON, C'MON, HURRY UP, C'MON!
OH, HI, PATRICK. WHAT'S UP? BESIDES US?
SPONGEBOB, WE GOTTA...WAIT, WHAT'RE YOU WEARIN'?
IT'S MY NEW FEETY-PAJAMAS! LIKE 'EM?
OOH, THEY'RE SO COOL! I GOTTA HAVE ME SOME!
YEAH...
AHA HA HA HA!
SO, UM, WHAT'D YOU WANT, PATRICK?
OH, RIGHT!
LET'S GO GET THAT CANDY WE HID LAST WEEK, SPONGEBOB-- AND LET'S EAT IT!
AT 3 A.M.?
IT'S A LITTLE KNOWN FACT THAT CHOCOLATE TASTES BETTER AT NIGHT, WHEN NO ONE SEES YOU HAVING IT!
REALLY? KINDA MAKES SENSE...

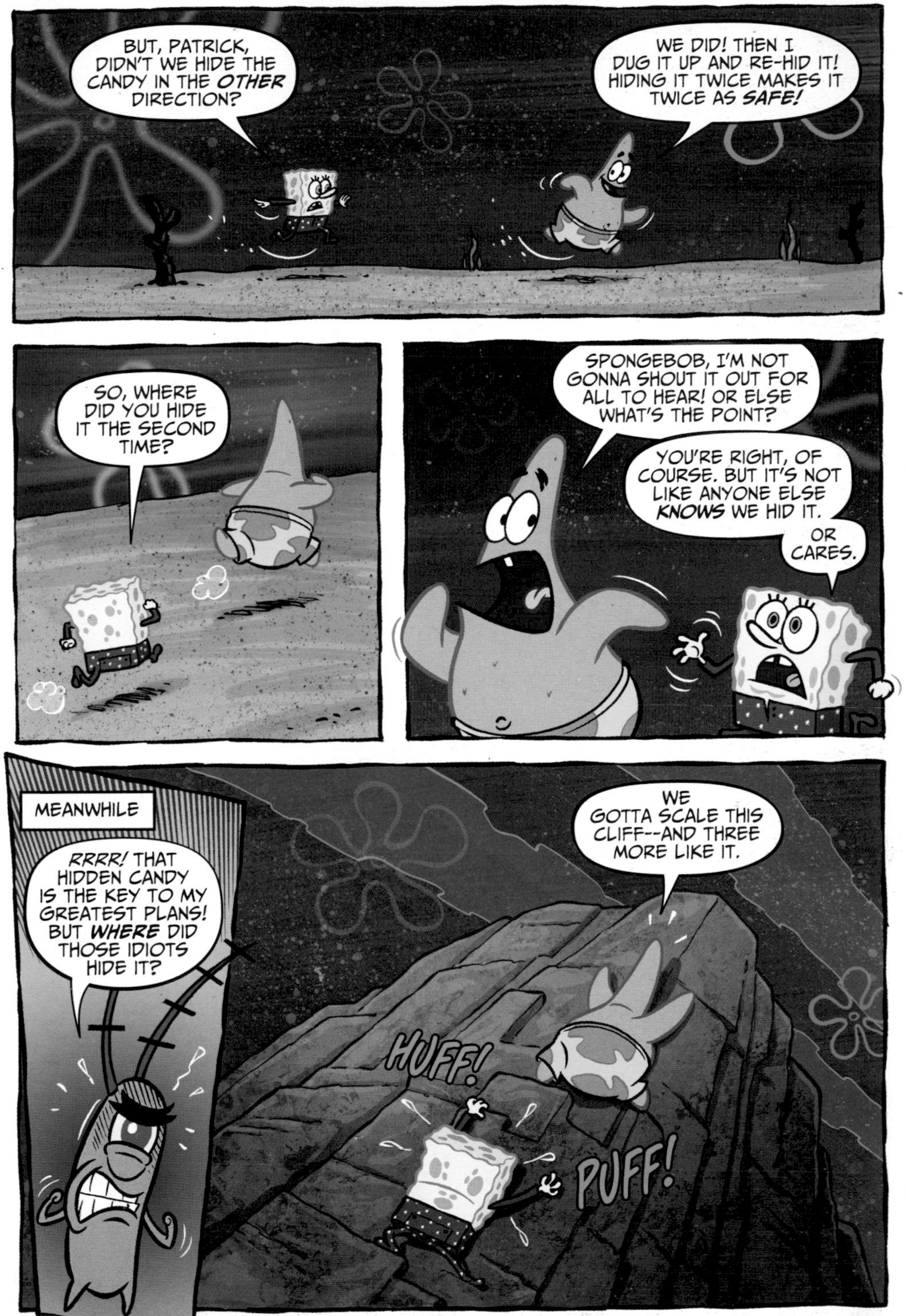
BUT, PATRICK, DIDN'T WE HIDE THE CANDY IN THE *OTHER* DIRECTION?
WE DID! THEN I DUG IT UP AND RE-HID IT! HIDING IT TWICE MAKES IT TWICE AS *SAFE!*
SO, WHERE DID YOU HIDE IT THE SECOND TIME?
SPONGEBOB, I'M NOT GONNA SHOUT IT OUT FOR ALL TO HEAR! OR ELSE WHAT'S THE POINT?
YOU'RE RIGHT, OF COURSE. BUT IT'S NOT LIKE ANYONE ELSE *KNOWS* WE HID IT.
OR CARES.
MEANWHILE
RRRR! THAT HIDDEN CANDY IS THE KEY TO MY GREATEST PLANS! BUT *WHERE* DID THOSE IDIOTS HIDE IT?
WE GOTTA SCALE THIS CLIFF--AND THREE MORE LIKE IT.
HUFF!
PUFF!

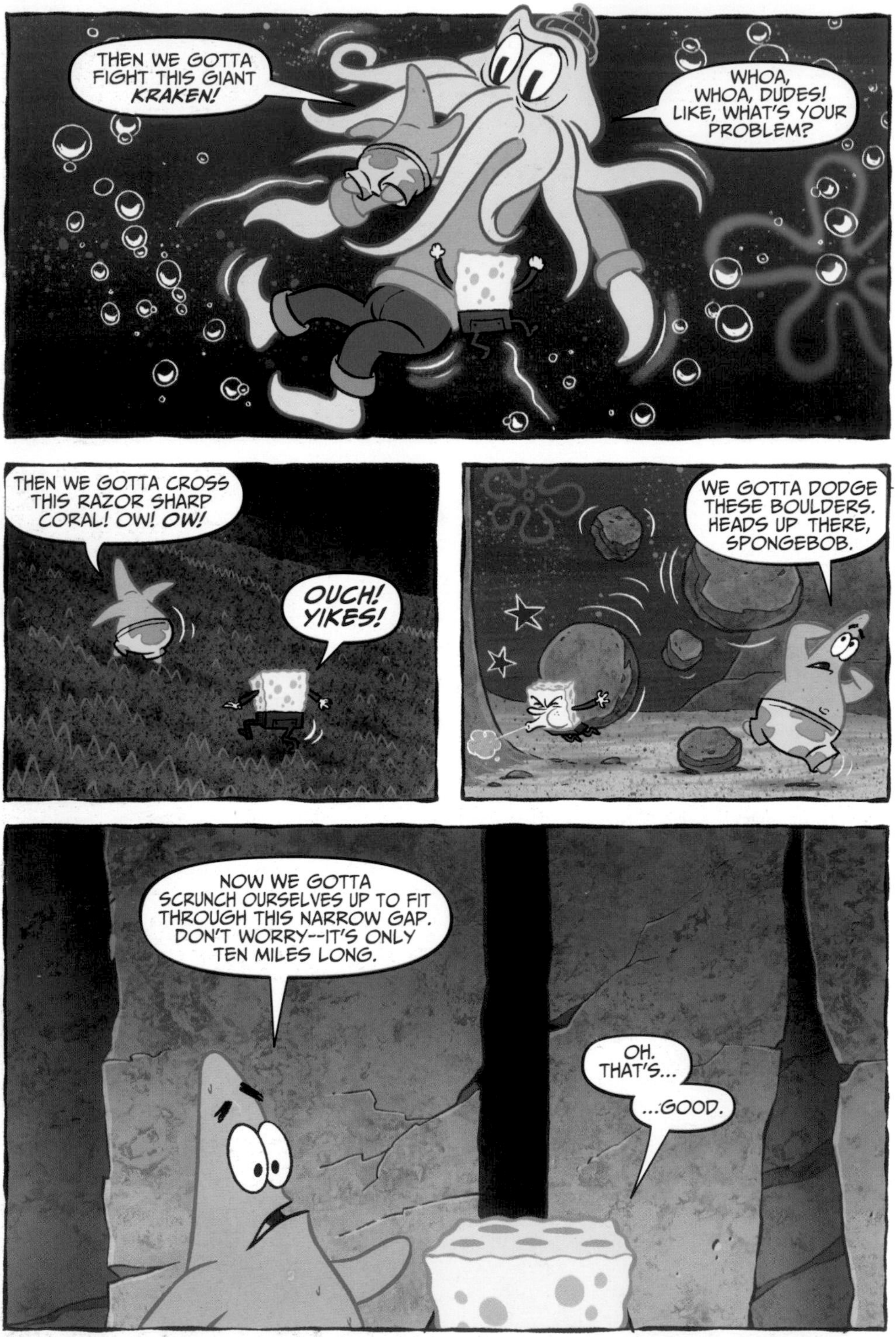
THEN WE GOTTA FIGHT THIS GIANT *KRAKEN!*
WHOA, WHOA, DUDES! LIKE, WHAT'S YOUR PROBLEM?
THEN WE GOTTA CROSS THIS RAZOR SHARP CORAL! OW! *OW!*
OUCH! YIKES!
WE GOTTA DODGE THESE BOULDERS. HEADS UP THERE, SPONGEBOB.
NOW WE GOTTA SCRUNCH OURSELVES UP TO FIT THROUGH THIS NARROW GAP. DON'T WORRY--IT'S ONLY TEN MILES LONG.
OH. THAT'S...
...GOOD.

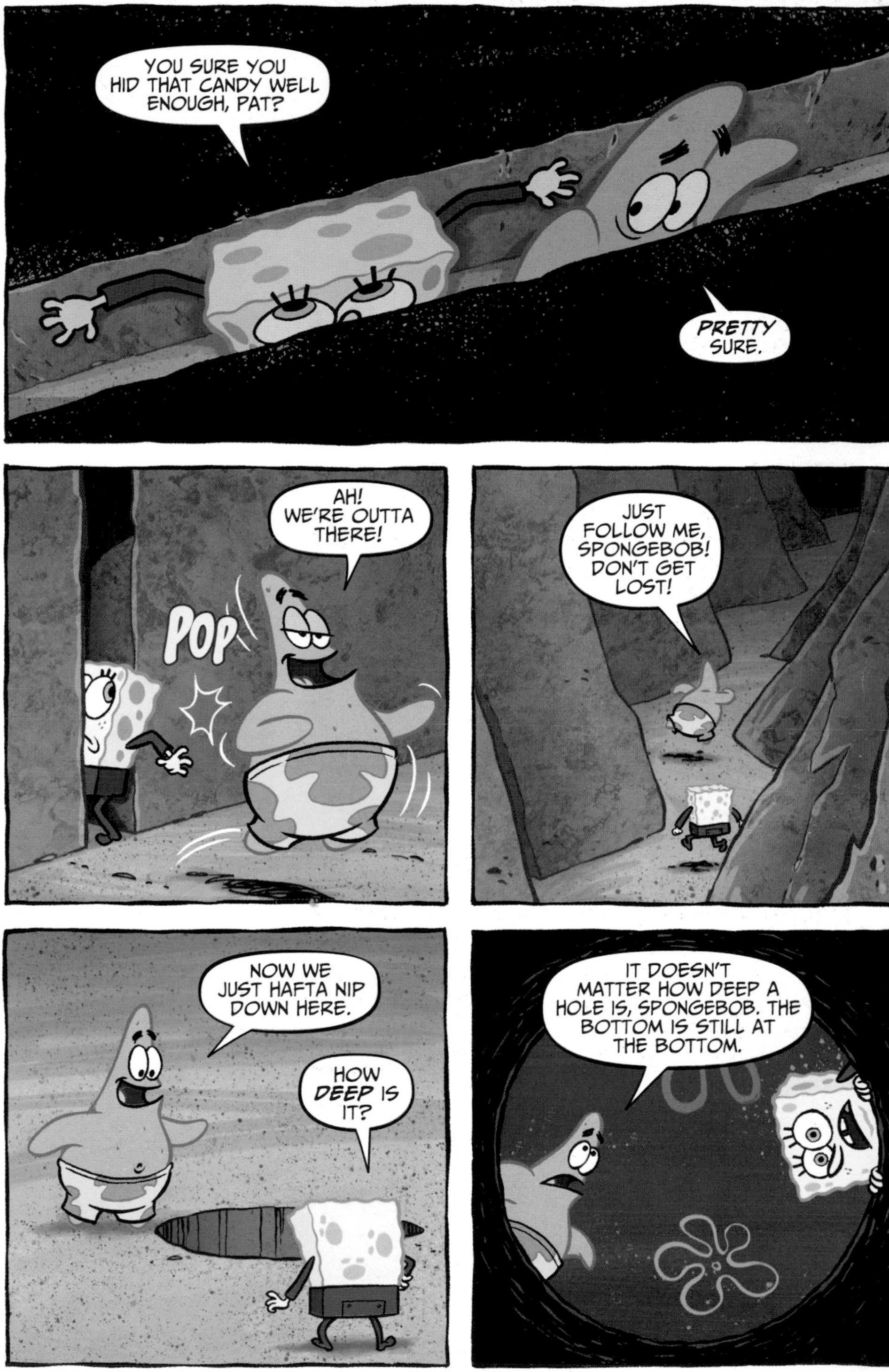
YOU SURE YOU HID THAT CANDY WELL ENOUGH, PAT?
PRETTY SURE.
AH! WE'RE OUTTA THERE!
POP
JUST FOLLOW ME, SPONGEBOB! DON'T GET LOST!
NOW WE JUST HAFTA NIP DOWN HERE.
HOW DEEP IS IT?
IT DOESN'T MATTER HOW DEEP A HOLE IS, SPONGEBOB. THE BOTTOM IS STILL AT THE BOTTOM.

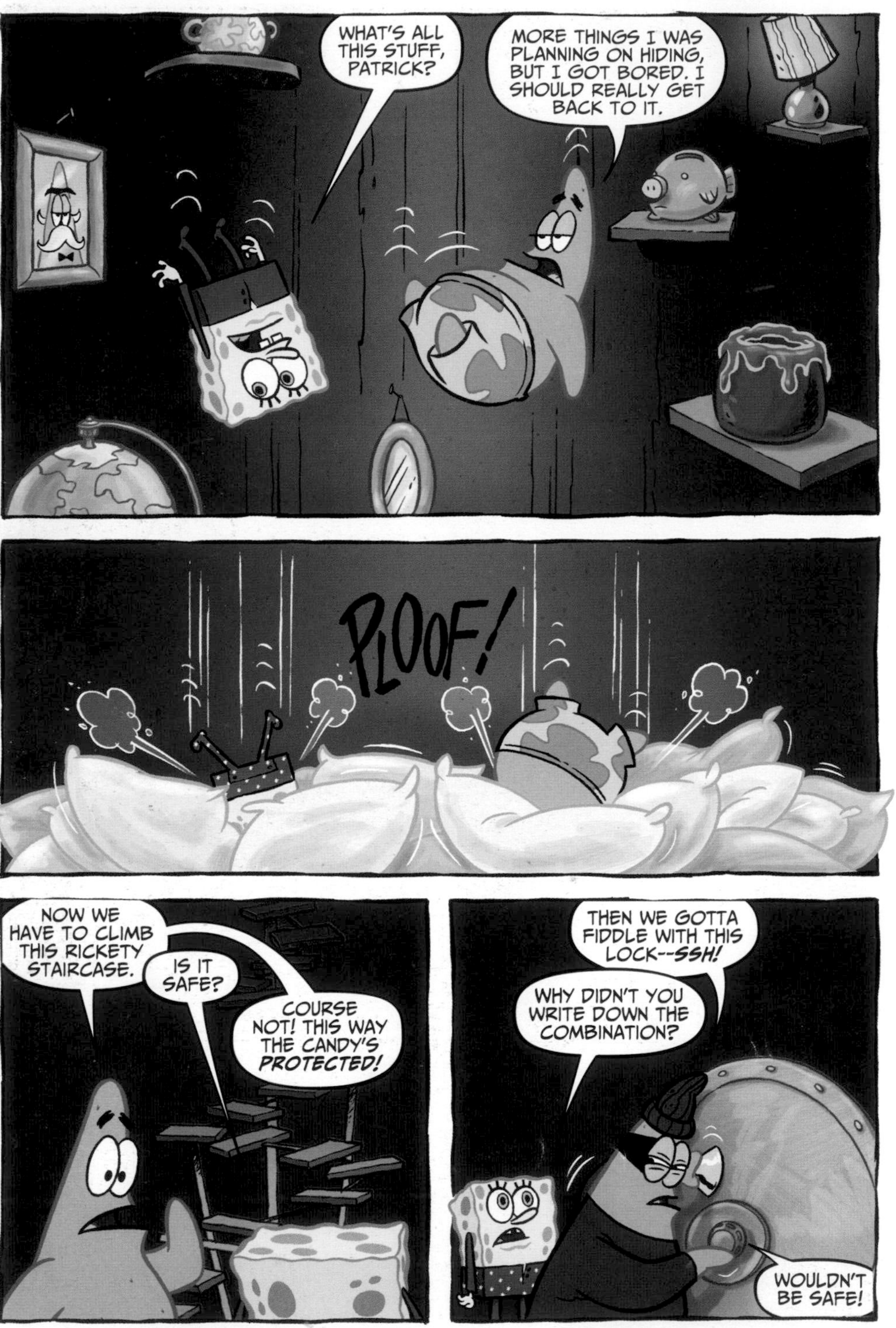
WHAT'S ALL THIS STUFF, PATRICK?
MORE THINGS I WAS PLANNING ON HIDING, BUT I GOT BORED. I SHOULD REALLY GET BACK TO IT.
PLOOF!
NOW WE HAVE TO CLIMB THIS RICKETY STAIRCASE.
IS IT SAFE?
COURSE NOT! THIS WAY THE CANDY'S PROTECTED!
THEN WE GOTTA FIDDLE WITH THIS LOCK--SSH!
WHY DIDN'T YOU WRITE DOWN THE COMBINATION?
WOULDN'T BE SAFE!

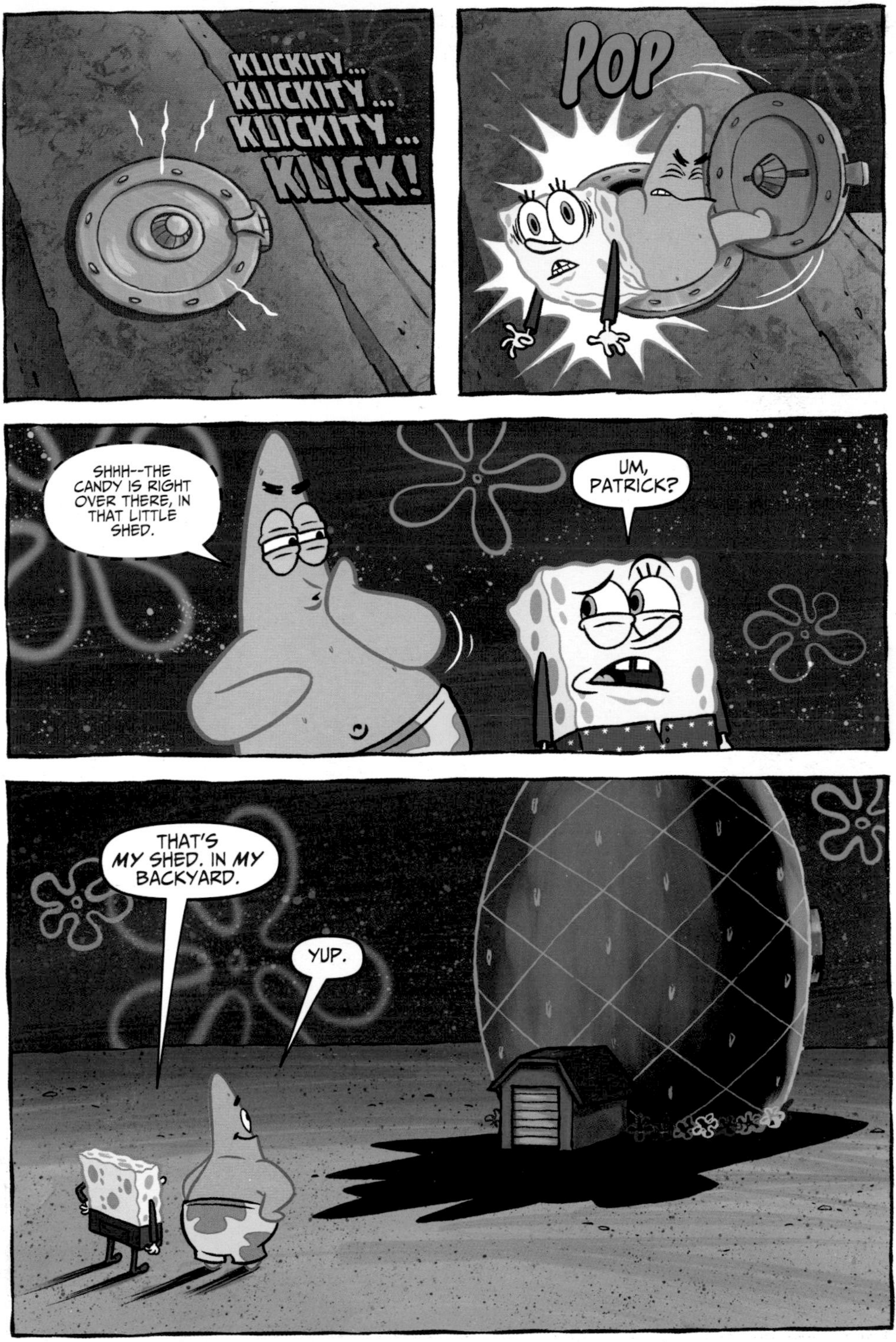
KLICKITY...
KLICKITY...
KLICKITY...
KLICK!
POP
SHHH--THE CANDY IS RIGHT OVER THERE, IN THAT LITTLE SHED.
UM, PATRICK?
THAT'S MY SHED. IN MY BACKYARD.
YUP.

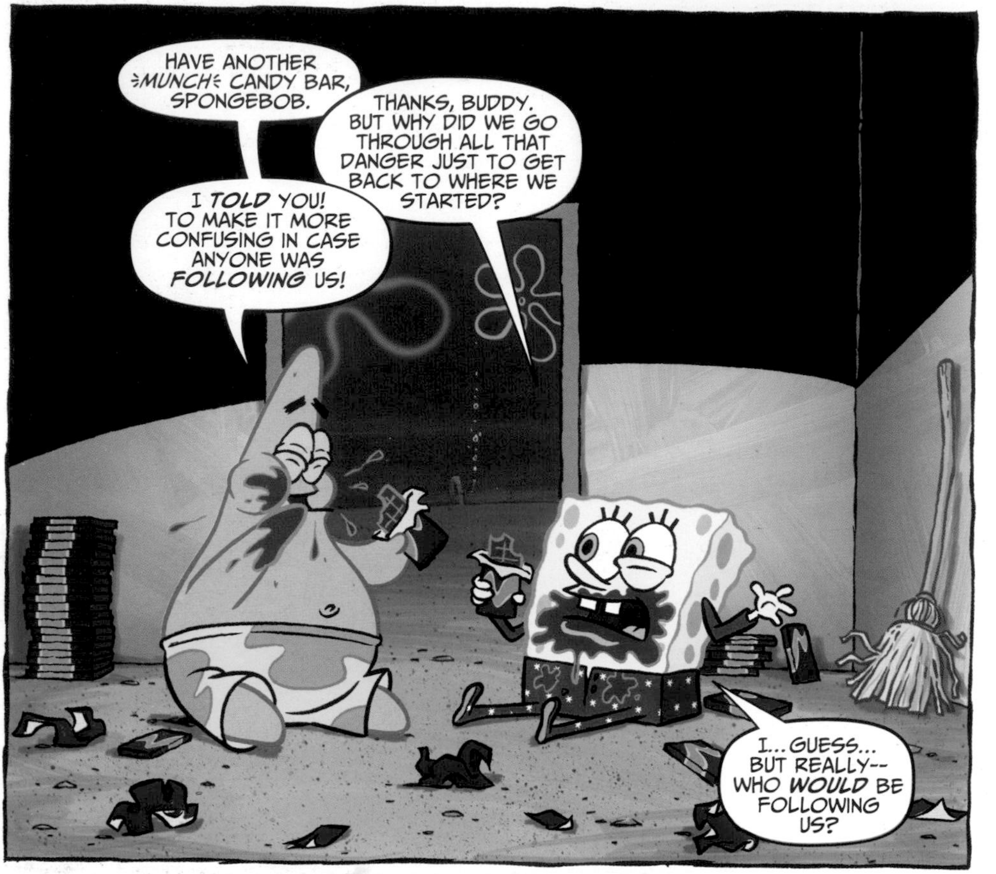
HAVE ANOTHER MUNCH CANDY BAR, SPONGEBOB.
THANKS, BUDDY. BUT WHY DID WE GO THROUGH ALL THAT DANGER JUST TO GET BACK TO WHERE WE STARTED?
I TOLD YOU! TO MAKE IT MORE CONFUSING IN CASE ANYONE WAS FOLLOWING US!
I... GUESS... BUT REALLY-- WHO WOULD BE FOLLOWING US?

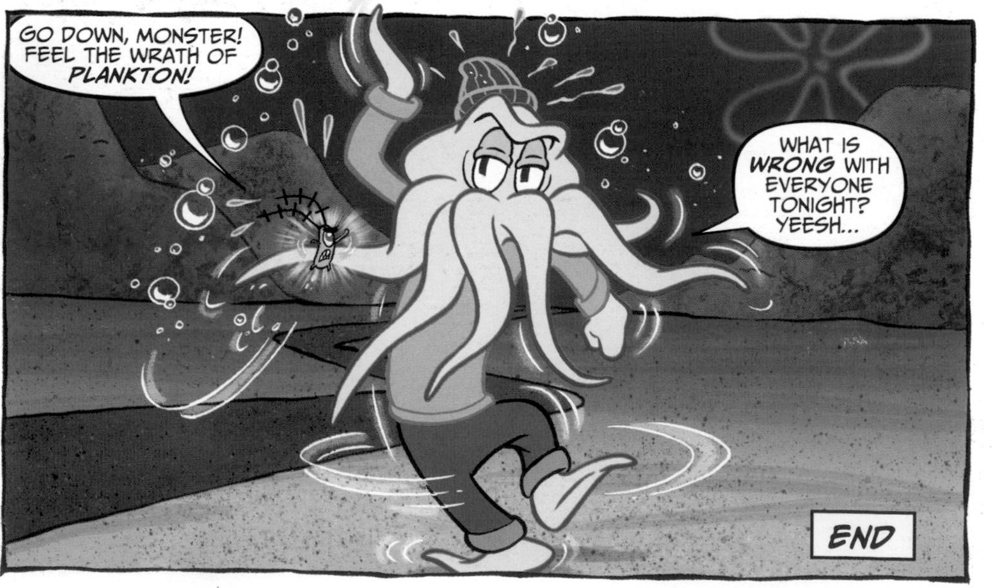
GO DOWN, MONSTER! FEEL THE WRATH OF PLANKTON!
WHAT IS WRONG WITH EVERYONE TONIGHT? YEESH...
END

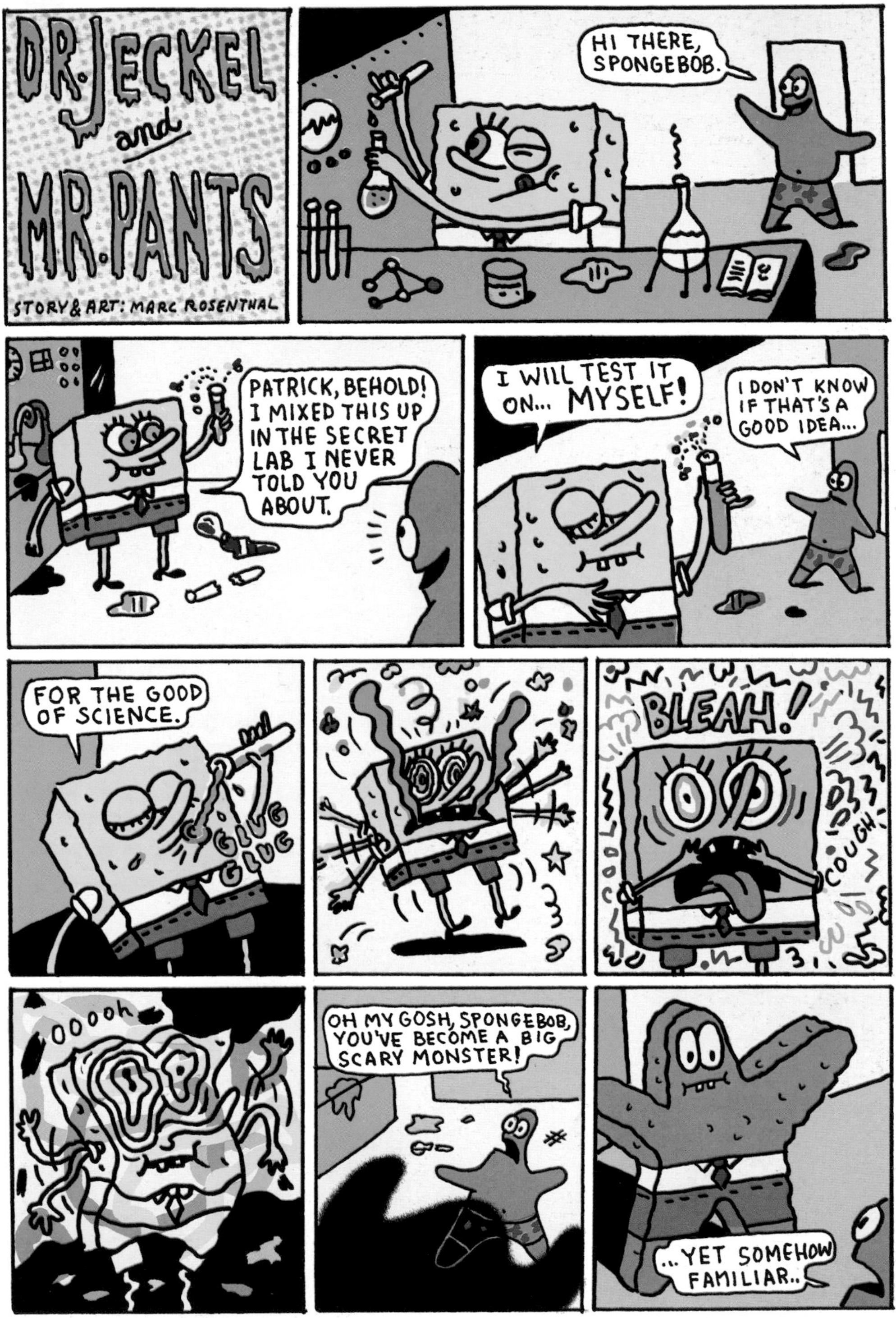
DR. JECKEL and MR. PANTS
STORY & ART: MARC ROSENTHAL
HI THERE, SPONGEBOB.
PATRICK, BEHOLD! I MIXED THIS UP IN THE SECRET LAB I NEVER TOLD YOU ABOUT.
I WILL TEST IT ON... MYSELF!
I DON'T KNOW IF THAT'S A GOOD IDEA...
FOR THE GOOD OF SCIENCE.
GLUG GLUG
BLEAH!
COUGH!
OOOOh
OH MY GOSH, SPONGEBOB, YOU'VE BECOME A BIG SCARY MONSTER!
...YET SOMEHOW FAMILIAR..

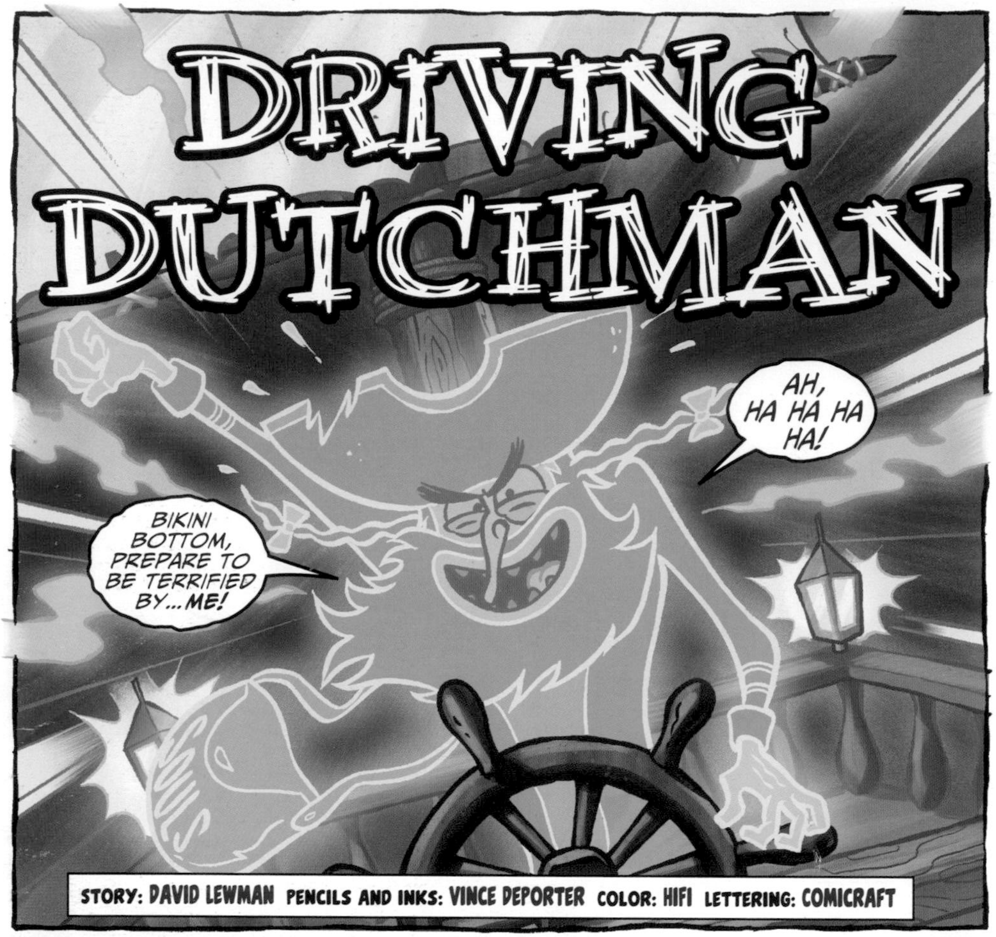
DRIVING DUTCHMAN
AH, HA HA HA HA!
BIKINI BOTTOM, PREPARE TO BE TERRIFIED BY...ME!
STORY: DAVID LEWMAN PENCILS AND INKS: VINCE DEPORTER COLOR: HIFI LETTERING: COMICRAFT

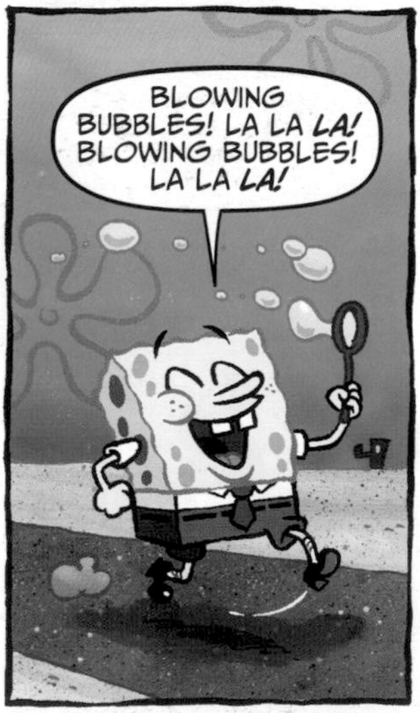
BLOWING BUBBLES! LA LA LA! BLOWING BUBBLES! LA LA LA!

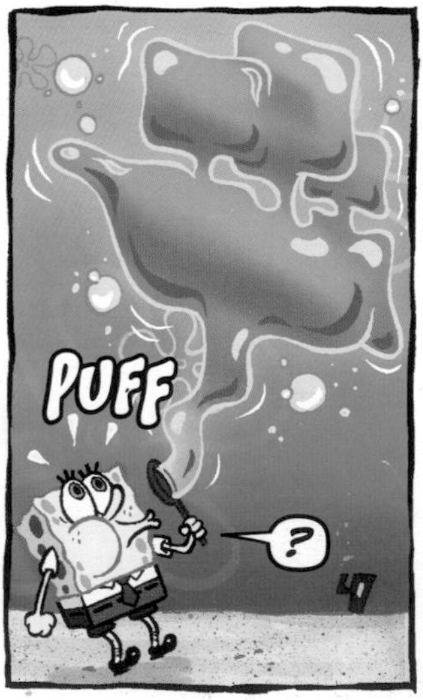
PUFF
?

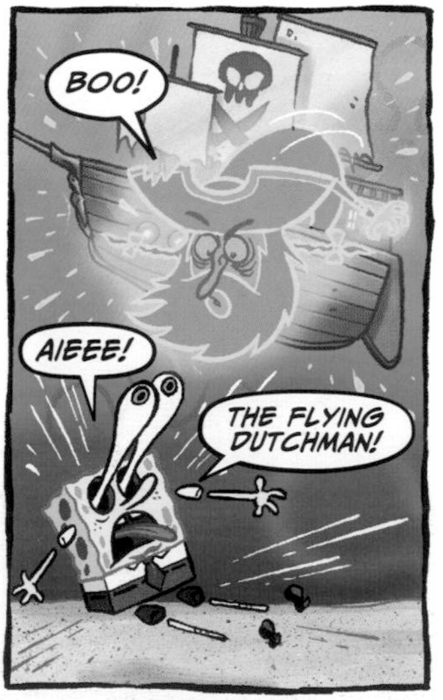
BOO!
AIEEE!
THE FLYING DUTCHMAN!

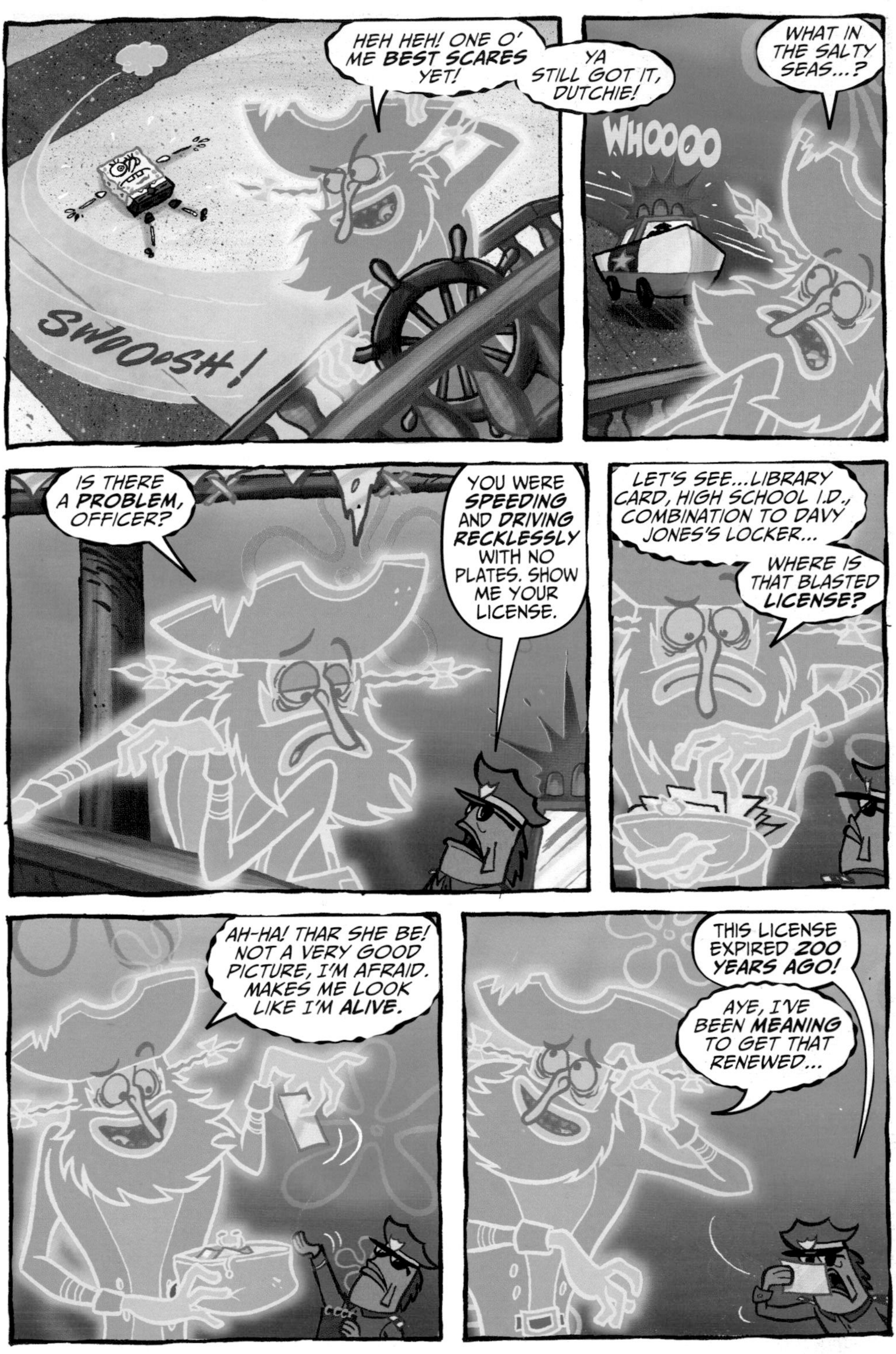
HEH HEH! ONE O' ME BEST SCARES YET!
YA STILL GOT IT, DUTCHIE!
SWOOOSH!
WHAT IN THE SALTY SEAS...?
WHOOOO
IS THERE A PROBLEM, OFFICER?
YOU WERE SPEEDING AND DRIVING RECKLESSLY WITH NO PLATES. SHOW ME YOUR LICENSE.
LET'S SEE...LIBRARY CARD, HIGH SCHOOL I.D., COMBINATION TO DAVY JONES'S LOCKER...
WHERE IS THAT BLASTED LICENSE?
AH-HA! THAR SHE BE! NOT A VERY GOOD PICTURE, I'M AFRAID. MAKES ME LOOK LIKE I'M ALIVE.
THIS LICENSE EXPIRED 200 YEARS AGO!
AYE, I'VE BEEN MEANING TO GET THAT RENEWED...

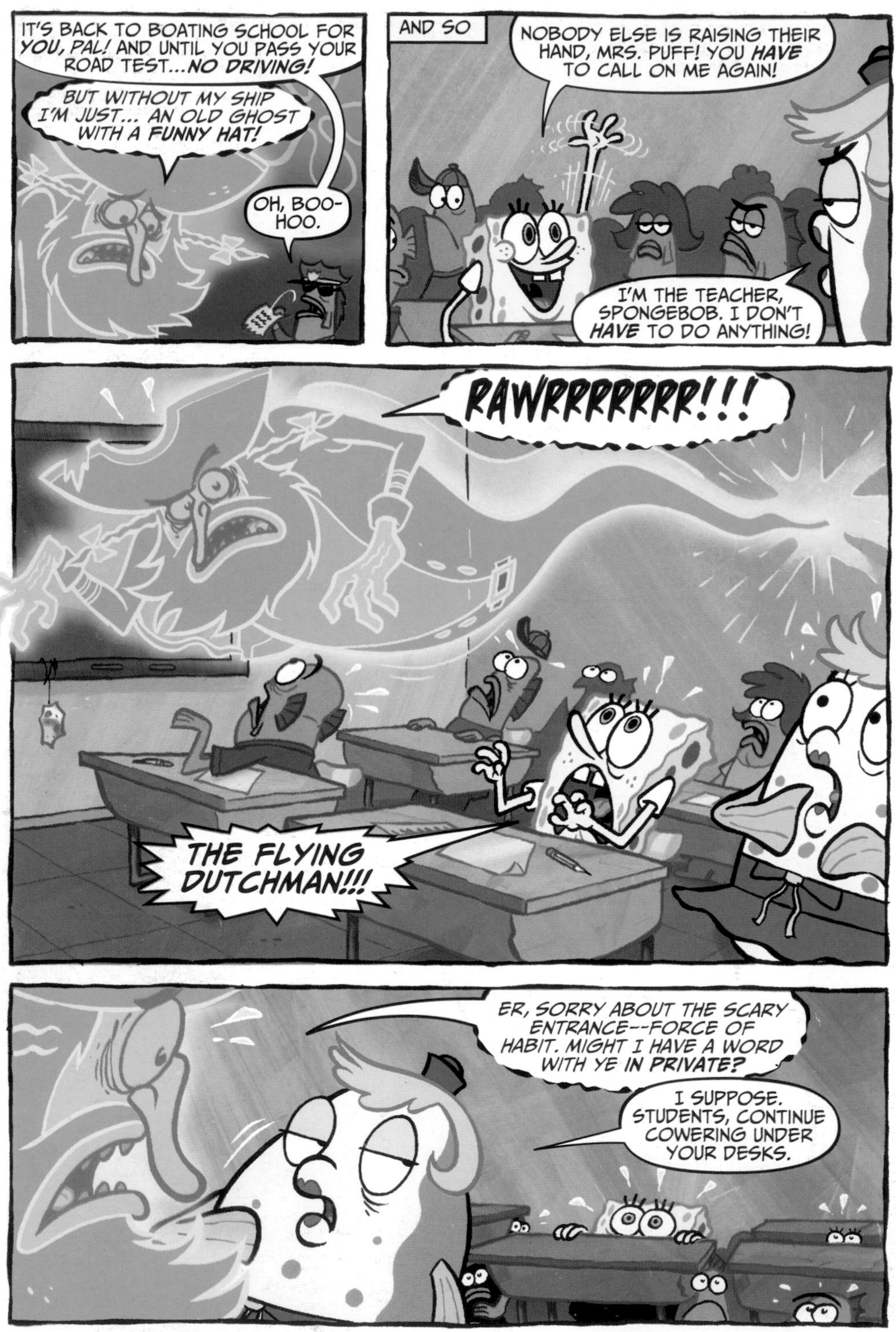
IT'S BACK TO BOATING SCHOOL FOR YOU, PAL! AND UNTIL YOU PASS YOUR ROAD TEST...NO DRIVING!
BUT WITHOUT MY SHIP I'M JUST... AN OLD GHOST WITH A FUNNY HAT!
OH, BOO-HOO.
AND SO
NOBODY ELSE IS RAISING THEIR HAND, MRS. PUFF! YOU HAVE TO CALL ON ME AGAIN!
I'M THE TEACHER, SPONGEBOB. I DON'T HAVE TO DO ANYTHING!
RAWRRRRRRR!!!
THE FLYING DUTCHMAN!!!
ER, SORRY ABOUT THE SCARY ENTRANCE--FORCE OF HABIT. MIGHT I HAVE A WORD WITH YE IN PRIVATE?
I SUPPOSE. STUDENTS, CONTINUE COWERING UNDER YOUR DESKS.

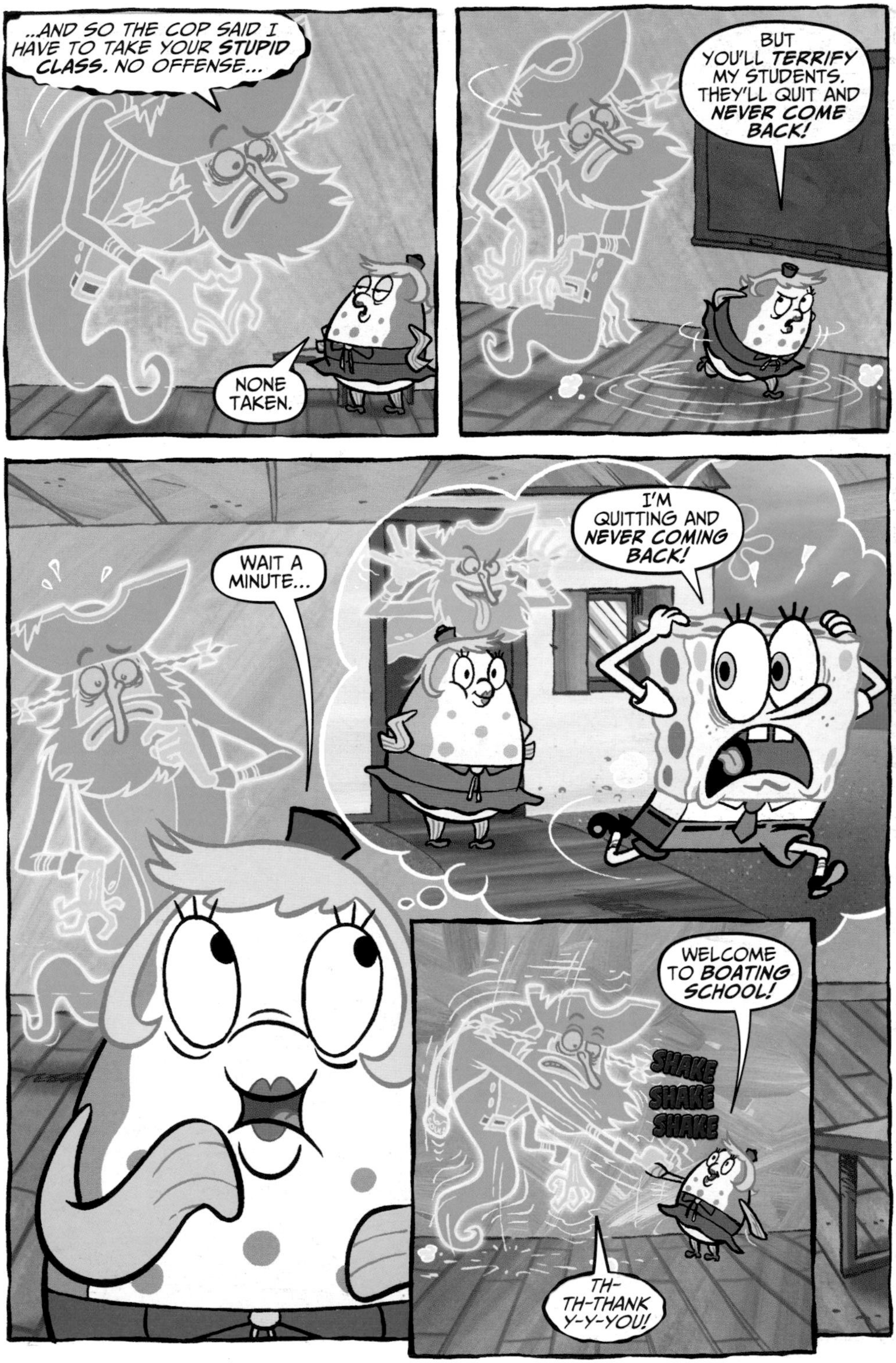
...AND SO THE COP SAID I HAVE TO TAKE YOUR STUPID CLASS. NO OFFENSE...
NONE TAKEN.
BUT YOU'LL TERRIFY MY STUDENTS. THEY'LL QUIT AND NEVER COME BACK!
WAIT A MINUTE...
I'M QUITTING AND NEVER COMING BACK!
WELCOME TO BOATING SCHOOL!
SHAKE
SHAKE
SHAKE
TH-TH-THANK Y-Y-YOU!

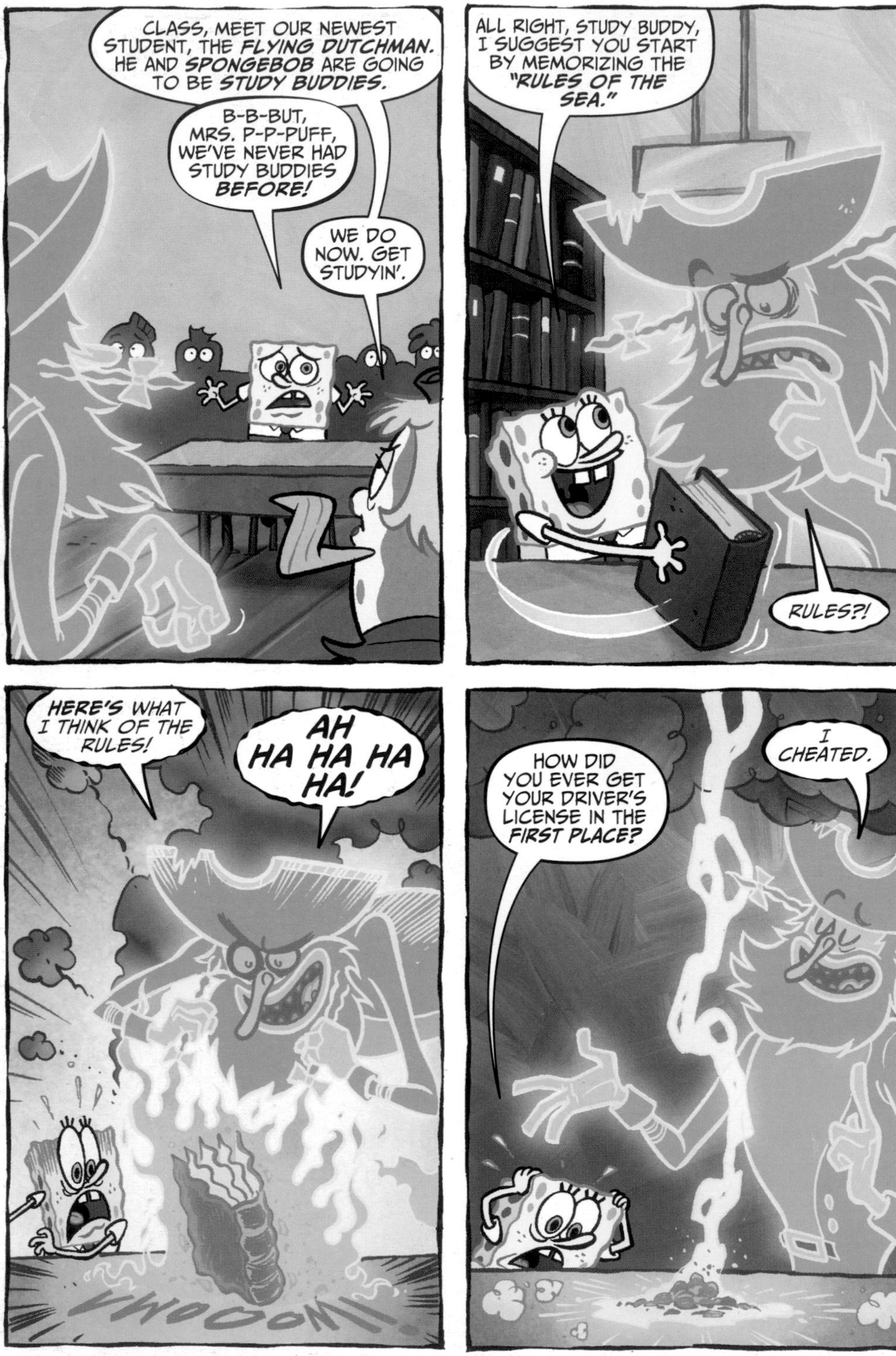
CLASS, MEET OUR NEWEST STUDENT, THE FLYING DUTCHMAN. HE AND SPONGEBOB ARE GOING TO BE STUDY BUDDIES.
B-B-BUT, MRS. P-P-PUFF, WE'VE NEVER HAD STUDY BUDDIES BEFORE!
WE DO NOW. GET STUDYIN'.
ALL RIGHT, STUDY BUDDY, I SUGGEST YOU START BY MEMORIZING THE "RULES OF THE SEA."
RULES?!
HERE'S WHAT I THINK OF THE RULES!
AH HA HA HA HA!
VWOOOOM!
HOW DID YOU EVER GET YOUR DRIVER'S LICENSE IN THE FIRST PLACE?
I CHEATED.

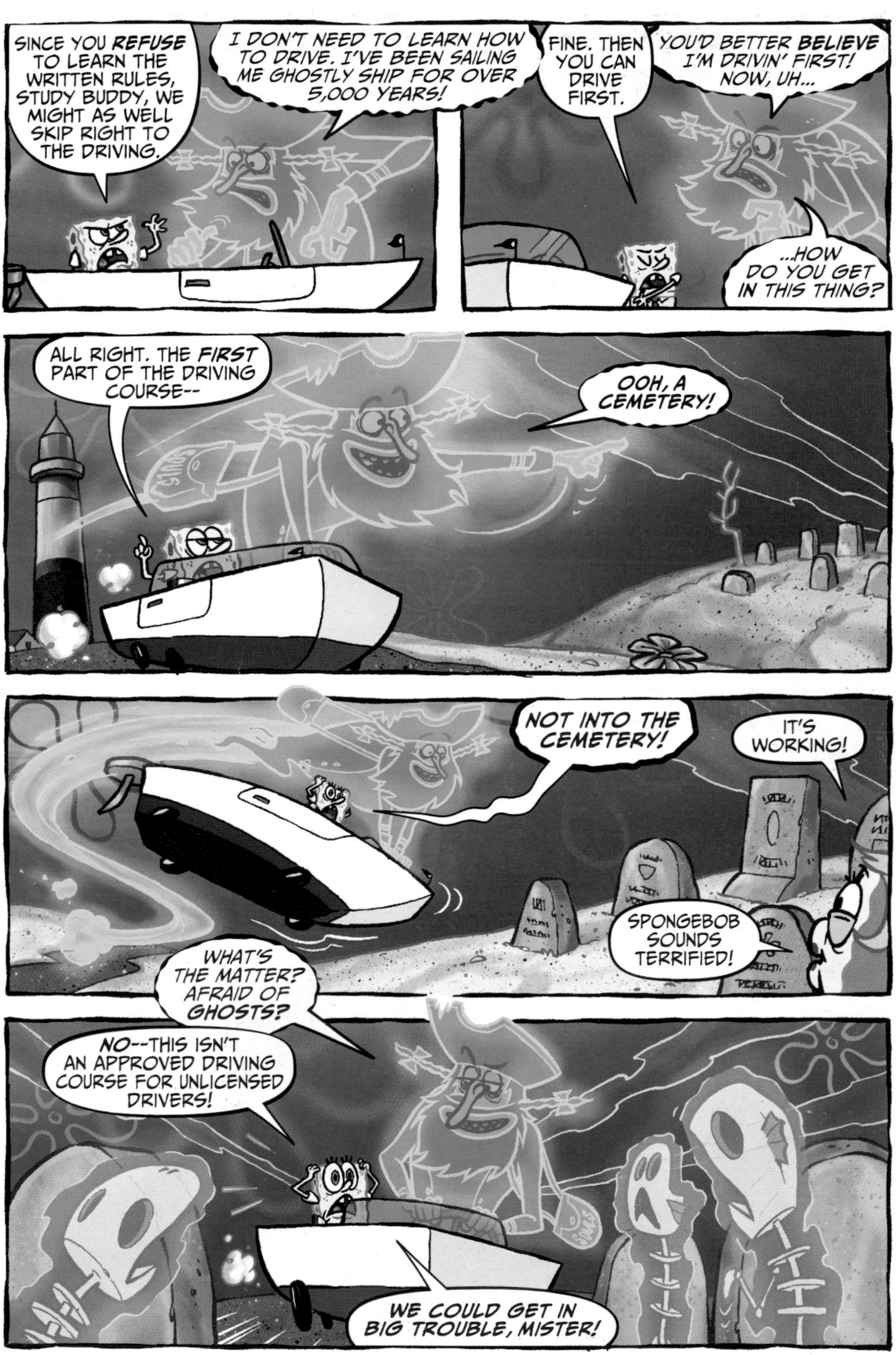
SINCE YOU REFUSE TO LEARN THE WRITTEN RULES, STUDY BUDDY, WE MIGHT AS WELL SKIP RIGHT TO THE DRIVING.
I DON'T NEED TO LEARN HOW TO DRIVE. I'VE BEEN SAILING ME GHOSTLY SHIP FOR OVER 5,000 YEARS!
FINE. THEN YOU CAN DRIVE FIRST.
YOU'D BETTER BELIEVE I'M DRIVIN' FIRST! NOW, UH...
...HOW DO YOU GET IN THIS THING?
ALL RIGHT. THE FIRST PART OF THE DRIVING COURSE--
OOH, A CEMETERY!
NOT INTO THE CEMETERY!
IT'S WORKING!
SPONGEBOB SOUNDS TERRIFIED!
WHAT'S THE MATTER? AFRAID OF GHOSTS?
NO--THIS ISN'T AN APPROVED DRIVING COURSE FOR UNLICENSED DRIVERS!
WE COULD GET IN BIG TROUBLE, MISTER!

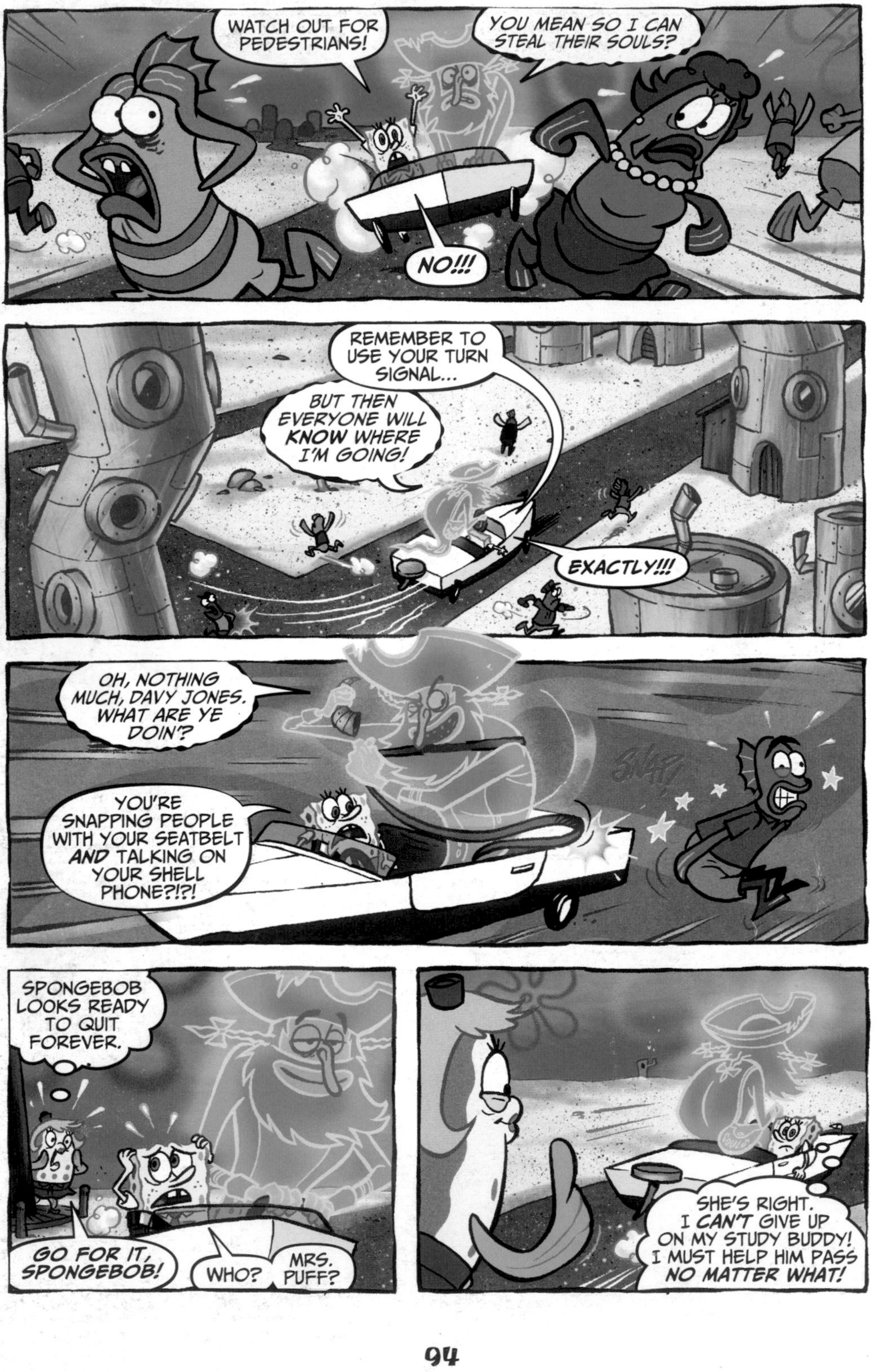
WATCH OUT FOR PEDESTRIANS!
YOU MEAN SO I CAN STEAL THEIR SOULS?
NO!!!
REMEMBER TO USE YOUR TURN SIGNAL...
BUT THEN EVERYONE WILL KNOW WHERE I'M GOING!
EXACTLY!!!
OH, NOTHING MUCH, DAVY JONES. WHAT ARE YE DOIN'?
YOU'RE SNAPPING PEOPLE WITH YOUR SEATBELT AND TALKING ON YOUR SHELL PHONE?!?!
SPONGEBOB LOOKS READY TO QUIT FOREVER.
GO FOR IT, SPONGEBOB!
WHO?
MRS. PUFF?
SHE'S RIGHT. I CAN'T GIVE UP ON MY STUDY BUDDY! I MUST HELP HIM PASS NO MATTER WHAT!

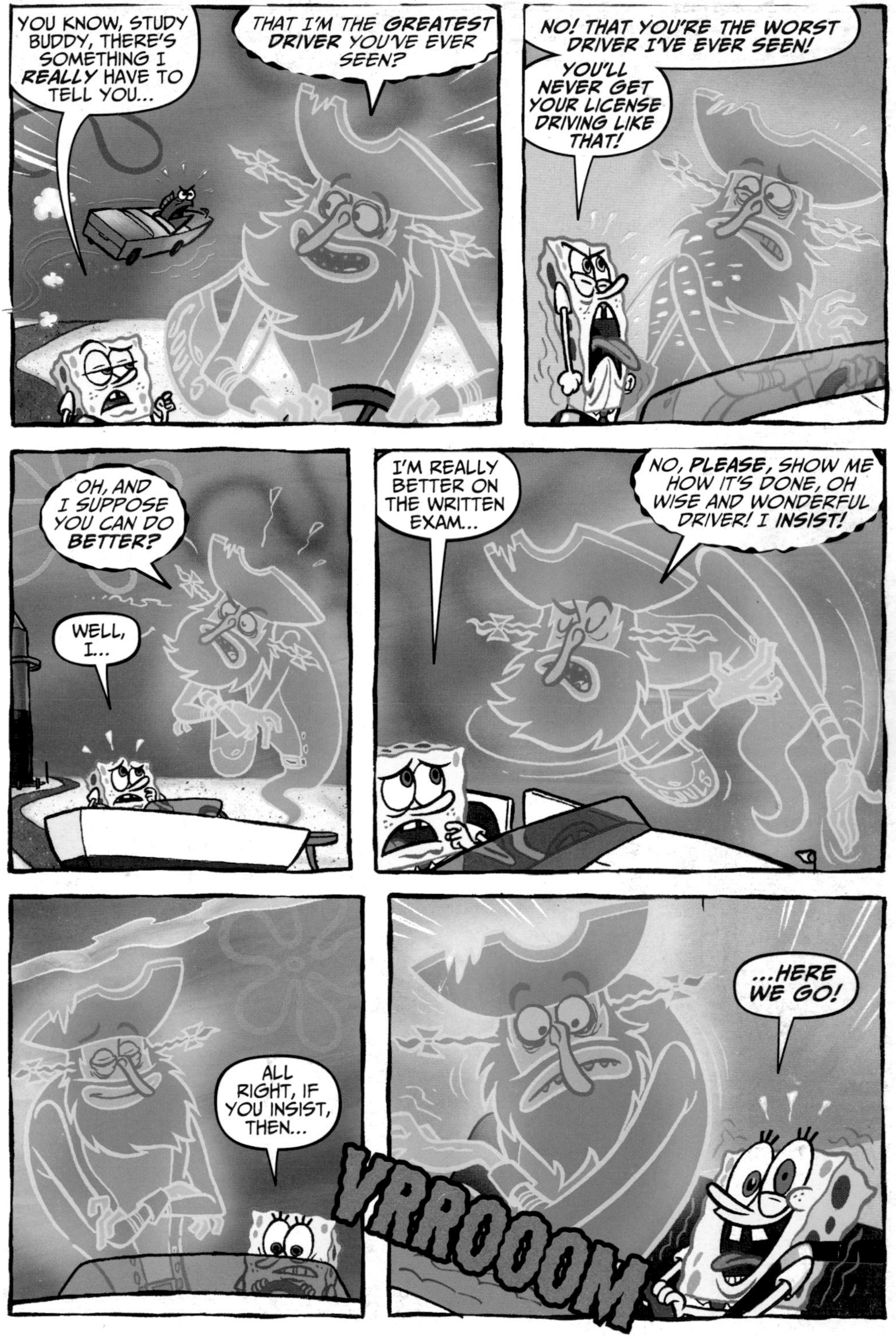
YOU KNOW, STUDY BUDDY, THERE'S SOMETHING I REALLY HAVE TO TELL YOU...
THAT I'M THE GREATEST DRIVER YOU'VE EVER SEEN?
NO! THAT YOU'RE THE WORST DRIVER I'VE EVER SEEN!
YOU'LL NEVER GET YOUR LICENSE DRIVING LIKE THAT!
OH, AND I SUPPOSE YOU CAN DO BETTER?
WELL, I...
I'M REALLY BETTER ON THE WRITTEN EXAM...
NO, PLEASE, SHOW ME HOW IT'S DONE, OH WISE AND WONDERFUL DRIVER! I INSIST!
ALL RIGHT, IF YOU INSIST, THEN...
VRROOOOM
...HERE WE GO!

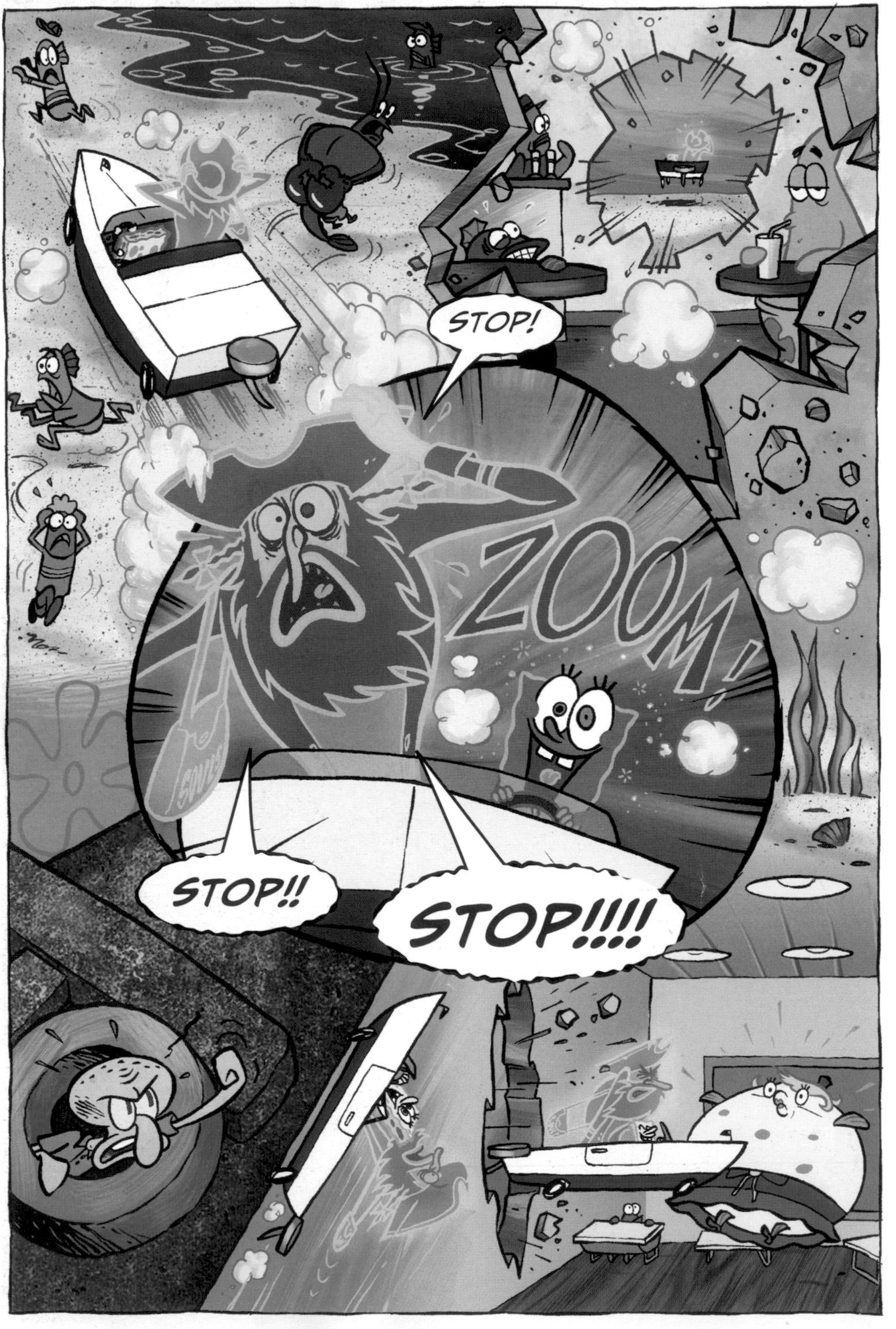
STOP!
ZOOM!
STOP!!
STOP!!!!

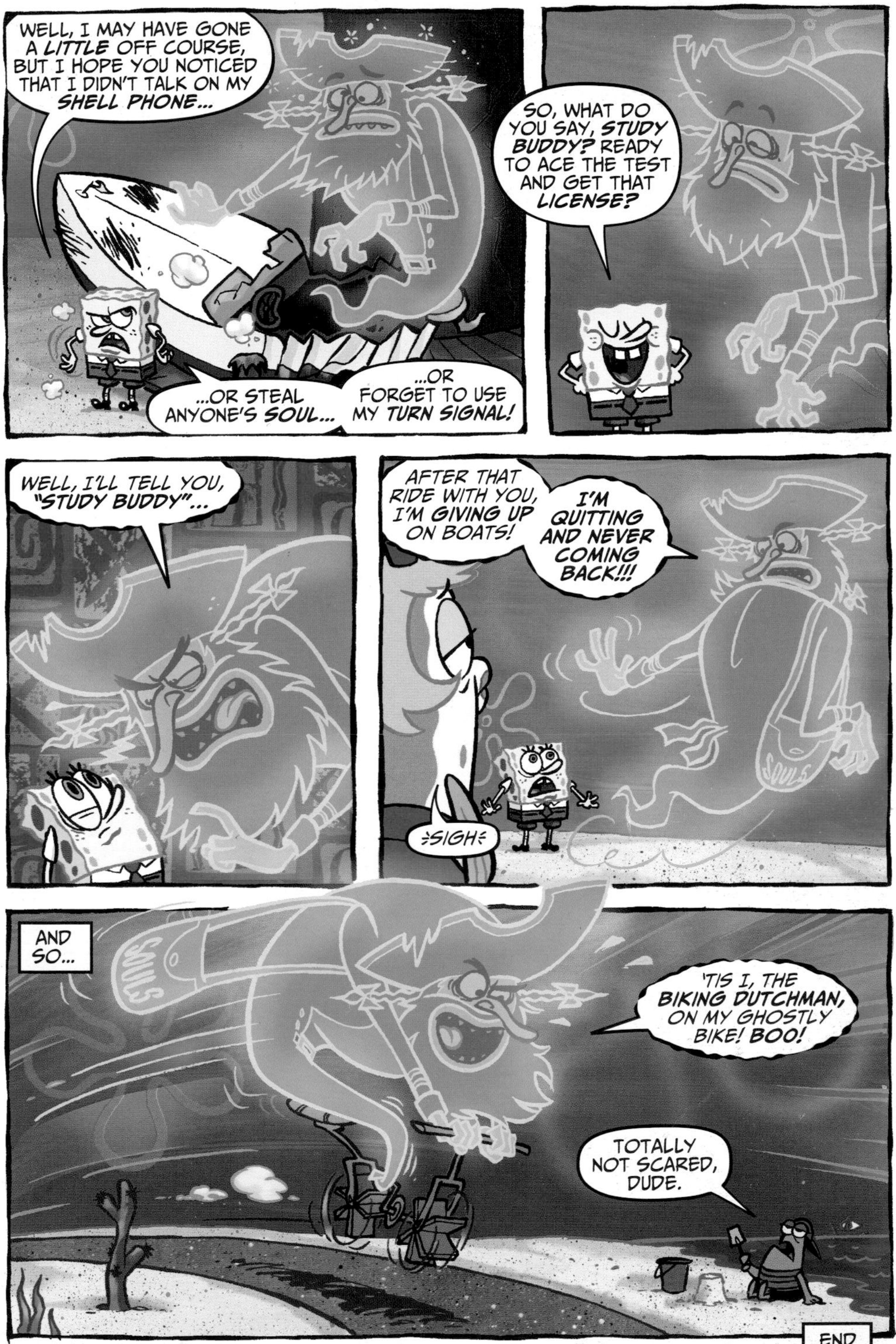
WELL, I MAY HAVE GONE A LITTLE OFF COURSE, BUT I HOPE YOU NOTICED THAT I DIDN'T TALK ON MY SHELL PHONE...
...OR STEAL ANYONE'S SOUL...
...OR FORGET TO USE MY TURN SIGNAL!
SO, WHAT DO YOU SAY, STUDY BUDDY? READY TO ACE THE TEST AND GET THAT LICENSE?
WELL, I'LL TELL YOU, "STUDY BUDDY"...
AFTER THAT RIDE WITH YOU, I'M GIVING UP ON BOATS!
I'M QUITTING AND NEVER COMING BACK!!!
SIGH
AND SO...
'TIS I, THE BIKING DUTCHMAN, ON MY GHOSTLY BIKE! BOO!
TOTALLY NOT SCARED, DUDE.
END

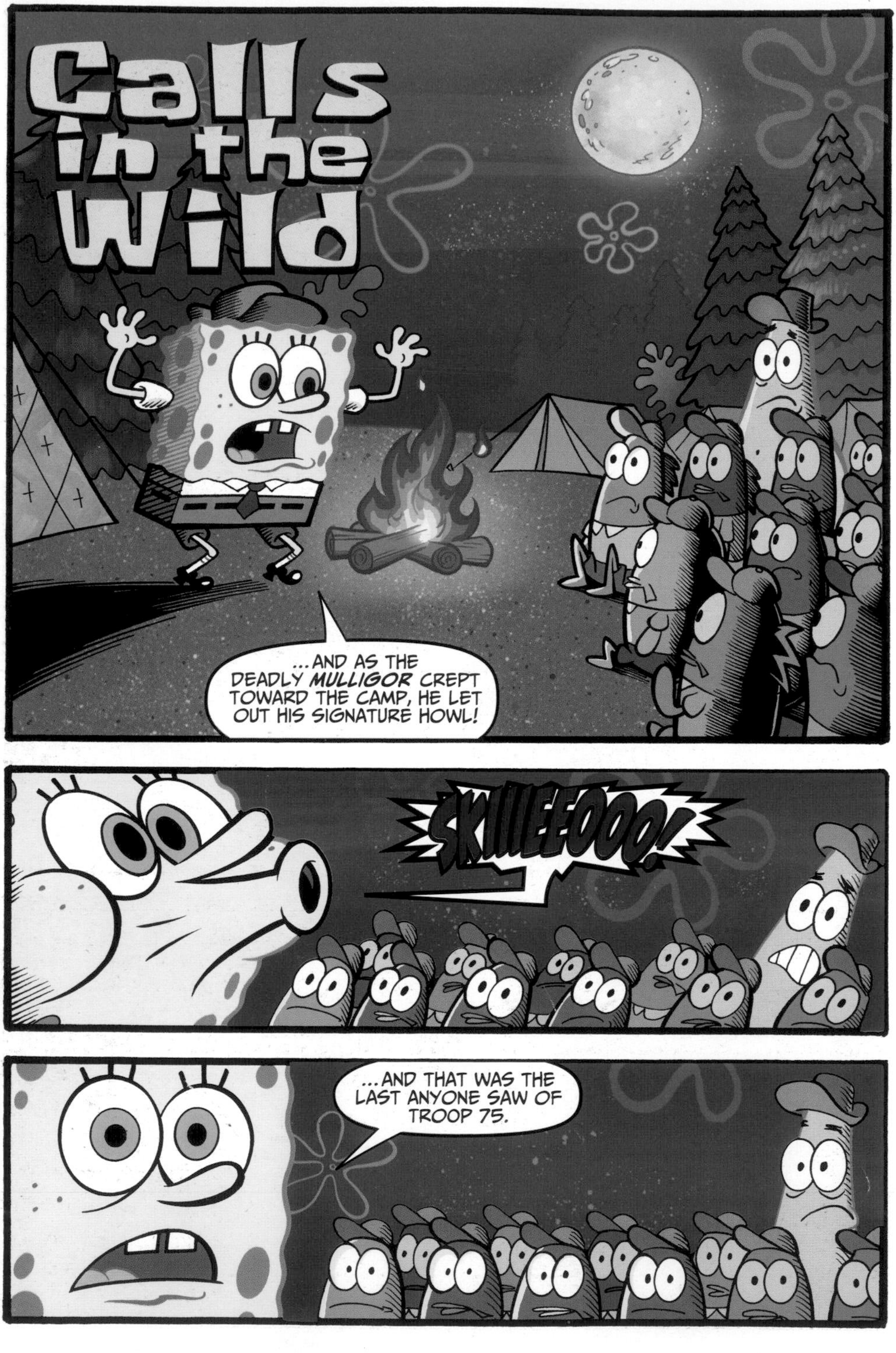
Calls in the Wild
...AND AS THE DEADLY MULLIGOR CREPT TOWARD THE CAMP, HE LET OUT HIS SIGNATURE HOWL!
SKIIIEEEOOO!
...AND THAT WAS THE LAST ANYONE SAW OF TROOP 75.

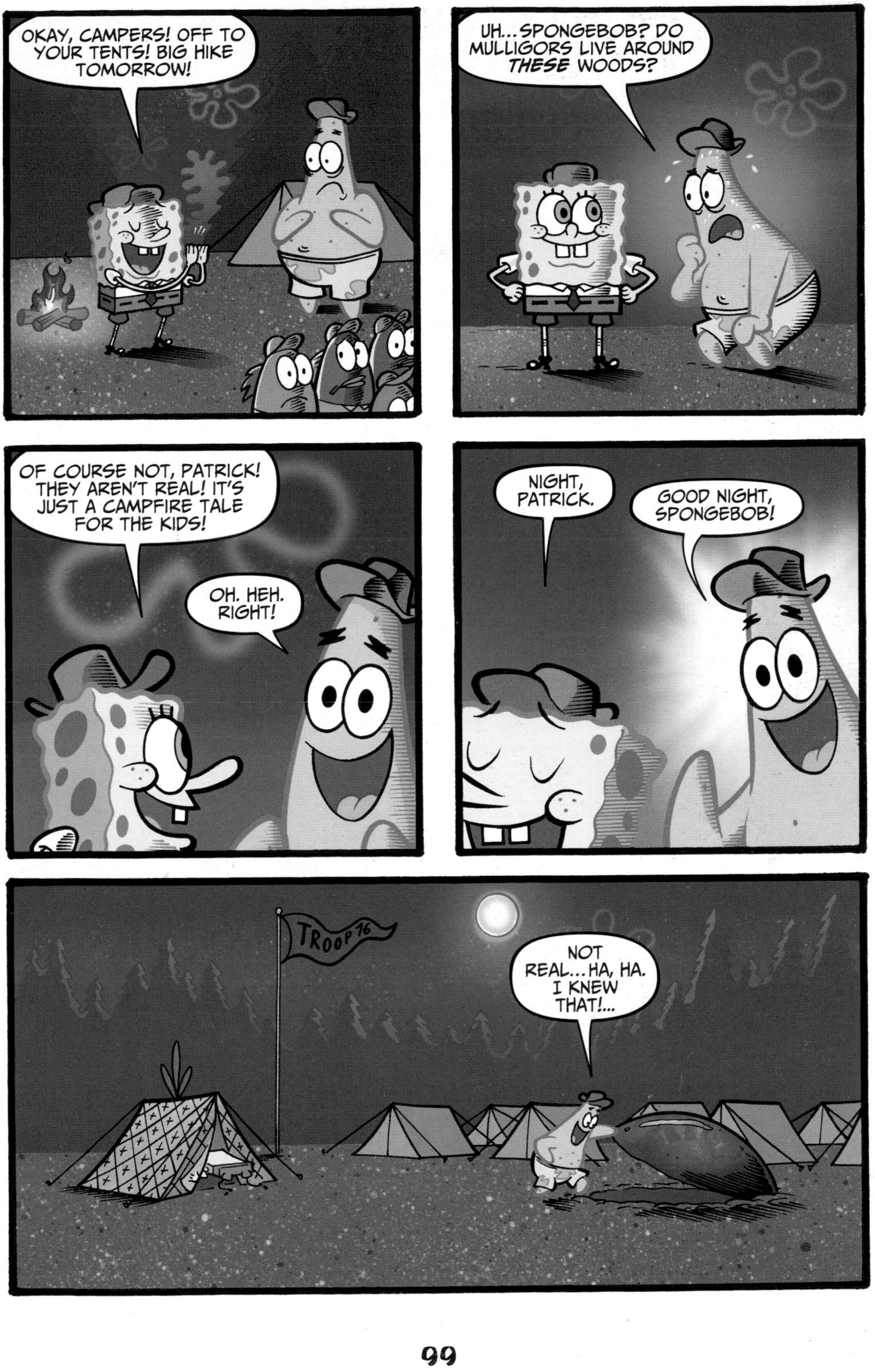
OKAY, CAMPERS! OFF TO YOUR TENTS! BIG HIKE TOMORROW!
UH...SPONGEBOB? DO MULLIGORS LIVE AROUND *THESE* WOODS?
OF COURSE NOT, PATRICK! THEY AREN'T REAL! IT'S JUST A CAMPFIRE TALE FOR THE KIDS!
OH. HEH. RIGHT!
NIGHT, PATRICK.
GOOD NIGHT, SPONGEBOB!
TROOP 76
NOT REAL...HA, HA. I KNEW THAT!...

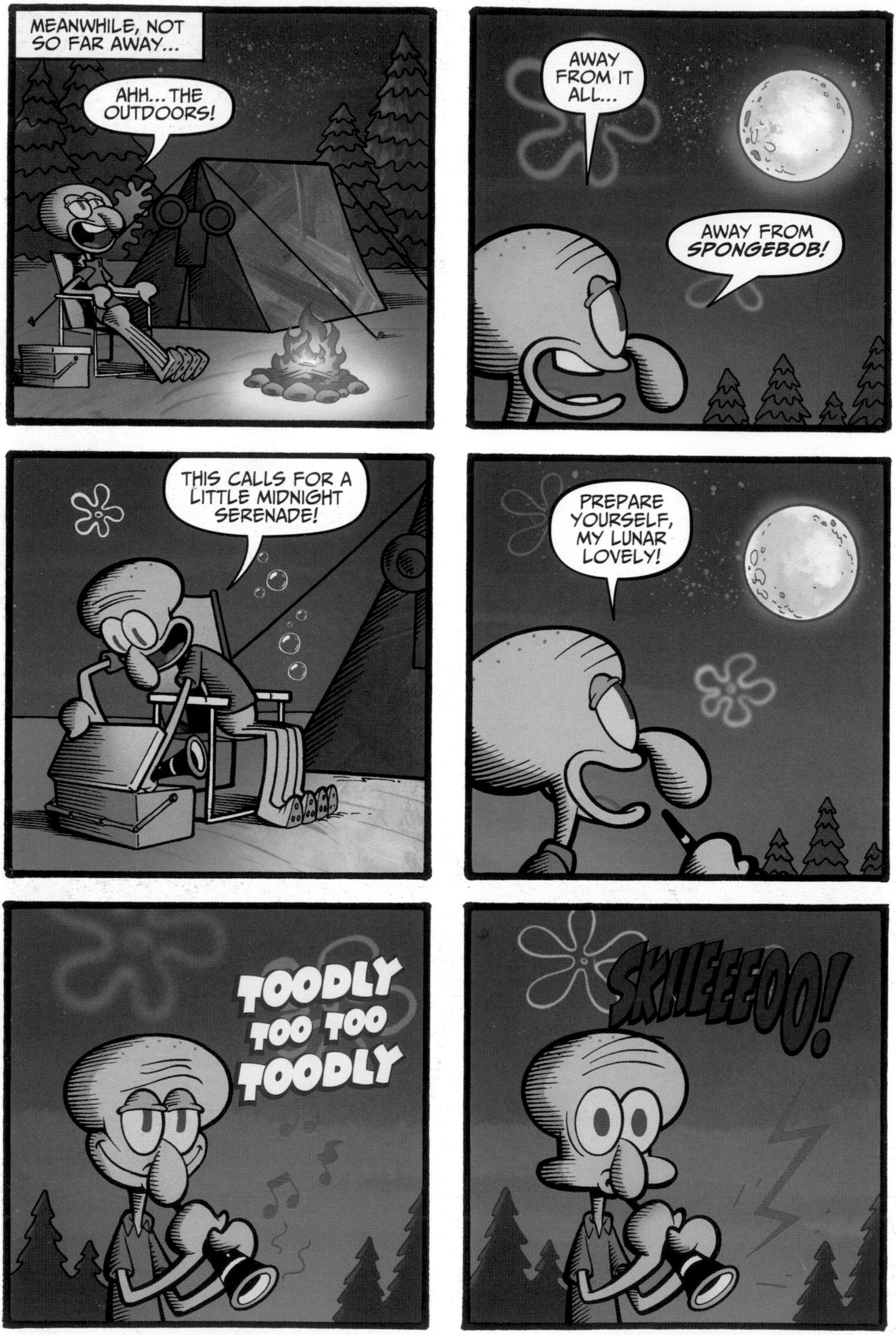
MEANWHILE, NOT SO FAR AWAY...
AHH... THE OUTDOORS!
AWAY FROM IT ALL...
AWAY FROM SPONGEBOB!
THIS CALLS FOR A LITTLE MIDNIGHT SERENADE!
PREPARE YOURSELF, MY LUNAR LOVELY!
TOODLY TOO TOO TOODLY
SKIIEEEEOO!

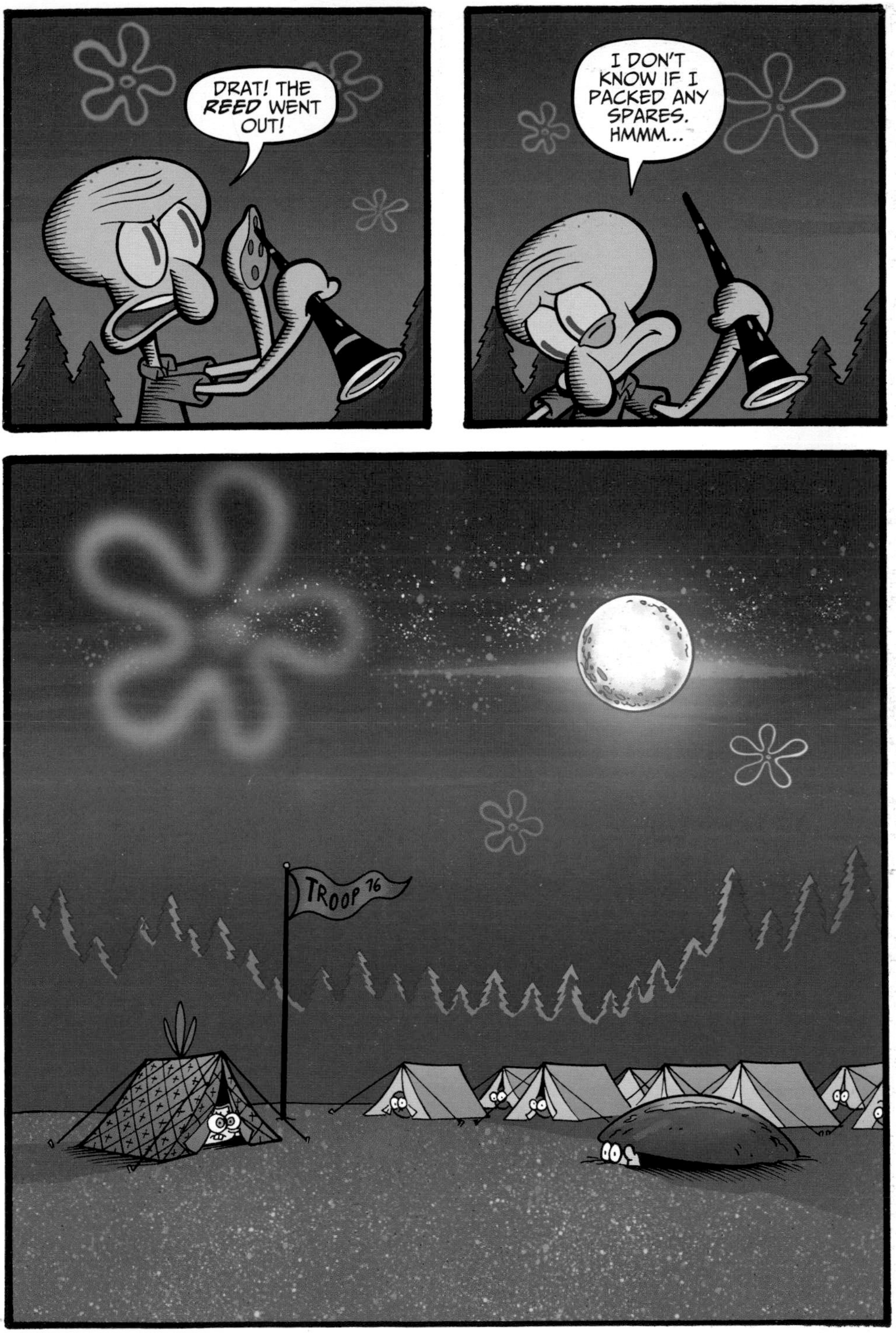
DRAT! THE REED WENT OUT!
I DON'T KNOW IF I PACKED ANY SPARES. HMMM...
TROOP 76

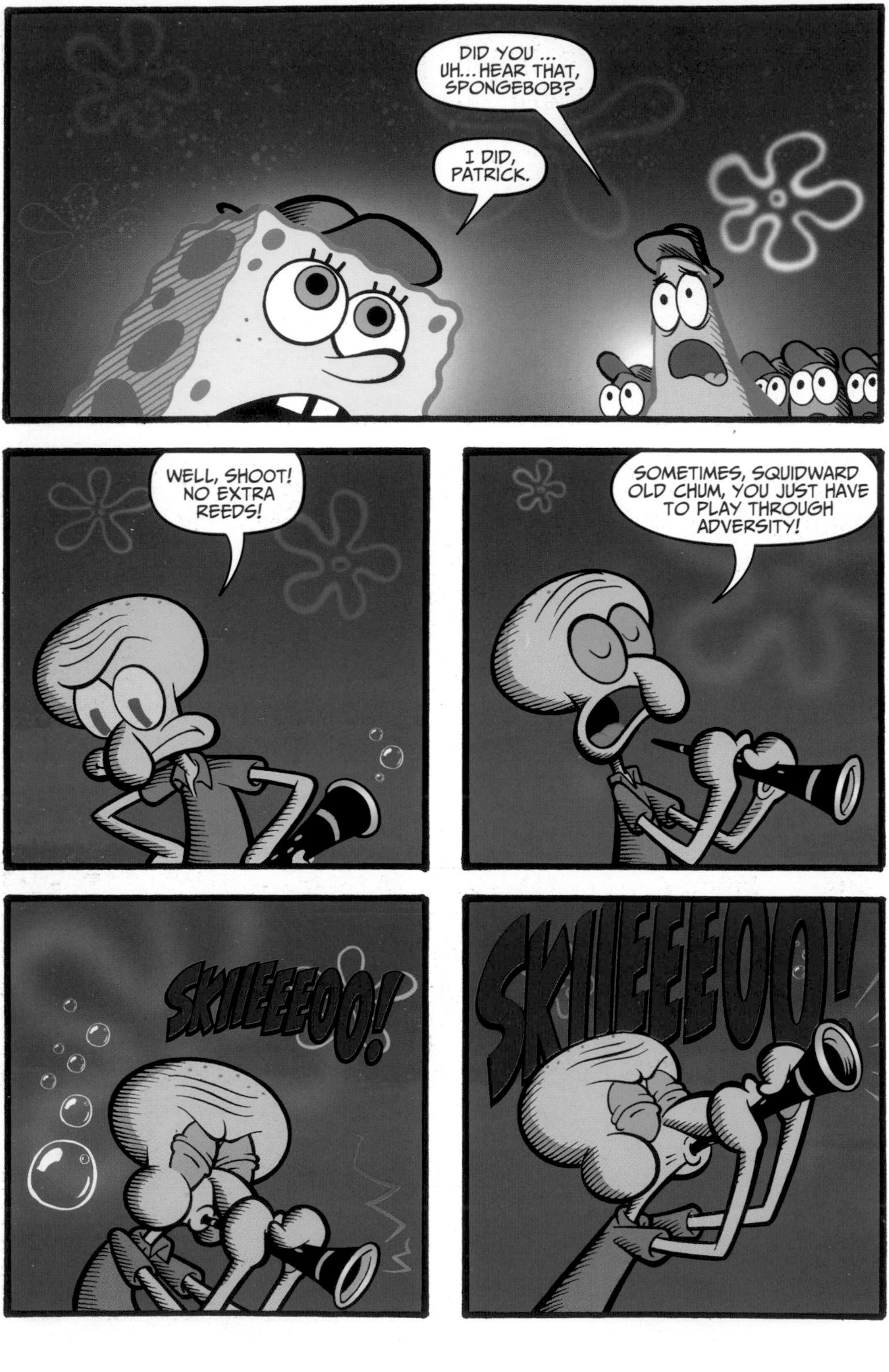
DID YOU ... UH... HEAR THAT, SPONGEBOB?
I DID, PATRICK.
WELL, SHOOT! NO EXTRA REEDS!
SOMETIMES, SQUIDWARD OLD CHUM, YOU JUST HAVE TO PLAY THROUGH ADVERSITY!
SKIIEEEOO!
SKIIEEEOO!

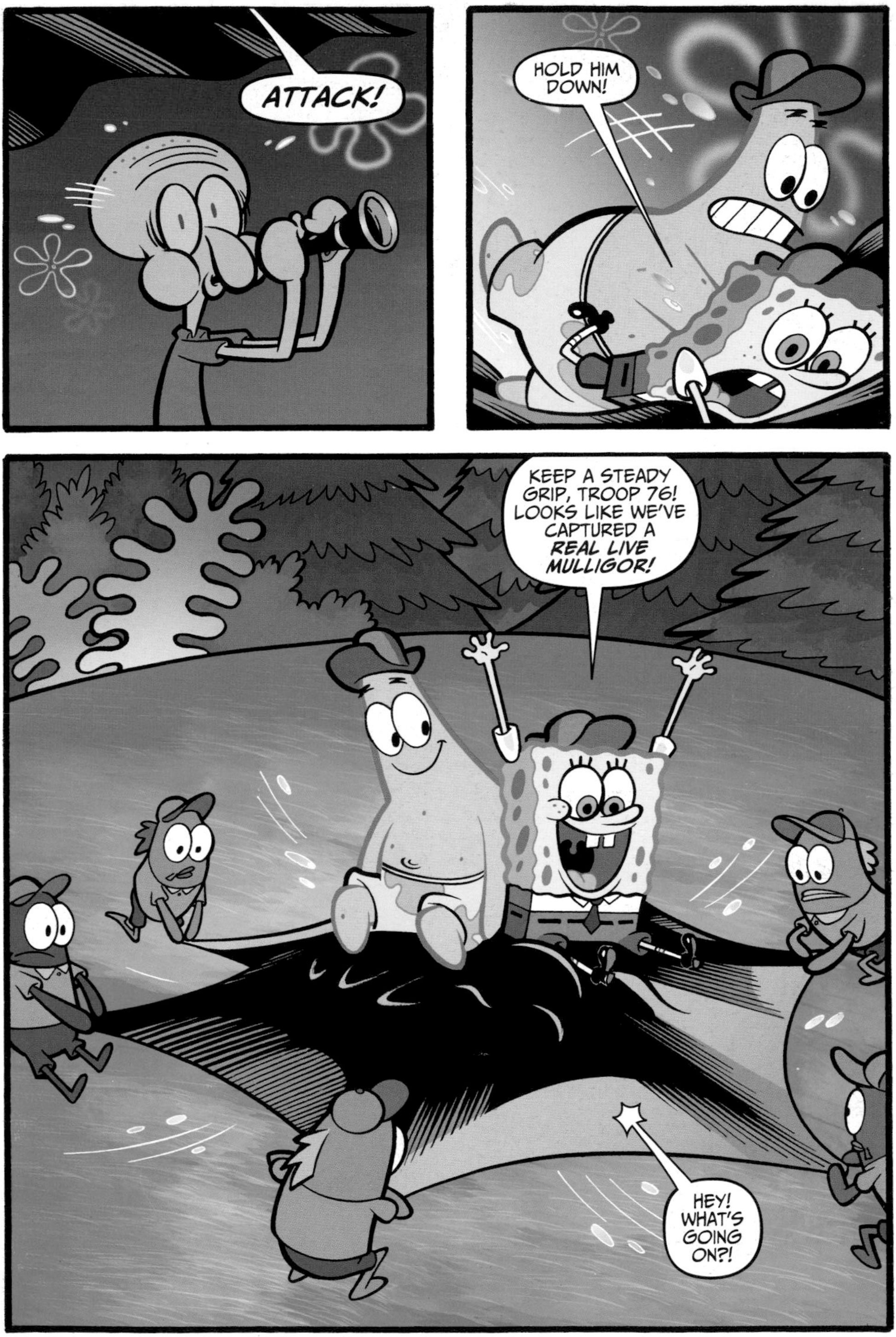

ATTACK!
HOLD HIM DOWN!
KEEP A STEADY GRIP, TROOP 76! LOOKS LIKE WE'VE CAPTURED A REAL LIVE MULLIGOR!
HEY! WHAT'S GOING ON?!

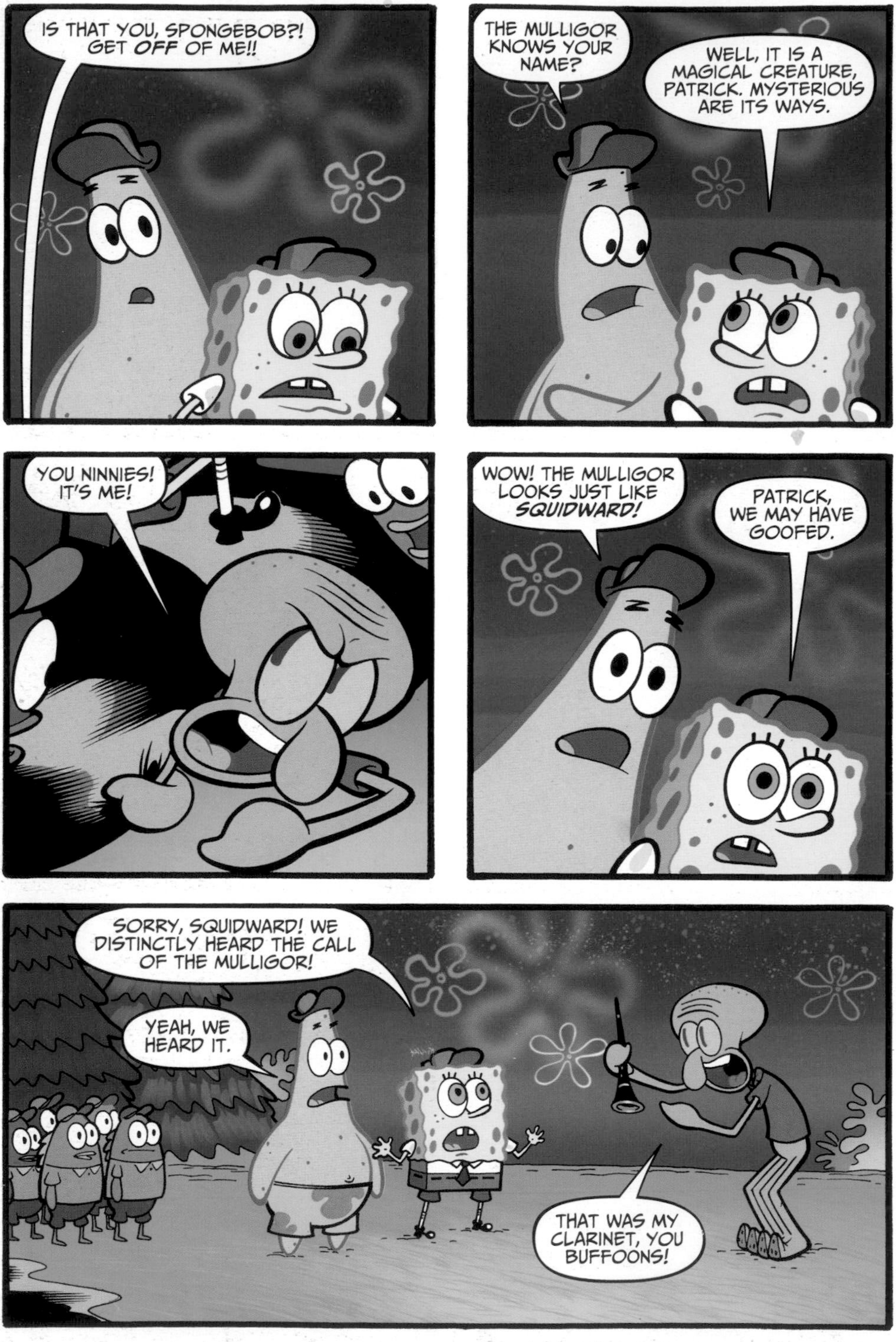
IS THAT YOU, SPONGEBOB?! GET OFF OF ME!!
THE MULLIGOR KNOWS YOUR NAME?
WELL, IT IS A MAGICAL CREATURE, PATRICK. MYSTERIOUS ARE ITS WAYS.
YOU NINNIES! IT'S ME!
WOW! THE MULLIGOR LOOKS JUST LIKE SQUIDWARD!
PATRICK, WE MAY HAVE GOOFED.
SORRY, SQUIDWARD! WE DISTINCTLY HEARD THE CALL OF THE MULLIGOR!
YEAH, WE HEARD IT.
THAT WAS MY CLARINET, YOU BUFFOONS!

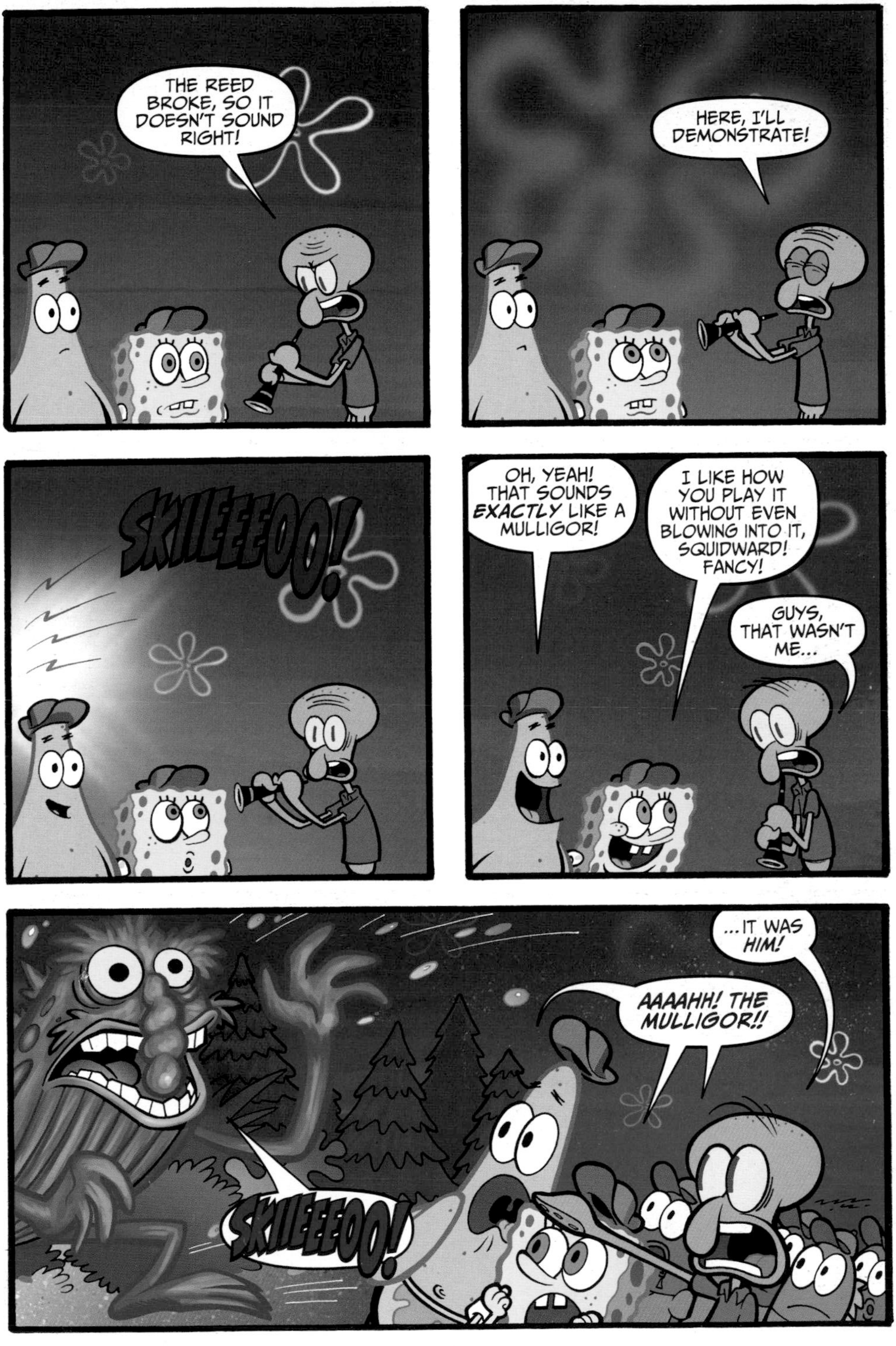
THE REED BROKE, SO IT DOESN'T SOUND RIGHT!
HERE, I'LL DEMONSTRATE!
SKIIEEEOO!
OH, YEAH! THAT SOUNDS EXACTLY LIKE A MULLIGOR!
I LIKE HOW YOU PLAY IT WITHOUT EVEN BLOWING INTO IT, SQUIDWARD! FANCY!
GUYS, THAT WASN'T ME...
...IT WAS HIM!
AAAAHH! THE MULLIGOR!!
SKIIEEEOO!

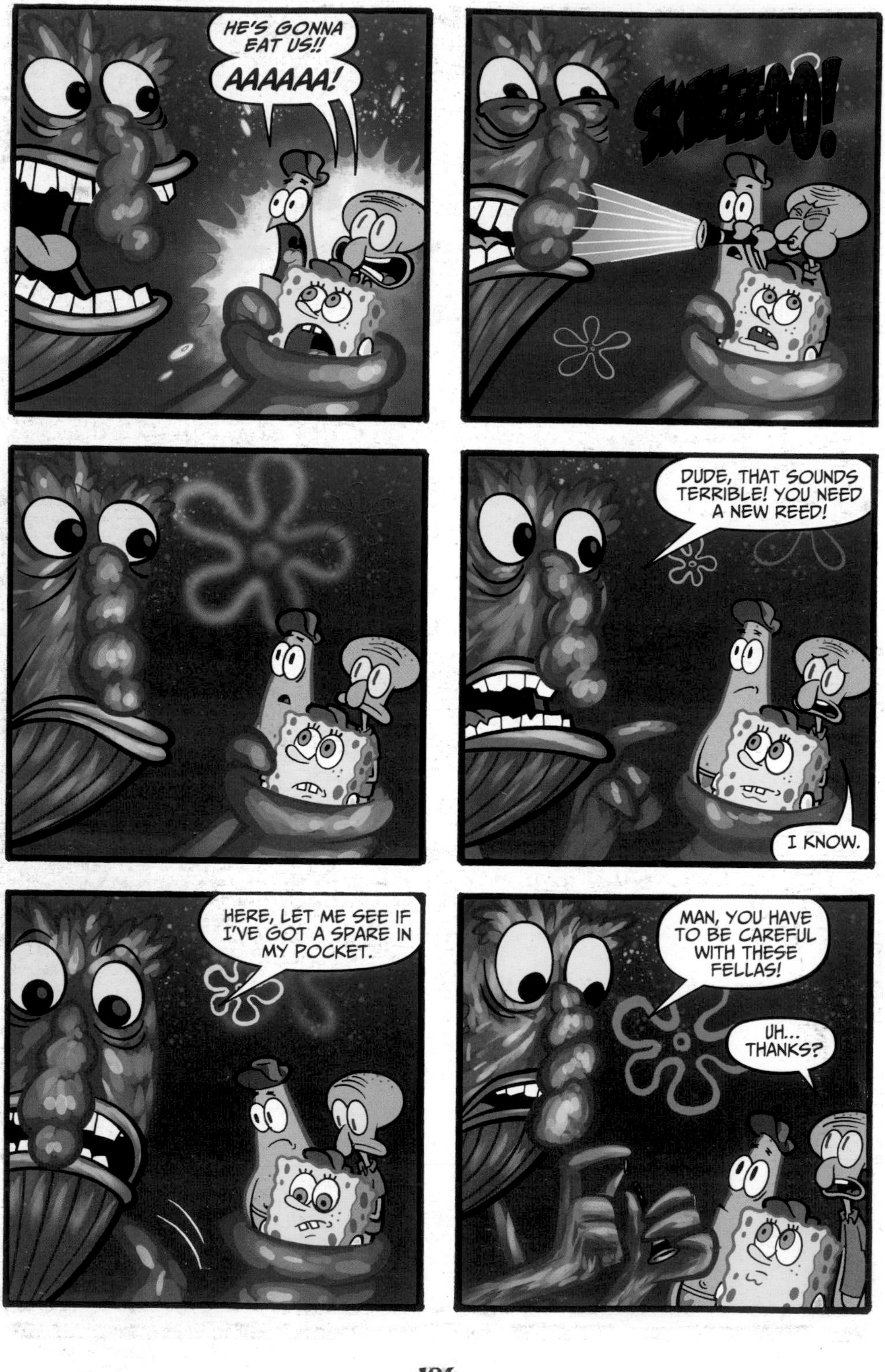
HE'S GONNA EAT US!!
AAAAAA!
SKWEEEOO!
DUDE, THAT SOUNDS TERRIBLE! YOU NEED A NEW REED!
I KNOW.
HERE, LET ME SEE IF I'VE GOT A SPARE IN MY POCKET.
MAN, YOU HAVE TO BE CAREFUL WITH THESE FELLAS!
UH... THANKS?

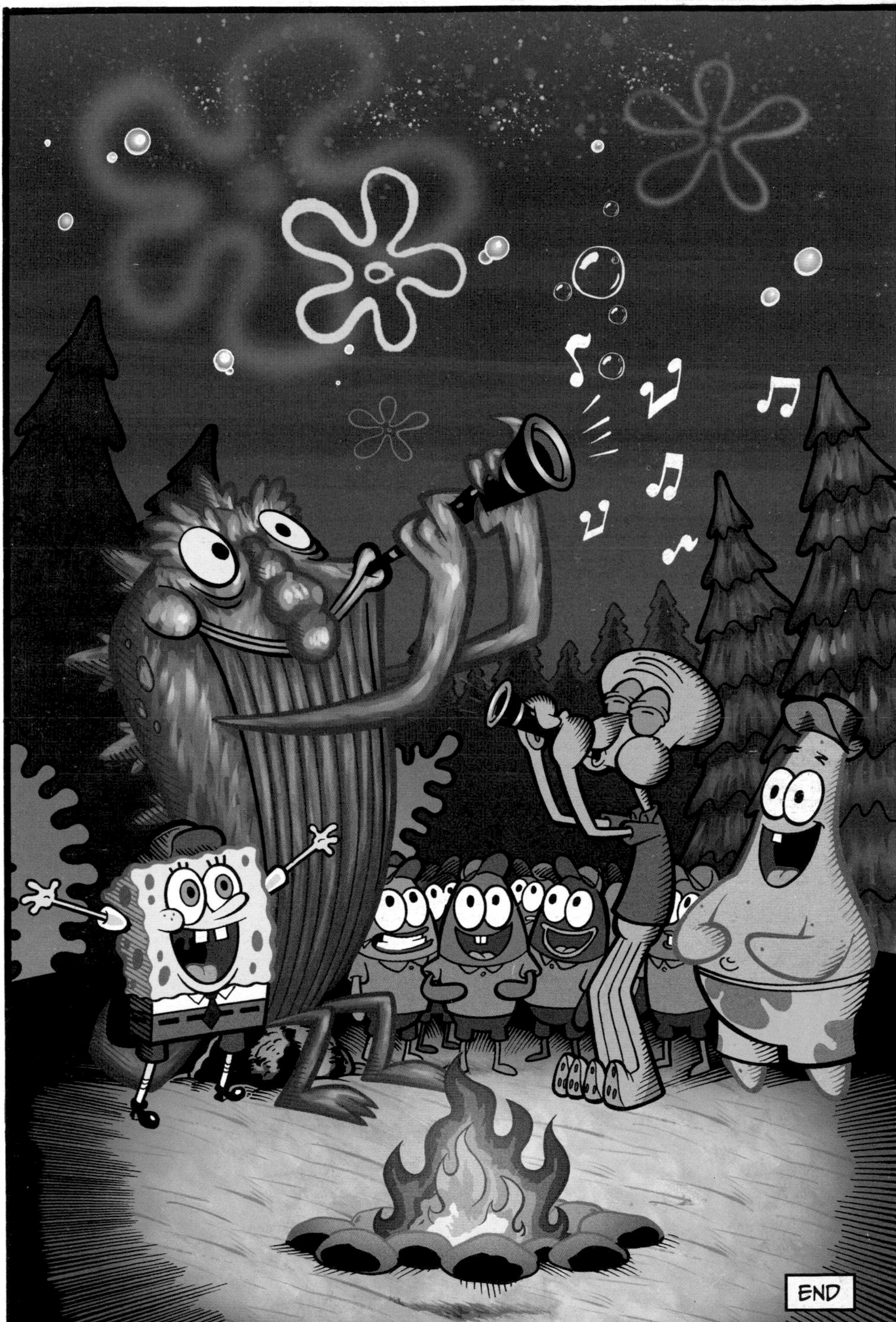
END

STORY: GRAHAM ANNABLE PENCILS: GREGG SCHIGIEL INKS: ADAM DEKRAKER COLOR: MONICA KUBINA LETTERING: COMICRAFT

The CURSE o' COMICS CAVE!

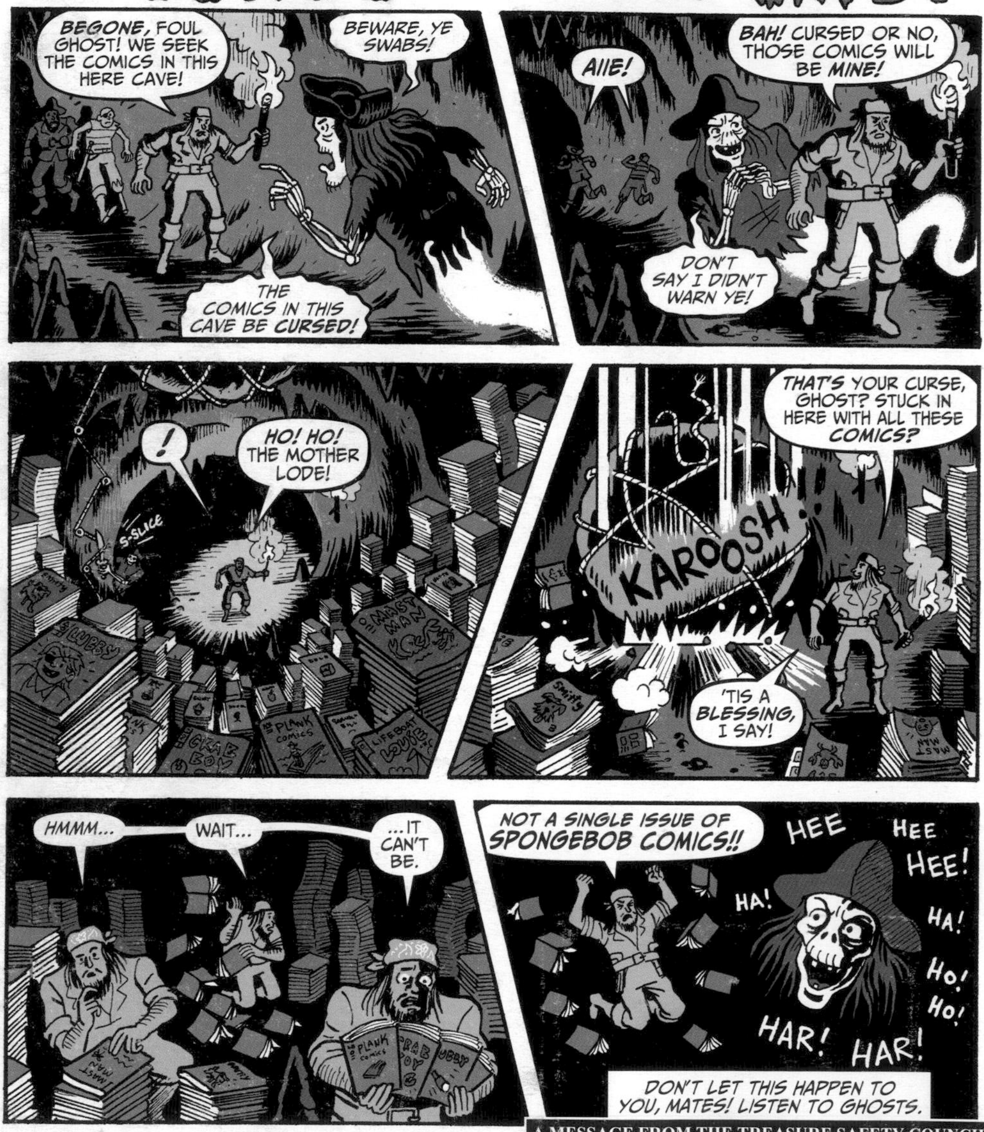
BEGONE, FOUL GHOST! WE SEEK THE COMICS IN THIS HERE CAVE!
BEWARE, YE SWABS!
THE COMICS IN THIS CAVE BE CURSED!
AIIE!
BAH! CURSED OR NO, THOSE COMICS WILL BE MINE!
DON'T SAY I DIDN'T WARN YE!
!
HO! HO! THE MOTHER LODE!
S-SLICE
KAROOSH!!
THAT'S YOUR CURSE, GHOST? STUCK IN HERE WITH ALL THESE COMICS?
'TIS A BLESSING, I SAY!
HMMM...
WAIT...
...IT CAN'T BE.
NOT A SINGLE ISSUE OF SPONGEBOB COMICS!!
HEE HEE HEE!
HA! HA!
HO! HO!
HAR! HAR!
DON'T LET THIS HAPPEN TO YOU, MATES! LISTEN TO GHOSTS.

A MESSAGE FROM THE TREASURE SAFETY COUNCIL.

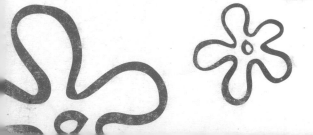

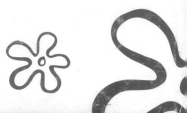

Story and art: Nate Neal. Lettering: Comicraft.